THE
GREAT LIBRARY
of TOMORROW

THE BOOK OF WISDOM TRILOGY: BOOK I

THE GREAT LIBRARY OF TOMORROW

ROSALIA AGUILAR SOLACE

TEXT PUBLISHING MELBOURNE AUSTRALIA

The Text Publishing Company acknowledges the Traditional Owners of the country on which we work, the Wurundjeri people of the Kulin Nation, and pays respect to their Elders past and present.

textpublishing.com.au

The Text Publishing Company
Wurundjeri Country, Level 6, Royal Bank Chambers, 287 Collins Street,
Melbourne Victoria 3000 Australia

Published in Australia, New Zealand and the UK by The Text Publishing Company, 2024

Interior art and cover image and design by TL International BV / Tomorrowland
Typesetting by Blackstone Publishing

Printed and bound by CPI Group (UK) Ltd, Croydon, CR0 4YY

ISBN: 9781911231455 (hardback)
ISBN: 9781923059184 (ebook)

A catalogue record for this book is available from the National Library of Australia.

The Forest Stewardship Council® (FSC®) is a global, not-for-profit organisation dedicated to the promotion of responsible forest management worldwide. FSC defines standards based on agreed principles for responsible forest stewardship that are supported by environmental, social, and economic stakeholders.

MIX
Paper | Supporting
responsible forestry
FSC
www.fsc.org
FSC® C171272

ROSALIA AGUILAR SOLACE grew up in Mexico City, the scion of a long line of writers. Finding Rosalia can be a challenge, as she splits her time between her hometown, where you might catch a glimpse of her writing in a bookshop café, and the Great Library of Tomorrow. But whether she's at home with family or researching future work, you can be sure of one thing: magical stories follow.

www.thegreatlibraryoftomorrow.com
Instagram and Facebook: @rosaliaaguilarsolace

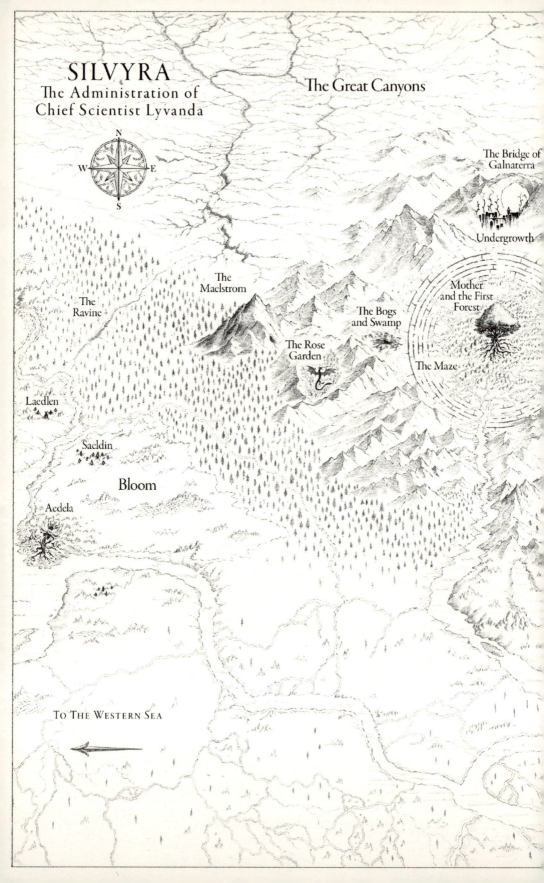

SILVYRA
The Administration of
Chief Scientist Lyvanda

The Great Canyons

N
W   E
S

The Bridge of
Galnaterra

Undergrowth

The Maelstrom

The Ravine

The Bogs
and Swamp

Mother
and the First
Forest

The Rose
Garden

The Maze

Laedlen

Saeldin

Bloom

Aedela

To The Western Sea

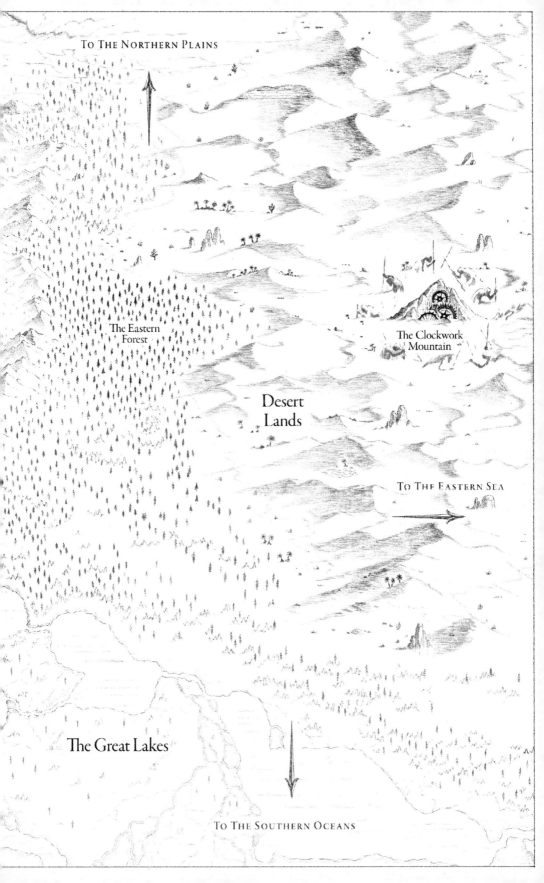

TO THE NORTHERN PLAINS

The Eastern
Forest

The Clockwork
Mountain

Desert
Lands

TO THE EASTERN SEA

The Great Lakes

TO THE SOUTHERN OCEANS

PROLOGUE

The ash blew like snow across the dried ocean bed.

The lone figure hurried past the few scattered corpses without breaking stride. There was no time to dwell on what he saw. He ignored the unnaturally twisted limbs and torn faces scattered across the sand. The skulls with jaws locked open as though silently screaming—a choir of agony frozen in time.

The bones lay around the crumbling hulks of rotting ships, where evil had devoured them.

That the darkness had won made it all the more appropriate the meeting should take place here, in the first realm that fell to its power. Once a location of light and love, its twin stars shining over lush forests, green mountains, and deep oceans, it had become the first realm to be consumed by the malevolent evil the figure served.

Now it was a benighted landscape in which only the hardiest survived, especially where he trod now. Where this once vast ocean had stretched was now a desert lowland. Desiccated remains of great sea creatures littered the ground, with mournful mountains of dead coral reefs looming large over the lifeless sands.

The man stumbled as his boot crunched through someone's rib cage.

He quickly shook the crumbling and charred remains of the unfortunate soul away from him and carried on climbing the slopes to where
the swirling winds of cinders were strongest.

His destination: the towering skeleton of bleached bones of the legendary Copper Sea Monster, rising like the ruins of an ancient cathedral
from the vast, unending desert.

He was suddenly glad he'd kept his human form for this visit, choosing not to take the more agile and faster form of his merciless hound-like
self. It was more subservient and fitting to serve the Harbinger of Dark
Stories as a human. Although, in this fragile state, the threat of death
churned hard in his stomach. The deep desert cold bit across his skin,
especially around the eye socket where he carried his shrunken companion, Myrtilus.

The Orb vibrated against his skull, Myrtilus's little pulses of energy
communicating in that peculiar way all Orbs did. Not quite speech, but
enough of a pattern to be understood.

We're close.

Ahead, the cloud had grown thick, drifting like a shroud over the
bone cathedral, giving only shimmering glimpses of what lay within.
And now, as he knew it would, the ash began to fall heavier. Thick flakes
swept across his path, an unnatural and bitter rain that smelled of the
destruction of life.

He suddenly noticed hundreds of faces peering in his direction
through the cinders and bones. The corrupted folk and the wild creatures that accompanied them.

The huge beasts, like hounds of the devil, were all matted fur, fe-
vered eyes, and teeth. But it was the people who fascinated the man.
The foot soldiers of the dark. He hadn't seen them up close until now,
and it drew his breath to witness their appearance firsthand. The otherwise normal faces—albeit worn and battered by living in this brutal
world—were covered with seething, crawling script flowing across their
skin like molten ink.

The man saw that these words were of the darkest stories known to
humankind. They were carved upon the skins and hides of every being

here, bending them to evil's will. Each word burned like fire across man and monster alike.

That was a sign they were ready to kill.

The man eyed them warily but continued moving into the ash cloud. They were not here for him. They were here to accompany the figure who was beginning to materialize through the gloom.

Immediately, the man dropped to his knees. "I have come as ordered."

The new figure stepped forward, pulling his glowing coat of embers around him more tightly as if to wrap himself in its protection. The air stank of burning flesh as he approached. Globules of fat spat out from beneath the coat and fizzled on the drifts of ash that collected around his feet.

The cloud cleared enough to reveal the figure's ghostly white head and seemingly featureless face.

Have you undertaken my orders as instructed?

The voice was felt rather than heard. A physical manifestation of fear reverberated and rattled through every bone in the man's body, the words wriggling like worms beneath his skin, drowning out all rational thought.

It was the primal and delicious feeling of pure evil.

"I have done everything required, and the preparations are now complete," he said, bowing his head. "The taint is flowing in the realm of Silvyra . . . and beyond. Your time for revenge is at hand."

Good. We have been waiting a long time for this. As have—

The figure didn't finish. Off to the side, one of the bone pillars cracked and collapsed, sending the being who had been leaning on it stumbling forward. It was a young man, or at least he had been before his own story had been replaced by the corrupted language of Discordia. He fell on all fours before trying to scramble back as if there was a chance his interruption would go unnoticed.

It did not.

Without hesitation, the featureless figure raised a hand and twisted his fingers. The young man screamed as the words on his skin grew even more alive with flame. One by one, they burst open, creating fissures of fire, like volcanic vents, all over his body.

Another twist of the fingers pulled the writhing mass of agony into the sky. A tearing sound echoed from above as he was pulled apart in several directions at once.

The figure turned his head back as it rained blood around them.

And what of the dragon protector?

"Subdued, my liege. The realm of Silvyra is all yours for the taking. You and these . . ."

He gestured around at the assembled masses, burning text dancing about their exposed flesh.

My Unwritten.

"Of course."

There was no obvious sign of emotion from the figure, but he seemed pleased by the news of the dragon. He raised his arms before him and his coat of embers sparked, growing bright with fire.

Now we can finally finish what I started all those years ago. I will show that cursed Book the power of the dark stories. She may have tried to shut them out and pretend they did not exist, but her betrayal will cost all of Silvyra dearly.

His blood racing, the man was barely able to contain his excitement at what lay ahead and his pride in his part in bringing it about. Inside his skull, Myrtilus pulsed eagerly.

What comes next is the most important.

"Yes, my liege."

Return to the Great Tree and destroy all evidence of the work you have undertaken these many years. Kill anyone who is a threat. Create chaos and sow the seeds of fear. Those who oppose us will be blinded by their own ignorance. The battle will be over before it even begins. The way will be paved for our dark stories to feast.

"Of course." He bowed his head. "And what of your invasion?"

I will rid Silvyra of its troublesome protector and finally unleash death in the mother of all realms. I will give them a glimpse of what is coming to all of Paperworld.

The faceless figure had been trapped in the darkness for centuries, yet he clearly remembered how to wield his power. He reached out and sliced his finger across the air. He made the action five times, drawing slivers of silver that bent and wound around each other, before he violently shoved both hands into the center and tore the edges back.

Through the gash, another world could be seen. A glimpse of what some might consider paradise.

With the unnatural act complete, the featureless figure stepped through.

Now. It begins.

CHAPTER ONE
AMBUSH

The blue moss of the Rose Garden was slick with blood. Two lines of it trailed behind them like tram tracks, Xavier's life force seeping out through the slashes on his legs. Helia dragged him as best she could toward where she hoped help could be found.

"How much further?" Xavier asked. His words were ragged and weak, as he himself looked, but there was an urgency to them, full of concern, which was unusual for him.

Helia tried to bury the desperation that tore at her insides—the thought of losing him—but failed spectacularly.

Vega, her Orb, sensed her panic. Floating close by, he flashed an anxious message in swirls of green. She frowned at him and shook her head.

Xavier saw the exchange and tried to laugh, but it came out wet and pained. She glanced down to see a splatter of red on his lips.

"That bad, huh?" he said.

"You're going to make it," she replied, hoping it wasn't a lie. She blew her cheeks out under the strain of his weight. It was a weight she had always loved. A reassuring, comforting mass of muscle and good humor that provided a rock in whatever storm she faced. But right now the weight was dragging them both into danger, and she didn't know what to do. She staggered and almost lost her footing. "I'll get you to safety."

He saw right through her forced optimism, as he always did. He was the Sage of Truth, after all. It was his gift and often her curse.

"It was a trap, Helia. Leave me and get back to the Great Library. Or he's going to find us and burn us both into cinders. That's what the stories say he does. He hasn't changed his ways."

"You don't know it was him, Xav."

"It was him."

Her Orb flashed his agreement.

She glared at Vega as her mind spun, ferociously trying to remember what had happened. But it was impossible. Her memories of the last hour were gone, swathed in fog, a malaise brought on by whatever had caused the gash across her forehead that was now dripping blood into her eyes. Had she fallen? Hit her head somehow?

She couldn't remember a thing that had happened since the ambush. *That* was still vivid in her mind, at least. The surprise of it, the ferocity. The fact it had come from nowhere, a sudden blight of violence in the one place she had always felt safe and at peace.

She could still taste the cloud of ash that enveloped them as they had stepped from the portal and felt the familiar spongy moss beneath her feet at the periphery of the Rose Garden. There had been no sky welcoming them upon their arrival. None of the usual oranges, pinks, and purples of the light dancing through the drifting clouds, casting the majesty of this otherworldly garden—the deliciously green foliage, the swaying flowers, the rock fountains—in sunset hues. There had only been glowing figures and clawed fingers reaching from the sudden suffocating gloom.

But worse—far worse—was the sense of what lay in the mist beyond.

A presence as dark and evil as any she had felt across all the realms she had ever visited.

Suttaru was his name. Although she knew him by another.

The Ash Man.

It had to have been him. The one from the founding of the Library—a time long before even Helia's arrival. A figure of menace that was now only whispered about in the quietest corridors and nooks of the Great Library, uttered by students and scholars trying to frighten each other with campfire stories.

It didn't seem possible that it was him. And yet the truth seemed plain, especially to the man who was dying in her arms.

Beautiful Xavier always recognized the truth of things, as was his talent. A seeker and protector of truth. She should have known better than to doubt him.

"Helia," he whispered. A lover's whisper. Her heart collapsed inside itself at the sound.

"It'll be all right, Xav. I promise."

He was almost lost. She had to hurry.

The cloud still at their backs, she continued to pull him toward the center of the Rose Garden. The dragon Perennia would surely save him—wouldn't she?

Helia's head burned in agony at the thought of the dragon, white-hot pain exploding right behind her eyes. It was as if there was something in her mind, some kind of information she needed to know, but was obscured by trauma. All she knew was that she had to move forward. There was nowhere else to go.

That was when she saw it clearly. The truth of what was happening.

"Helia, why are the roses gray?"

She didn't hear Xav's question at first. All her energy was being directed to her limbs as she tried to heave him down the last incline, her arms hooked under his, his feet still trailing behind. But as she finally pulled him onto the emerald path, hoping to feel comfort in the familiar and usually beautiful surroundings, she could no longer ignore it.

The flowers that should have been blooming all around them were gone.

In their place was a mass of curling, dying petals, all of them cinder-gray, as if they had been drained of life by some strange magic, leaving them ghosts of their former selves.

Corrupted.

Beneath the twisted, withering vines were the dead and dying bodies of the Garden's creatures. Pink-tipped humming bees, moon swallows, and tufted jackrabbits lay scattered through the leaf litter. Some still alive rustled as they passed, perhaps sensing salvation, or perhaps reaching out in their final death throes. But most did not move.

Helia's Orb pulsed a long, solemn blackish green—as close to a cry of anguish as he could manage—and drew closer to her.

The horror of their situation spiked, as did her adrenaline. That was enough to give her the strength for one final push.

She crunched her heels into the emerald path as she heaved Xav onward, gritting her teeth, pushing every sinew of her body until she burned from the inside out.

And at last they came to the center of the Rose Garden.

To find nothing.

Perennia was gone.

Helia's legs buckled, and she collapsed, bringing Xav down beside her. He was too far lost now to cry out in agony, but as he struggled through his own pain, he must have sensed the despair that was crashing over her and took her hand.

She stared at his pale face, and with what remained of her strength, she pulled him against her chest and cradled him. His beard was matted with blood. His lips twisted in a grimace as he adjusted himself, trying to dig in the pocket of his long coat to retrieve his Orb.

"What are you doing?" she asked, though she feared she already knew the answer.

"Antares shouldn't leave your side!"

He pressed the ball, now only the size of a marble, into her palm.

"No, Xav. As soon as we get you back to the Great Library, we can get you to a healer, and they will take care of you both and have you back to rights again. *Unite forever*, remember? It means your Orb too."

"We have no choice now, Helia."

He took her fingers and clasped them over his lifeless companion. Little Antares was surprisingly cold to the touch. There was no movement or color, no pulsing or vibration. Not like there should have been. Helia suddenly wondered whether Orbs could actually die. It wasn't a question she'd ever had to consider before, but in all the centuries she had been in the Library, she'd never known one to shrink like this.

Her own Orb, Vega, drooped mournfully beside her and nudged her hand, trying to wake his friend.

"It'll be okay," she whispered as Antares remained still. She tried to sound calm, confident, as she knew she must. Not just for her Orb, who could already sense her mood, but for Xavier. It wouldn't do to let him hear her voice break. Hope was needed here if he was to survive. Hope was the light that always led people from the darkness.

Dum spiro spero, she thought, trying to calm herself. *While I breathe, I hope.*

As Xavier's chest rose and fell in shallow breaths, she pocketed his Orb in the folds of her cloak and stared at the emptiness around her.

"Perennia's gone," she said, and the pain came again. Her vision blurred, but she blinked it away. "I can't believe it. Why isn't she here, Xav? Where is she?"

His brow creased in a frown. Weakly, he reached up and touched a finger to her forehead. "Are you all right?"

She nodded, placing her hand over his and squeezing. There was something in her memory she knew she needed, but right now it eluded her.

"I hit my head. I think?"

"You don't remember what happened?"

"Only the attack, but after that . . . it's all gone."

"Vega?" he asked the Orb.

Vega swirled a frustrated pattern that confirmed it. Because of the Orb's ties to Helia, he'd lost that part of his memory too.

Xavier was about to say something else, but then they saw the first dark speck of death twist and spin as it fell from the sky.

Ash.

Suddenly, Helia could smell the stink of burning and smoke again, coming closer, fierce enough to burn the back of her throat, causing her eyes to water. The wind carried the threat of fire on the horizon.

"He's here," Xavier said, not bothering to look. "You have to get away. Now!"

Helia twisted to look behind her, seeing the blur of the shadow mist that was cresting the hill.

Fear roiled deep inside, reaching parts of her that she hadn't felt since her last morning on Earth. A thousand panicked crickets were trapped in her chest, vying to get out.

Yet she still clung to the hope she was known for and the power she had learned to wield. She reached out to the spirit of the Rose Garden and sought any spark of the life it used to hold.

A knot in the fabric.

A thread to pull on.

It was weak, but it was there. And when she found it, pull she did, whipping back her hand and drawing the magic out.

Thorny tendrils suddenly sprouted from the decaying garden, a whole mass of them, writhing across the path and curling around each other as they twisted up into the heavens. She pushed her energy into the wall of foliage, feeding it until the green mass was as high and thick a defensive barrier as she could manage. When she was finished, it circled the entire Garden in a protective embrace.

It wasn't much, but it was all she could manifest with the little energy she had left. Even with the help of their Orbs, using powers in Paperworld was always draining for a Sage. It was not enough to hold up against such evil, she knew that, but it might buy them some time.

"We leave together," she said, trying to lift him.

He used what was left of his strength to push her away.

"Call Amare. Do it. She can get you out of here."

His words were barely audible. Behind her, Helia felt the shudder in the air as the shadow mist met her magic. She glanced back and saw the barrier of foliage begin to blacken.

"I'm not going without you, Xav."

"You have no choice. Call Amare and ride her back to the Library. Find the others and tell them what's happened. No time to grieve. In the face of evil, the Sages need to remain united and stand together . . . or we will all fall."

Helia looked over her shoulder again, unwilling to listen. "Amare is powerful. She can carry us both."

"No. Only one may wield her magic to travel between the realms."

"How is it you always know more than I do?"

He gave her a weak smile. "I'm not the most experienced, Helia. But like the botanists of the Great Tree, I've always had a nose for such things. Now go. Call Amare. And, Helia, whatever happens, whatever you need to do next, hold on. You are the Sage of Hope, after all. Hope must always endure."

Helia bent down and brushed the damp strands of hair away from Xavier's face. She kissed his forehead tenderly.

"There will never be another you, Xav."

"That is true," he replied tiredly, laying his head down on the dirt.

Biting back tears, she crawled to her feet again, taking care not to look back at the thick black smoke for too long. It engulfed her wall of vines and thorns, the enemy beginning to pass through it.

She staggered across the clearing, her mind blank. She succeeded in avoiding thoughts of all the times she had spent here with the dragon, conversing through their connection with nature and learning from each other. Neither did she stop to wonder what had happened here. Or where Perennia had been taken, not trying to retrieve the elusive memory that had been knocked out of her head.

Those were thoughts for another day.

Her focus right now was on finding a place to use her power to call Amare, using her abilities to tap into the magic of the realms beyond their own, as the Sages discovered long ago. Helia's talent was to harness nature, which meant she just needed to find a sign of life to let her cry for help ring out. Was that even possible here, now? Was anything left that hadn't been burned or corrupted in some way?

There.

Buried beneath the death and decay on the other side of the circular nest, she sensed something. Seemingly small and insignificant, it now felt like a blazing beacon of hope.

A single white rosebud that hadn't blossomed yet. A survivor in this wasteland.

Getting on her hands and knees, she inched her arm through the brambles. Vega was hovering behind her, his anxiety pulsing. He vibrated furiously to tell her to be careful, but she let the thorns scratch through her sleeves and dig into her skin without much care. She was only focused on the bud.

She grasped it in her fingers.

Her mind quickly traveled into the flower, into what roots were left, then out up into the air, through the wind, and around the rings of the sun.

The call for help she unleashed was as primal and instinctive as any that had ever existed.

It was suddenly as if she was everything and nothing at once. Part of the great fabric of existence. The glorious weight of all those sensations bore down on her, causing her to squeeze her eyes shut as she waited for a sign. A response. For Amarc to appear and save her.

The intensity was overwhelming, filling her with so many feelings she could barely stay conscious. Her fingers tightened, and her knuckles popped. She dug her free hand into the charred dirt and grasped at it for support.

How long she waited, she didn't know. It was probably only seconds, but in that moment, before she received an answer, it felt like she'd lived a billion years.

A screech tore through the air above her head, and the withered foliage swayed en masse as a colossal and magnificent bird appeared overhead. In a blinding flash, it was upon her, swooping low, its fiercely multicolored feathers rippling and sparkling in the light.

Amare circled once and landed gracefully next to her.

Helia tore her arm out of the foliage and hurried over. She climbed onto the bird's back. Vega floated after her, and she let him nestle safely in her lap. In her pocket, Antares was still motionless.

She looked over to Xavier and opened her mouth to say something, but he was already waving her off.

"Go. Go!"

The great bird, Amare, had been shifting uneasily on the grass, having noted the absence of the dragon. But with the sound of the crackling wall of vines across the Garden, she understood that danger was upon them.

The bird jolted and lifted them in a steep climb. Up and up and up, at such speed that Helia could barely catch her breath. It was not until they were high above the wall of vines that she saw the writhing sea of monsters below, their fire-ravaged forms now parting to reveal the evil leader in their midst. She gasped involuntarily.

She leaned over the bird's neck and tried to yell down to Xavier, to warn him, but her words were lost on the wind. Vega pulsed against her, unmistakably afraid. She had never known him to do that. She didn't even know Orbs could feel fear. There had never been a reason to be afraid of anything across all the realms of Paperworld.

"Xavier!" she screamed again. Could he hear her still? Could he sense what was coming?

Grasping Amare as tightly as she could, her fingers digging into the bird's thick feathers, she leaned over as far as she dared. Xav was still where she'd left him, watching her.

For an instant, the wildness of the air abated, and she managed to catch one single word.

A parting gift. It was weak, but undeniably him.

"Live!" he shouted.

She knew then that their moment of existence together, as fleeting as the elderly Sages had always said it would be, was over. She had to do as he said. Time had run out.

The shadow smoke had finally eaten through her magic.

From the center of the razed wall of vines, a figure materialized, wrapped in a glowing, burning cloak and shimmering within the rain of ash that fell around him.

The Ash Man barely seemed to notice the injured Sage as he walked past him. The evil being simply waved his hand, causing Xavier's body to convulse, before his entire being turned to cinders and blew away.

Helia screamed. Properly this time. A cry of rage and fear and anger and despair.

The malignant figure tilted his head toward the sound, his featureless white face looking straight up at her.

I am coming for you all, said a voice reverberating through her. *My Unwritten will find you. There is nowhere you can run, Sage.*

She almost found herself calling out for the bastard to burn her up as well, to rid herself of the agony she knew would haunt her.

But her fate was out of her hands.

Amare opened the fabric of time and space and carried her through the rift. And Helia found herself fleeing from smoke and ash and death for the second time in her life, leaving behind those she loved.

CHAPTER TWO
A MEETING IN THE GREAT LIBRARY

Helia's fingers tightened around feathers as she clung on to the bird, pressing her cheek into its neck as the universe buffeted her.

As a Sage, she'd been allowed to travel between realms many times over her long life, though always through the single portal in the Great Library that led here. That was the usual method of travel for Sages and their Orbs when leaving to explore the vastness of Paperworld.

Stepping into the other realms through the Great Library held a moment of magic known as the Glimmer, a tremor that ran through one's entire body, as though a multitude of emotions was washing through the body and filling it up for one glorious moment with all the joy the universe has ever known.

This transition was not like that.

Amare was a ball of light and a comet of fire and ice, which broke the normal rules that bound Paperworld. For those in dire need, Amare could be called on to carry people where they needed to go; however, traversing the boundary between realms was difficult and dangerous.

Across the universal winds they flew, through storms the size of planets, skirting rivers of electricity and around bends in time and space. Helia held fast as they swooped and dived, feeling her stomach in her throat with every jolt. Around them, new stories were born in fire, and trails of ancient stories burned fiercely in a river of words. She cradled a panicking Vega in her lap. She could feel her Orb trying to talk to her, but she was too focused on hanging on for dear life to try to translate his terrified pulses. She hoped that, in her pocket, Antares had remained shut down to avoid the experience altogether.

She wished she could have.

Her fingers dug into Amare until she knew she couldn't hold on any tighter. Then all that was left was for her to trust in the bird.

There was a deafening screech, and they entered a tunnel of light. Concentric rings of blue and gold swept past them, carrying them onward faster and faster, pushing them toward their destination. Through this passageway between realms they flew, until finally the light burst into fireworks before Helia's face and Amare swept gracefully into the center of an underground cavern, pulling back her wings to catch the air and slow their descent.

She landed softly on the brass-railed platform in the center of the space known as the Nest. It was carved deep in the rock of the island that held the Library, near the location where the first magic was discovered. The glow of bioluminescent pools across its floor made the dark place safe, underneath the ancient metal landing pad that held them now. It was a place built specifically to welcome Amare in the times she should ever be needed, which to Helia's memory had only been a handful.

Helia slid gratefully off her back, with Vega in her hand.

"Still with me, little one?"

Her Orb pulsed once, a sickly green swirl. *Let's never do that again*, he seemed to say.

He wobbled from her grasp, easing back into the air like a new-born balloon.

She turned back to the bird.

"Thank you," she said, her words a hushed echo that filled the otherwise empty cavern.

She placed her hand on the bird's beak, smoothed the feathers beneath her eye, and pressed her face into the comforting plumage. A quiet awe overwhelmed her, momentarily easing the sorrow gnawing in her gut. All the stories had not done this magnificent creature justice. And now she had ridden her. Xav would have been thrilled.

Amare leaned her head down briefly, returning the gesture. Then she nudged Helia. An unspoken message.

Stand. Carry on.

Helia stepped back, took a breath, then turned with Vega in tow. Despite the weight of grief on her shoulders, she hurried down the winding stairs and across the bridge to the door—with a care not to jostle Xav's small, exhausted Orb still in her pocket.

There was a flash behind them, and when she glanced back, Amare had gone.

"Let's find Mwamba," she said.

Vega swirled in agreement.

Nu walked along the Concourse lightly, enjoying the snippets of excited whispers she caught, dressed in colourful clothes, with her long dark hair swishing around her neck. Those gathered around the tables continued in their clusters of wisdom.

An arm waving in the throng caught Nu's eye, and she spotted two people passing by on the other side of the space. There was suddenly a warmth in her chest, and her breath caught. Not at the tall, goofy Will in his consistently rumpled tunic but rather the blond-haired Triss, with that swish of freckles across her nose that matched her star-embroidered dress.

Nu felt the warmth spread to her cheeks as her friends pushed their trollies over, each one was stacked with tiny mountains of books destined for a return to the shelves to be found anew. Will gave his usual lopsided grin and Nu returned it, while straightening her top as best she could, wishing she'd worn that much more elegant dress.

Then Triss drew up in front of her, flashed a wide smile, and began signing.

"Nu! I was hoping to see you today." She pointed in the direction of the nearby dining booths. "Would you like to meet tonight for dinner and drinks?"

Nu couldn't respond for a moment. Her brain was racing. Was Triss asking her out? Could this actually be happening? She glanced at Will, who was still grinning. No, wait. Was it a general invitation to join the pair of them? Or maybe more? Perhaps Will was going too.

Or maybe he was grinning because he knew what Triss had asked, and he was enjoying the momentous climax of months of Nu's awkward flirting finally paying off.

Nu gave Triss a thumbs-up.

She immediately regretted it—such a lame response!—and tried to reply properly.

Nu's signing wasn't perfect, but there were enough classes at school in order for everyone—from students to Sages, hearing-impaired or not—to be able to communicate with each other when needed. Of course, the magic of the Great Library was such that sign language wasn't always needed, as the Book of Wisdom ensured there were no language barriers here. When people passed into these hallowed halls, they would find themselves able to understand each other no matter where they were from or how they communicated. It worked for the books too—it didn't matter what language they had been written in; anybody could understand them.

But Nu had wanted to experience real, authentic communication with Triss. To be able to properly speak to the friend she had grown up with . . . and had discovered feelings for at an early age. Nu had worked hard to ensure she could make herself understood, and now she could. All that remained was to actually have the courage to express the words.

"I'd love to. I should be free after work."

Those weren't the words she wanted to say. But they were *some* words. A proper response. And who knows, perhaps this was going to be her first date with the girl she had loved from a distance for so long.

"Great!" Triss signed back. "I'll see you then."

As her friends moved off, Nu was halfway to doing a little jump of delight when Will looked back and added, "See you!" He then went back to chatting amiably with Triss, who read his lips and kept signing in response.

See you? Now what did *that* mean? The butterflies in her stomach froze midflight.

Was Will joining them? Or was it a general "see you"?

She stared at the pair moving through the crowd, trying to draw on that gut feeling she was so familiar with, her fingers flexing and clenching by her side. Using her *knowing* wasn't something she often did to read how people were feeling around her. She felt it somewhat of an invasion of privacy. Yet right now she didn't care. This was important! And people used all kinds of ways of determining how someone felt, right? Body language. Tone of voice.

This was hers.

"Focus," she muttered. "*Focus.*"

But she came up short.

Soon they were lost to the crowd.

She took a slow, deep breath.

"What will be will be, I guess," she said, rather too loudly, startling a passing scholar who almost dropped his scrolls. She gave him a smile, then turned on her heels and kept walking in the other direction, trying hard to shift the rush coursing through her veins back to focusing on the exciting job she had ahead of her.

Not long out of her schooling—although, in the Library, one was never done learning—Nu was content to help out in any role she was asked to perform. Most who reached adulthood here were the same. If you were born in the Library, you grew up understanding the part everyone had to play in making this magical, important nexus of knowledge what it was—a place to hold the discoveries in the realms beyond, to guide the dreamers who ventured here in search of answers, and to sow inspiration into their fertile minds.

Nu especially loved the roles that took her closer to the outside world. Today her task was a greeting, which perhaps might not be seen as exciting as other roles that could take her farther afield on Earth itself, but it was enough for her. She loved meeting new people and getting glimpses of the exciting and fascinating lives they led, even if it often left her dreaming about one day having a higher purpose. Sometimes she envied the visitors she welcomed into the Library—how they were called here for a reason and would find their lives changed forever as they were guided toward the answers they sought.

There were many ways to find yourself in the Great Library of Tomorrow. There were portals scattered all across Earth, although most were hidden, like wooden doors weathered with age and tucked away at the back of rarely visited alcoves, or vine-covered stone archways at the end of mossy paths.

Those particular entrances weren't staffed by anyone. There was magic at work that ensured nobody paid the least bit attention to these magical gateways into the Great Library, save for those chosen people who found it when it was the right time.

Yet people's destined paths changed all the time, and the Book of Wisdom was wise enough to know that sometimes a helping hand was needed to gently nudge someone from one world into another. And that was where Nu found herself useful, occasionally tasked with waiting at these magical portals to help guide whoever it was into the Great Library.

Hurrying on, she wove through the streams of captured starlight that puddled across the marble floor, wondering where she'd find herself today. Passing the corridor that led toward the Sages' Gallery, she was delighted to see Sage Maïa and her companions as they left that chamber. She instantly recognized the Sage of Integrity, with her high cheekbones and cunning gaze befitting her middle age.

Maïa had been the first Sage who Nu had seen walking these halls. Back from one of the realms, the Sage had been walking along, nodding and smiling to those she passed. Which just happened to include a young Nu, off running errands for her parents. The light glinting in the woman's eyes, the sly grin, and the heady scent of summer flowers as she breezed past were enough to form a memory within Nu that she knew she wouldn't fast forget. It made it difficult not to stop and stare.

The woman was wearing a flowing green dress to match her eyes, with her crimson hair spun in circles around her head. It was a bright and colorful look, stunning, even by the standards of what people usually wore within the Great Library. And although Maïa often dressed a little sharper than the others, her outfit today was elaborate enough to indicate she was again on her way beyond this world.

Nu watched, wondering which realm was lucky enough to be receiving her as a visitor.

The Sage turned in the other direction and headed for the Haven, where the Book of Wisdom and the portal to other realms could be found. The woman's Orb floated at her shoulder, and a small black cat trotted dutifully alongside her feet.

Funnily enough, Nu heard rumors that a few Sages had been called away again today for various reasons back into Paperworld. She considered it a sign of good luck that, before she left on her own mission, she had managed to catch a glimpse of one of their number.

What it must be like to have such responsibility, she thought with wonder. *To know every step you took carried you forward for a greater cause.*

Passing the majestic theater-style entrance to the Auditorium, she could hear one of the inspiration sessions. The booming laughter of Sage Veer reverberated from inside, accompanied by a multitude of otherworldly rhythms, each running to its own time, each overlapping the last, yet somehow all perfectly in sync. The poster adorning the Auditorium wall—showing the Sage standing at the center of a huge circular arena—suddenly came to life as she passed it. Veer's mustache lifted as he grinned, and he started to chat amiably, encouraging Nu to join them in learning about some musical wonders he had recently discovered. As he leaned out of the poster, she couldn't help but shuffle aside quickly. She knew it wasn't real—only a little of the Library's magic—yet there was an intimidating presence to Veer, even in poster form, that made her feel a little shy, as though the man himself was actually talking to her.

She lifted her hand in apology and hurried on, taking a shortcut into the sweet-smelling domain of the kitchens.

"Hey, Nu!" Grindlepuffin, a boyish cook, greeted her. Noticing the bounce in her step, he said, "Off to work, I take it?"

She nodded and paused only to snatch a handful of dark chocolate beans from a platter of food he was preparing, before bouncing away through the culinary artists from all backgrounds on Earth.

She herself had been born in the Library. Her parents—her mother Australian and her father Burmese—had found this place long ago, back when they were science-obsessed twentysomethings, and eventually settled here. But Nu had not yet had a chance to visit her ancestral homes, though she desperately wanted to see where they had grown up.

Like many others here, she had spent her entire life in the Great Library. She felt the urge to explore beyond its magnificent walls grow as she got older, the outside world as fascinating to her as the magical realms of Paperworld. It seemed strange to yearn for things unknown to her, outside of seeing them in books. But yearn she did.

Yes, she was able to talk to people from all over Earth, and she often snuck into the Observatory, where she could see events through an ingenious mix of technology and magic.

But there was simply no substitute for being able to glimpse it for yourself.

Which is why she loved it whenever she got to go and greet visitors, like the one she was on her way to meet.

Helia raced through the passageways toward the Sages' chambers; through the caves of heated springs, where one could soak and rejuvenate among the stalactites and stalagmites; past the crystal hall, where any noise made was turned into music by the living rocks around them; then into the upside-down gardens beneath swirls of green shoots from which hung colorful fruits and vegetables.

Life in the Library was continuing as normal. Nobody was the least bit aware of what had happened. Helia hoped that would be the case for a while, although she didn't know what was going to happen now—she just hoped her old friend Mwamba would have an idea about what to do.

Luckily, the man she sought was exactly where she expected him to be.

As she and her Orb burst into the room, it felt like stumbling into a cherished memory: The safe embrace of a parent when one awoke from a nightmare as a child. A time in life when comfort and warmth were easy to find.

Sage Mwamba's preferred reading room was often like that. It was one of her favorite places in the Library for just that reason. Now, though, it felt muted and flat. Not enough to dispel the sadness gripping her heart.

An old, worn desk rested in the center, covered with scattered scrolls and a teetering pile of books and surrounded by mismatched chairs. Bookshelves filled to the brim lined the walls in the flickering shadows, beckoning you to come closer and explore their pages. To one side sat an easel with a half-finished painting of the ocean and a rugged coastline. Above the roaring fireplace hung a haunting portrait of a proud Black woman in a blue dress, the barest hint of mischief captured in the corners of her eyes.

Helia often found Mwamba in here sunk deeply into his plush, green armchair, staring wistfully at the woman. The painting was his pride and his solace, though he had not revealed to anybody who the woman was. He'd simply smile whenever he was asked.

He wasn't smiling now.

Helia's eyes shifted from the painting to the chair beside the fireplace as the man resting in it lowered the dusty tome he had been reading. The Sage of Knowledge's normally cheerful demeanor was held in restraint, his powerful gaze twitching from confusion to grim understanding as he saw the state of her and the fact she had returned alone.

"Helia," he said, quietly shutting the book and placing it carefully in his lap. His long fingers clasped together over its cover, as they always did when he was ready to listen. The scar that ran the length of his face, from the side of his left eye to his chin, twitched as his jaw hardened.

Canopus, his Orb, flew down from where he had been working among the bookshelves to hover at Mwamba's shoulder.

Helia straightened as best she could. In her mind, she could still see Xav's face as they'd parted, willing her to be strong. And while she could feel the churn of an ocean of loss inside her, she would do her best to stay afloat. The Great Library needed her. Mourning would come later.

"Mwamba," she said, looking into the eyes of her friend and colleague of many centuries, a man who had loved her like a father all these years. "We're in trouble."

As she went to sit down in one of the chairs, ready to tell him everything, she reached into her pocket to check on Antares, only to discover the little Orb, her last remaining physical connection to Xavier, had gone.

Nu hurried beyond the dining rooms and halls, out into another smaller atrium, and followed a path that ran underneath towering bridges, which crisscrossed above them. Some of the bridges were aqueducts, carrying water from the wellsprings deep in the Library. And then there were those that carried the marvelous tram around various parts of the city. In fact, she could just about hear the clickety-clack in the distance and pictured the graceful assemblages of brass and steel and hardwood—veritable works of art on wheels—chugging around, carrying its passengers sitting in luxurious upholstered seats.

Yet it was down here, among the people, that was Nu's favorite place to while away her time. There was something about being in the hustle and bustle of it all that filled her with glee. It was as if she was able to soak in all the hopes and dreams of scholars, workers, Sages, and visitors by walking among them.

This also came with a growing feeling of longing, that need to have a purpose, as all those others did. She didn't have a clue what her purpose might be, but she did love helping out around the Library. All she knew was there was a blossoming need inside her to be doing *more*, to be contributing even more positivity to the Library and the Earth and the realms bey—

Her daydreaming was suddenly interrupted by a commotion ahead.

She had made her way back into the network of corridors near the Sages' reading rooms, where in front of her a door burst open, and two figures swiftly rushed out. It didn't take much to recognize them from the back: the regal man on the left was Sage Mwamba, and his companion, with dark curly hair befitting her Mediterranean heritage, was Sage Helia.

And while it certainly was rare to have seen three Sages in a single trip across the Library, that wasn't what made Nu stop in her tracks and frown.

Helia looked like she'd been in a battle. Her traveling tunic was charred, torn in several places, and looked very much like it was covered in blood.

Her blood?

The idea that one of the Sages was hurt sent Nu's brain into a wild panic. Should she go and help? Or would that be insulting to Mwamba, who was already clearly assisting her?

More importantly, what could have happened?

Nu wanted to run after them, but something held her feet where they stood. She knew something was very wrong. She also knew it was not appropriate for her to interrupt them right now.

Knowing such things was something Nu became used to over the years. She often wondered if the Book of Wisdom knew of her strange talent too. Maybe that's why she had been chosen for the kind of work she was undertaking today.

Yet even as she hurried somewhere, another knowing nudged her insides and told her to wait. And in that moment, she looked down and saw a small shape in the center of the corridor.

It was so small that at first; she wasn't sure if it was real or a speck of dust in her eye. A tiny ball, not much bigger than a marble. As she peered closer, it appeared to move, and she gave a small yelp of surprise, at which point it started rolling weakly along the carpet toward her, bouncing up and down every so often, like a newborn bird learning to fly.

An Orb.

Unsure of what exactly was happening, she knelt and held out her hand, allowing the small ball to roll up her fingers and into her palm.

Only Sages had Orbs, and they very rarely went anywhere without each other. What's more, she'd never seen an Orb this size before. Had it been shrunk or damaged somehow? There was no way of telling.

"Hello, little one," she said gently, so as not to scare it. It seemed to tremble in her hand. "And where have you come from?"

The Orb went still for a moment, as though out of breath.

Nu lifted it up. The small being trembled again weakly, but it was doing its best. It gave her a tiny buzz of vibration, like a whisper she couldn't quite make out.

She ran a gentle finger over its smooth surface.

"You're trying to speak to me, aren't you? I'm so sorry. I'm not a Sage, so I don't understand you as much as I would like."

The Orb shook once more, just barely, then was still.

Nu frowned. She didn't understand why, but there was that feeling again. A knowing about this little companion's state and what lay behind it. The harmless being before her held shadows. It was not just an Orb that had depleted in strength but one that had been through something she couldn't yet imagine.

She knew it needed her.

She stroked it again and stood carefully, making sure the little thing didn't fall from her grasp. Her eyes glanced up to the end of the corridor, where she'd seen the two Sages disappear, and wondered whether it belonged to one of them. But then she remembered that each had been accompanied by their own Orbs, so it couldn't be.

No matter. There wasn't time to dwell on the puzzle. She had somewhere to be, and she needed to hurry now. It was almost time for her to be at the portal, and she couldn't stand the thought of letting anyone down, especially if the Book had deemed the visitor she was to meet worthy of coming here.

She whispered to her new friend, "Don't worry. You can come with me for the time being. I promise I'll look after you. Then we'll see about getting you back to wherever you need to be, okay?" She popped the ball gently into the pocket of her hooded jacket, hurried up the corridor, and took the turn away from where the Sages had gone.

CHAPTER THREE
CELEBRATIONS AT THE GREAT TREE

It was late at the heart of Silvyra, the Great Tree.

As Dzin reached up to pin the end of the vine with glowing berries to the top of the shelf, he felt the stool wobble underneath him. His lanky black hair fell over his eyes, and his elbow accidentally nudged a stack of research papers.

The crinkle of the paper reminded him again that his own work still sat quietly on his desk on the other side of the room. He'd been staring at his formula proudly all afternoon, twirling his beloved walking staff in his hands, enjoying the sheer joy and relief at having managed to get it right. His very own formula for the Elixir of Life! All the hard work had paid off; he'd undertaken this labor of love to apply the philosophy of the Seed of Life, which all botanists—and prospective Runners in particular—held sacred. Now he just needed to remember to put the scroll in his shirt pocket ready for tomorrow's ceremony. It was the one thing needed to complete the ritual—the scroll handed from student to teacher to prove he was ready to become a Runner.

It would be just like him to forget it and turn up empty-handed.

"Concentrate, Dzin," Monae urged as the vine almost fell from his grasp. "A Runner's focus always needs to be switched on. How else do you think they locate the ingredients the refinery needs for the Elixir? They must have the keenest concentration, a mind like a pollen trap, always ready to catch whatever clues to resources they might happen across."

Monae's eyebrow was raised as she looked up from where she stood watching him. Her blueberry-colored eyes scoured the length of the vine, judging the distance between the illuminated berries to make sure they were even and perfect.

"Rot and canker, Monae, I *am* concentrating! Besides, we haven't even graduated yet, and I'm not searching across the realm right now, am I? Can't you give me a night off?"

She harrumphed good-naturedly, and he did as she asked anyway. Monae always liked everything *just so*, and while his arm hurt from hanging the ornaments and lights, Dzin understood her excitement.

They'd already decorated the extensive leaf-roofed gazebo outside the front of the laboratory. This was where the party would burst into life the next day around the specially carved centerpiece—a circle of figures representing the five graduating students, each chiseled and sculpted from golden heartwood by the finest Silvyran craftswomen. Monae had then decided to use the leftover ornaments and lights to brighten up the inside of the laboratory too. And why not? Their friends and family would be here to celebrate.

Dzin had experienced the festivities before, of course, as the whole Great Tree celebrated the achievement of the students. But now he would be the focus of the celebration, as one of the students themselves. It meant everything to him to be embraced by his community in such a way. To feel their pride and to know he had done something of worth with his life, as his parents had always wanted. As *he* had always wanted.

It hadn't always been easy. He hated that his journey here had almost come apart, and he'd almost let himself be thrown from the path, spiraling into his usual panic. Yet, with a little help, he had rallied. Overcome the obstacles. And he had *made it*.

All that was left now was to enjoy the moment. A confirmation of his value.

The hairs on his arm rose at the thought of the excitement that awaited. The air would be infused with a blend of magic and music and song. The trunk of the Great Tree would vibrate with deep and power-ful beats all through the night, until the glorious golden sunrise filtered through the leaves. And the elder musician of the community, Pulse, would regale them with his storytelling melodies, until the music was brought to an end, and the exhausted and joyful gathering would stum-ble contentedly back to their homes.

Monae nudged his leg. "Come on, we're almost done. A little more to the side, now up. For petal's sake, be bolder with it, Dzin! Where's that famous sense of adventure that brought you into the school, eh? Wait . . . stop . . . yes. There! Pin it quickly!"

Dzin blew his hair out of his eyes and silently corrected her that it had always been more of a love of traveling—rather than a thirst for adventure—that had attracted him to the Botanical Education School. In his experience, nobody ever understood the differences between the two, with one involving new sights and smells and a different way of viewing the world, and the other involving danger.

And the problem with danger was that it tended to involve risks that could bring on his anxiety.

But he said nothing to his friend. It was not worth getting into that whole debate again. So he simply did as he was told, then climbed down and stood next to her as they admired their handiwork.

"Perfect," Monae said, happily following the curves of the green vine and its beautiful berry lights as it swept like colorful waves around the room. She gave him a grin. "I think that does it!"

"Thank Mother for that." He gave her a begrudging smile, re-lieved he didn't have to adjust anything more. They'd been working from light into darkness on these decorations already. He felt the sweat against his neck, and he pulled at the collar of his shirt to try to get some air in there.

"So how are you feeling?" Monae asked. It would have been per-fectly innocuous from anybody else, but with her it carried weight. She was checking in on him, as usual. "Are you ready for all this, Dzin?"

Only she knew how he had struggled to find his last ingredient.

He'd been too stressed to think straight, too consumed by wanting to do a good job to actually be able to do it.

He nodded gratefully, feeling a sudden lump in his throat and unwilling to chance saying anything in response. She accepted that, though, and went off to continue her preparations.

It was growing increasingly warm in the laboratory, high up on the topmost branch of the Great Tree—or Mother, as Dzin had always known her—despite the night's chill that rattled the seasonal golden leaves and plump popping berries that hung outside. The coziness was perhaps not helped by the fact that all five students were now crammed into the room. And though it was a generous space, the excitement and effort of decorating was making them all red in the cheeks.

The other three Silvyran students were still bustling around. Dzin was used to seeing that during the many rotations they'd been working hard at researching, experimenting, and perfecting their formulas for the Elixir of Life—a liquid, applied like an ointment, that could heal any ailments that befell a person. Yet now the movement of his friends was fraught with nervous anticipation. The Elixir had demanded perfection from them to get right, and all the students wanted to make sure they carried that through to the end. Nobody wanted to be the ones to make any mistakes. The very thought of it made Dzin's chest ache. Their big day had to be *perfect*.

He thought it fitting they should celebrate their last night before graduation here. It was, after all, a place they had come to call home—not least because they saw it more than their actual cubbies in the Tree. Whenever they returned from traveling to faraway lands, having collected ingredients for their Elixir, it always felt like returning to family. Because they *were* a family of sorts now.

He looked over at his closest friend, Monae, the colorful beads in her hair complementing the silvery-green hues of her skin. He chuckled at her need for order, her workstation obsessively neat as always, and the real reason they were tidying the laboratory before the ceremony. *I mean*, he thought, *it's a lab! It's supposed to be cluttered!*

He glanced over at Pyruc, the lad's lanky form striding over to put his Threbolometer back on the shelf with the other instruments before Monae turned her attention to him once she'd finished with Dzin. Gaeloc and Atraena, collectively known as "the Twins"—he with hair like the sun; she with hair of the blackest blackbird—were doing their part, although Gaeloc was already sneaking gulps from the fountains of nectar that were dotted around the place, while Atraena was testing and retesting the root sound system, through which the music would be carried all around Mother.

"Just the sprite leaves to go, and then I think we're almost ready," Monae said proudly, hands on her hips. The other three across the room grinned at her excitedly. She turned to Dzin. "Can you believe we're here now, on the cusp of graduating? All these moons of dreaming about being Runners, and here we are about to join their number. We did it!"

He beamed back, feeling that same glow as his friends, that sense of satisfaction and glee that comes with working hard enough—and perhaps also from having that stroke of luck in the first place to discover an ambition that can blossom into a reality.

We did it, he repeated to himself.

Making the Elixir of Life was a ritual that took place every alignment of the two moons. Each time, five students in the Botanical Education School were selected, those with the most powerful sense of smell, the keenest botanical skills, and the greatest thirst for adventure. Their job was to discover formulas and brew the potion that the Great Tree was famous for—the Elixir of Life—before it was then bottled and shipped across the world. Each vial contained the results of a unique and personal concoction that always led to a magical liquid that when dabbed on your skin would heal whatever ailments had befallen you, be they physical, emotional, or something else entirely.

It could take many moons to find the ingredients that made up each student's own special formula. Entire seasons might be spent away from their home looking for them, before they returned to focus themselves on the work of crafting a formula to brew their very own version of the Elixir of Life. Then they would graduate to become the latest Runners, who would not only be responsible for locating the ingredients needed for the refinery to produce the Elixir on a widespread scale but they would also teach the next generation of students.

The graduation celebrations were famed throughout Silvyra for shaking Mother to her roots. Dzin was nervous, but he couldn't wait to be a part of such a historic experience.

He tried and failed not to dwell on how this could all have been very different had he not found that last ingredient. Thankfully, one of his teachers—the stocky and balding Tywich—had been eager to help. And even though Dzin had always been a little wary of the eccentric man and his strange blank stare, which sometimes made it feel like he wasn't really present, he had been grateful for the assistance.

At his lowest ebb, Dzin had sought out and talked with the man. Tywich had helped by asking questions about his childhood, as they tried to determine where he might best find his final ingredient. As with all the ingredients, it had to be personal to him. This was how, a few nights earlier, the pair had ended up climbing from bough to bough, down through the settlements of Mother to the roots of the Great Tree, away from any watching souls, and where only the tiny flying Bugscrubs and insect-like Crunchers could see them.

"You talk often of your parents, Dzin," Tywich had said as they stood there in the mulch, listening to the sniffles of the creatures around them. His face was lit only by the soft fingers of moonlight that drifted through the leaves above, giving him an appearance that looked like the dead rising. "You say you want to make them proud. Thinking of them has guided you to the precipice of success, with nearly all your ingredients gathered."

Dzin nodded, saying nothing. His parents died when he was young, forcing him to grow up sooner than he would have liked. Not that he resented them for that. It just . . . made him feel different to everyone else. His friends had grown up with their families, large and small. Dzin only had Yantuz now, and though he loved his brother, he missed his mother and father fiercely.

The idea of making them proud didn't make any sense. Yet it had driven him. Always pushing him forward, through bad times and good, toward a goal they could only hope beyond hope to reach.

Tywich seemed to understand that. He gestured beyond the roots, pointing a chubby finger toward a place that all in the Tree knew: the graveyard of the Tree folk.

"What if they are guiding you still?"

And that was when Dzin knew what his final ingredient was. Now they were here, it was obvious. Using his walking stick, he'd stumbled through the leaf litter and over fallen branches, passing the markings of so many others until he reached the calm and quiet of his own parents' resting place.

As he'd approached, a rush of memories hit him: their sudden loss and the feeling of their absence in the cubby; how after their deaths he had seen his mother's staff—now his walking stick—how he'd picked it up and been unable to let it go; and then there had been the immense pressure, knowing that he was now responsible for raising Yantuz, being both an older brother and a substitute parent.

Yantuz had been too young to really understand what was happening, beyond the immediate grief. So as he got older, he'd been able to let go of their memories more easily. Dzin hadn't. He'd carried that loss every day since, some days heavier than others, while always trying to do his best for them. So much so that he feared he had fallen into the routine of perfectionism, constantly feeling anxious he was falling short.

The symbol he and his brother had carved into the bark was still above their graves, a little dirty and covered in moss, but clear enough for him to recognize it. Two curves of the twin Silvyran moons. One for each of his parents. He smiled when he saw it, but then he was beset by an overwhelming sadness.

Grief all over again, combined with a heady mix of anxiety and the fear of failure. He had let them down, hadn't he? After all the work he had done, in the end, he had to be led here. He hadn't found the place by himself; he had needed the help and guidance of a teacher.

What kind of Runner would need that?

Worst of all, he still hadn't found the last piece.

In that moment, Dzin had almost broke down and wept over their graves. Even now, under the lights of the laboratory, he could still feel his breath that night coming in shallow, labored gasps as it always did when he panicked. The shivers of the white-cold fear burrowing under his skin. The tightness across his chest and along his limbs, and his vision, blurring.

At the gravesite, he had gripped the walking staff hard, trying to hold on to the constant of its rough bark beneath his fingers, to hold the panic at bay. But he was otherwise frozen. A statue of anxiety, battered by a hurricane of emotions that wanted to crumble him into dust.

Until.

His eyes caught a glint of something unusual growing in the soil nearby.

The fat, damp, silvery stalks of mushrooms, each barely bigger than a finger, with a thin brown cap on top, and only really visible if you happened to be standing right in that exact spot.

The storm in his mind almost immediately blew itself out. The weight of emotions in his chest dissipated, and his fingers released their grip on his walking staff as he reached down to gather the precious ingredient.

This is it.

"I think I've found it!" he said to himself.

"So you have," Tywich replied, looking satisfied as Dzin returned to show the collection of mushrooms he clutched in his hand.

After that night, Dzin had needed to hurry to finish the formula and brew his Elixir. But he'd managed it with time to spare.

Now he was here, getting the place ready to celebrate their graduation. His graduation. And his potion sat proudly on the shelf along the back wall, in a curved glass vial next to those of his fellow classmates. He noticed his bottles were a little less full than the others, which was odd, because he was sure he'd managed to fill more than he could currently see. But it had been a tiring process, and Tywich had insisted upon Dzin getting some rest when he was done. His teacher had been talking to the advisor of the Great Tree at the time, and the advisor himself had asked for the honor of checking Dzin's Elixir for him, which was unusual, but what was Dzin to say?

Perhaps the advisor had simply taken a little more than the usual amount to test it.

Patting his multipocketed coat to feel the collection of tiny fungi still hiding inside, he made a mental note to store them in the ingredients archive next time he was in there. Once all this decorating was finally finished.

Little did he know, he would never get the chance.

CHAPTER FOUR
WHAT MAGIC STILL EXISTS

Nu navigated the twisting network of corridors before finally entering a place just outside the heart of the Library—the Annex.

She stepped into the perfectly square rock-cut room and headed for the twisted oak desk, where a man sat beside a doorway that glimmered with silver.

"Hey, Nu," Halbeard said, his cheeks rosy with good cheer. He swept through the virtual pages of his diary. "Where are you off to today, then? Ah, I've found you. Today it's a bookshop!"

"Oh, how lovely," Nu said immediately, bouncing up and down on her toes. She lived her whole life in the Library, but there was something about those bookshops back on Earth that was every bit as magical. "I can't wait. Whereabouts will it be?"

"Mexico City, it says here, where it is"—he flicked to another page and frowned slightly—"currently thirty-seven degrees Celsius, with some torrential rain."

He gestured for her to continue, and she pressed her palm to the broad leaf that was sticking up from the vine around the desk. It scanned her and pulsed once, a glorious and bright shade of green, acknowledging her journey ahead.

"You may proceed," he said. "Good luck!"

Nu gave him an excited grin and stepped toward the door. It blazed into life, pouring golden light out into the room, and she had to shield her eyes against it, but she moved forward all the same and let the light wrap around her like a warm embrace.

Her head felt light, and for a split second, she felt like she was spinning through the universe. Then she arrived at her destination and was once more surrounded by her favorite things in all the world—books.

It wasn't a real bookshop, of course. It was an extension of the magic of the Library and served as a more powerful and obvious portal for those visitors who needed a little more of a nudge to step between realms.

She stepped up to the wide window to breathe in a rare glimpse of the world outside the Library—a city street that shimmered beneath the rain lashing down the buildings and streaming over the sidewalks and road. The locals hurried past, giving the sky above them dirty looks as they scuttled between the patches of shelter along the street.

But Nu had no mind to worry about such things right now. She was just happy to be here, able to see the world in person. She looked down at the clothes she'd appeared in, created by the Library's magic to enable her to fit in here—a long checkered skirt and a white blouse, topped off with the brightest white trainers. She did a twirl and then bounced back to behind the counter, where she needed to be.

With a contented sigh, she stared through the glass, wondering with a growing excitement who she was about to meet and why they might be coming to the Great Library.

The rain was heavy, even for a July afternoon in Mexico City.

Arturo stared at the browning and now waterlogged shrubs and dying strips of grass that were meant to breathe life into the space outside the modern office building he had just left. He knew he should go straight home, but a huge and persuasive part of him wanted a quick trip to the cantina to begin his week off work with a much-needed drink.

Unfortunately, the rain was only part of his problems. As he loosened his tie—he *knew* the damn thing was a silly idea, but his ex-wife, Elena, had convinced him that dressing professionally might help with his focus—he accepted that he was at a loss for what to do with his life. The rainy season finally chose that moment to appear, two months too late, its dark clouds shrouding the sun, *el sol sangriento*, before unleashing those long-awaited torrents of water . . . well, it only compounded his mood.

"Are you with us, Arturo, or have you started your holiday early?" Juan, the twenty-nine-year-old creative director, had joked during the last of the day's meetings.

Arturo had not been entirely present. He had been staring out of the window, fixated on his usual daydream of books he wanted to write, creating worlds in his head and giving voices to characters who had appeared to talk to him. He had long ago given up trying to keep up with the agency's team of young, energetic writers.

As he'd smiled apologetically, he could almost see their eyes rolling collectively. He ran a hand through his hair, trying not to be self-conscious of the fact there had been even more gray in it this morning, a discovery that made him even more aware of the fact he'd outlasted all his old colleagues. He was now at least a decade older than everyone in the room and knew that if he'd taken a different path he could potentially have been the one running the meeting—or indeed the whole agency.

But that's not what he wanted. He enjoyed writing. He loved the process of crafting meaning from certain words, pulling them into line, observing them from every angle, and breathing life into them in new and interesting ways. So he had stayed a copywriter while others climbed the corporate ladder.

And that had been enough, for a time. Occasionally, the work that came along allowed him to express his creativity in a positive way that could do some good—sometimes they worked with a charity or a cutting-edge business that was looking to help the world—but lately Arturo was finding his attention drifting more and more toward the stories he would much rather be telling. He needed more to sate the growing hunger inside him to be doing the thing he always felt, secretly, that he should be doing.

Ever since he had been a child, he wanted to tell real-life stories and bring some positivity into peoples' lives—to show them where to find inspiration and hope in the world when they needed it the most, and to hold on to those hopes as they grew. An important lesson that . . . well, hadn't most of us forgotten over the years?

He certainly had.

His writing had lost its magic. With all his talents, all he did now was write superficial copy that only aided the very worst of capitalism. Besides, the older he got, the more he realized he should be doing more for the world that had given him so much. Especially for his daughter. Wouldn't it be something special to be able to say that he'd helped fix the world for her—no matter how small a part he'd had to play?

"Tell me a story, Papa," she'd ask him every night without fail. And every night he would tell her a new story he conjured up on the spot, never the same, always something new.

He cherished those moments creating stories with Rosa, and he wished he had more of them. But too many times in recent years he'd let life get in the way. The demands of his job and paying the bills especially. The stresses of parenting. Then navigating a deteriorating marriage, which had come to an amicable, if not a little heartbreaking, end not so long ago.

It had all got between him and what he loved doing.

"Writers write" was a saying he knew all too well. So why hadn't he written?

More importantly, was it too late to pick it up again?

Turning his back on his office building, Arturo walked away, taking a left at the end of the street and splashing across the road between the cars that zipped past.

Two blocks up, he then pulled into a side street he loved and feared in equal measure. He saw the facade of *La Celestina Oscura*, and his lips suddenly felt far too dry. The smile faded a little.

Just the one caguama today, he thought, as if the act of making a silent pact with himself would make any difference. *Just the one, Arturo. Enjoy the beer and a botana, just to take the edge off your frustration and the humidity.*

Yet as he made his way over, trying to keep beneath the shelter of the trees, he realized something about the scene wasn't quite as expected.

The disused alleyway between the bar and the shop next door was no longer empty. The scattered boxes and overflowing garbage containers were nowhere to be seen.

Instead, was a very small, very thin, and incredibly familiar bookshop with rain washing down its windows. An entire building that looked as if it had always been there, nestled quietly between the others beside it, waiting for him.

There was a hand-painted sign above the window.

La Luna, it said in dreamy white letters.

It was his childhood bookshop—or at least it looked a lot like how he remembered it. *La Luna* had been his favorite haunt as a child, when his mother would take him there as a treat after school, not always to buy, but to breathe in the different worlds that existed across the bookshelves. While in there, he would always feel the universe of possibilities around him.

It was a cozy, warm, loving memory. One of his favorites.

Which made it all the stranger that it had appeared here—real and colorful and alive—when Arturo knew for a fact the actual bookshop he remembered so fondly had been located on the other side of the city and was torn down years ago to make room for apartments.

He frowned, glanced at the cantina, then back at the bookshop, which was still there, refusing to become any less real.

How can that be?

The question lingered for a moment, and he tried to gather his senses. But they would not be gathered. Instead, he felt a very strong urge to run over to the memory made real, grab the slick, wet door handle, and go inside.

Which is what he did.

"*Buenas tardes,*" said a young woman behind the counter—the very same counter he remembered peering up to as a child, pushing some saved coins across the desk as he bought a comic or a picture book. The woman didn't seem to mind his look of utter shock as he stared around him. She simply waited until his gaze returned to her, before she beamed a smile that lit up her whole face. Arturo found himself grinning back. There was an energy to this girl that immediately set him at ease.

"*Buenas tardes*," he replied. He half gestured to the room around them, ready to ask the quite ridiculous question about how exactly this bookshop had appeared here, when the woman continued speaking.

"Is it your first time here?"

He forgot his question and felt himself shake his head, then nod.

"Um, I don't know," he eventually settled on.

Her warm smile widened, putting him back at ease, and then she gestured breezily to the back of the shop.

"Head down the stairs, then look for the second aisle on the left. You'll find what you need there."

"What I need?" he repeated, scratching his head. Why had he come in here again? "I'm not sure I understand. What do I need exactly?"

For the briefest second, he considered leaving and heading to the safety of the cantina and some alcohol, but his interest was piqued now. He felt like the other Arturo again, the old Arturo, the storyteller who right now wanted to know what lay down the stairs, in the second aisle on the left.

So he followed her directions, heading back into the deeper recesses of this strange shop, until he found himself faced with aisles of books.

"I'll know it when I see it," he muttered as he wandered, only slightly aware that he could hear voices in the distance. Yet there was nobody else here. He listened closer. A buzz of activity. He wondered if it was coming from the cantina next door. His mouth instantly dried up at the thought of that cool bottle of beer. But something in him kept his eyes gazing over the shelves, even though there was nothing remarkable about the books he saw. They were dusty and old and had titles he didn't recognize.

Until he came to the aisle he had been told to find.

It was labeled simply. Two words in black on a small white sign. But it might as well have been emblazoned in neon with a flashing sign saying "Here, Arturo!" such was the impact they had on him.

Pequeño escritor.

Little writer.

The connection with his past overtook him; he sensed the embrace of his mother, who always called him that whenever he handed her one of his scribbles. Two words whispered delicately in his ear as she hugged him, as if confirming the path she could see him taking.

That feeling of nostalgia only grew when he saw the first book on the shelf. He stopped in his tracks. It was a picture book he remembered from his childhood, with five birds on the front set against a stunning orange sky—the very same book he'd read to his daughter when she was a baby. Next to that was another fond classic whose cover with the excited children and the big tree he recognized instantly. Then another from when he was eight, with a beautiful, fantastical landscape and two riders on horses in the foreground looking up to a city in the sky. Then another from the same series; he'd read that one when he was a little older. Then there was a whole stack of graphic novels from his teenage years, epic books he'd spent all his time devouring while holed up in his bedroom.

He ran a careful finger over them all, his gaze lovingly caressing each spine as his feet shuffled him from memory to memory.

Then, for one beautiful moment, some primal force stirred within him, as though the pages of his own story were being quickly flicked through by a strong breeze.

He realized he had reached the end of the shelf.

The final title staring at him, bookending the others, was the very last book he had read. He'd finished it only last night.

What strangeness was this? He had read every book in the entire row, as if the selection of books had been carefully curated from his entire lifetime's reading.

Yet this wasn't the only strange thing he noticed now. Because the cheap pine shelf he had started along had somehow morphed into something grander, a bookcase carved of the finest dark oak. The noise he had heard earlier was now thick around him—the hushed whispers of people talking, books being shuffled across desks, the odd *whoosh* as something else flew past. And in the distance, there was the very clear sound of wheels upon a track and a hiss of steam.

At which point he looked up and his mouth gaped open as he saw he was no longer in the bookshop.

He was standing on the edge of a book *city*.

CHAPTER FIVE
THE BOOK OF WISDOM

Helia and Mwamba moved quickly through the wood-paneled corridors, away from the quiet reading rooms, where the Sages and their assistant scholars often retreated to deliberate and find peace, and toward the Haven.

Helia knew it must be approaching evening here. Even as far underground as they were, hidden away within the depths of the island mountain upon which the Founder had long ago come ashore, she could tell by the type of glow that poured through the artificial windows. During the day it was a perfect stream of light, warm and golden from the stored sunlight that was captured on the surface and guided down by some ancient architectural magic, to be distributed through the Great Library's windows. Yet now the glow was a slightly paler twilight, with just the barest sprinkle of starlight held within its beams.

Despite the late hour, Helia found that the Great Library of Tomorrow was still bustling and full of life. It always was, even out here in the labyrinth of corridors, rooms, kitchens, and gardens, away from the hustle of the Main Concourse. There were always people looking for learning. "Knowledge seekers never rest," Mwamba had once said. And he would know; that was his talent and power. He was the most knowledgeable of them all, not only because he was the wisest naturally but also because of his innate desire and determination to know what he did not.

The groups politely greeted each other as they hurried past, yet Helia could almost feel their glances burrowing into her back as she hurried along, drying her eyes. They were likely wondering what could possibly lead two Sages and their Orbs to move with such haste through these sacred halls.

She wouldn't have been able to tell them, even if she had the time. She barely understood it herself.

She hadn't wanted to utter the words about what had happened, because then there would be no taking them back. It would be true, and she wanted more than anything for it all to be a lie.

Yet there had been no choice. She'd told him about the ambush upon their arrival at the Rose Garden, how she and Xavier had fought and he had been injured; the Rose Garden's withered state, its color and vibrancy stripped away, along with the animals that had called it home; and how the dragon, the great protector of Silvyra, the realm of the Great Tree, was gone.

And how she left Xavier to be killed.

If that wasn't bad enough, she'd then had to reveal that Antares was missing. Xavier's little Orb, who he'd trusted her with, was gone. Had Helia dropped the companion while she'd been riding Amare? No, she didn't think so. She distinctly remembered feeling the Orb in her pocket as she'd arrived and hurried to find Mwamba. And her pockets were deep, too, so she couldn't have been dropped while hurrying through the Library.

Perhaps Antares regained a little strength to deliberately leave her. But why? And where had she gone?

Sage Mwamba hadn't offered any answers as he'd listened to the story tumble out. A patient man at the best of times, he was like a rock in the storm now, though as she reached the part about Suttaru, his brow finally broke into a troubled furrow.

"Are you sure?" he had asked. "Suttaru is practically a figure from legend, Helia. From far beyond even the time of you and I, despite us having lived for so long. He is a symbol of evil that only exists in the Library's memory now, from the time of the Author and the creation of the Book of Wisdom. His true name is barely remembered by most. He has himself become a story as the Ash Man. Something parents use to frighten their children into doing their chores. Are you *sure* he's who you saw?"

"Yes, I am. And he's not alone—he has a legion of wild beings at his back. His 'Unwritten,' he called them. My memory is mostly lost, but I can feel them tearing at me still. They were people, and their flesh was carved with words of fire. They had beasts with them too—hounds or wolves of a sort, all with the same script. Although it was a language I do not remember seeing before."

"Dark stories," Mwamba muttered, his voice like a rumble of distant thunder. "It's how he was said to be able to corrupt others."

Immediately taking her hand in his, he led her out of the room and across the Library, heading toward the Haven—the only place where answers might yet be found. A place of sanctity and magic, a place that students whispered about as they passed its doors, slowing to wonder about what astonishments lay beyond.

"Do you think the Book will know what's happening?" she asked as they caught a glimpse of the doors at the end of the corridor. There was a spark of hope in her chest that kindled into life, as if they were in sight of some kind of explanation to cut through the horror. "Will she be able to tell us about Suttaru, if indeed he has returned? Or even how he's managed to do that? In the stories I've heard, he was supposed to have died."

"I have faith she will," Mwamba replied. "The Book of Wisdom was created to counter his threat. And though that momentous event took place centuries before even you or I arrived here, we only have the stories to remind us, and those stories often have a kernel of truth in them."

"So Xavier always insisted."

"He was a smart man."

As they reached the end of the red-carpeted hallway, Helia expected them to stop and knock. Mwamba always knocked here at the Haven. In this sacred place, the literal heart of the Great Library, he would knock. Because he understood what lay inside deserved his utmost respect.

Not today, however. There was no time for even the faintest formality. Mwamba grasped the spiral handle and pulled the door open, stepping through and letting it swing shut behind them when they'd both entered.

They stepped into a vast, airy space, as large as any cathedral and as hushed and quiet as a tomb. In the center of this sacred place lay the Book of Wisdom, resting upon a grand podium fashioned from wood so fine it could almost have been carved from the Great Tree herself.

Some were surprised to learn that the Book appeared as a physical book, such were the tales of its magic, majesty, and power. It was a humble, moderately sized tome, with a gilded red cover. You certainly wouldn't have recognized it as the most revered book in history, created by the Scholar. With the Great Library's own knowledge of technology and magic, in combination with the influence of the endless stories and realms that existed beyond the Library, the Book of Wisdom held every secret imaginable.

But the Book of Wisdom wasn't *just* a book, of course. It was the beating heart of this city of stories and a power greater than—Helia suspected—even the older Sages considered possible. Xavier in particular had enjoyed regaling Helia with tales of the Book. He knew them better than anyone, being besotted with the truth of any story. He'd studied them constantly, always looking to rediscover delicious details that had been lost to time, in the hope he could furnish future retellings.

The story of how the Scholar had evolved into the Author had especially interested him. The sacrifice that the woman called Fairen had made. How she had become one with the Book of Wisdom to counter the evil brought about by Suttaru and his dark forces.

How her sacrifice had saved everyone and everything.

Now Xavier had made a sacrifice of his own to save Helia.

The thought stung, but she knew he would have liked that similarity. He would have laughed, in that gleeful way he did. Such a beautiful, throaty laugh. She could still hear it in the back of her mind, even now.

Biting her lip, she tried to maintain the facade of calm expected of the

Sage of Hope, even if inside she was struggling to keep her head above the waters of despair. She blinked and watched as Mwamba stood in front of the pedestal and placed both hands on the lectern. He bowed his head for a moment. Not in prayer, she knew that now. But a silent pause of respect.

The Book of Wisdom didn't just hold words; it held the Author too, making it the consciousness of the Great Library. Helia had witnessed the Author speak from within the Book many times, and it was always either a moment of grand occasion or a moment of great need.

The shortness of Mwamba's pause marked this occasion as most definitely the latter.

"Are you ready?" he asked, and she nodded. With that, he pressed his hands together in front of him, his fingers splayed out and their tips touching. Then he faced his palms upward and began to speak in the way the ritual demanded: his lips moving quickly, the words firm, spoken with a rhythm and tone that was as if he was reciting a poem or song. It was like providing a gift of words, a wondrous collection that held such beauty and power they never failed to rouse the ancient spirit within.

Helia now joined him, palms face up, offering her own words alongside his, slipping them in between, as though providing a harmony to his melody. Their separate incantations soon became a singular song of splendor, celebrating the unity that represented everything the Book had intended for the Sages.

Even as her lips moved, Helia could feel it working. The hairs on her skin rose as the cover of the Book shuddered, and a great light and energy began to spill out from the pages within, cascading around the room with a strength she could barely describe—something akin to the feeling one might experience if they drank a glass of sunshine, an ancient warmth that filled one's entire being, a fierce strength of knowledge and, as she had always considered, hope.

But as she lifted her head to soak it in, embracing the heat as it forced away the heartache that threatened to consume her, it vanished again.

The cover stopped moving and remained closed. The room grew dark again.

Mwamba glanced over his shoulder to confirm she had witnessed this too, his contorted look of surprise telling her something had gone wrong. He had never looked unsure before, not in all the years she had known him.

What's happened to the Book?

There was always the Book. Always. It was the constant in all their lives, the heart and soul of the Library. While Helia represented hope for many, she found her own hope in the Book.

It was safety. The parental figure you might run to if you were hurt or in trouble. The superior force that would make it all better.

And now it wasn't working. Which, after what Helia had already witnessed that day, filled her with dread.

Mwamba wiped his fingers on his tunic to dry the sweat and then placed his hands on either side of the Book, speaking more firmly this time.

The cover shuddered again, but the light from within was fainter and more tentative. It failed to pour into the room as it had done moments ago, as though it was holding off, knowing it was beaten and trying to maintain its strength.

Helia's eyes grew wide, and Mwamba cursed under his breath. It was unusual of him to do so—he was usually so calm and considerate, even in trying times. But she didn't blame him. What they were both witnessing stoked the despair in the depth of her gut, riling it into a churn that made her want to flee to her quarters.

The elder Sage shifted uncomfortably on the spot, then held his hand over the cover warily.

Only now was Helia shaken to move. It was as though he had taken leave of his senses.

She touched his shoulder, wanting to pull him back to reality.

"Mwamba, no. That's not the way. Are you even allowed to touch the Book? To touch *her*?"

The look he returned, like a child about to do something he knew would get him into trouble, sent a shiver rippling through her.

"I have no idea, Helia. This isn't something I have had to contemplate before. But you are seeing what I am seeing, aren't you?"

She nodded and withdrew her hand.

"Then I must try it, for all our sakes."

His fingers flexed uncertainly, then lightly touched down.

Mwamba was a big man, tall and strong, with arms as thick as the trunks of ancient vines and hands as wide as their bowl-like leaves. Yet as his hand lay fully on the Book of Wisdom, Helia noted how tiny and insignificant it seemed.

The power of the Book was still evident. It still dominated the space, as it should. It still had the ability to force Mwamba into an exhale—he must have felt the whispers of the stories and realms that lay beyond the cover.

Yet even as he spoke to it again, his words now more urgent, tumbling out like boulders rolling toward an ocean, she could tell it was having no effect. As the boulders found the water, they created only ripples and sank without a trace, leaving the ocean unmoved.

Helia glanced at Vega. Her Orb flashed its concern, and she nodded.

"I can feel it," Mwamba said after a moment, although his tone was less positive than Helia had hoped. The Sage reluctantly removed his hand from the Book and stepped back, a little boy lost in this strange new world without guidance or direction. "I can feel *her*. The Author is still present in the pages. The life of the Book of Wisdom vibrates as I believe it should."

"Are you sure?"

He nodded and gestured to Canopus, who was still bobbing around his head, looking as concerned as he.

"The Orbs are connected to the Book. If she was lost to us, so would our companions be . . . and yet they are still here, alert and active."

Canopus and Vega both flashed in the affirmative.

"Then . . . I don't understand." Helia was feeling weaker by the minute. Her mind whirled. "What's happening? Why isn't she talking to us?"

Mwamba silently conversed with his Orb, then shook his head. "I do not know. But take a look around you. It's not only our Orbs. The Great Library is as it always is. The life breathes here still, and so our heart is intact. It's just . . . she is unable to talk to us. Her voice has been stilled."

Helia felt her knees begin to give way, yet she did her utmost to stay standing, despite the day's shock and fatigue trying to drag her down. She didn't want to believe any of this was happening. It seemed like a nightmare, one from which you couldn't wake.

"Has it been corrupted?"

"I'm sure the Book is beyond such things," Mwamba said, though he sounded unconvinced. He paused and considered. "But there is a problem. She appears . . . blocked. Or trapped."

That word instantly sent Helia back to the ambush that had greeted them at the Rose Garden. Her pulse quickened, and her thoughts spiraled back to that dark place.

Suttaru took the dragon and killed my beautiful Xavier. What if he has done this too? What if his powers have somehow reached into the Great Library and spread his darkness here as well?

Mwamba's sudden movement as he strode away from the silent Book shook her out of this disturbing line of thought. She watched him pull a cord on the wall, ringing the bell twice. It chimed around them, quietly enough that at this time of the evening it would not stir anybody it shouldn't, but significant enough to bring an assistant running.

Not thirty seconds later, a panting middle-aged scholar, Thomas, knocked on the door. Mwamba bade him enter, and he poked his head around. As he noted Helia was there too, he wrapped his evening robe around him even more tightly, and then approached the Sages. His expression at first seemed confused, then grew quickly into one of concern.

"Good evening, Sages. How can I help?"

Mwamba had regained some semblance of control. His face now wore its usual calm, stoic expression, unwilling to reveal the clues that would alert others to their desperate situation. Helia knew only a little about Mwamba's former life, before the Library, but whatever he had been, he had seen and done enough to never be rattled for too long.

Helia wished she could feel as calm as he looked. She'd had many lifetimes of experience at the Library that could be used as a crutch in this moment, but she could remember nothing in all that time that had been quite this terrifying.

"Thomas, what Sages remain in the Library?" Mwamba asked.

"Not many, I'm afraid. Several of your number have left throughout the day, for various destinations across Paperworld." His brow creased as if trying to recall information he had not been expected to relay. "I believe

Sage Robin is still on Earth, although she is due to return soon. And I've just left the Auditorium, where Sage Veer was finishing up another of his enlightening sessions. Which leaves you two and Sage Xavier—"

He looked to Helia as though confused why Xavier wasn't with her, as he usually was.

She immediately dropped her gaze.

"Thomas, would you go back to Veer and ask him to join us?" Mwamba waved away the assistant's question before the poor man could even open his mouth and turned to Helia.

"What's the nearest settlement to the Rose Garden?"

Helia understood what he was thinking. Suttaru may well already be on his way out of the mountains down to wreak more devastation. The poor people wouldn't stand a chance.

"The town of Aedela," Helia replied. "It's in the land of Bloom. It also happens to be where the ruler of Bloom, the Petal Queen, resides."

Mwamba nodded and addressed Thomas again. "If Veer asks, tell him someone is needed to take a journey to see the Petal Queen in Aedela, and it's a matter of the highest urgency. Don't stop and talk to anyone else. Go to him directly and ask him to come back to me with all haste. As quickly as you can, please."

Helia watched Thomas's quizzical gaze drift over Mwamba's shoulder to where the Book of Wisdom lay.

"Of course, Sage. Although, if I may—"

She knew what he was going to ask, but he didn't get the chance. The sudden flame-orange swirl of Mwamba's Orb, Canopus, and its low vibration, like an impatient growl, made Thomas take a step back, his cheeks burning a fierce red to rival any of the Rose Garden's flowers.

The elder Sage himself only raised an eyebrow, content to let his Orb do the talking for him.

"Very well," Thomas said, before giving a quick bow and hurrying out of the room.

Helia and Mwamba looked at each other as he shut the door behind him.

"What now?" she asked.

CHAPTER SIX
NEW FRIENDS

Nu shouldn't have let herself be distracted so easily.

She'd done everything right, as she always did. The visitor had arrived in the bookshop, and she had given him the once-over. She had stretched her senses out and understood instantly he was here at just the right time, as the Book of Wisdom must have foreseen. So she smiled and guided him onward, to take the leap between worlds alone, as all needed to do.

A rite of passage of sorts.

It should have been easy enough to follow him and meet him in the Library, to properly introduce herself and then show him around. Not all who wandered between Earth and the Great Library of Tomorrow got such a welcome. Most found their way in their own time and were only too happy to explore by themselves. But when the Book required someone like Nu to greet someone, it was protocol to take them on a tour, to ease them into the transition.

Unfortunately, Nu's attention had been lacking in that moment. Because as soon as the man had moved off to find his bookshelf portal, there had been a buzzing in her pocket.

"The Orb!" she'd exclaimed excitedly. Reaching in, she pulled the little being out and placed her in her palm.

A weak thread of light drifted over the Orb's surface.

Nu didn't understand it. Only the Sages understood their Orbs and how they communicated, but she felt . . . something. A message pass between them.

"Are you trying to talk to me?" she asked, lifting the little companion up to her eyes. "As I said before, I'm afraid I'm not a Sage. But I am glad to see that you still have a little life about you."

The Orb showed two threads of light this time. A little straighter and more defined.

Like tiny strikes of lightning. Then she was still.

For a moment, Nu panicked, wondering if that had been the end of the being's life. She held her up again, staring for a few minutes as she waited for some kind of sign she was still alive. Finally, there was a very faint buzz. It felt almost critical, as though telling her off for something.

Which was when she realized that the man had entered the Library already. She leaped up from the counter and rushed to her own portal to find him.

Moving unsteadily from the safety of his shelf of memories—as though attempting to walk for the very first time—Arturo walked toward the center of the magnificent circular hall he found himself in. In his chest, a strange mix of cautiousness and rising excitement battled for supremacy. His heart thumped like a drum of war between them.

A few seconds ago, he'd been in *La Luna*, in the heart of Mexico City. Now he was here in this . . . this . . . well, what *was* this place?

As tall as his city's beloved cultural center, the *Palacio de Bellas Artes*, and as spacious as any sports stadium he'd been in, the hall was a marvel of sight and sound. It was filled with people dressed in all kinds of wonderful, colorful clothes and styles from around the world. They were all walking and talking with each other, their pleasant chatter echoing across the interior like a gentle whispered symphony of humanity. A semicircle of ancient bookshelves fanned out from behind where he had appeared, and as he glanced to either side, his mouth fell in astonishment. A couple of other people materialized, as if they, too, had slipped into existence, like characters from one of the books on the shelves.

Overhead all manner of flying contraptions zipped around. He had to duck as a small bird-shaped blur with a bright red chest gave him a chirrup as it nearly clipped him, its tiny golden wings fluttering as fast as any hummingbird. It flew from the hall into a towering corridor of ramshackle wooden structures that looked like they contained thousands more bookshelves. He heard a hoot, and suddenly an elaborately decorated tram snaked across the floor to pull its ornate carriages alongside a small platform.

As if to answer his own question, his gaze was drawn up to the walls to the intricate mosaics that circled the chamber. And suddenly he knew. Not anything specific as to the *where*, but he now understood the *what* at least. Because the striking images that soared toward the distant ceiling told a story: from detailing the earliest cave paintings, depicting humanity's wonder and awe of the world around them, to pictures of the beginnings of the written word, showing scribes recording information on clay tablets and scrolls. Arturo spun on the spot, soaking it all in, watching history unfold, until his eyes came to rest on a masterfully crafted mosaic that showed a whole array of beautiful books and portrayed someone perfecting the process of bookbinding.

It was a celebration of stories and storytelling. Instantly, Arturo knew that wherever he was, it was a place that cherished and protected such things.

It was a place he belonged.

A noise startled him from his awe, and he jumped back as a sphere floated into view. A shiny gray metallic ball about the size of a volleyball and glowing a soft campfire red across its surface. As he peered closer, he saw it seemed to have several layers beneath its outer surface, each spinning in their own way and flashing their own patterns and shapes. It hovered in front of him as if sizing him up.

Hello, it seemed to say.

Arturo had no idea if that was the case, but the enthusiastic swirls of crimson symbols that danced like fractal flames across its surface suggested it was offering a friendly greeting.

Somehow he was filled with a sense of warmth and peace.

There was no danger here. Just acceptance and understanding.

The sphere spiraled some more intricate designs across its surface as it bobbed and watched him.

"Um, hi . . ." he said unsurely.

"I didn't know you could speak Orb," a teasing voice came from behind him. The owner of the voice swept around and joined the sphere, studying him in much the same way the Orb had. "His name is Centauri, by the way. He's with me."

Arturo was relieved to find the woman standing in front of him was another human. She appeared to be Indian British—he had worked with plenty of English clients, and he recognized the slightly cheeky London accent—and she wore a dress that at once seemed from an era long past yet wouldn't have been out of place in a movie set in the distant future.

She pushed back her thick dark waves of hair, which were intertwined with strands of golden tinsel, and looked him up and down. A wicked, knowing grin lit up her face.

"Oh, I do love meeting visitors," she said, her wide eyes glinting with mischief, seemingly taking delight in his bemusement. "It's quite a trip, yeah? Stepping through from wherever you came from and feeling that sensation as if you're being carried through a magic divide directly into your favorite story. I can't get enough of it, personally."

She didn't give him a chance to respond beyond a nod, before gesturing around her.

"Well, let me be the first one to say welcome to the Great Library of Tomorrow! I'd ask if you're new here, but it's written all over your face, my friend. You look like you're either about to faint on the spot or run back through the portal—and I would kindly beg that you do neither, because that's no fun at all."

She reached out a hand.

Arturo took it and gave it a quick shake. "Uh, nice to meet you?"

The woman laughed. "You don't sound like it is."

As their hands parted, her sleeve rolled up, and he saw that she had a tattoo. Arturo couldn't help but stare at the quote that had been inked onto her arm: *Love turns the Earth.*

"Oh, that?" she said. "Yeah, I'm a big fan of the concept. I think I read it in a book somewhere, or maybe I dreamed it up. Anyway, I got the tattoo as soon as I was old enough. These words have been my moral compass ever since." She paused and tilted her head thoughtfully. "Not that I need a moral compass, you understand. I'm generally pretty nice. But sometimes it's good to have a reminder of what you stand for in life. And I believe it, although there's always one person who sees this and can't help but bleat on about how it's not love turning the Earth but the sun's gravitational pull. You know the type, right? Whatever. In my experience, it's love that steers us all, guides us, protects us, breaks us up to start anew. Don't you think?"

Her scattergun burst of talking hit a momentary pause, and she waited for him to respond.

He took a breath, wondering what he could possibly say. Did he even need to respond?

Or was it a rhetorical question?

The air was cozy and warm in here, like his favorite café in winter. It smelled like it too; there was an unmistakable scent of warm cinnamon drifting through the hall, mingled with other spices and quite possibly some exotic coffee.

Together with the comforting whiff of old books, this place felt like home.

The grin flashed across her face again. "This place is pretty amazing, isn't it?"

"Yes, it is astonishing," he said dreamily. Then he realized she was still staring, and he checked himself. "Arturo. That's my name. Sorry, I should have said that before. And it *is* nice to meet you, whoever you are, and wherever this is."

"Arturo, well met. My name's Robin, and you've already met my Orb, Centauri, here." The Orb confirmed this with a swirl of color. Robin gestured proudly around them, her hair swishing around her shoulders as she turned. "And this place you've found yourself in is the

Foyer of the Great Library. Truly a marvelous place and a lovely way to start your journey into one of the greatest wonders in the world, even if only a fraction of humanity will ever see it or come to know it exists."

"The Great Library?" Arturo repeated, before Robin grabbed Arturo's hand and led him onward, in what seemed to be the start of a guided tour.

"The Great Library of Tomorrow." She sighed happily. "A place beyond the boundaries of what you and I know. A place of great learning and stories and magic. An oasis in the desert of time and space. I still don't yet understand how it all works myself, not like the others do at least. But sometimes I wonder if I even need to understand it. Maybe I just need to believe in it?"

She smiled again as if making a joke. The weird thing was, he could almost feel what she was getting at. As he stared at the ceilings, then at the walls of bookshelves, the vast diversity of folk milling about, the wondrous flying contraptions, and now this Orb . . . it certainly felt like the kind of place you couldn't simply understand. You just had to believe in it.

They walked out of the Foyer and into a slightly more subdued, more hushed corridor that also held a number of towering bookcases.

The sense of age and majesty here was immense, as though one could feel the hand of those who had crafted it long ago. And it must have been centuries, because the beams seemed rough, and some had even been handcarved for some other purpose—it was as if they had been stripped from some ancient sailing vessel and reused to house the books that now sat upon them.

Robin's voice quieted as she explained more. "These are the Stacks. One of the first parts of the Great Library built by the person who founded this place." Scattered tables lay around the vast sea of space, full of students and scholars, even this late in the afternoon. Their heads collectively bent, poring over old scrolls and ancient tomes laid before them.

"He was known, funnily enough, as the Founder. A great man who traveled the world collecting stories."

"And how did *he* get here?" Arturo whispered, feeling silly for asking such a specific question when he didn't even know where here was.

"Oh, he landed here a very long time ago, quite by accident. Ship-wrecked."

"Shipwrecked? You mean we're still on Earth?"

Robin responded with an enigmatic smile. "Yes, we're still on Earth. Where? I don't really know myself. A lost and remote part of the world, I imagine. Don't worry. It always takes a while for visitors to acclimatize to the idea. One minute you're wandering around wherever you live, and the next minute—*bang!*—you've stumbled through a portal into a completely different part of the world!" She tapped the side of his head, then ran her finger down to his chest. "It can screw with your mind a little if you let it. I've always advised people to accept it in their hearts and move on."

He stared down at her finger resting lightly on his shirt. "Lots of people do this?"

"Oh, you have *no* idea," she said brightly, leading him out of the Stacks and deeper into the Library. "The Great Library welcomes all. The centuries of collected knowledge here always draw in the bright and curious minds that need it most—usually the people who held the greatest potential toward changing humanity for the better. Come on, lots to see!"

They wandered through corridors adorned with paintings of places that could only be other realms, saw reading rooms and discussion chambers, and even a series of underground gardens that grew all kinds of foods for those who resided in this wonderful place. And, according to Robin, there were many of them here, from all over the world—along with some temporary visitors looking for answers to big questions in their lives.

Again, he saw the machines flying about, mechanical and magical flying machines of all shapes, designs, and roles.

"What are these?" he asked his guide.

"Ah, the Volare Machina!" she said, her tone delighted. She stopped and looked up as a cluster of them flew, fluttered, buzzed, swooped, and soared. Some had wings, others had rotors, each hurrying about its business.

"They have a multitude of functions. Some are helping visitors like yourself"—she paused, looking at him closely, as if thinking, *Perhaps not quite like you*, before continuing—"while others are maintaining the collection's indexing system, the Codex. But all use a sprinkle of the Library's ancient magic in their workings . . ."

"And which category do you fall into here?" he asked as they stood before a fountain with sprays of different colored waters. The streams seemed to defy physics as they bounced in unnaturally beautiful ways around the carving of an underwater city. He pointed to Centauri. "I haven't seen anybody else with a companion like you have."

"Ah, well, we Sages have a different role to everyone else."

"Sages?"

"That's right. There are ten of us, and each was chosen by an Orb sent by the Book of Wisdom. We are . . . well, I don't want to toot my own horn, but you can think of us a little like guardians and explorers. Protectors of Earth, the Great Library, and what lies beyond. And the Orbs that chose us—Centauri here is mine—are our constant companions and our connection to the Great Library of Tomorrow. They're also our passport to the places that most don't ever see or even know about."

Places that most don't even know about? Arturo didn't know what that could mean. He'd spent enough time on Google Earth exploring the world, and he figured there wasn't anywhere humanity hadn't visited by now, which had been a significant disappointment for the adventurer in his heart.

He opened his mouth to ask for clarity, but Robin was on a roll now.

"While on our travels, we observe and learn what we can to add to the knowledge held and protected in the Great Library. Not only that but we have a responsibility to uphold the values we embody. You see, the Orbs chose us for very particular reasons. We each embody a particular value that's important to the very best of humanity. A virtue, you might say."

"Do you have a virtue?"

"I do."

"And it is . . ."

She gave him a sidelong glance, a twinkle of mischief in her eyes, but said nothing.

He laughed. "Fine, keep your secrets, mysterious Sage. I suppose it's in keeping with everything I've experienced today. One minute I was in a bookshop, the next I'm here. Wherever *here* is."

"A bookshop, eh? That's cool. Are you an author or something?"

"A writer. I used to want to be an author. Of children's books, something fun and fantastical, you know? Something to inspire children to make the world a better place."

"And what do you write now?"

"Yesterday it was a commercial for waste pipes." He sighed. "You know, for toilets."

She laughed loudly, startling a group of men unrolling maps. "Oh, I'm so sorry. That must be really *shi*—"

He held up a hand. "I've heard all the jokes, thank you. Now, seriously, can you at least tell me why I'm here? What strange and otherworldly force has drawn me to this Great Library of yours? Is there a reason I've fallen into this place or just a happy accident?"

"That, my friend, is a very good question indeed," Robin said. "We get lots of visitors stumbling into our wonderful home, and there is *always* a reason for them finding us, even if they don't always understand what it might be. Perhaps they are seeking answers to a great conundrum in their work or personal life. Perhaps they want to change the world, and it is here they find the inspiration to return to Earth and make it happen. The Great Library is open to everyone, yet you have to be a certain kind of person to find your way here." Her gaze met his again, and she narrowed her eyes ever so slightly, chewing her lip. "I wonder: Which one you are?"

At that moment, there was a shout from behind them. It sounded as if someone was shouting for a Mage. Not for the first time since arriving, Arturo wondered if he had indeed made it to that cantina and was now drinking himself into some kind of stupor, while his inebriated brain ran wild making up bookshops and libraries. It wouldn't be the first time he had dreamed up new worlds as he slipped into unconsciousness, losing himself in his own fantasies.

Yet even if there was indeed some kind of sorcerer-related issue, he didn't *feel* drunk.

And this didn't feel like the kind of wonderland his addled mind would conjure up.

Robin grabbed his hand again and led him through the meandering folk, toward a girl with long black hair and flushed cheeks who was running toward them.

"Sage coming through!" Robin said, pushing the onlookers away with some urgency.

Ah, Sage, he thought.

They stopped when the girl reached them and to his surprise, Arturo recognized her as the girl from the bookshop. If she recognized him too, she gave no sign. She was too busy gasping for breath as she tried to tell Robin something, before finally giving up and holding out her hand to reveal a much smaller Orb in her palm.

Luckily, nothing more needed to be said, because Centauri immediately flashed with what seemed like concern and drifted over to talk to his fellow sphere with a series of waves of fractal lights. The smaller Orb's attempts to communicate in return were far weaker, the patterns across its surface tiny and visible.

Finally, Centauri returned to Robin. Slowly and hesitantly, he relayed something to her, which drained the life from her face. She listened with a growing horror.

"You're kidding?!" she said, glancing down to the other Orb. "Oh, Antares. I'm so sorry."

Unseen by her, Centauri's strange symbols softly lit up across his surface. To Arturo, it suggested in no uncertain terms he was serious. But Robin was already looking at the girl.

"And who are you?"

"Oh, I'm Nu," she replied through gasps. "I live here, and I was on my way to work earlier when Antares rolled up to me. I didn't know what else to do, so I thought I should bring her to a Sage."

"She rolled up to you?" Robin repeated. She digested this information for a moment longer, before gently touching the girl's shoulder. "Thank you, Nu. You did the right thing."

Arturo could have sworn he saw a sliver of golden light, the same color as the tinsel in Robin's hair, spread from the Sage's fingers. It swept across the girl's arm and enveloped her briefly in an aura of warmth.

Nu immediately stood a little straighter and more confidently, her cheeks still flushed, but now more like she'd received a compliment.

"How can we help Antares, Sage Robin?" she asked.

"I'm not sure," Robin replied. For the first time since they'd met, Arturo sensed the woman didn't have all the answers anymore. "I think we need to see the other Sages, starting with Mwamba."

Nu's eyes widened. "We? Oh no. I'm sure you don't need me."

"Antares came to you for comfort. That to me suggests otherwise." Robin turned to Arturo. "I'm very sorry, but I think I have to cut our tour short. We need to speak with my friends. You should get on with whatever reason you have been drawn here. Let me find you someone who can help induct you properly, and maybe then—"

"No," the young woman said quietly, yet firmly. She was looking at Arturo strangely. Not just in recognition now—there was something else. It was the same kind of knowing look she'd given him in the bookshop. Then she blinked and looked aghast as Robin stared at her.

"No?"

"Oh, Sage Robin, I'm so sorry!" Nu blurted out. "I don't mean to be rude. I was the one who guided him here, and I should have followed him to carry out his induction, but I got caught up in the bookshop. Then you found him, and I can't explain it"—she gestured to Antares resting in her palm—"but I suddenly have a feeling this *is* the reason he was brought here. We should take him with us."

Robin looked as though she was about to argue, when Centauri spun a pattern of impatience across his surface and nudged her arm. She frowned at him, glanced between Arturo and Nu, then relented.

"Fine, we all go together, then," she said, brushing her fingers against Arturo's arm again as she guided him ahead of her. "Let's go and get some answers to this conundrum, shall we?"

Arturo went without a fuss, feeling a strange mix of excitement and belonging creep through him.

CHAPTER SEVEN
THE LEGACY

"How do you feel, Dzin?"

The words were soft and meandering, like leaves on the wind. They blew over Dzin's shoulder and into his ear, though they were perhaps not as comforting as they should have been. Questions about his feelings never were.

He shifted along the hammock bench that swung gently from the bough outside the laboratory so he could let his teacher sit down. Tywich gave him his usual appraising look. It was the same one he always reserved for Dzin, as though watching an experiment that could either yield excellent results or blow up at any time.

Tywich said nothing more for the moment. He hardly ever followed up on his initial questions, preferring to wait silently until his students simply had to reply to fill the dead air. "I think I feel good, Runner Tywich."

"You *think*?"

Dzin's face grew warm under the heat of his teacher's slow smile. He knew the man meant well, but he really found no enjoyment in these mind games.

"I meant . . . yes, I feel good, thank you."

Was it even true? He wasn't sure, but he had to say something. And he supposed he felt good in a way. The laboratory was decorated, and Monae was now busy bossing Pyruc and the twins around inside. They were trying to rouse some of the sprite leaves into unfurling so that the glowing, ethereal strands could be hung around the branches in the morning, just before all the guests arrived for the graduation.

"Do you feel you made your parents proud, Dzin?"

Tywich still looked at him. It wasn't an unkind gaze, and his teacher had certainly helped enough over the last few seasons for Dzin to know that he understood his internal struggles. Yet he couldn't help feeling uncomfortable now, being quizzed like this.

"I can only hope I did," he replied.

He was being casual with the truth, of course. Had he failed with his Elixir, he didn't know what he would have done with himself. That he had succeeded meant that at the very least he hadn't let his family down. He still harbored concerns that, come the moment he stood in front of his entire community, he might make a fool of himself.

"Good. There is something to be said for that when all is said and done. What drives us all is inconsequential. Be it pride from the grave or a simple desire to be more than you are. To do great things. None of it really matters. What counts is achieving what you set out to do, regardless of how you got there. Wouldn't you say?"

Dzin said nothing, unsure of what he could say to all that. He offered a shrug, and thankfully the man looked away, content to sit quietly again, letting the swing move them back and forth, enjoying the comforting rumble of the Great Tree.

Distant chatter of people and creatures alike drifted up the branches, fluttering the leaves. A flock of night owls swooped up the trunk like spooked ghosts, their wings grazing the bark with enough of a motion to cause the ancient faces in the gnarled knots to stir from their secret discussions. One mossy beard crinkled as he mouthed an old Silvyran curse, before he went back to communicating with the others in a conversation that Dzin knew could take years to finish.

Then, above where they sat, he heard the unmistakable crackle of blooming galaxy seeds, which came out at this time every night. Within a few moments, he and Tywich were watching the spiraling star systems fall like snow around them, on and over the branch, before exploding with tiny pops to sow their magic.

Owlings hooted in the distance, an airship rumbled nearby, preparing to land at the pad, and there was now a trickling of sap through the rivulets of the bark beneath their feet, before lapping could be heard as some unknown creatures drank their fill.

It was all the sound of home. A comforting symphony that Dzin had grown up with and always appreciated. It helped him to center himself. Even tonight, despite it being punctuated by Monae's groans of frustration and Pyruc's defensive retorts as the pair struggled with the notoriously stubborn sprite leaves inside the laboratory.

"You have accomplished something magnificent and wonderful," Tywich said to Dzin, his voice even quieter than before, barely audible above the breeze, as if he was now talking to himself. Dzin shivered. No longer leaves on the wind, the man's words sounded more like tiny insects scurrying across bark. "The Elixir of Life is at the heart of all we do here at the Great Tree. What you have done here will change everything, Dzin."

Dzin glanced at the man, unsure of what to say. Yes, he'd made an Elixir of Life, a great thing, but it was nothing that hadn't been done before by the other chosen students, new and old, of the Botanical Education School. And besides, they both knew he never would have done it without help. Not in the state he'd been in, trying to find that last ingredient.

"Thank you, Runner Tywich. But all of us created the Elixirs, as we were meant. I did nothing special."

Tywich's smile was faint, but it was there. The man continued staring at Dzin. No, he wasn't staring at him, Dzin realized, but *through* him, at some unseen thing in his mind's eye.

Tywich's eyes were almost glazing over, the smile growing tighter.

"What you created, Dzin, is something special indeed. You fashioned your very own personal brand of the Elixir of Life from the world around you. A unique Elixir, far different from any that your colleagues made. Once you graduate from the school, you will leave with quite the legacy."

The words should have been comforting. They were the kind of words Dzin had fantasized hearing from his mother and father, had they still been here.

But they did not soothe him as he thought they rightly should. There was an undercurrent of something else beneath the praise. One that set him on edge and triggered the anxiety that was always hovering around, waiting to blow up a storm inside him.

He fidgeted again, wanting to get up and leave. He tried to calm himself. It was just the pressure still getting to him. Making him hear things that weren't there. Panicking when there was no need. He wondered if the other students had suffered similar bouts of it recently but knew they had not. At least not to the same extent. He was different, always had been. Smiling on the outside, while inside he was often falling apart even as he continually attempted to build himself back up again. He collected worries and concerns that others wouldn't see, and they would rattle around noisily in his chest until his entire being seemed alive with a maelstrom of panicked emotions and thoughts. A panic storm that would overwhelm his mind and often encourage him to shut down.

The panic storm seemed on the verge of starting again right now, in fact.

He spoke quickly, to try to distract himself.

"We all achieved something great here," he said, trying to stamp out the guilt that was bubbling up. He didn't like being singled out for such praise he surely didn't deserve. Praise that wasn't warranted. "I did nothing out of the ordinary, Runner Tywich. Other than run a little late with my collection of ingredients. Though I am still very grateful for your help."

"It was my honor," Tywich replied.

There was a crackle of boots on leaves behind them. Dzin looked around to find a tall, thin figure standing near the back of the laboratory, near the entrance to the archives. The man's face was gaunt in the low evening light, but even from here Dzin could see the reflection from his cold silver eye.

It was the advisor to the Chief Scientist. A man who most at the Great Tree knew of only by title, although the students sometimes saw him around the laboratories from time to time.

He nodded to Dzin, then spoke directly to Tywich. "I need to speak with you. Urgently."

Tywich continued to stare through Dzin, his face thoughtful and his smile distant. But he had clearly heard the advisor's words.

He got up, smoothing down his shirt. "Why don't you go inside with the others now?" he said to Dzin. "Enjoy the last of your time as students, for all too soon the festivities will be upon you, my boy."

"Oh, of course," Dzin replied, relieved he had an excuse to get away from the awkward situation.

He got to his feet, bowed his head to the advisor, then hurried off back into the lab to help the others. He hoped they could finish the decorations off and try to get some sleep in what little remained of the night. He would need as much rest as possible ahead of tomorrow.

Because Tywich was right. Everything in his life was about to change.

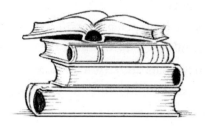

CHAPTER EIGHT
SIGNS

Helia felt the heat of the fire as she ran.

She didn't know where she was running to, only what she was running from: flames as high as the sun, a tsunami of flaming destruction sweeping across the plains behind her.

And ahead, Xavier was calling her name.

"You have to keep going, Helia!"

But she was tired now. As the steam began to rise, her feet were slipping and sliding across the mud, and the ground baked beneath her shoes.

"I'm trying," she whispered.

Looking up, she couldn't see him now. Death was at her back, and the cloud of ash was raining down around her as it had done all those years ago. Smoke filled her lungs. She stumbled, coughing, and fell to her knees, knowing that if she didn't get up, that was it.

This was the end.

"Xavier!"

The word brought her back to reality, although it took her a second or two to realize the cry had come from her own lips. Before the tears could form at the corners of her eyes, she pushed aside the plush dandelion blanket she'd once been given at the Great Tree and pulled herself upright on the edge of her bunk.

It had been barely a nap, and despite Mwamba's good intentions she felt even more exhausted after it. But she got up anyway, because that's what you always did when others were counting on you. Even when you felt numb with grief.

You got up. You carried on. You took the next step.

Xavier was the first thought on her mind. Her mind filled with images of him, not only from the nightmare but happier memories too. She could picture him as they picnicked beneath the pink clouds of the sky lakes on Zuliya, his slim, handsome face a picture of joy as he told her a story. For a moment, she felt relief, a slackening of the weight of the guilt she was carrying. But then all too soon it came flooding back, the situation only magnified by the loss of Antares too.

Helia made her way to the wardrobe and slipped on clean clothes, then poured herself a fresh glass of juice from the tap and drank it in one go. Her lips were still a little blistered, her throat raw too, but one of the healers had brought her some medicine that had helped soothe both, and now the cold drink eased the pain some more. She took a long, deep breath and tried to center herself, repeating her mantra again.

Dum spiro spero.

Helia wasn't going to let Xavier down.

While I breathe, I hope.

Vega appeared through his porthole entrance above her door. His emerald light shifted in intricate patterns across his many layers as they spun, one beneath the other. The tiny leaflike symbols that were his favorite swirled around him as though caught on an invisible wind. But Helia saw the patterns. She had long ago deciphered his particular way of communicating, to be able to understand him in more detail than any other Sage might.

Such was the bond between a Sage and her Orb.

You look tired, he suggested unhelpfully.

She couldn't help but laugh a little, sad though she was. "Yes, I am, but I'll be okay. I'm guessing you bring news?"

Mwamba needs us.

She nodded, placed the glass down next to the sink, and followed her companion back out of the door, hurrying as she went.

On the way, Vega would occasionally swirl something, although whether to her or to those they passed, she didn't really know. She knew people were staring, but her mind was too lost in what she could remember of the Rose Garden. She knew she'd never be able to forget the gray rain of ash falling around her, just as it had on the slopes of Vesuvius that fateful day she had first come to the Library. Nor Xavier's beautiful face as it crumbled at the hands of Suttaru. Nor the sense of emptiness she'd felt as they'd discovered the dragon was gone, leaving Helia with a sense of hopelessness she'd been too horrified to acknowledge at the time.

That last thought was especially troubling. All these years, she had been the one everyone could rely on to protect and nurture hope. What did it mean now that she had felt its absence, even if just momentarily?

All she knew was that she couldn't allow herself to feel that way again. Whatever happened, she had to remember to hold on to hope. It was a part of her title, after all. A guardian of the Book of Wisdom and protector of one of the key values of humanity. Whatever lay ahead for them all, she resolved to not let her friends down. The fate of everything depended on them now.

A few minutes later, she was back in Sage Mwamba's reading room. The fire was still burning in the background, but it was too low for her to pretend that it was the reason for the heat still flushing in her cheeks.

Robin stood, arms folded, studying her with a concern Helia couldn't help but appreciate. They had been friends ever since the young British woman had wandered into the Library all those years ago with that wide-eyed curiosity and endless compassion of hers. Nobody could resist the glow that seemed to surround Robin.

Veer was there too, his thick mustache stoic and still, his jaw set hard. The man's cloak swished gently against the backs of his legs as he shifted his stance. Helia was glad of his presence. The Sage of Strength would be needed in the coming days, of that she was certain.

There was also a younger woman with beautifully long, dark hair. Helia recognized her from various places around the Library. She was one of those born here, growing up in the warm embrace of this magnificent repository of knowledge and insight. A talented girl, always smiling and happy and eager to do her part—apparently born with an instinct for things, Helia had heard.

She couldn't help but wonder if that was why she was here now. Mwamba must have a reason. It wasn't often anyone other than the Sages gathered in these rooms, especially in a moment of such importance.

This thought drew her attention to the fourth attendee. A complete stranger. A man with scruffy hair and a cropped beard, who was hovering in the background. He was eyeing everything and everyone with a barely concealed look of astonishment. There was definitely a reason he was here too.

As she took a seat, Mwamba retold her story so she didn't have to. As he did, the others glanced her way with a mix of horror, pity, and confusion as it became clear what had happened.

Suttaru is back.

That revelation still made her feel nauseous. There had been no way to get used to such an idea; it was still overwhelming and terrifying.

Worse still, she didn't know how or why he had returned. There was no clue to his goal. All she knew was that chaos and fire had found the Rose Garden, a place Helia thought safer than any other because of its protective dragon guardian. And now Perennia had disappeared. Without her there to protect them, the whole realm of Silvyra itself would be left open to attack.

And as the mother of all realms, that meant trouble for the whole of Paperworld.

Helia pinched her eyes shut for a moment, certain there was more to the story, something she had forgotten. Her fingers touched the wound on her forehead absently as she wondered what she might have missed in those forgotten minutes. The pain she had felt before was less now, but still shrouded the memories, unwilling to let her through.

Had she seen the dragon? Witnessed what had happened to her or where she'd been taken? She couldn't help but feel she must have. If only she could remember. Yet the moments between being trapped in an ambush with the Unwritten and finding herself dragging Xav into the center of the Rose Garden were inaccessible.

Where is Perennia?

She could almost hear Xav's voice in her head, laying out the truth of the matter.

You need to find her, or Silvyra will fall. And if Silvyra falls, so will the other realms, because they are all connected through the River of Letters. Each of the realms of Paperworld will succumb to the evil brought back by Suttaru, one by one. And as Paperworld crumbles, so Earth will suffer. It will be a chain reaction the likes of which could spell the end of humanity, in all its guises.

A small part of Helia's soul, the one that would always belong to Xavier, twisted into knots, but she did not waver or collapse as others might. She held firm, unwilling to dwell in the darkness.

She was needed now more than ever.

The tale told, the mood in the room had darkened.

Arturo looked from face to face, wondering what to say, if anything. He settled on the Sage known as Helia and offered his best apologetic smile. It didn't seem nearly enough for what the poor woman had been through, but she returned his smile as she stood up from the chair, straightened her blouse, and brushed down her sleeves.

"I'm so very sorry," Robin whispered to the woman, reaching over to touch her arm.

Helia put her hand over hers and held it for a moment.

"I know. Thank you. But now is not the time for sorrow, Robin. Remember? We must live today, love tomorrow, and unite forever. That is the way of the Great Library of Tomorrow and we Sages who protect her, and it is important to hold to that now. We must stand united in the face of what approaches."

"Trouble," the old man Mwamba said, looking to Arturo as though he might have aged a little more in the last few minutes of recounting Helia's trauma. "That's what approaches."

Helia took a breath and inclined her head ever so slightly, acknowledging what might be. "Yes, it does. We have been fortunate to have enjoyed many centuries of peace here, my friend, but it seems that the Great Library of Tomorrow is once again called upon to fight." She looked around the room, as if half hoping to see someone else there. "Are we sure that no more of us will be joining?"

"I'm afraid not," Mwamba said. "We four are all the Sages in the Library. The others are in various realms."

Realms?

Arturo looked to Robin, who noted his unspoken question and gave a subtle shake of her head. Similarly, Centuari flashed a symbol that he was sure must have meant "not now."

Arturo bit his tongue and said nothing, wondering what on Earth that could have meant.

Helia had already moved on, approaching the young woman who had come in with him and Robin. Nu seemed equally as out of place as Arturo, although he knew that was from a lack of confidence rather than her being new to the Library. Her dress was in a similar style to the Sages here, if a little more flamboyant, with swirls on her blouse akin to the ones the Orbs used to communicate.

"Sage Helia," she said, jumping from her chair as Helia approached and offering her hand. "It's good to see you again, though I am terribly sorry for . . . well, everything."

"Nu, isn't it?" Helia replied as the two shook in greeting. "It's a pleasure to see you again also. But I admit I'm unsure as to why you might be here today. I know you are always so helpful around the Library, for which we are eternally grateful, but how is it you can help us now?"

Nu looked immediately to Robin, who nodded. The young woman

then tentatively put her hand into her pocket and drew out another Orb and held it out before her.

"Antares!" Helia cried.

She leaned over the little Orb, clearly full of relief to see it again. For its part, Antares gave a pale flicker of light like a weak light bulb. It was enough to confirm they were all right.

Her eyes watering, Helia lifted her gaze to Nu. "Oh, thank you," she said, her voice beginning to waver. She seemed exhausted, on the edge of collapsing, but reached out to take the Orb anyway. "I don't know where you picked her up, but thank you for looking after her. Antares means a lot to me."

To Helia's obvious surprise, Antares rolled backward, further into Nu's cupped hands. The Sage frowned and flinched a little, while Nu herself looked suddenly aghast. She pushed her hands forward, but Helia had already drawn back.

Arturo saw the bemused glance between Helia and Mwamba, while the Sage known as Veer had his arms crossed and was twirling the ends of his mustache thoughtfully.

"How did you find the Orb, Nu?" he asked, his American accent strong. Arturo would have guessed he was from the West Coast, maybe Seattle.

Nu did well not to buckle under the pressure of having everyone stare at her. She cupped her hands further around Antares, as though warming herself, and raised her face to meet the Sage's gaze.

"She was in the corridor outside here. And she found me. She'd been with Sages Mwamba and Helia, I think. At least, I'd seen them in the corridor just before she headed straight for me, as if she knew I'd be there. I thought something was wrong and wanted to get her back to you as soon as I could, but I had a visitor to greet." She glanced at Arturo.

"Anyway, Antares needed my help, I guess."

Helia's smile seemed tinged with something as she regarded the weak Orb in the woman's palm. She reached over and gently closed Nu's fingers over it.

"Can you look after Antares for me, Nu? It is of the utmost importance."

Nu nodded, her face a mixture of emotions. Excitement and confusion mostly. But there was a determination there as well.

"I will."

"Thank you, my dear," Helia said. Then she turned to Mwamba. "We need to talk about the Book. Have you discovered anything more?"

"The Book of Wisdom is still unable to communicate with us, I'm afraid," he said. "I have tried everything I know to rouse the Author and get her to speak, yet she remains silent—although she is conscious enough to continue to run the Library's operations. It is nothing I have ever seen before, and I have consulted enough of the books here to know it has never happened, even before my time. Sadly, I am at a loss."

"That explains it," Robin said.

Arturo watched Centauri drop down to her shoulder to pulse what felt like a quick *I told you so*, before Robin waved him back up to the chandelier. "Back on Earth, Centauri mentioned he hadn't felt anything from the Great Library in a while. I just thought there was some kind of interference. Like shoddy Wi-Fi or something."

"Shoddy Wi-Fi?" Mwamba repeated, eyebrow raised.

"You know what I mean. There are a lot of weird things happening around the world, Mwamba. Not just ecosystems out of balance but other things too. The last thing I saw, clouds were gathering around all the extinct volcanoes across the world and more volcanic islands have appeared across the oceans too. Activity on a global scale. Although nobody knows why. The media is going around in circles trying to explain it. I just figured whatever is happening was causing problems with communication between Centauri and the Library. I had no idea all this other stuff was happening."

"And that is currently one of our problems. None of the Sages know what is going on, and without being able to call them back through the Book, we cannot do much at all. Half our number of Sages are traveling across the realms."

"What can we do?" Veer asked. He stood tall and proud, ready to help.

Arturo got the impression he was a man of action, always thinking of the next move, how to fix the problem, how to help. "You said that what happened in the Rose Garden was deliberate. You said it was Sut-taru. And these Unwritten? If that's the truth of the matter, I should go to Bloom and confront them before the fiends can do any more damage."

"No!" Helia said firmly. "I'm sorry, Veer, but he's too powerful. We all know the stories of what he did. How can we forget what he did to the Library itself when he was last here? Razing the entirety of the Central Terrarium, burning scholars alive and destroying several gener-ations of rare flora collected from around the globe. Had the Book not stopped him then, he would have ended the Library for good, forever disrupting the balance between the realms of Paperworld and Earth."

As Veer's eyebrows arched, she softened her tone slightly. "Look, I've seen his power for myself now, and I tell you that we cannot tackle him alone. We need to unite . . . and we need Perennia back."

"But Mwamba said you can't remember what happened to the dragon, Helia. Can you?"

Helia bit her lips, before shaking her head. "I took a knock in the fight. I have lost part of my memories, perhaps only a fraction of what we experienced in Silvyra. But enough that I cannot recall if I saw Peren-nia or what might have happened to her. I can only remember reaching her nest in the center of the Rose Garden to find nothing there. She was gone. I think *he* must have taken her."

"And what about *him*?" Robin asked, her lips pursed together as though finding the words she was saying distasteful. "This *Suttaru*. I thought he was dead?"

"He was supposed to have died long, long ago. That's what the sto-ries have always told for as long as we have known them."

"Yet he's back again? How can a figure of such evil return? How is that even possible? He's from a long and distant history—most people think he's an urban legend. Does it have anything to do with the Book, do you think?"

Robin looked around the group, but Arturo saw that nobody had an answer.

"Who's Suttaru?" he asked. It came out louder than he intended, and he felt like a fool, but he had heard enough now that he needed answers.

Every face in the room turned his way. He straightened and coughed nervously.

"Arturo!" Veer boomed. "Ah yes, why are you here again?"

"Nu seems to think the Book brought him to us in connection with whatever is happening," Robin said, studying Arturo in that manner of hers that made him feel both special and a little like a particularly interesting museum exhibit.

Arturo swallowed and clasped his hands together in front of him. "I'm sorry to have asked what might be an obvious question to you all. But if I'm here, I might as well try and understand. This Ash Man. Who is he exactly?"

It was Mwamba who replied. "He was one of three friends who were among the first to inhabit the Great Library. The Great Library of Tomorrow is a wondrous place," Mwamba intoned loudly, his voice amplified as he spoke, echoing around the walls that wrapped around them. "Yet, as you are now finding out, there are other realms that lie beyond it. The first of our number to discover this was a wise and adventurous woman called Fairen, the brightest and best of the three friends. Our youngsters"—he paused and nodded at Nu—"learn about her in their studies. She was the first scholar here, who—during her exploration of the Library—happened upon a most unlikely doorway. And it was this doorway that led her into the place we know as Paperworld, a vast collection of very real stories—indeed, entire realms—that can be visited and explored, and even lived in.

"Her friend and colleague Adi, as he was then known, was an educated scholar with big ideas and an even bigger confidence to tackle them. Yet his work was said to have strayed too close to evil. It drew the attention of a malevolent power in the universe, a devourer of light and stories and realms. This entity lured him away and corrupted him. Made him its ally and forced him to turn on the Great Library and his friends."

"But why? What did it want?"

Helia continued, "Mwamba and I have been at the Library for centuries and even we don't know the truth of the matter. The stories of its existence were old even when we first arrived. The entity is said to have come into being in one of the darker areas of Paperworld. You see, Arturo, Paperworld is a vast universe of different realms, entire worlds built from words and stories, created from the River of Letters, a force that gave birth to all life. Yet it is believed that in a shadowy corner of the river flowed darker stories. Nightmares. In the natural order of things, these pooled in their own secret corner of the universe, a realm of torment that we came to know as Discordia. This is where this *thing* escaped from."

Arturo raised his eyebrows. "By these *realms*, do you mean different worlds? You're saying there are different worlds out there?"

"Cool, huh?" Robin said. "Are we melting your mind yet?"

He gave a nervous laugh. "Just a little! So let me get this straight: People visit the Great Library from Earth through many different portals. But there is also a single portal here that leads to other realms? This . . . *Paperworld*?"

"Correct. Although that one is just for us Sages to travel through with our Orbs. No visitors go through, and similarly nobody from Paperworld can visit the Great Library. It's only for the Sages to use to explore and learn, before returning to expand the Great Library's repository of knowledge."

"We still don't know exactly how or why our Library is connected to these other realms in such a way. But what we do know is that this universe of other stories is infinite, flowing from a limitless Source, full of constant change and creation. A parchment patchwork of all tales ever told, existing in a dimension of its own, where the River of Letters flows freely, along endless channels, forming into words, sentences, and ultimately, stories. And through some magic we could not hope to describe—and gave up long ago trying to—these stories have each become a realm of their own. Realms we can learn from and through which we can enrich our own."

Sage Helia took over the tale. "You see, Arturo, we have come to realize that much like how nature exists on Earth—not in any singular identifiable form but as a collective force—Paperworld is another foundation of our existence. Just as life cannot exist without nature, humanity cannot exist without stories. We are nothing without them. They tell us who we are and where we've come from. They let us glimpse our possible futures. They have long reassured us as to our small and humble place in the unknown, and when we'll have long since passed from the real into the beyond, they will act as our legacy to others. Stories . . . are everything. And the universe beyond the Great Library is where they are held and nurtured and protected."

"By the Book of Wisdom?" Nu's voice was soft, a tiny note in the melody of the machine at work. She looked nervous at her interruption.

Mwamba and Helia nodded together. "And the Sages and their Orbs," he replied. "A united force."

Arturo rubbed his eyes and blinked them clear again, trying to take it all in. He'd learned so much growing up—from schooling, working his whole life, and reading books on everything from history to pulp fiction—but this information he was learning now, in this grand place with these Sages, felt far more real.

The excitement of all the possibilities rose in his chest. Yet it was quickly tempered by the feeling that there was more to be said about the threat on the horizon.

Arturo rubbed his face, the whiskers on his upper lip coarse against his finger. He was nodding slowly, trying to wrap his head around what he was being told. It was like trying to follow one of those fantastical shows he enjoyed on TV, but only after being dropped into the middle of season six.

"What happened when this entity turned the Scholar into Suttaru, or whatever you call him? You say he attacked some people?"

"There was a great and terrible fight. And it was only thanks to the Book of Wisdom that he was stopped. Defeated. And killed."

"Or so we thought," Veer added.

"And now he's back, and he wants revenge," Helia said, and they all turned to her. "I know this because it wasn't just destruction I witnessed in the Rose Garden. It was hatred of the beauty and life at the heart of Silvyra. Of the fabric it holds as the mother of all realms, the spirit of her nature flowing from the roots of the Great Tree out across the River of Letters to the other trees in so many other realms." Helia paused and swallowed. "And of us. I could sense his rage at Xav and I and what we stand for. It was there in the heat that surrounded him. A burning need to kill us. Whatever happened to him back then, he's returned to seek retribution. I think Silvyra is just the start."

Veer clenched and unclenched his fists. Despite the stoic look on his face, he appeared to be trying to calm himself. "Well then. Regardless of his motivation, we Sages, appointed guardians, must stop him. The question is: How do we do that without the dragon?"

"Or the Book," Robin added. "Without it, we will be fighting blind against a foe only the Author inside truly knows."

Nobody said anything to that.

"You say you were a writer, Arturo?"

Arturo was startled to hear this. Mwamba was looking at him, sizing him up.

What does that have to do with anything?

"A copywriter, yes," he replied, trying not to feel silly that he was answering such a mundane question in the midst of a discussion of the fate of the universe. "I used to want to write books, to become an author. I was thinking just that, in fact, when I saw the bookshop that brought me here."

Mwamba pondered that for a moment, before nodding again.

"You are probably wondering why you are here, and I do not know for certain if there is an answer we can give you right now. People find the Great Library in all kinds of ways and for every reason you can imagine. Here they will discover more than they could ever know and find the answers to their most ardent questions. Then they return to Earth enlightened and ready to make the best of themselves." His eyes grew kind. "But sometimes the question asked is ours and the answer we require is to be found in those who come here. And that is when the Book of Wisdom plays a more proactive role in bringing people to us."

"Nu suggested as much," Arturo replied. "But you said the Book isn't working, so how can that be?"

"The Book of Wisdom is the heart of the Library, and the Author is the consciousness within it. And although she cannot communicate with us at present, the Library itself is still functional. The Orbs are working and the portals from Earth to us are open. As is the portal from here to the realms beyond the Great Library. Nobody is any the wiser about what is happening. The Book of Wisdom is silent in voice only."

"So, what's blocking her? Is she sick? Can books here get sick?"

"I've never heard of a book getting sick," Veer said, though he didn't look at all sure.

Mwamba's gaze flickered in Arturo's direction again. "What I think is that it is rather fortuitous that an author-in-waiting walked into our midst at the moment we lose the voice of our very own." He gestured to Robin. "Robin, this is an unusual request for a Sage, but I think it would be important for you to be Arturo's guide while he is here. Can you acquaint him with the Library and find him some temporary visitor quarters? He may be with us for a day or so while we try to figure out what is going on. It may take an author to help us solve the mystery of the Book."

Arturo didn't know what to make of that. He felt comfortable in this place and had a burning desire to go exploring, but being forced to stay here wasn't what he had in mind.

"Wait, I'm not—"

But Robin tugged his arm gently, cutting him off.

She nodded to the others. "I am happy to look after Arturo and show him around until we figure out what to do next. What about the rest of you?"

"I'll go to Silvyra," Veer said immediately, throwing a look to Helia that dared her to defy him again. "I will not go to fight, but to protect. I can make sure they are prepared for what might be coming their way. Helia, any suggestions for where to leap to?"

Helia didn't look happy about it, but she didn't argue.

"His force was huge. There were hundreds of his . . . well, I think they were once people. Their attack is likely already underway. I fear they will simply spread out from the Rose Garden and raze what they come across.

Veer nodded. "The town of Aedela is the closest settlement in Bloom to the Rose Garden. Perhaps I can meet with their leader and confirm the enemy's movements from there. And, if needed, do what I can to protect the inhabitants."

"Thank you," Mwamba said.

"And what of you and Helia?" Robin asked the man.

"I will talk to Helia about what we need from her next."

"That's all well and good, Mwamba, but we can't possibly ask her to go back out there again so soon after what's happened. Not without another Sage with her. I'll go."

"I'll be fine, Robin," Helia said. "You know how this works. The Sage of Knowledge remains in the Library, with the Book. This is where Mwamba's powers are strongest. And it's clear you're needed with Arturo to offer him your particular brand of guidance. I'm the Sage of Hope. And hope must continue to work its magic in the world."

Mwamba held up both hands, heading off any further protests. "Robin, you are right. Helia cannot go without help." And with that he directed a tired smile at Nu, who almost stumbled back and fell over her chair with shock. "This is all quite unorthodox, my young friend, but can you help us, please? Time is already running out, and we have a map to read."

With that, he, Helia, and Nu left through one door, with Veer waving them goodbye before disappearing through another.

Arturo and Robin were left alone.

"I guess you're stuck babysitting me, then," he said, trying to lighten the mood.

She frowned at him.

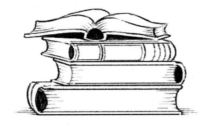

CHAPTER NINE
THE ORRERY

Nu followed the two Sages out of the reading room, a rising tide of eagerness and nervousness inside her. Helia's Orb, Vega, and Mwamba's Orb, Canopus, hovered on either side of them, and inside her pocket she could feel Antares stirring, as though eager to join her friends.

It was all a lot to take in. One minute she'd been doing her usual job, the next she was standing in Sage Mwamba's reading room, part of a monumental conversation about the fate of the realms.

Everything seemed different now. It was as if she was seeing the Library in a new light and truly feeling its importance for the first time. She had turned a new page and was becoming a part of its story.

From the fine red carpet beneath her shoes to the crystal lamps that grew stronger as the group passed—their presence producing the charge to light them—Nu took it all in with humility and excitement, especially the paintings, which had always fascinated her as a child: ruined cities, beams of light, islands in the sky, the Great Tree in the center of the Maze. They seemed bigger, bolder, more real, as if these realms that had always felt out of reach were now calling to her.

"Quickly, now," Mwamba said as he led them on. They were heading toward a part of the Library that Nu had never visited before.

The ocher-painted name above the double doors spelled out "The Hall of Finding." Only the Sages and the occasional scholar would ever need to come here, yet being a curious sort, Nu had learned all about it. As they entered, she saw that it was as astonishing a place as she had always imagined. A vast and cavernous space, filled with high shelves of bound atlases and travelogues, and innumerable scrolls—a seemingly endless array of cartographical information about the Earth and the realms beyond. Entire constellations of globes were dotted around the room in every conceivable size and scale.

Nu had heard they didn't just hold physical maps here but also those with more emotional or spiritual sensibilities—those that charted the course of a person's dreams, for example, or the landscape of a child's imagination as they played in the backyard.

It was still a room of stories—not quite the same as those held elsewhere in the Library, but important in their own right.

The great machine that rose before them drew her attention most. A complex assemblage of brass and steel and crystal filled the vast space around it, like some kind of ancient and magnificent organ in the center of a concert hall, ready for someone to come and play it and dazzle an audience of thousands. But Nu understood this wasn't a musical instrument. The multitude of concentric rings that spun and twisted on individual axes and orientations—tiny galaxies in a machine universe— had an altogether more special purpose.

Nu watched silently as Canopus buzzed around the panel, pulsing different patterns at Mwamba, like a tiny composer. She realized the Orb was guiding his Sage, even as the man continued to talk.

He stepped up to the machine and stood before one of the many panels resplendent with knobs, dials, and levers. Only now did he glance over his shoulder to ensure Nu was watching.

"You said we needed to go on a journey," she said. "Is that why we're in here? To see where to go?"

"In a way," Mwamba replied, still working away at the controls. "This magnificent contraption is the Orrery, a one-of-a-kind design from an Italian genius Helia and I once knew."

Helia sniffed. "Genius is pushing it a little."

"Even so, he was brilliant enough to design *and* build this contraption, leaving it here as his secret legacy to the world, knowing only a few would ever truly appreciate it. Because, Nu, the universe beyond the Library is bigger than you or I could ever imagine. What you learned at school—that it contains all the stories ever told—is no exaggeration. There are a multitude of realms out there, and we Sages spend a lot of our time traveling and learning about them."

"Like literary anthropologists—that's what they taught us."

He paused a moment to beam at her. "A little like that, yes. And this machine, the Orrery, finds them for us. To master the controls takes years of training, and even then, making inquiries can only be done with the help and guidance of one's Orb." He pulled another lever. "Yet it allows us to locate any Sage and their Orb, whichever world's story they may be visiting or exploring."

At that moment, far above, one of the millions of sparkling crystals that were scattered like stars across the great machine burst into the blue glow of a supernova. Canopus flashed in what seemed like relief, and even Mwamba himself seemed to breathe a little easier under his breath.

"Veer's arrived in Silvyra," he confirmed as he studied the three-dimensional map. "Let us hope he's in time to help, if help is needed."

"Help *will* be needed," Nu said.

She didn't know why she said it. The words were suddenly out of her mouth and no amount of the embarrassment that followed would take them back, even as Helia glanced sideways.

Mwamba nodded and adjusted the controls some more, letting the mechanisms whirl and spin. Then there was a strange flash. Not as before, nothing bright or colorful, just a lighter gray, a bit like a glimpse of headlights in fog.

"Was that another Sage?" Nu asked.

Helia shook her head, still watching the Orrery. "No, just a glitch. One of the ghosts in the machine, so to speak. It used to appear when you ran a trace in one of the other crystals, but the glitch has been stuck in there, in the Great Tree, for a few decades now. Nobody has been able to figure out why." She peered closer. Vega pulsed something, and she nodded.

"The glitch doesn't affect the locator though."

"No, it doesn't," Mwamba said with a sigh. "Which means none of our number are at Mother—the Great Tree—presently. I had hoped we might be lucky, yet that is not to be the case."

Nu didn't know what this meant, but she could tell Helia was upset by the implications of what was being discussed. The woman shifted uneasily, yet straightened and lifted her chin determinedly as she spoke.

"We can't expect Veer to protect the whole of Silvyra himself. If he is the front line of defense against any attack that flows from the Rose Garden, we should make sure that one of us is there to protect the Great Tree. She holds the balance of Paperworld, of everything, within her." She glanced at Nu, who knew she hadn't hidden her confusion very well. "You see, Nu, the Great Tree isn't only important to the realm of Silvyra. Her roots connect all things. They weave through the soil not only under her own realm, but their magic stretches into the River of Letters itself, communicating with all other realms. Mother is her name, for that is truly what she is—the Mother of all nature across Paperworld. Her survival is our survival. We cannot stand by and allow her to be at the mercy of those who would seek to disrupt the balance. It would be catastrophic."

"So, you will go?"

Helia's tight nod answered Mwamba's question. "How could I not? There is no one else who can help, and my powers have always been suited to Silvyra. I will protect the Tree and the people there as best I can. Your place is here. It is what must be done."

Mwamba's sad smile indicated to Nu the regret he might hold over what Helia was saying. It was the look of a man who might feel a little trapped by his role, despite the importance it held. For the Sage of Knowledge was known to be the constant at the Great Library, the Sage who was almost always here—able to utilize the wisdom contained within these hallowed halls in more powerful ways than the others— while his colleagues traveled to other realms.

He spoke of none of this, however. His voice was calm and measured as he replied, "Thank you for your courage, Helia. And there is perhaps another reason I think you should be the one to go. Perhaps of even greater importance than as a protector. Because I believe the Elixir of Life Silvyra is known for might be able to help you recover what you are missing. It heals all ailments, after all. And if you can recover your memories of what happened to Perennia—"

"Then we might be able to find her? I was thinking the very same thing. Perennia is the key. Wherever she has gone, we need to rescue her."

"If she is still alive," Mwamba said quietly.

Helia smiled. "I am not the Sage of Hope for nothing."

Nu looked between them both, her head swimming with what was happening. Discussions involving Silvyra, the connection between the Great Tree and all things, a missing dragon . . . and a villain from legend. None of it felt real. At least not the kind of real that she was used to in her everyday life in the Library.

The burst of excitement that had warmed her insides upon accompanying the Sages was easing off. Fear and doubt were now flowing into the void left behind. She didn't belong here.

Maybe I should go back to work, she thought, taking a step back.

Yet just then she felt a small vibration in her pocket as Antares spoke to her. Not in words yet. She was still too weak, but she reminded Nu of the truth. The truth deep in her heart that this was where she needed to be.

Helia must have sensed her unease. She placed her hand on her shoulder and squeezed it gently. "Just wait," she said.

It was enough to steady Nu's nerves and push that creeping doubt back into the shadows.

Mwamba stepped away from the controls. Canopus followed him, glimmering in the flittering lights of the room. To Nu, he looked like some aged sorcerer. Kindly, but tired.

His eyes fixed upon hers.

"Whatever happens in the realms beyond the Library will affect us all, Nu. We are all connected, and the impact of Suttaru's actions in

Silvyra would be felt far beyond the edges of her reality. There are so many realms of beauty and life in Paperworld, and they all need to be protected because their loss will be the undoing of humanity here on Earth. All of which brings me to what comes next. Helia cannot go to Silvyra alone. You already know that, don't you?"

As Nu fumbled for a response, she watched the man's wrinkled finger gesture to the pocket in which she had been carrying Antares.

"One of our Orbs has requested your help, Nu. And I trust the decision Antares has made to bring you into this tale. So I must do the same. Will you accompany Helia to Silvyra to help her—and us—protect the Great Tree and maintain the balance across all things? Can you help her find the dragon, if she can be found?"

Nu felt the fluttering in her chest as she balanced precariously on the edge of this momentous decision. After all these years growing up in this magnificent place, often feeling like part of the background, this was her chance to do something more.

Yet she was terrified of what this all meant. Of the magnitude of what was at risk and the fact she was now partly responsible for its outcome. That didn't seem right. She was nobody here! Certainly not a Sage with powers and the ability to do great things.

She was just Nu.

And yet . . . wasn't this everything she had wanted? To do more? To become more? If the Sages needed her help, she must give it. "When do we leave?" she asked, fixing a smile to her face as the nerves fluttered around inside her.

CHAPTER TEN
THE END OF AN ADVENTURE

"It's time!" Monae said brightly, throwing her arm around Dzin's shoulders and gesturing around at the decorations. "We're done and everything is *perfect*. Don't you think?"

Dzin nodded and smiled. Everything was done, it was true. But his mind was playing tricks again, making him nervous, making him wonder if somehow his Elixir would be found wanting in some way. That he'd be revealed to be not good enough to graduate after all.

He tried to tamper the anxiety down again. Pictured the unease sliding from his shoulders like rain from a scuttlebug's back. The amusing visual worked a little.

Pyruc stopped alongside them, brushing himself down after clearly sneaking a handful of dandelion-seed caps meant for tomorrow. He beamed at the both of them.

"It really is, isn't it! We've done a great job, all of us. Because, and I cannot lie, I found the unfurling of the sprite leaves harder than creating the Elixir. So for us to have finally got those blasted things up makes me want to weep for joy."

The twins and Monae laughed. Dzin smiled with him. The five students were full of good cheer and comradeship, as friends at the end of one adventure and the beginning of the next. Bonded by a mutual experience that few would have and many yearned for.

It was then the ground fell out from beneath their feet.

There was a commotion beyond the laboratory—the smash of glass and equipment falling to the floor. For a few moments, nobody could place where it had come from. Dzin realized in the silence that followed that he could hear something in the next room of the botanical building.

A *click*, *click*, *click* of something moving along the floor toward them. Claws.

Before anyone could move, a spray of orange flames exploded through the door to the archives, sending them all screaming and ducking for cover.

Gaeloc was the first to spring back up. The first to cry out in shock.

Dzin couldn't make out what he was seeing, but the terror was obvious in the noise his friend was making. What was going on? Was the Tree on fire? Or just the archives?

Then he saw the cause of the destruction.

A monstrous creature—a wolf or hound of some sort—padded out from the fire.

Its fur was soot-black and rippling with flames. Its snout was long and its glowing red eyes bulging and fierce.

Dzin's own cry caught in his throat and died. He wanted to move, but his body had given up. He could hear its heavy breath—the rhythmic, eager breath of a predator. He felt the waves of cold panic flow through his insides, before coming up against the wall of heat that was cooking his skin.

He had never before imagined such a terrifying beast, let alone seen one on his many travels. He was locked in place, his limbs frozen, his heart racing, beating so loud in his own ears he couldn't believe the creature hadn't heard him and sprung in his direction. His breath came short, and his limbs began to tremble with fear as his eyes swam out of focus, dizziness hitting him hard. It was like he was back in his home, being told his parents were gone. The shock, the paralysis. He wanted his brother's soothing arms to comfort him, to protect him. But his brother wasn't there. Just his classmates and their screams. In the end, his inability to move saved him. As the students fell back in cries of shock, its lip curled up to reveal bloodied teeth, and it leaped for the first to try to run: Pyruc.

There was a scream of horror from Pyruc as he was pounced on, two flaming paws landing on his back and pushing him down, mixing with the sound of breaking bones, then cut immediately short with a wet gurgle and sigh as half of his neck was ripped out.

It wasn't the sight that did it for Dzin. That was too much, too visceral in the moment to take in properly.

No, it was the sound of tearing skin that snapped him from his panic.

"Monae!" he cried, reaching out for her.

But she didn't hear him. She was too focused on the beast as it leaped toward Gaeloc and Atraena.

The twins should have parted ways, and if they had, one of them might have made it. But they held fast together, and it was together they fell. Under fire they were dragged down, two pairs of arms trying to fend off the monstrous beast, trying to protect each other, until the arms went limp, and there was no more fight left to give.

Dzin's heart was doing circuits around his chest. His mind went into overdrive. *What was this thing, and why was it here killing them? How did it even get so high up the Tree, and why was it on fire!*

He stared helplessly from the beast—still ripping at the twins with its teeth and claws—to the archives. All the past formulas for the Elixir of Life were being turned to ash. His gaze swept across the shelf of vials of their Elixir, watching as the heat shattered each one, spilling their pride and joy everywhere.

Suddenly, he realized he'd backed up against his own desk. *My formula.* It seemed a silly thing in such a moment, but it was something to focus on. His work. He couldn't let it be lost.

As quickly as he could, he slipped his hand inside the desk and retrieved his scroll.

Then he grabbed his walking staff and held it out to Monae so he could pull her after him. "*Quickly,*" he gasped through the heat and steadily amassing smoke. Her eyes were wide with terror, her lips moving as though whispering something to herself repeatedly. She saw the staff, and for a moment, he was sure she would take it.

Then the flaming nightmare found her.

It stood there bathed in fire, dripping blood and gore. A thing from the darkest nightmares. Dzin tried to get between them, but he wasn't quick enough. His breath caught in his throat as the fire beast finished with the poor twins and leaped over the table, spilling blackening foods and setting drinks to the boil just by standing next to them. It fell upon his friend.

Despite his fear, Dzin felt some kind of instinct take over. He lifted the staff, his limbs no longer trembling with fear, but instead with rage, and swung it, trying to drive the creature off. The staff was a rare piece, fashioned from a fallen branch of the Great Tree by his father, and would make a fine weapon if needed. Unfortunately, he soon realized that didn't make any difference. While the staff didn't catch light from the fire, the beast just absorbed his withering blows. His wiry limbs, lean but muscled from his travels and life as an apprentice Runner, were no match for this creature. Its teeth bared at him, causing him to stop flailing with the staff as the fire continued to ripple like fur across its body.

Dzin heard Monae whimper. He tried to take a step toward her. Perhaps he could yet reach her. Pull her away from this madness.

Yet again, the beast stepped forward, too, and the fierce wave of heat that it carried with it forced Dzin back, tears stinging his eyes as he felt the clothes on his back singe and start to smoke.

"No!" he cried out, yet there was nothing he could do. Stumbling back, he tried to block out his friend's scream, but with his hands clasped around the staff his ears went unprotected, and the horrifying sounds of the creature as it tore into her made him howl with impotent rage.

He was alone. His friends were dead. Taken in the blink of a bat's eye. He was next.

Get out, his mind screamed at him. *Get out!*

The creature turned, lifting its jaws, Monae's blood now dripping from its teeth as it slowly strode toward him.

Then there was a shout.

From behind him, Dzin felt a breeze of cold air, a temporary relief before the wind whipped the flames around even more fiercely. They had already spread across the blackening tables and up the bookshelves where the vials of Elixir bubbled and shattered. Now the gust of wind caused the flames to curl above him and lick their way across the ceiling.

He glanced back to see a pair of Tree guards burst in, hands to their faces to shield them from the flames. Tall women dressed in lightweight plant armor. They looked around wildly, then, spotting Dzin, they drew their spear-swords.

Help, Dzin thought desperately, unable to give voice to his words. His eyes must have been bulging from his head to try to get their attention. *Help me!*

Their reaction wasn't what he expected. Instead of the horror at seeing some nightmarish creature from hell having come to life, the revulsion in their gaze seemed to be reserved for him.

"What have you *done?*" one of them half cried, choking on the last word as they looked at the scene of devastation and then back to him.

Confused, he swiveled back to cast his eyes on the beast but now saw that it was gone.

There was nothing but fire and a swathe of blackening bodies being consumed by the flames.

It was just him. Alone with his dead friends.

"No, wait," he mumbled, looking at the stick he was still waving in his hands as though still warding off a monster. "This isn't . . . I wasn't."

Another figure ran in behind the guards.

"Dzin, no!" Tywich cried out. "The laboratory! The archives!" Then his eyes found the corpses littering the floor. "No!"

He ran further into the lab, taking care not to get caught on any of the tables around him that still remained ablaze. Though, not carefully enough, Dzin noticed, for one sleeve of his cloak had already caught fire, the material at the hem slowly beginning to curl up.

"How could you do this?" Tywich continued, wailing as he fell before the first body he reached—Pyruc's.

Tywich's reaction was everything Dzin had feared—and everything the guards needed to understand what had happened here. They thought *he'd* done all this. That he was responsible for all this fire and devastation and death.

He wanted to explain what had really happened, but, in his fear that they wouldn't believe him, no words would come. He lurched toward the guards, beseeching them to listen with their sense of reason, but he was still waving his staff, and they must have thought he was about to attack.

They raised their batons.

"Stop him!" Tywich yelled, pointing directly at Dzin.

The guards took a step forward.

To his surprise, Dzin didn't panic. He didn't have time before his instincts kicked in.

He lashed out with his staff, enough to ward them off and create a space for escape.

Which is exactly what he did, bundling the guards out of the way and scrambling into the cool night air.

CHAPTER ELEVEN
PORTALS

They were to depart immediately.

Nu barely had time to pass a message to one of her friends telling her family not to worry, before Mwamba and Helia began to lead her onward to the outfitters. She struggled to hide her glee at getting to select a costume to wear, something one always had to do in order to better fit in when arriving at another destination. And for them to be visiting the Great Tree, a place she had heard so many stories of as a child, perhaps her favorite of all the realms she had come to know by story only . . . well, it seemed a dream come true. Even in the face of the danger that possibly lay ahead.

As they hurried along, Mwamba told her stories, some of which she knew, and quizzed her on what she knew of Silvyra already, asking her about the Great Tree and the Elixir especially. She couldn't figure out if he was nervous about sending someone untrained or was simply making conversation to ensure nobody they passed interrupted them or noticed their alarm.

He retold the story about the three scholars, including Fairen, who found the first portal into Paperworld; how the Founder of the Great Library was lost to that same portal and then of how Fairen was betrayed by her closest friend. He spoke of the battle that followed and of the creation of the Author as Fairen joined with the Book of Wisdom. And how this new combined force had then been enough to help the Great Library fight back against her friend—who had become Suttaru. After which there followed a great moment in Paperworld, reflected in Earth's history, full of relief and joy and a resurgence of creativity and spirit.

She already knew a lot of what Mwamba was saying, either from her school teachings or from the tales people told around the Library, but it was something else to hear the stories in such a personal setting.

They moved into a whole new section of the Library, into the living, breathing, underground forest that had been grown here long ago. Nu loved it here because it spoke of the nature of the outside world, except that here people lived in harmony with it.

The leafy floor bounced pleasingly as they strode across it. Above, petals of reds and pinks and blues tickled her hair from where they hung from the upside-down gardens on the ceiling. Two gray-haired women were chatting animatedly about books in a vine-covered alcove, pausing to collect the sweet-smelling liquid that dripped out of the center of a newly blossoming flower nearby, filling the chamber with a waft of chocolate and spices.

Beyond that were fountains of nectar two stories high, entire hexagonal wall combs full of bright yellow bees making honey, and the occasional bursts of color as balls of dandelion-like seeds drifted into the air and exploded like tiny fireworks around them.

Heads turned their way as they walked by. Nu saw them all as they first looked up to the Sages, then their Orbs, and finally her. That's when she would look away, feeling self-conscious, especially when she saw people she knew, others who had grown up here like she had. Their mouths gaped open in unanswered questions—what could she be doing in such illustrious company? And why? Nu didn't know how she could possibly explain. Even she wasn't quite sure how she'd ended up here today, only that it seemed right.

She let her hand drift up to touch the pocket that held Antares, feeling a strange comfort in the firm shape of her new companion beneath the material.

Eventually, they reached a small room off a main corridor. Mwamba held the door open for Helia and Nu, gesturing for them to go inside. He continued to talk from the doorway. "One of the rules you might already know about travel beyond the Library, Nu, is that we do it not officially as Sages, at least not openly. Only a few select folk know our true identity. We have to be discreet and blend in where we can."

"I understand," Nu called back, trying to rein in her excitement. She and Helia stood in the middle of a hexagonal dressing room, large enough for two people. Five tall, gleaming mirrors surrounded them.

"You'll enjoy this," Helia whispered.

Within seconds, the images in the mirrors changed. Not their faces, but the clothes they saw themselves in were different.

In her reflection ahead, Nu was dressed in a fine blue dress that shimmered like the sea, as was Helia. To the mirror on the right of that, she was in a sleek all-in-one suit, with a brown headscarf wrapped around her head. She bent and twisted her body to admire herself, realizing all the visages around her were moving in unison, as though she were really wearing multiple outfits at the same time.

Unfortunately, she wasn't quick enough to get to see what other fantastic outfits were displayed in the other reflections. Helia walked up to the mirror to the left of the sea-blue dress and pressed her fingers to it. Suddenly, all the images showed the same outfit: an embroidered white tunic, comfortable—if not baggy—brown trousers, and a short green cloak that looked as if it'd been made of freshly pressed leaves.

Nu blinked as she realized Helia was now wearing that exact same outfit. Even more surprisingly, she looked down to see that she had somehow changed into the same clothes too. All perfectly fitted to her size and shape, and incredibly comfortable. She ran a finger down the smooth fabric of her sleeve.

"H-how is that possible!?"

"A little magic from long ago," Helia said, gesturing that they go outside again. Vega swirled his approval from above, and Antares managed a small vibration from where he had moved into the pocket of Nu's updated outfit to let her know she was still there. Helia brushed her hands down the material and pulled the cloak around her waist. "It's not the finest fashion of the realm, I'm afraid, but not the worst either. We will blend right in."

Nu raised her hand and realized she was wearing a light, gold bracelet, with exquisite circular designs sweeping across its surface. She also noticed Helia was wearing something similar around her neck—a beautiful, gold-threaded amulet with flecks of silver like lightning bolts shooting out of it.

"These seem a little excessive if we're trying to blend in."

"That's for Vega and Antares," Helia replied. "Not everyone is comfortable with Orbs. Sometimes they raise questions, and we don't always have time to supply the answers. Some Orbs can cloak themselves, but in this case, Vega will shrink down to the same size Antares is now and they will hide on us. It allows us to maintain our bond and connection, while remaining discreet."

Mwamba fell into step beside them as they strode toward the Concourse. Soon they found themselves at the Haven—the home of the Book of Wisdom. A place that was only ever talked about in hushed whispers and a place only the Sages ever saw.

Nu paused hesitantly, even as the other two walked in.

Was *she* really going to get to see the Book of Wisdom and even travel through the portal in the Haven, as all her heroes in the past had?

"Come on," Helia said encouragingly. "You can do this."

She held out her hand. Nu took it and stepped through. She didn't have a chance to look around, as much as she would have liked. The hall was magnificent, so vast and beautifully lit, with an air of magic permeating everything, as she had always dreamed it might do. And there, *there* was the Book, sitting on its pedestal.

Yet Helia's hand firmly led her on, indicating this was not the time to linger. Straight to the other side of the Haven they went, with Nu unable to take her eyes off the Book . . . at least until an empty frame of a portal—a magical rectangle of aquamarine, shimmering like a vertical pool of pristine waters—rose before them.

The portal to Paperworld.

"This is where the scholar first found the other realms," Mwamba said. "Where the magic of our connection to Paperworld was first discovered. It is where we Sages take the first step of our journeys. And now you will too. Are you ready, Nu?"

Nu nodded without saying a word. She couldn't. What could she possibly say? She was too excited to even think straight.

Suddenly, Antares lifted out of her pocket. She swirled in reds and golds, still faint, but stronger than before.

I'm with you, the Orb seemed to say.

Helia was watching on with a strange, sad look on her face. Until Vega nudged her arm and she shook herself back from wherever she had been.

"Vega, take us in at the highest bough of the Great Tree," she said.

Whatever the Orb did next Nu didn't know, but as his colors swirled faster and more furiously around his surface, there began a hum in the chamber. Low at first, then building in power. It felt like a wave of energy or magic or something in between, and it suddenly brought the portal to life in a burst of light as waves of colors from the frame bled out into the center and swirled around inside it, shimmering like the surface of an otherworldly ocean.

Mwamba placed a hand on both their shoulders. Then he stepped back, with Canopus following.

"Helia, Nu . . . the journey ahead may be dangerous. We don't know what you will face in the coming hours, so keep your eyes and ears and wits about you and be there for each other." He touched two fingers to his heart. "Be safe and travel well. Warn the Great Tree. Find the dragon. We're relying on you."

Helia did the same. "You can rely on us."

With that, she pulled Nu closer to her, making sure Vega and Antares were hovering around them, then they stepped into the light.

CHAPTER TWELVE
A FORMULA FOR DISASTER

The logs of the wooden suspension bridge rippled beneath him as Dzin raced away from the Great Tree, causing the inhabitants going about their evening business to stumble and mutter.

"So sorry," he called out to one particularly disgruntled couple he pushed past, waving his treasured staff in one sweaty hand, his scroll clutched tightly in the other. The woman sniffed haughtily, her olive skin flushing with anger as she tried to hit him with her leaf umbrella. Dzin kept going. "Can't stop. Emergency botanical business!"

That was a twist on the truth, of course. It was an emergency, certainly. But to the guards, who he'd temporarily lost a few branches back and whose high-pitched snail whistles he could occasionally hear as they called reinforcements, it was an emergency of Dzin's making.

Which obviously didn't make any sense that he could fathom. He'd just witnessed his colleagues being killed and his laboratory burned down. He couldn't understand what had happened. Where had the fire beast gone? And why had Tywich been so quick to point the finger of blame at him?

As he crossed the bridge, then ran around the spiral staircase, all these questions vied for attention in his head. He reached the airship docking tree.

Down though. Not up.

Up might yet be the better option. Up would lead straight to the multitude of huge woven platforms that were suspended like sky-bound lily pads, each awaiting their next airship occupant. Up would give him the chance to run away to a faraway land beyond the bounds of the dark and deadly Maze that surrounded them, allowing him to escape properly, leaving behind the accusations and punishments that he knew would now follow should he be caught.

But no, there would be no airship for him tonight. The formula was one of two important things in his life. The other was the responsibility he was bequeathed when his parents died.

He clutched the scroll in his hand even tighter and kept running down the tree, rushing through an unsteady gathering of traders who, judging by the stink of the clouds of their curses, were coming off an afternoon in the nearest fermented sap tavern. Down, down, down.

To find his brother.

He reached their small bark cubby, and at the circular door, he jiggled his key in the lock. It was bolted from the inside.

"Yantuz!" he hissed through the window. "Yantuz, open up quickly!"

An inquisitive face appeared at the window, framed by the cozy, orange lamplight inside—strong cheekbones, eyes the color of green roses and tousled blond hair. Yantuz had certainly grown up to be the popular, handsome brother. Dzin, meanwhile, had eyes the color of rock, his hair was flat and brittle, like rock, and his face unremarkable . . . like rock. Luckily, he wasn't one to harbor resentment; otherwise, he'd be stowing away on an airship right at this very moment.

"Have you been for a run, brother?" Yantuz asked, stifling a yawn. "That's most unlike you."

"In a manner," Dzin replied, his pulse still racing as he glanced around. He could almost feel the spindly hands of a Great Tree guard grasping his collar and hauling him off to be interrogated. "Now, please, hurry. Open up and let me in before they find me."

"Who's that now?"

Another long, high-pitched whistle was blown, somewhere in the distance.

From the direction of Mother.

"Oh no . . . no!" he whined, crumpling the scroll further in his hand as his heart continued to slam against his ribs, playing them like musical wind chimes. He banged on the door with the staff, even as he heard the bolt being slid back.

"Hold on, I'm opening it like you asked. See?"

Yantuz's welcoming grin faded as Dzin burst into the humbly furnished room. He wanted to grab things, but he knew he couldn't. There was only one thing on his mind now.

"We have to go, Yantuz."

"Not another expedition for ingredients?" Yantuz said, stretching as he leaned lazily on the still open door. "I thought you were done with all that. You're bloody well graduating tomorrow, Dzin! Anyway, I told you I was hoping to get an early night. Promised I'd take Junic up to the highest branches before your ceremony to catch the dawn. He's visited us so many times, but he's never seen it, you know? Oh, goodness, he's going to love it. Remember how beautiful the light always looks filtering through Mother's leaves in the summer mornings? Nothing like it in all Silvyra."

Dzin stopped dead and raised a finger to his younger brother. "Please listen. Something terrible has happened and a misunderstanding has occurred that I don't think can be undone. I can't explain, but we need to go before we—before *I* get into trouble." He thought of the creature and grimaced. "Or worse."

Yantuz blinked a few more times, then pointed to the scroll. "Isn't that your formula?"

Dzin shoved it into his coat, while more snail whistles could be heard, rising to join the first chorus. All getting closer. "Leave everything. We have to go."

Dzin knew his brother was many things—flighty, annoyingly fun, a lover of teasing and taking life at a pace that some might consider lazy—but tonight he was grateful for the fact that Yantuz trusted him implicitly. He took only a few moments to change into his day clothes and ready himself.

By the time they left the house, the alarm had been well and truly raised. Dzin led the dazed Yantuz around the wooden trails, ignoring the variety of olive-and-brown-bark-colored faces poking out of windows and leaning out of doors, their attention on Mother, and they ran past in the other direction.

It wasn't long before he heard the whistles closer. The guards were now streaming out across the network of bridges from the Great Tree. Dzin wondered whether they would recognize him if they saw him, then realized what he must look like: he must be charred all over and his clothes a state. He looked exactly like the kind of person you'd want to stop and detain if you knew something was wrong.

Spotting a guard moving toward them from the other direction, drawn by the whistles, he ducked behind a trader's stall and yanked Yantuz down with him.

"What did you *do*?" Yantuz whispered.

They watched the guard pass by, before they leaped out and kept running. Dzin had to keep pulling on Yantuz's arm to drag him along as his brother's gaze kept drifting back.

"I didn't do anything, but something happened at the laboratory that I can't explain. Something bad. There was an attack. A fire. And . . ."

His voice trailed off as he pulled Yantuz onto another suspension bridge, and they bounced across into the glassblowing district of Crooked Limb, known for its beautiful strings of glass pearl lights that zigzagged above the walkways.

As they passed rows of stalls set up around the trunk of the Great Tree, each full to the brim with the tiny vials used to house the Elixir of Life, he couldn't help the words from getting stuck in his throat. It was as though he was afraid to utter them.

"And what?"

Dzin gritted his teeth and forced it out. "There was a beast, a hound, its fur full of flames. It burst into the lab, setting everything ablaze. The other students . . ." He turned to his brother. "I tried to help Monae. I really tried!"

Yantuz stared at him in confusion. "I believe you. Whatever happened, I believe you. But why are we running if there was an attack by someone else?"

"Some*thing*. And that's the problem. The guards didn't see it. I don't know what happened, but one minute the creature was there, and I was trying to defend myself against it, then the guards arrived, and when I looked back, it was gone."

Yantuz pointed to the staff. "You're trying to tell me you defended yourself with your comfort stick?"

"No!" Dzin hissed through gritted teeth, frustrated by Yantuz's mocking term for his staff. Then he paused and said reluctantly, "Well, yes. But it's not a comfort stick; it's Mother's walking staff. And I was trying to save Monae from the beast."

The image was still clear in his memory. One moment the creature had been there, its paws on his friend as it growled at Dzin and his feeble attempts to attack it with the staff. The next it was gone, scared off by the guards and Tywich. He was discovered alone, with no logical defense of himself to offer.

"Surely you can explain—" Yantuz began, but Dzin cut him off.

"I saw the looks in the guards' eyes, Yantuz. I heard what Tywich said. They all think I did it."

"But you're one of their best students! They knew what they were doing when they selected you, and until now you've given them no reason to doubt you. You're the Silvyran with not only a superior sense of smell and knowledge of flora but the greatest love of traveling, experiencing new places, and seeing the world. They have to understand that this is just a misunderstanding."

Dzin listened while another voice in his head tried to interrupt.

What are you doing here? Do you really think you can run away from this? How is that even possible?

His head was full of questions he didn't have answers to, and now his breath was coming in ragged gasps. That, at least, wasn't surprising.

Despite his adventurous spirit, he wasn't a particularly physical soul. At heart, he was simply a student of botany . . . at least until today.

Yantuz, of course, was breathing fine. As they ran, Dzin watched as his brother causally nodded to a glassblower he knew, but waved away the inevitable greeting that would follow.

"They know you, Dzin," he continued. "They know you wouldn't do this."

Dzin let out an exhausted, pained rasp of acknowledgment as his lungs threatened to give in. He pulled on Yantuz's arm to slow him down, in an effort to get him to understand.

"My friends, the other students—they're all dead. The fire gutted the laboratory and the archives. All the formulas are gone. Our Elixirs, gone. Everything we worked for—"

He didn't get to finish the sentence. A piercing whistle split the air not far behind them as a guard caught sight of his blackened tunic. Dzin risked a backward glance, only to see the tall, lithe guardian raise a muscled arm in their direction before blowing his snail shell again.

"Stop him!"

To his credit, even as Yantuz must surely have been wondering about how much trouble they were in, his speed didn't slow a jot. If anything, he was dragging Dzin, such was his loyalty to his older brother.

Through the stalls they ran, leaping over crates and pushing past astonished workers. More guards could be heard pouring into the trail behind them now, the clack-clack of their branch boots rising to a crescendo as they chased the pair across the tree city that surrounded Mother. Dzin felt his spirit beginning to flag—and his energy along with it—but Yantuz seemed to know what needed to be done.

"We have to get out of here," he said.

"Airship?" Dzin asked in between gasps.

Yantuz shook his head heavily, as though that was the silliest idea ever. "We'll never be able to double back and get up to the docks. We could get trapped up there. And you definitely can't climb in *that* state. The only way out is down now."

"But down is the Maze . . ."

"And?"

"You know about the Maze, Yantuz! It guards us—it keeps us in just as much as it keeps other Silvyrans out. The feeling you get stepping in there . . ." He shivered, remembering it all too well. "It's like it *knows*. And do you know what? It does. There's a reason they say any who aren't pure of heart disappear in there!"

"And? You've been in there before on your search for ingredients. You're as worthy as any of us. You can do this."

Dzin wondered about that. To get through the Maze, his heart needed to be pure. But was it? He had surely done everything he could to save Monae, but he had still failed. The sliver of guilt continued to inch its way through his insides. All his friends had died. He hadn't and yet now he was being blamed for it.

"Besides," Yantuz continued, "we don't really have a choice now, do we? It's either that or the root dungeons for the both of us, now you've dragged me into this little mess of yours. We go down."

The way ahead was suddenly blocked as a gathering of wood folk dressed in all kinds of outfits, from crumpled bed gowns to leaf-leather overalls, crammed onto the bridge.

"Stop them!" came a yell from behind, followed by more whistles.

Suddenly, those keen-eyed people blocking their way understood. As one, the crowd surged forward toward the pair.

"Quickly, over the side," Yantuz said, grabbing his arm and forcing him to the railing.

"Over the *what*?"

Yantuz leaped first, straight into what appeared to be nothingness. That was until Dzin leaned forward and saw the winched platforms below them, hanging by vines. Yantuz had landed nimbly on his feet and was now beckoning for Dzin to follow.

With a sharp intake of breath, Dzin jumped, only to crash face-first into a stack of hay boxes, knocking them all over the place and spilling their contents—berry biscuits wrapped in wax leaves. As he lay amid the debris, something squealed next to his head. A gray mass of hair unfurled itself to reveal a large flying squirrel that had been curled up, quietly hitching a ride up the Tree.

For a moment, Dzin and the startled creature stared at one another, each more shocked than the other, before the squirrel's dark eyes narrowed into a glare. It gathered up its nuts, and quickly leaped off to glide to another platform.

Yantuz yanked Dzin back to his feet and pushed him onward. There was another platform of goods being winched up only a short leap away. And on the other side of that was a third platform going in the other direction.

So they jumped again. And again. They watched for hidden hitchhikers as they moved from platform to platform around the great trunk—leaping down, then being winched back up a bit, then jumping down to the next one. Crashing into all manner of goods as they slowly slipped further and further toward the ground.

Above them there was chaos. Dzin glanced up to see one of the guards had leaped over in an attempt to follow but had got himself caught in a bramble of thorns that wound its way across a branch. The wood folk were trying to rescue him, still yelling down at the two of them.

Whistles were sounding in every direction now. A multitude of faces appeared at the windows carved into the trunk, accusing fingers being pointed in their direction.

But nobody managed to catch up, and quickly enough, the brothers' boots found the hard, unwavering soil in between the giant tree roots. They started their long journey across the mossy loam and First Forest surrounding Mother. It was easy enough to begin with, moving in the generous spaces between the trees nearest the Great Tree, all the while watching the rope bridges above them in case they were seen. Yet the further away they got, the denser the forest became. Thankfully, despite how strenuous their movement was, they were still able to move at a clip, darting between the thickets of gnarly, thorn-filled bushes and moving through the landscape at speeds those born outside the Tree's borders would only have been able to marvel at. Until, finally, they reached the towering wall of vegetation that circled them. Kept them safe. And held them in.

Wearily, they stumbled toward the opening.

The Maze beckoned them in.

Dzin stared up at the towering jungle of dark flowers, leaves, and vines that framed a single corridor leading into the unwelcoming place. He felt the dread of what lay within.

What he might lose if he should step foot in there.

It would ensure only the worthy would pass unscathed.

Was he worthy?

He could feel the panic rising in his chest. Should he go in and risk it or to stay here and be caught? A white heat billowed within him which spurred him on. The only way to avoid the panic was to outrun it, to keep moving.

He looked to his side to see Yantuz tearing off the sleeves of his shirt. He handed one to Dzin, before tying the other over his eyes.

"We need to go blindfolded."

"I *know*," Dzin muttered as he stared at the material. One of the rules of venturing into the Maze was to put your trust in it completely, which meant shielding your eyes and using your other senses to find your way. And although it was true he had done this before, this was a part of the journey he had never particularly enjoyed.

"We'll be fine," Yantuz said.

If he was trying to offer reassurance, it was sorely lacking in enthusiasm.

Dzin tied the blindfold around his head, unable to stop picturing Monae's face as the beast devoured her. He could have done more. He *should* have done more. She was one of his closest friends. Now she was a void within him. An empty place at a table where usually there was laughter and love.

"We'll be fine," he repeated, just as unenthusiastically.

He linked arms with his brother.

They stepped into the Maze.

CHAPTER THIRTEEN
VISITORS IN A NEW WORLD

Helia made sure to hold Nu's arm as the two women stumbled onto the thick bark of the bough at the top of the Great Tree, followed closely by their Orbs.

She'll get used to it, Vega's patterns flashed in observation as Nu almost fell to her knees.

"The crossing can be a little tricky," Helia said, trying to bolster the young woman's confidence even as she held her up. The poor girl had already been thrown into the deep end, as it were.

To her credit, Nu wasn't panicking. She brushed herself off as she stared around the Tree, sweeping away the leaf litter and curls of bark that had picked up on her trousers.

"I feel like I just fell through a painting," she said breathlessly, unable to help the grin that swept from cheek to cheek. "One of sunsets and clouds and mountains and an ocean. Except we weren't falling or even flying . . . it was like becoming a part of something bigger, being something more than just yourself. Like you were suddenly connected to the rest of the universe."

Helia nodded, remembering the first time she had traveled in such a way. In fact, her first trip had also been to this very bough when she had first become a Sage, spilling out from the portal, all excitement, panic, and joy.

"It's what we call the Glimmer. The transition between realms. For a moment, you *are* a part of the universe, connected to the River of Letters. It's quite a feeling, isn't it? Like you can do anything."

"The Glimmer. Is it always like that?"

"Almost always."

Nu's face glowed. "I could get used to it."

Helia smiled and gestured to Vega to lead the way.

Her Orb had done his job and brought them to one of the highest limbs, which normally afforded a view over the Maze and beyond to the desert lands. But it was the fifth season now, so the majestic leaves were in full bloom all around them, providing only glimpses of the horizon in the distance.

This didn't stop Nu from gawking though.

It was so early in the morning in Silvyra that the sunshine only hinted at appearing, yet there was already enough colorful activity to marvel at on the Tree itself, especially on the many lower limbs that stretched out from the great trunk below them. In between the houses and apartments— Helia remembered they were called cubbies—people milled about on the bark of the wide branches. Traders had their market stalls open. Someone was leading a cart that looked like an upside-down acorn lid piled high with food. Another followed close behind, carrying barrels. Words from all kinds of dialects and in various accents rang out through the markets, the air filled with the scents of delicacies from all over the world. People were grouped everywhere—along the limbs, up the spiral staircase around the trunk of the giant tree, and across the bridges that connected Mother to the neighboring trees, which held even more settlements.

Helia noted the fauna of the Great Tree was just as active this morning. Bees, like those from the Rose Garden, buzzed past. A scurry of giant flying squirrels glided in circles overhead, while butterflies swooped over and around the crowds in the market. The air was full of the sounds of titters and chirps as winged pollinators fluttered from home to home, delivering notes.

"Oh, I love it," Nu whispered, her eyes darting from sight to sight, soaking up all the details she could.

Antares swirled around next to her ear, and Helia watched as the woman grinned and nodded. The pair of them were already beginning to form a bond of communication.

Nu turned to her, eyes wide with awe. "I'd heard all the stories of Silvyra, of course. Everyone born and raised in the Library knows of these beautiful realms. The Great Tree was always my favorite of the tales, though, and it doesn't disappoint."

Helia understood. It was truly a delicious scene in all its beautiful chaos.

And yet something was off.

She'd felt it the moment they'd stepped through the portal, but it had taken a moment to pinpoint what it was. Usually, simply being among the Great Tree's sheltering boughs or smelling the sunlit fragrance of her blossoms was enough to give you a deep-seated sense of belonging, of oneness with the natural world, of being a part of a grand continuity of life that stretched both far into the distant past and forward into the unimaginable future. But today the energy was different. She could feel it as it flowed from the roots, up the trunk, and out to the flowers at the tips of her outstretched branches. It felt tender and bruised.

Even in the chaos below, Helia could see the signs that others felt it too. The atmosphere wasn't quite as raucous as it should have been. People's faces were downcast.

There was very little laughter or joviality.

Everything felt muted.

"Something is very wrong," Nu said, as if reading Helia's thoughts. She seemed surprised to find the words coming out of her mouth, as though perhaps she hadn't been the one to think them. The glee in her wide hazelnut eyes was fading quickly.

Helia nodded slowly but said nothing, giving Nu the space to find her way.

The young woman walked toward the towering trunk, reached out, and touched the bark. For a moment, she held her fingers tightly against the wood, frozen fast. Her face was suddenly clouded and troubled. As Helia stepped up beside her, Nu blinked and shook whatever it was away.

"Are you okay?" Helia asked.

Nu nodded, although it was clear something was worrying her. Nu led the way now, following whatever feeling she was having. Helia let her, understanding that this was instinct taking over now. She had seen it before.

"Anything of the Chief Scientist?" Helia whispered to Vega as the Orb slipped into her necklace to hide.

He didn't answer the question.

"Vega?"

Fire, he replied.

"Where?"

Follow her.

Up they went, climbing the path that spiraled around the great trunk, until they saw the black drifts of cloud pouring into the sky. The smell then hit them hard, the bitter tang of wood smoke making them both pull faces as they reached the top bough and found the still-burning remains of a building.

There were some people standing around it, watching helplessly as a wall made a cracking sound and crumbled inward. Helia realized there would be little water up here to spare to put the fires out. There was nothing anybody could do.

"The Botanical Education School Laboratory," she said, realizing what this place was. She tried to stamp down the feelings of anxiety, but the events of the Rose Garden were too fresh. The same smell of smoke and death lingered here as it had there, bringing with it thoughts of Xavier. And although she tried to suppress them, for a moment she couldn't help but see his face and hear his voice calling out to her. She swallowed hard, covering her nose and mouth.

"The whole place has gone."

Nu blinked as she stared at the scene of destruction. It seemed within reason for her to be struggling with what she saw, but there was definitely something behind her eyes now.

That was not a look of shock. It was horror . . . and understanding.

There was something happening inside her head. And while it would have been easy to ask what she was experiencing, Helia had a feeling she already knew.

Besides, this wasn't the moment or the place to inquire about such things. There was too much here and too many people around. She stamped down the desire to ask.

And yet you know it's true, Xavier's voice echoed in her head, before laughing at his own secret joke. *I'm not irreplaceable.*

Helia couldn't even bring herself to smile at the thought of him, but it was enough to help strengthen her spirits.

"Quickly," she said, placing a careful hand on Nu's shoulder and turning her around. The heat from the fire, though low, was still fierce. They needed to move. "We need to find the Chief Scientist. Vega, anything?"

The Orb buzzed from the amulet at the nape of her neck.

I've found her.

As they made their way around the trunk, they pushed through a drift of cloud. Nu barely saw the wooden fort that had been cut into an off-shoot of the branch.

She was too busy trying to understand what had just happened.

It had been a dream. That was the only way she could describe it. A dream while awake. As soon as she'd touched the trunk of the tree, her mind had been deluged with images. They had been vivid, but not. Distinct, yet blurry. As though she were adrift on the ocean and barely keeping her head above water.

She had seen a laboratory full of decorations. Figures standing around, happy and cheerful. She had been among them in a way, present without being seen. A voyeur of sorts, watching on from another plane of existence.

Then, in an instant, the room had disappeared, replaced with waves of fire. The figures around her disintegrated before her eyes. She watched in horror as their faces had been pulled in expressions of torture as their flesh had become burned and charred.

Worst of all, stalking through them had been a ferocious beast, a hound with a thick red mane.

No, it wasn't a mane. The creature was *ablaze*.

Flames rippled along its muscular torso, down its limbs, and across its thick, meaty paws. Its eyes glowed red, like hot coals. And when it snarled, Nu had been assaulted with the very definitive scent of seared meat.

Then she had realized she wasn't alone. There had been another figure present. A short, thin man with olive-silver skin and wide, terrified eyes. He had been holding a stick, trying to ward off the beast, while in his other hand he clasped a small scroll.

Then it was over. As quickly as the images had appeared, she had snapped out of the dreamlike trance and found Helia looking at her strangely.

"Are you well, Nu? You look pale."

Nu waved away the question. "Yes, yes, I'm fine. Please, carry on." *Why didn't I tell her?*

As she led Helia toward the wooden fort, Nu considered what had happened. And why she had been so quick to hide it from Helia. There were possibilities behind the vision's meaning, that was for sure. Important ramifications.

Yet the further they walked away from the trunk, the more the doubt curled its fingers around the memory and tried to take it from her. The images began to feel fantastical. Unrealistic. Could she really bring that to a Sage? What would Helia think if Nu started talking about waking dreams and beasts with fire for fur? She'd likely send Nu packing back to the Great Library.

As much as she liked stories, Nu was not one to give into fantasies. She had always liked to deal with the facts and the truth. And the truth of this was that she had no idea what had happened to her or what it meant.

So they continued in silence.

The fort rose above them, impressive and imposing. An entirely circular vertical branch, carved into a tower. It had little landing pads

sticking out of its outer wall at various levels—for what craft or creatures, Nu could only imagine—and there were several arched windows
dotted in between.

Vega pulsed something at Helia's neck, and the Sage shrugged.

"It's been a while, Vega. They clearly figured they needed a new
headquarters, and this is as good as any. The view you get from up there
overlooks the docking pads. A perfect place to oversee operations."

Another colorful message lit up the Orb.

"No," she agreed with a sigh. "I don't think it's something she would
have done either. Igina didn't care so much for the docks, even though
it was a part of her job. She much preferred looking out over the people
themselves, not the economic comings and goings. I guess we better be
prepared for someone new."

"So it's not your friend up there?" Nu asked, following closely behind.

"The Chief Scientist changes from generation to generation." Helia
drew up to the beautiful stained-glass door and rapped loudly. "But the
role always stays the same. Whoever it is takes charge of all operations
at the Great Tree, overseeing everything from the Botanical Education
School to the refinery down below and the distribution networks around
this world. Yet it's been a while since I was last here, so anyone could
have taken over from my old friend Igina."

"How long did it take for you to learn their language?" Nu said,
wondering to herself at the Sage's long life and all she must have seen
and learned.

"Ah," Helia replied, her eyes lighting up. "Many years and more
than one Chief Scientist! But worry not—thanks to the Orbs, the Book
of Wisdom will translate for us and those around us, as she does in the
Great Library, even local colloquialisms."

Nu nodded, amazed that the Book's power could extend even here,
realizing that her world had just become so much *more*. The Sage could
travel anywhere, talk to anyone. Learn the stories of any world they came
to, all thanks to the Book. It was humbling, yet she felt in her heart the
stirring of a desire to know more. To learn everything that she could
about these magical places.

The bark above the door rippled and twisted. Then a face appeared, a wizened, ancient visage that looked as though it had been carved into the wood eons ago, with wide eyes and a long, pointed chin.

"Security," Helia whispered.

The wood creaked as the face emerged and stared down toward the visitors. Nu immediately stood straighter, feeling the eyeless gaze sizing her up, before it moved on to Helia.

Then, with a gruff, sandpapery sound, the mouth opened, and a call echoed from its lips and reverberated through the walls, back into the building. Almost immediately, they could hear the sound of footsteps beyond, and the face sunk back into the bark as if it had never been there.

A pane in the glass door slid aside, and a pair of steely eyes peered out. "Yes?"

"We need to see the Chief Scientist," Helia said, getting straight to the point. "It's important. They will want to see us."

She waited patiently as the eyes in the doorway blinked and considered the request.

"Is it about what happened at the laboratory?"

Helia nodded curtly, perhaps sensing this as an easy way in. She tugged at the sides of her leaflike cloak as she responded.

Helia wasn't one to mislead anyone in order to get her way. Yet Nu understood why Helia was acting like this. This mission was too important.

The eyes framed by the hole in the painted glass blinked again, then disappeared into the darkness. The pane slid shut. For a second, Nu wondered whether Helia had made a mistake. Perhaps the person behind the door had seen through the facade, and they were, right this second, rushing off to fetch someone to arrest them and throw them in the dungeons.

On her wrist, Antares made a low, concerned vibration, as if sensing her worry, and perhaps even thinking the same. Nu shushed her and waited.

Thankfully, there was a sudden squealing creak as the door swung outward and the eyes, which were still regarding the pair carefully, were revealed to belong to a tall, lithe, and beautiful guard, whose skin was as pale as a silver birch. They were dressed in the manner of what Nu imagined a guardian of a Great Tree might look like: a short brown cloak, with a green tunic underneath, which had a symbol woven into the padded chest—a great and powerful tree, its limbs stretching out across twin moons behind it.

They wore boots up to the knees, and a short dagger had been tucked into their belt. Their hand rested at their hip, their brown-gloved fingers flexing momentarily over the hilt, as though waiting for someone to do something they shouldn't.

"Come," they said firmly, gesturing to Helia and Nu. "She is waiting."

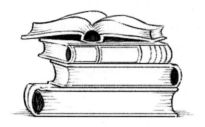

CHAPTER FOURTEEN
A SHORT STORY

Robin and Arturo had left the meeting with the intention of finding Arturo a chamber to stay in, yet not before he had argued with Robin about getting back to Earth.

"I can't stay here overnight," he had said. "My daughter, Rosa . . . she'll be wondering where I am. Yes, she's staying at her mother's for a few days, because this is supposed to be my week's holiday. But I usually try to send her a message every so often to check in." He had paused then. "Of course, she hardly ever keeps her phone charged to respond, so maybe she won't even notice."

His enthusiasm for the argument had been half-hearted at best, and he knew Robin could tell. The desire to get home was certainly not as strong as the enthusiasm he had for wanting to stay here and see more of this beautiful new world. When else might he have such an opportunity to wander halls filled with centuries of words and wisdom? At the very least, it might inspire him to do more with his life when he got home.

Fortunately, Robin was understanding. "The draw of family is a strong one, Arturo. I know it all too well, having just been home to see mine. So, if you like, we can check on your daughter later." When he gave a grin of acceptance, delighted she'd given him a chance to feel like a responsible father as well as enjoy this little adventure, Robin took his hand and gave it a squeeze. "Good! Then that's what we'll do. Because I would love for you to stay. This is the Great Library of Tomorrow, after all! A place of mystery and magic. A repository of knowledge and all the stories you have ever known. A legend in some societies and only a slippery rumor in others. It would be a shame if you didn't see a little more of it while you were here."

Centauri swirled his colors in a way that seemed to suggest he agreed with his Sage.

They then embarked on the tour.

Now, Arturo was definitely glad he'd stayed. Not only had he seen so many wonderful sights but he'd also learned a great deal about the Sages, including how old some of them were.

"You'd be surprised," Robin said, bounding along next to him as she showed him the gardens where all the food was grown to feed the city. "Some of our number have lived here much longer than convention usually allows in the outside world. Helia, for instance, left Earth in the seventeenth century. She escaped a volcanic eruption at Vesuvius and found her way here."

"Wait. *The* Vesuvius?"

"That's the one. It's erupted a few times, as I'm sure you know. The last big one—around 1631, I think—well, she was almost caught in it. Luckily for her—and us—Vega, her Orb, had been sent to collect her. He brought her out before the town was overwhelmed, and that's when she was selected as a Sage."

"My God," Arturo whispered as they pushed through a set of double doors. They were met with a cloud of mist that was settling across greenery, rising in magnificently leafy spirals from floor to ceiling. Various colors of vegetables hung off them. "She's really that old?"

"Yeah, she's been around for a while, throwing herself into her work, exploring the millions of stories whose doorways are held within these walls. Whenever she returns from these trips, she adds to our knowledge. I guess that's why she still looks relatively young, considering her age. If the Library is like a book, where the story moves at a different speed than reality, then us Sages are like the characters within that book. So, once you become a part of the story, time is no longer linear; you cease to age."

Arturo let out a sigh, his head fuzzy and his imagination struggling to keep up.

They entered a corridor full of paintings, and his gaze moved toward an image of a woman sitting down in what looked like a cave full of books. She was bent over an open page and was reading beneath a flickering lamplight.

He reached out toward her, letting his fingers touch the image. He felt the paint shifting beneath his skin.

The painted woman kept reading, unaware of the visitor watching on.

"That's Andora, one of the first Sages," Robin said, appearing at his shoulder. "She died long ago."

He crouched to get a better look at the book Andora was reading. He could just make out the emerald letters emblazoned on the side as she flipped to the next page. *Great Trees of the World*, it read, and within the pages were sketches and drawings of forests and a maze.

It was a delightfully illustrated book. One that told a story he badly wanted to understand better.

What's more, seeing it gave him an idea.

Arturo's pencil wavered over his favorite notebook.

It was small and blue, with a soft moleskin cover. He grinned at the memory of his daughter giving it to him for his fortieth birthday. Ever the animal lover, she had reassured him, "It's not a real mole's skin, Papa. That's just the name of the material."

He always carried a notebook, usually slipped into the inside of his left jacket pocket, along with a small pencil. Some of his favorite writers had done the same; you never knew when inspiration would strike or that elusive sentence you were looking for would reveal itself. He might not know what he wanted to do with his craft, but he still took it seriously. If you were a writer, you wrote things down when they happened. And there was nothing like the feeling of putting pencil to paper and having the words spill out of you.

That's where the magic lay.

He'd only meant to make a few notes as he sat in the chamber he'd been assigned, waiting for Robin to return. Yet after he'd written one quick reminder to buy the fox plush toy that Rosa kept telling him about, the notes about his adventure here quickly became a short story.

He had traveled to this wondrous Library, met some ancient Sages, and heard all about this incredible Book of Wisdom; it was inevitable the notes would weave themselves into a fantastical narrative detailing his time here.

As he wrote, with the pencil scratching against the paper with increasing speed as he found his rhythm, he began to scan the room around him for even more inspiration.

Someone had left a book on the oval oak desk. Pulled from one of the many bookshelves around the room, it sat across from him now. Hefty as anything, bound in what looked like tree bark, and as thick as any of Stephen King's mammoth novels.

"Favorite Hymns of Melodia" was imprinted in gold leaf on the spine.

It was a beautifully crafted piece of work. So much so it had him thinking back to the Book of Wisdom, he had been told about, but was revered in ways he couldn't comprehend. The Sages considered it a higher power, and although he loved books himself, this felt special on a whole different level.

So that's how he introduced it in his little story.

Only . . . as soon as his pencil had placed the period at the end of the paragraph, something very unusual happened. He'd written about an "all-singing, all-dancing" book. And that's what he saw.

The table shuddered, and he looked up to see "Favorite Melodies of Melodia" leap onto its side, spin on its corner, then start sashaying across the oak veneer.

"What the *what*?" Arturo gasped, feeling his jaw go slack.

The pencil fell from his fingers and rolled over to where the book was dancing. The tome barely paused, and with a flick of its cover, it picked the pencil up and started twirling it like a baton. From within its pages then came a cheerful melody.

"I . . . I . . . what's happening?"

It was probably for the best that the book didn't respond, because Arturo feared that might have sent him completely over the edge. As it was, the thing seemed harmless, just intent on enjoying itself.

He looked down to his notepad.

All singing. All dancing.

No talking though.

What he'd written had come to life before his very eyes. It was the most amazing and unexplainable thing he'd ever witnessed, save for the birth of his baby daughter. But at least back then he had been given some level of expectation of what was to come.

This was unprecedented. He knew that storytellers considered themselves artists, breathing life into imaginary things, but *this* was something else entirely.

He whistled for the book's attention and held out his hand.

The book duly obliged, doing a cartwheel and dropping the pencil into his fingers, before tap-dancing away again.

He was losing his mind. That was the only thing he could think of. He'd left work, disillusioned with his life and dreaming of a better tomorrow, and had a nervous breakdown, or a stroke, or something. He was probably in a hospital right now, plugged into machines with annoying beeps and tubes who knew where. A magical Library? Portals to other worlds? Worlds made of stories? A magical notebook? *You idiot*, he thought to himself. *Walk out of the dream, wake up, open the door, and you'll walk back to your life.* He did it, walked into a corridor of stone and wooden bookcases, marvelous workmanship, and people going about their business. There was a young woman sitting on a reading bench near his door, watching him. He moved toward her, and she politely rose and met him partway, although her gaze looked troubled by what she was seeing.

"Miss!" he said, his voice high and not very reassuring, he supposed. "Miss, where are we, really? I'm afraid something has gone terribly"— *wonderfully*, his subconscious whispered to him—"wrong."

The young woman pointed to a pad in her hand and signed at him.

He knew of sign language, of course, but wasn't conversant in it. "May I?" he asked, pointing at the notebook.

She nodded her approval, and he brought up his pencil, still clutched in his hand, and wrote: *Am I going crazy, or is this all real?*

She frowned and wrote back: *My name is Triss. Are you okay, sir? I was asked to watch your room and fetch Sage Robin if you needed anything.*

He wrote back: *Ah, I wish I could sign and tell you not to worry about me. I think I'm just facing information overload.* But before he could hand back the notebook, it happened again. A pair of hands appeared in front of them, startling them both, and started signing to Triss. She gaped, backed away, and started signing back, frantically, but the hands just hovered in midair, like a mime waiting for their next show. He grabbed the notebook back and wrote one again: *Get Robin. Something very strange is happening!*

The hands sprang into action, and Triss, startled once more, ran down the corridor in a most un-Library fashion.

Arturo gazed after her, still clutching the notebook, and looked at it as the floating hands slowly dissipated. *There's no way I could dream all this up*, he thought, then said aloud, "Now, let's see what I can *really* do." He headed back into his room and leaned over his notepad once again.

CHAPTER FIFTEEN
THE CHIEF SCIENTIST

On Helia and Nu's short journey up the various levels of the Control Tower, the guard didn't speak once. Neither did they. Whether or not their disguises had worked, the guard clearly had more pressing matters to consider.

Against Helia's neck, Nu could see that Vega was muttering to himself in low vibrations and snippets of color. Helia would nod every now and then but didn't say anything.

Nu could tell both were on edge.

The tower was grand and stunning. Not in the way the Library was, with its halls and wings; its exquisite architecture; and the feeling of history imbued in its hallways, bookshelves, and even the diversity of the people within. It was more earthy than that. More organic rather than designed. A fortified branch that had been hollowed out and filled with levels upon levels of chambers.

It was all a hive of activity. Other Tree folk, in similar uniforms to the guard, strode around with intent, fiddled with strange contraptions, or stared at odd domed screens that looked very much like large drops of dew and wobbled as gloved hands were ran over them, adjusting unseen controls.

Whatever had happened at the laboratory had caused quite the disturbance.

They finally reached the end of their journey: the topmost level, which they reached by using a vine-pulled lily pad lift. Here they disembarked into a small hallway and were immediately met with the sounds of an argument in full flow ahead.

"And I asked *you* a question, Advisor. How do we know it was the student who caused the fire and killed his colleagues? What possible motive could he have had for such an act? It seems unlikely."

"I wholeheartedly disagree, Chief Scientist," a sneering voice replied, a man's voice that Nu instantly disliked. His words were like tar in her mind, sticky shadows that held contempt for their recipient and whose tone conveyed nothing good. "He was the only one still alive when the guards arrived on the scene, and what's more, he was found to be attacking another student! I have already sent someone into the Maze to retrieve him and bring him in for punishment."

"The Tree is our house, and it is my duty to protect all my children in it. All of you. That is the role of the Chief Scientist, and it is a role I take very seriously."

"I wasn't suggesting otherwise."

"Yes, you were. You think I am weak because I do not wish to judge on the basis of happenstance."

"With respect, Chief Scientist, not only did we lose four valuable students but we lost the entire archive as well, and even the stores of Elixir kept at the Botanical Education School. This is a serious crime, for which the surviving student must be suitably punished."

"And that he will," the woman's voice continued, her patience clearly running thin. "Because the Maze will do as it sees fit. If what you are suggesting is true, then we can be assured the Maze will sense it and not let the student leave. Ever. He will be met with his punishment."

"But—"

"You may be quiet now, Advisor. I have guests."

The guard motioned for Helia and Nu to step into the room, which Nu now saw was a carved hollow encompassing the entirety of the fort, with a curved wall that ran in a circle around them and three long clear windows evenly spaced around the circumference, giving them a 360-degree view of the world of the Great Tree.

It was like a control tower of sorts.

They were high, just poking up above the canopy of leaves that had shaded the branches below. And now Nu could see properly the airbound activity across the top of the tree. Twenty or thirty giant leaves rose above the others, each a bright green against the wide blue sky, and within them were nestled airships of all sizes and colors. Most were stationary, with people hustling around beneath them, unloading glass barrels and prickly containers that looked to Nu like huge chestnuts. In one direction, three stout men wrestled with a wide box full of whirring cogs being spun by what looked like hummingbirds. In another, a tall woman was loading boxes of gleaming light onto the back of a majestic dragonfly, whose wings were buzzing impatiently.

As Nu watched, she saw one airship rise and take to the air, before little puffs of steam sputtered out of the back, where the engine was strapped underneath the balloon. The craft jolted away from the tower and pulled into the sky.

"*Wings of Crimsonia* is away," said a woman from the back of the room, where a group of people sat staring out at the docks and scribbling down records of whatever they saw.

"Good," replied the Chief Scientist. She was Black and fiercely beautiful. Her brown eyes burned beneath golden eye shadow, her perfectly smooth skin was freckled with glitter, and her curls of midnight hair were held back in a golden crown decorated with moon slivers across its front. She was dressed unlike any kind of scientist Nu had ever imagined, wearing a gold high-collared sleeveless gown, with flowing patterns of leaves and flowers stretching down the curves, each of which seemed to move of their own accord, as if fluttering in some unseen wind.

She stood in the center of the room, behind a magnificent oval tree stump serving as a table, which was about a foot thick and resplendent with thousands of rings across its surface. She didn't bother looking at the person who had spoken. Instead, she rested her hands down on the table and fixed her intimidating gaze on Nu and Helia.

"Keep the other airships moving. These shipments of the Elixir cannot be delayed."

"Yes, ma'am."

Silence descended, and as the woman studied them, Nu found her cheeks burning.

The Chief Scientist's eyebrow arched as she peered at the pair of them, focusing most intently on Helia. "I believe you asked to see me?"

"In a manner of speaking," Helia replied with a curt nod, choosing her words carefully. "We have come to speak with you, Chief Scientist, about an important matter that relates not only to Mother but to the lands beyond yours. We believe you can help us, and perhaps we can help you too."

The woman glanced around the room, her gaze finally resting on a man who was lurking in the shadows. He was tall and thin, with a strange, unnaturally silver eye, and was watching them intently. The advisor, Nu realized. She resisted a shudder; he looked as creepy as his voice sounded, like a stick insect forced into an ill-fitting suit that hung off his boncs.

The Chief Scientist tilted her head toward the door.

"Will you excuse us, Advisor?"

He gave Helia and Nu a curious glance—one that Helia gave him in return, Nu noticed, as though she knew him somehow but didn't quite know why—then, with his lipless mouth thinning, he glided around the table, then disappeared through the door.

The Chief Scientist nodded to the guard. "Make sure nobody else comes in. I will take these two to the roof, where we can get a bit of air."

Her gown swished like leaves in a breeze as she turned and made her way to the spiral staircase on the other side of the room. Helia silently followed, with Nu behind.

Up the stairs they went, emerging onto the top of the tower, where they could hear as well as see the activity around them as the sun rose over the world: people yelling to each other; the hum of engines waiting to ignite properly; large creatures buzzing past them; and the delicious ruffle of the wind through the canopy of leaves, like ocean waves breaking on a beach.

The Chief Scientist walked immediately to the railing that ran around the roof and peered out over the airship dock. She patted the wood gently, her golden bangles clanging against it, then she glanced over her shoulder and gave Helia a childlike grin. "I was wondering when I'd see you again."

CHAPTER SIXTEEN
OLD FRIENDS

Helia watched the Chief Scientist's shoulders relax as she casually flicked her hair from her eyes, then adjusted the crown on her head. A slim finger slipped under her collar and undid the clasp at her neck. It fell open a little, and she sighed with relief.

"As soon as I took on the mantle of this role, I knew there would come a time when you'd come back," she said, with a wry grin. All sense of authority was gone from her voice now that they were alone, just the three of them. Vega flew out of Helia's necklace and grew to his normal size, buzzing excitedly around the woman, and she reached out to touch him in greeting. "Oh, how I have dreamed of this moment, Helia! To see you and your little ball of fun again. Although I am both glad and worried that it happens today."

Helia couldn't help but smile back at her old friend, trying to keep the underlying worry at bay. She reached over, and they clasped hands.

"And I hoped if anyone would be meeting us instead of Igina it would be her daughter. Although I am surprised you so easily recognized me, Lyvanda! It was a long time ago I was last here."

"How could I forget such an event in my young life? A mysterious stranger and her floating friend coming into my mother's orbit and changing it so dramatically? Don't forget—I spent many hours playing with Vega here. It was a formative experience. Even if he used to cheat at hide-and-seek."

Helia felt Vega's glee at remembering how he'd played with her as a child. His symbols flashed through his many layers as he laughed in his way. He nudged her shoulder again, looking for more petting. Her smile grew wider still.

"How are you, little balloon?"

He flashed something, and Helia translated.

"He says he's missed you. Although you remember it wrong; you were just bad at hiding, so it was always easy to find you."

"That may be very true. I was very young and not as smart as I liked to think I was."

"Oh, come now, Lyvanda. We all knew you had your mother's intuition and were as smart as any of her cohorts. It was only a matter of time before you took over." Helia looked out over the Great Tree wistfully, her fingers tightening on the barrier, trying to remain in the present and not lose herself in the memories playing in her head. A much different period of her life. Infinitely calmer and more fun. She sighed. "Time . . . is a funny thing. How long has it been?"

Lyvanda tilted her head and thought for a moment. "I was but a child, so I would say about thirty cycles for me. But by the looks of it, time has no meaning for you. You haven't aged at all. It is as though you stepped out of our lives that day and were frozen until you returned to us now. Although you look far more tired than I remember. I hope you don't mind me saying that."

That was the truth of it, plain and simple.

"Much of it is from the last day," Helia said. "Which is why I'm here."

The mood changed in an instant, transitioning from two old acquaintances catching up to a Chief Scientist and a Sage. Helia regretted that. She would have much preferred to have chatted amiably as she used to with the girl's mother.

"I thought there must be a reason for your visit, Helia. Since we last met, I have learned more of the Sages and your part in the great scheme of life. My mother told me all she knew and passed on the secret of your duty to the Great Library and to the realms beyond this one, concepts that remain only myth and legend here, told in the darkest corners of taverns and in the fairy tales we tell our children. I have kept your secrets so I would be prepared for the next time you appeared."

"And I am grateful for your discretion, Lyvanda. Although right now that is the last thing on my mind." Helia paused, reluctant to go on. Yet she must. Time was of the essence, and she could not avoid the inevitable discussion. She steeled herself and continued, "We saw what happened at the laboratory, and we caught the end of your discussion downstairs. Your students were murdered by one of their own?"

"That's what my advisor would have me believe," Lyvanda said, her gaze dropping to the floor. Helia couldn't tell if it was through anger or sadness. "Unfortunately, what he's saying holds up. It's what the evidence suggests. There were witnesses to the attack, and the sole survivor seemed to have a weapon. He had apparently killed his colleagues and set fire to the laboratory and archives. Dzin then ran off, taking his formula for the Elixir of Life with him. We sent the guards after him for questioning, but he escaped, aided by his brother, into the Maze." She paused and looked up again, frowning as if only now realizing something.

"But that happened not so long ago. It cannot be why you're here."

Helia held more tightly on to the barrier at the rim of the roof as though she might be about to topple over it. "No, that's not why we're here. Although I wonder if the two events are connected somehow."

"Two events?"

"I'm afraid there's been an incident, Lyvanda. The Rose Garden has been burned and corrupted. Everything there is dead or dying. And Perennia is missing. Abducted, we think."

"The dragon?" The blood seemed to drain from Lyvanda's face. Her eyes grew watery and weak—a look Helia recognized: someone seeking some kind of hope and finding none. "But she is the essence of our land. A symbol of our strength and the force of nature that has always protected us from harm. She can't be gone."

"And yet she is. Without her protection, it was decided I should come here to the Great Tree to offer my assistance in any capacity I can to counter whatever might be coming. In light of what we have found here, however, I'm not entirely sure we will be enough . . ."

"How so?"

"I'm afraid to say we believe the danger will spread beyond the Rose Garden and into the land of Bloom. One of our number has gone to Aedela to coordinate an evacuation, but the population will need somewhere to shelter. The Great Tree is a beacon of hope and enlightenment that has shone for eons, but it will be a long and perilous journey for them with the enemy at their heels. Will you ensure those people who need a home get there safely?"

"Of course. But you should not stay here, Helia. I have no idea of your powers, it is true, but in the face of a danger that has already claimed the Rose Garden and threatens to sweep into Bloom, too, I cannot believe you can do much good here."

"I have feared as much myself," Helia replied, wondering how much she should say.

Her powers of connection with nature were strong here, more powerful in the realm of Silvyra than anywhere else. Yet she had witnessed Suttaru's destructive capabilities. She could not stand up to him alone.

"Then why are you really here?"

"Because I need your help."

"How? Tell me and I will do whatever it is you require."

"I cannot stand up to the destruction that comes our way. But Perennia could. She is what's important now. She is the great protector of Silvyra. Without her here to guard this realm, the taint of evil could spread beyond to all the other realms."

"But I don't know where she is. How can I help you with such a thing?"

Helia shuffled awkwardly on the spot. "I was there, in the Rose Garden, when it happened. We were ambushed by a monster named Suttaru and an army of corrupted souls—the Unwritten, he called them—and I was injured. I hit my head as we tried to escape, and I lost my memories. Not of everything, just a few moments, but enough that I cannot remember what I saw. I believe I witnessed what happened to Perennia. I can almost see her in my mind's eye, but the memory is clouded. I need to unlock that memory to know what it is I can sense and then use that to help me start looking for her."

In truth, Helia didn't know how much of her memory was going to help. They had landed in the Rose Garden, stepped out from the portal and straight into the heat of battle. Then she had fallen under a mass of outstretched arms and limbs and snapping jaws, and the rest had been a blur, just colors and noise and pain.

When she had returned to the present, Xav had somehow managed to save her, at great cost to himself. She'd had to step up and drag him the rest of the way, only to find that Perennia wasn't where she normally was.

There were so many questions she needed answering: How had she been injured? Had she hit her head after falling, or had she been clobbered by one of those creatures that had attacked them? And how exactly had Xav managed to get her out of there? She remembered a vivid, powerful light and knew that was his power at work—the light of truth, which he had used sparingly in all their time together. Perhaps that had pushed back the hordes enough to give him time to get her out of there.

But the biggest question fell to the dragon herself.

Helia knew that if such an attack had happened on the edge of the Rose Garden, Perennia would have been roused from her deep slumber. She would not have stayed where she was, in the center of the roses, which is why they had not found Perennia there. They would surely have seen her as they fought from the portal and made their way to where she normally lay.

So where was she, then?

The elusive memory niggled under Helia's skin, like a splinter she couldn't visibly see to remove. When it came down to it, all she had was hope that the information about the fate of the dragon was in her head. But as with so much in her life, hope was often enough.

The memories were there to be unlocked. And here in Silvyra was the key she needed to free them and find Perennia to help save them all.

"I need to use your Elixir of Life," Helia said. "And I need to use it now."

Nu had been watching the interaction intently, standing behind and to the side of Helia, trying to remain discreet and quiet. That the two were old friends was obvious, and Nu had no wish to interrupt such a reunion.

Yet as Helia stated the real reason for them being here, Nu couldn't help but speak up. Something had happened within her. A moment of panic, of . . . wrongness. That was the only way she could explain it to herself.

Something was wrong. She just didn't know what.

"Are you sure the Elixir will work?" Nu asked suddenly.

The two women turned to her with puzzled expressions, and even Vega swirled patterns that showed he was unsure of what she was saying. Her cheeks went warm with embarrassment, yet the feeling had been strong.

Real and tangible. She wondered what it meant.

Lyvanda only seemed to notice Nu for the first time now. Her eyes twinkled, and Nu shuffled uncomfortably under her magisterial gaze. Antares hovered almost protectively at her shoulder, and for that, she was grateful.

The Chief Scientist glanced at Helia, who gave a very slight nod—a "she's with me" gesture, which instantly made Nu feel more relaxed. Like she belonged here.

"What is your name, friend?"

Nu stood a little taller. "My name is Nu, Chief Scientist."

Lyvanda offered her hand, which Nu grasped and shook, feeling a little starstruck. As they parted, she looked down and saw her palm was covered in gold sparkles, like glitter, except it seemed to have been fused to her skin.

"What was your question, my dear?"

"Oh, well . . . the Elixir of Life heals all ailments, doesn't it?"

"It does."

Nu frowned. The feeling was still present, roiling around inside her like an ocean caught in a storm. Were they here on a fool's errand? Perhaps the Elixir couldn't help Helia after all.

"Even memory loss?" she asked.

As soon as the question was out of her mouth, she felt instantly silly. Surely Helia would have known the Elixir would help her. She was a Sage of many centuries' experience. She had been to Silvyra many times before and likely knew more about the Elixir of Life than any at the Great Library.

Yet if Helia was offended at having her mission questioned, she showed no sign. And Lyvanda took care to smile and answer the question sincerely and without judgment.

"Yes, even memory loss, Nu. The ancient Silvyrans learned how to use the flowers and leaves and sap of the plants around us to improve their lives, to help cure illnesses when they were sick and to relieve pain when they were injured. Eventually, they discovered a process by which they could create an Elixir that would protect them from illness altogether and help to extend and improve their lives. That is the very same Elixir we brew today, although the formulas that create it are many and varied, even if the result is the same."

"The formulas are different, but they create the same Elixir?"

"Yes. The formulas we follow can only last so long, so upon each cycle, five botanical students, those with the keenest sense of smell, are chosen to brew their own personal variations of the Elixir. And just as each of our paths to happiness are different, so are the formulas that lead these students to their own brewed potions. Our famed Elixir is of such great healing powers it is known the world over." She sighed, long and loud, turning back to Helia. "Unfortunately, the laboratory is now destroyed, and the archives—all the records of our past formulas for the Elixir—are ruined. The one remaining formula is with the fifth student, Dzin, who is on the run. We only have what's currently being brewed in the refinery and those last stores of Elixir you see being loaded up on the airships before you, ready to transport across the world. Fortunately,

I happen to have my own here." She reached for the small, curved glass ornament that was hanging delicately at her neck, which until now Nu had assumed was simply jewelry, despite the way it seemed to be glistening with some special magic. In fact, it was a vial with a blue ointment inside. Lyvanda unclasped it and handed it to Helia. "May it help you uncover what was lost."

Helia let out a sigh of relief so long and exhausted that Nu wondered if the Sage might deflate on the spot.

Lyvanda's fingers tenderly lifted Helia's chin. It seemed as if she, too, had noticed her grief. "You were not alone, were you? In the Rose Garden? Your handsome counterpart . . . where is he?"

Helia's jaw must have clenched, because Lyvanda removed her hand quickly, her eyes full of pain and understanding. She nodded.

"I am truly sorry. I knew how much you two loved each other, even back then, when I was a girl and didn't truly know what love was exactly. But I saw it with you both."

"Thank you," Helia replied quietly.

Then something strange happened. As Nu watched the two women, she felt a warmth emit from Antares, and she suddenly saw the Sage's appearance change right in front of her.

Helia was still there, but it was as if an overlay had been placed over her. Another version of her, in another realm. A spirit with tears streaming down her cheeks, her mouth moving as though talking to someone. She appeared to be cradling a figure.

A powerful feeling washed over Nu, full of sadness and desperation and anger. A fraying of the edges of hope.

Yet she knew it wasn't her feelings she was experiencing.

What's happening to me?

Nu squeezed her eyes shut to try to block it all out, terrified at these sudden bursts of emotions that were not her own. Was Antares doing this? She turned to her, but the movement caused her to sway unsteadily on her feet.

And then suddenly her mind was somewhere else.

Nu found herself with Veer.

The Sage of Strength stood nearby with a small group of people at the edge of a settlement, overlooking a sight as grim as any she could have imagined. Veer was trying to remain calm, but Nu could sense the turmoil broiling within him as intensely as if it were her own.

She had no idea how she knew. It was just a gut sensation, an awareness. Unexplainable and yet beyond denial.

The thick black cloud on the horizon was getting closer by the second, bringing with it a sense of imminent death. The people of the town could sense it too, and everything was chaos. There was a manic, oppressive dread hanging heavy in the air, as though everyone was aware something was wrong.

Nu was glad they couldn't see the ominous cloud yet.

The shadow had come down from the Rose Garden in the east and hadn't stopped. A vast cloud of swirling smoke and cinders, lit by flickering flames from within, reached the foot of the mountain range and spread out across the forests and surrounding area like a disease. The colors of the wildflowers at the edge of the cloud began to fade, withering and wilting. Ahead stretched chaotic streams of destruction through the meadows. Rivers of nightmares, full of yowling, human monsters, their skin the color of hot coals, scrambling over each other in their race to be the first to burn the place down.

Nu watched Veer's fingers clench into fists at his side. He had clearly never seen dark magic like this before.

His Orb, Lynx, was hovering close by, uncloaked for the moment. Lynx's surface shimmered like clear sapphire seas, the symbols appearing across his various layers rippling over each other as if being pushed and pulled by ocean currents.

"The plan is solid, Lynx," Veer said. "We're sticking to it, no matter how concerned you might be for my safety."

A tall woman arrived beside him. There was an energy between them that was almost palpable. Nu got another sudden feeling in her gut. One of longing and regret. These two knew each other and clearly had for a long time. Theirs was a complex relationship, bridging the divides of realms. A relationship that may well have run its course now in the face of what's to come.

The woman stood a foot taller than the entourage of advisors and guards surrounding her, like a queen bee among her workers. She was beautiful, with muddy-yellow curls wrapped in tresses around her head, their ends hanging just shy of her wide shoulders. A true leader, whose strength was barely cloaked beneath the drapes of spun silver petals that made up the light armor she wore. Armor that sparkled in the light like water in moonlight with every breath she took.

On her chest, an embroidered rain of orange petals marked her as a part of the ancient line of rulers of this fine town.

"Petal Queen," Veer acknowledged.

"Sage," she replied.

Their impressive titles—one royalty, one an otherworldly power— didn't feel of much use in the moment. Nu could sense the helplessness of both, even as they stood stoically in the face of danger, unwilling to run like everyone else.

"What can we do?" she asked him quietly.

"Whatever we can," he said.

He looked to Lynx and began to channel his power.

Nu came back to herself in a rush of kaleidoscope colors and light. She almost staggered at the force of the change. One moment in the town with Veer, the next back here at the Great Tree with Helia.

What was that? she asked herself. She could still feel the lingering emotions of what she had witnessed. Chief among them fear and confusion. The hairs on the back of her neck were still raised, and her skin was cold and clammy. *What happened?*

Just as quickly came the answer.

A vision.

It wasn't a voice in her mind; rather, it was a feeling. She was getting used to that now, that indescribable *knowing*.

Had she answered her own question? Or had that knowledge been transferred to her by the vibration of Antares in her pocket? And why would the Orb be showing her this? How could it be showing her this? She wasn't a Sage, and while she'd been entrusted with Antares and brought into Paperworld, an experience usually reserved only for Sages, no one had told her she would have *visions*. Was she breaking some sort of rule or covenant between the Sages and the Book of Wisdom?

She badly wanted to ask Helia what was happening to her, but as she looked up, she could see Helia was now holding the vial of the Elixir of Life, ready to take it. Now was not the time for her problems. She would wait and see if it happened again.

Nu pushed down her questions for now. She blinked the remnants of the vision away, trying to focus on the moment and let the fear of what she had seen dissipate.

Helia looked the vial over once, took the lid off, and dabbed a bit onto the inside of her wrist. Rubbing it in with a finger, she closed her eyes and lifted her head back a little. The power of the Elixir was presumably felt internally, so when Helia's face started to pinch in concentration, Nu thought that the memories were flooding back in a rush.

Vega seemed to think it had worked too, for he was spinning his layers excitedly above them.

Yet when Helia opened her eyes again, they could all see the disappointment.

"It's not working," she said.

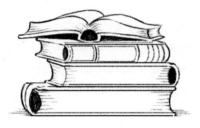

CHAPTER SEVENTEEN
A CHOICE

"What the bloody hell are you doing?"

Robin stopped short in the door of Arturo's quarters, surveying the scene with a shocked and disgusted look that suggested he might be in some trouble. He considered it fair, as his chambers did not look as they had when she had left him.

The dance troupe of books paused midroutine on the table. The toy spaceships that had been play fighting above his head now landed in tiny jets of steam, and a large moth stopped fluttering its dusty wings as it circled the lamp and came to rest on Arturo's shoulder.

He felt his cheeks grow hot.

"Things, er, got a little out of hand," he said, batting away the moth as it scuttled down his chest and tried to eat his pencil. "But it's okay— nothing's damaged. I've got it handled."

He scribbled lines through what he'd written and was relieved to see the books return to their piles on the shelves, the toy spaceships suddenly whizz past Robin's head and disappear back to whichever child in the Great Library they'd been pulled from, and the moth quickly shrunk back to its usual size and fluttered off. Robin tutted, and Centauri swirled something to her.

She shook her head. "Nope. Never in all my years have I seen such a thing."

Arturo got up from his chair. "I'm still learning, but what did you think? Did I do it all okay?"

"Do . . . what, exactly?" Robin gave the room a quick once-over to make sure she wasn't going to be surprised by anything else. "What did we just witness, Arturo? Because I've never seen anything like *that* before. Was that moth trying to eat your pencil? What were those books doing?"

"I was just doodling, really. I started with a few notes, and then it grew into a story, and suddenly I'm making books dance!" He waved his notepad at her as if in explanation, then shrugged. "The moth was admittedly a mistake. I thought it would be cute, but that guy was hungrier than I expected."

Robin frowned at him, in the way that sometimes his ex-wife did when he tried to explain one of his new story ideas to her.

"I literally don't understand."

"You don't understand . . . what? Isn't this just one of the many aspects of this curious Library of yours? I had figured this was something you would think was funny for me to discover on my own, with that keen British sense of humor of yours."

Robin shook her head slowly, looking from him to his notepad and then to the room around them. Centauri hovered closer to the books on the shelf, investigating. He swirled something in crimson red.

"Just regular books now, huh?" she replied, her increasingly suspicious look fixed upon Arturo. It made him feel like an exhibit at a museum. "Curious."

"Are you saying not everyone can do this?"

"No. What else did you write in there?"

"In where, my notepad? Oh, nothing. Just a note to get my daughter a plush toy."

"Did anything happen when you wrote that?"

Robin looked around as she said it, as though expecting to see a great fluffy fox run through the door.

"Not that I know of."

"Okay, then." That was all she could say for the moment. Her face pulled in several directions at once, seemingly perplexed and clearly unsure of how to deal with what she'd just discovered. Finally, Centauri buzzed and snapped her back into the present. "I'll have to flag this with the other Sages when we've time. For now, wizard writer, we've got work to do."

"Already? You haven't been gone that long. I was going to have a quick nap."

Centauri pulsed again as he flew near Arturo's ear—saying something derogatory, he was sure. Even though he didn't comprehend the secret language of symbols and patterns flitting across its surface, he seemed to understand the intent. Robin only confirmed it when she smirked and replied, "Not all writers are like that, I'm sure, Centauri. I've got a good feeling about this one. In fact"—she turned to Arturo—"don't let me down, please."

Puzzled by what had happened—*if it's not usual, why was I able to do that?*—he fell into step beside the Sage.

As they walked, he wondered about the plush toy. Which then led to thinking again of his daughter. What would Rosa have made of what he'd just done? What would she make of this whole strange and wonderful place? He smiled to himself, knowing full well she'd love it here, being the inquisitive little soul that she was. Supersmart, but curious with it. There would be so many questions—the Sages wouldn't know what hit them.

He suddenly felt a pull of longing for her little face and that voice that often talked to him nonstop, about the great many things that were on her mind. It didn't matter that he wasn't due to see Rosa until next week anyway; it didn't stop him feeling her absence and wondering what she was up to.

The look on his face must have spoken volumes. As Robin glanced at him, in that curious way of hers, she clearly saw what he was thinking.

Her hand found his back and gave it a little rub. "Shall we go and check on her? It might put your mind at rest."

Arturo nodded gratefully. "That would be wonderful, thank you.

Although how exactly do we do that? Are you about to whip out a crystal ball for me to peer into?"

"Something like that."

Nothing more was said as she led him on through the Library until they reached a dome-shaped room full of screens that wrapped around the circular wall. A desk ran along the outside, with chairs pushed underneath.

Robin pulled one out and gently ushered Arturo to sit.

"The Observatory is slightly bigger than your average crystal ball, but it uses the same kind of magic to allow us to see that which cannot usually be seen." Her fingers danced across the screen closest to them. Arturo couldn't really tell what she was doing, but various images and messages popped up, which she instinctively tapped or swiped away. Then the screen went black for a moment. "The Library allows us to check in on our loved ones, but we always need to receive approval first. You can imagine how people might otherwise misuse this place."

He didn't have a chance to respond before the screen transformed into an image he recognized.

Rosa's room at her mother's house.

"How?" he breathed.

It was like watching a video, but one that wasn't fixed, as though he were there himself, able to tilt his head and look around. He found himself crouching beside where Rosa was sitting on the carpet, watching her draw.

"An artist!" Robin said. "How delightful. You are a talented family."

Arturo watched Rosa for a few seconds more. "She loves the creativity in bringing lines and colors to life. She gets that skill from her mother—she's an excellent artist. I can't draw to save my life. Words are my paintbrush. Yet another difference that came between us."

He blew a kiss to his oblivious daughter, stood, then touched the original screen to end the transmission. He hadn't wanted to linger. It felt a little intrusive.

Yet as soon as the image of Rosa vanished, other visuals took its place: news feeds, breaking news banners, worried-looking reporters, and handheld footage being replayed from countries all over the world.

"Oh, what'd I do?"

Robin leaned over his shoulder, staring intently at the screen. "You just switched over to the general information observations. But what exactly is it they're observing?"

There were multiple images in front of them now. A mosaic of screens, each showing the same thing from a variety of angles and in vastly different places.

"Volcanoes?" he said. "Must be an eruption somewhere? But that's nothing new—"

Robin shushed him as they watched convoys of cars and trucks snaking out of a town in what looked like New Zealand. A reporter stood to the side, solemnly watching them, before the camera zoomed in on the background.

There it was. A triangle of darkness rising up from the horizon, beyond the rooftops and old satellite dishes. The volcano's vivid lines were only barely distinguishable from the thick clouds massing around it.

It was like something out of one of those American blockbuster movies about the end times.

"They were starting to wake when I was back on Earth," Robin said, her voice unnaturally solemn. Her whisper sent shivers up his spine. "The meteorologists on the TV were saying there was something unusual about volcanic activity on different continents happening simultaneously. Like it had never been seen before in recorded history."

"You mean, never?"

"Yep. *Never*."

They both flinched as the clouds around this particular volcano lit up in a blaze of lightning. Arturo then felt his jaw set hard as the footage cut to multiple images of similar weather activity, but—according to the captions underneath—from different countries.

Whatever was going on, it was happening *everywhere*.

"Shit, that doesn't look good at all," he muttered, almost able to see the clouds darken before his very eyes. "Why didn't I know about this?"

He wasn't one for watching or reading the news, admittedly. He'd given up long ago trying to determine which network or newspaper had an agenda and which was going to give him the truth of the matters he needed to know. But now he thought about it—he *had* seen something about volcanoes on his social media feeds. A few mentions here and there of something happening.

Only a few, though, and so Arturo had paid it no mind.

This though? This was something on a whole other level.

"It's escalating," Robin noted. She blew out her cheeks and straightened up.

Arturo glanced over his shoulder and caught her looking to Centauri. The Orb flashed a response that suggested he had no explanation for what they'd just seen.

"And what do we think *it* is?" Arturo asked.

Neither of them responded. The panic growing inside him began to gnaw its way through his gut.

Rosa was back there. He had no idea if there were any volcanoes near his home, but could he really take the chance one wasn't going to appear beneath the city? She had seemed fine in her room, drawing in her sketchbook without a care in the world. Things were obviously okay right now, but what if that changed? Things looked terrible.

"I should go home," he said firmly. "What if Rosa needs me, and I'm not there? I know I don't have her this week, but I should at least be around in case there's a problem."

Robin looked uneasy. It was a look he didn't believe she wore too often, such was the power of her energy and good humor he'd experienced so far.

Regardless, whatever internal concerns she was feeling, she reached over to take his hand in hers and gave it a reassuring squeeze.

"I don't claim to know what is happening, Arturo, but I understand how it must make you feel. It's natural to want to go back, to be near your daughter. I have to admit, I feel the same about my family. Yes, I saw glimpses of the news before I returned to the Library, but nothing like we've just seen." She lifted her chin and gestured around them. "But this place is where my power and strength lies. This is where I can do the most good. And from what I've seen, with your dancing books, the same can be said for you."

He blinked. "Are you saying I have a power?"

"I'm saying that perhaps the Book of Wisdom brought you here for a reason. There is a strange connection between Earth and Paperworld. Whatever is happening on Earth could very well be linked to what happened to Helia and the Author and the reappearance of Suttaru. Such is the strength of the connection. So perhaps—just perhaps—this is exactly where you are meant to be. To help us during the time of greatest need. Ours *and* Earth's."

Arturo wasn't sure what to say to that.

The voice in his head was telling him to go, to leave and find Rosa and make sure he was there if she needed him. Yet his gut was telling him to listen to Robin.

"Are you saying I can help stop whatever is going on back there?"

"I think there is a chance, yes. And look, nothing has actually *happened* yet. The volcanoes haven't erupted. Right now it's just the sense of a threat. Everyone is safe for now, and nobody needs to rush home. It looks like we still have time."

On any normal day, the idea of there being "a chance" he could do some good in the world might not have been enough to spur him into action. There was so much to fix—in his life, in his country, basically everywhere—and he had been feeling increasingly powerless to stop it. He was only one man. A man who hadn't even been able to hold his family together.

What good could he do, really?

But this was no normal day.

He'd experienced enough of the magic of the Great Library of Tomorrow to know there was something to be trusted in what this beautiful Sage was saying. That if there was "a chance" here, it was more than just a possibility. It could actually happen.

If he went home now, he would be powerless again. But if he stayed, he could help. Not only Rosa but everyone.

Arturo raised his chin and took a deep breath.

"Lead the way, Sage. I'm yours for now."

They walked out of the door and took a left, hurrying along a different corridor to the one they'd initially come down. Like earlier that day, he noticed the floor beneath the long red carpet seemed to give a little under his feet, while the lamps overhead pulsed a little more with every step. He'd been far too concerned with all the amazing sights to connect the two until now.

"It's kinetic energy, isn't it?" he asked, trying to take his mind off what was happening on Earth as he pointed between the floor and the lights. "Every step I take activates some kind of panel below the carpet, which triggers a burst of energy that feeds into the lights. It's what powers this whole place."

Robin's Orb flashed again in his direction, although this time his tone seemed to be slightly more complimentary.

"You've got a good investigative eye," she replied. "How'd you figure that?"

"Cause and effect. I noticed the lights flicker just that little bit brighter when people walk past them. You may keep talking about magic, but I get the sense there is a level of practicality to this Library too—a way of living that is sustainable from a human perspective, without relying on some kind of supernatural force. It's something I'm pretty good at, connecting the dots between the elements before me. I spent long enough trying to do this with my stories, and I eventually started doing it in reality too. The clues to how we live our lives, how we survive, how we interact with each other . . . they are everywhere. And there's always an explanation behind each one. You just have to tease it out."

"I guess Mwamba was right to ask you to help us figure this out, especially with our own great authorly mind unable to communicate with us."

They reached an alcove, and she gestured for him to stand on a subtly marked square. Then she stood next to him and pulled his arm tightly to press against hers. Centauri hovered between their heads.

"But don't forget," she said, reaching out with her other hand to a lever on the wall. "The reason you're here is because those supernatural forces brought you to us at our time of need. Magic always has its place, too, even though we tend to forget that back on Earth."

He sniffed. "I've always preferred practical—"

She pulled the lever, and the floor disappeared.

CHAPTER EIGHTEEN
GUARDIAN OF THE GREAT TREE

As night descended on the Maze, Dzin felt the blood soaking into his blindfold from the cut on his forehead. He'd gotten it up from running headfirst into a nest of hissing thistles, another dead end in this place of even deadlier endings. He tried using his sleeve to dab at it, but the blood continued to drip out of him, drenching the now ragged and damp blindfold Yantuz had fashioned to wear over his eyes.

"Does it hurt?" Yantuz asked. His voice was calm and close. He was still holding tightly to Dzin's arm, like a parent might hold a child as they led them through a dangerous area. Dzin was both humiliated and comforted by it.

"What do you think?" he replied.

"I think I told you not to run in that direction."

"Well, I know that *now*," Dzin snapped. He was feeling slightly woozy. "There seemed quite enough room in that direction. I heard no rustling of bughops or other beasts of the night that might have wandered in here. I thought it was clear."

Yantuz's sigh told Dzin that he was probably frowning, wondering why his older brother was so useless. "You know full well that's what the Maze wants you to think. Didn't you tell me yourself that it tests all who venture in here? It does its best to throw you off the scent of the path you want to take. Which, for us, is the closest damn exit we can find! Seriously, Dzin, coming into the Maze was literally part of your training. How are you so bad at this?"

Dzin felt the dampness of his own life force warm against his eyes. "I've had a very bad evening. I shouldn't have run. I shouldn't have dragged you into this."

"Yes, I was wondering when you'd get to that. But it's okay. I accept your apology."

"I *wasn't* apologizing! Just . . . thinking out loud."

Yantuz sighed again. Dzin had heard that sound an awful lot since they'd crept into the Maze, arm in arm, blindfolded and stretching out their free hands to guide their way. It had been even more difficult than either of them had considered. Their ears were filled with the orchestra of nature coming to life, the howls of beasts—vinetoads, Dzin thought— and the buzzing drone of the tiny but very loud insects that were singing a variety of mating calls. All of which had Dzin's nerves on edge.

It probably didn't help that they were on the run, and he was feeling a little weighed down by the guilt of not being able to save his friends. That he had watched them perish, while somehow, by luck, he had survived.

The feeling that he didn't deserve to be alive permeated his every moment. Why him and not one of them? Why had he escaped? It didn't seem fair. In fact, it seemed plain wrong. He knew logically it wasn't his fault—he hadn't been the one to attack the others; he would have died, too, had he not defended himself with his stick. Yet he couldn't help but feel he should have done something more. The horrible feeling clogged his every breath and threatened in every moment to bring him to a complete stop.

"At least we haven't been eaten yet," Yantuz said, pulling him along and trying to put a positive spin on things. He always did that, whatever the problems they faced, to the point it was almost annoying. "I'd say not being eaten by one of the Maze's flowers is a pretty good start. It's just the sign we need to tell us we might make it through this little adventure."

Ugh, adventures.

Dzin wanted very badly to latch on to the faint hope offered by his brother, but it was a stretch. Where Yantuz saw the positive in everything, Dzin was a realist. He always found it far too easy to see the reality behind the ideal. Some called him cynical. He took that as a compliment.

He had no idea what to think of tonight. The evening had been full of joy and excitement, and then suddenly there was fire, so many flames and so much heat. And, in the middle of all that, the beast. Where had that come from? What even *was* it? He'd seen plenty of strange and wonderful creatures on his travels, yet never something so terrible. It had been an abomination that shouldn't have been possible. A beast-like nightmare with fire for fur. A being so hateful you could feel the evil pouring off it. Why had it appeared tonight and killed everyone? And how had it disappeared? Where had it gone when the guards and Tywich had burst in?

"The Guardian of the Great Tree is designed to test your trust," Dzin said. He sighed, unable to stop the doubt from settling in. "Unfortunately, trust isn't something I feel much in myself right now."

"You're making no sense now, brother."

"Of course I'm not! I'm bleeding and terrified. Maybe we should just give up and accept our fate at the hands of the guards."

"Give up?"

"Maybe. There's no harm in admitting I panicked. Who could blame me, yes? The whole place was on fire. There was a beast. Maybe they'll understand why I ran."

"And if they don't? You'll languish in the cells, suffering in the dark and damp, down in the roots, far from life and having to fend off all the giant worms."

Dzin briefly wondered whether the fate that awaited them back at the Great Tree wouldn't be preferable to what awaited them in here. The blindfold was cold and sticky against his skin. He half considered holding it away from his face so he could rub his eyes clean underneath. But he knew even if it was lifted for just a moment, it would be enough for the plants in the Maze to notice and eject him. Likely in as rough and terrifying a way as possible.

It was difficult to tell how long they'd been in this place. It felt like several rotations, which meant it was the middle of the night. The majority of the Tree's millions of inhabitants—so many different people both Tree-born and those who had made this place their home—should all be fast asleep. He could just imagine what the Tree would usually look like right about now: A few pinpricks of light spilling out of cubbyholes dotted up and down the trunk and across the towns of the branches. Then the dawn of the morning would crack across the topmost leaves, and Mother would quiver as the world woke again, and her boughs would grow colorful with activity once more.

Except tonight hadn't been normal, had it?

Most of the Tree would likely be awake. The fire at the laboratory might still be raging. The flaming beast might still be on the loose. And people would be gathering to talk about the murders of the students. And the one who had run.

Now it was Dzin's turn to sigh.

"Shush now," his brother replied, an edge to his voice as he pulled Dzin along, almost as though he could smell the air of defeat that was currently pouring out of him. "You dragged me into this, and now I will drag you through it and out the other side. Assuming we can find the other side. Or any side. There are four gateways out of this place, right?"

"Four ways out of the Maze, to lands dreamt of in midnight's gaze," Dzin intoned, repeating the lullaby they'd both been taught as children, when they were just *little twigs growing within the canopy of the Great Tree,*" as their mother used to say.

"Right, so which way should we go, then?" Yantuz asked.

If Dzin could have effectively rolled his eyes and have his brother see it, he would have done so. But beneath the bloodstained blindfold all he could do was close his eyes and grit his teeth. "It doesn't matter. We literally can't see which way we're going. I will take any gateway we happen across."

"Where's the closest town?"

"Didn't you study anything in school?"

"Not especially, no. I was too busy making sure you didn't get thrown off a branch by whoever you had annoyed that particular day, remember? Now please, Dzin, I'm helping you. The least you can do is help me. You're the one who always excelled in class, who got chosen for all the awards and things. Stop making me jump through hoops. Where is the nearest town?"

Dzin relented, feeling the guilt grow upon his already weakened shoulders.

"It's Undergrowth. Through the north gateway."

"Then we should do what we can to find our way there. There should be plenty of places we can stay. Maybe get our bearings and figure out what to do. And—"

He stopped dead. Dzin stumbled into him. He went to cry out, only to find a firm hand clamped around his mouth.

"Can you hear that?" Yantuz whispered.

He released his hand, and Dzin crooked his head. "The unpleasant silence? Yes."

"Aside from that. I heard a growl. Is that a moonrat?"

Dzin could hear it too. His body went cold, the damp against his eyes sticky and suffocating. He had to concentrate hard to resist ripping off the blindfold and taking a quick look around.

"I—I don't think the Maze allows dangerous animals in here," he said hopefully, thinking back to the beast again. The evil silhouette covered in crackling flames that had come out of nowhere and changed the entire course of his life. Would it have come after him, trying to finish what it had started, for whatever reason it had been there in the first place? Could it be hunting him even now? He knew the Maze had strict magic around the humans who ventured in here, but did those magical rules extend to creatures? Suddenly, he wasn't so sure.

"Sometimes things wander into places they shouldn't," Yantuz said.

"What makes you think it's a moonrat?"

"I heard one once. A friend showed me a Flowtograph—you know, one of those moving pictures—that his aunt brought back from one of her expeditions into the mountain forests to the east. There's a town there with a shop that sells all kinds of trinkets from all over the world, and—"

"Concentrate, Yantuz. The moonrat."

"Right, right, yes. Anyway, the Flowtograph was of one. Maybe they'd tracked it into the wild, or maybe it was a tame one they'd found. But anyway, it made a unique sound. I heard it."

Dzin drew closer to his brother. "Are you sure?"

"Fairly sure."

"I don't think there are tame moonrats, Yantuz."

"I know," he replied, just before a throaty yowl issued forth from the trail behind them. "Run!"

Dzin stumbled after Yantuz, and with both of them clinging on to the other's arms, they pushed further into the Maze, scraping past a wall of thick, twisted branches as they found what seemed to be a smaller corridor off the main path they'd been on. Dzin didn't know for sure, of course, but the way the world went a little darker and the feeling of the brush of overhanging vines on his shoulders told him all he needed to know.

The Maze had been created to act as the Guardian of the Great Tree, and there was a wildness to the trails and corridors within it. Some were big, some were small; others felt like you were trying to squeeze yourself through a run used only by rabbits. The vines and branches often grew overhead, full of huge leaves and dark-hued flowers, ensuring very little light made it down to the ground. Not that you could see much with blindfolds on anyway. It certainly left no room for those Runners born with wings to navigate their way out.

The Maze had been grown by design, to protect the Tree from those it found unworthy.

Dzin ran and ran, the blood on his face now mixing with a cold sweat, stinging his eyes. He tried to rub them with one hand as the other held on to Yantuz, who was bullishly running down this ever-tightening jungle trail. But he was trying to do too many things at once now.

And he was tired. So damn tired.

It was only a matter of time until he stumbled.

He wished he could have blamed a root, but the fact was he just tripped over his own feet. Plummeting forward, he caught his brother.

Yantuz cried out in shock as he tumbled too, and with a soft *thwack* they both landed in something large and bouncy and sweet smelling.

Then, as the growl issued again behind them, so close he could smell the warm waft of meat from the creature's last meal, Dzin felt several large petals curl and lift him up.

He was tipped into a bell-shaped flower of what he sensed in a panic might be a voonusian mauler.

Carnivorous. And, if the Maze shared his increasing panic about his trustworthiness, perhaps even deadly.

A muffled shout of warning tried to burst forth from his throat, but it never made its way out. He found himself pressed against a sticky interior as the petals closed around him. All he could manage was to call out his brother's name before his head grew light with the perfume of a hundred pollen grains. And then the world around him disappeared.

CHAPTER NINETEEN
SEEDS OF CHAOS AND FEAR

Lyvanda held up the vial of Elixir to the light to inspect it.

"Its powers are almost always felt instantaneously. Are you sure nothing has returned to your mind?"

"I've taken the Elixir in the past," Helia said, trying to contain her disappointment—and fear for what this meant. "I know the feeling of its healing qualities. There was nothing there. It was like dabbing water on my skin."

Lyvanda's face hardened. She reached for her hip, where a thin-bladed knife was tucked into the sash at her waist. In one smooth motion, she drew it across her forearm. Helia saw Nu wince as blood trickled out of the cut, but Lyvanda paid it no mind.

She merely opened the vial again and tipped a few drops into the wound.

The bleeding continued. There was no healing to be seen.

Muttering a curse under her breath—of such exotic derivation even Helia didn't recognize the words—Lyvanda then raised her fingers to her lips and whistled. One of her workers appeared almost immediately.

"Do you have your Elixir, Tal?"

He nodded and reached into his pocket. "I have little left in this vial, but it's all yours, Chief Scientist."

He handed it over, and they all watched as Lyvanda dropped this potion into her cut.

There was still no effect.

"I don't understand," she whispered, her eyes darkening as she sought answers inwardly. She reached out to hand the vial back to Tal and motioned for him to leave, then began to pace across the roof. "No change. None at all. The Elixir's power isn't there. It's gone. How is that even possible?" Then she paused suddenly, before spinning around and drawing up in front of Helia. "The Garden."

"Yes?"

"You said it had been destroyed."

"That's right. What does that have to do with this?"

"Each Elixir formula requires the Cerulean Rose from the Rose Garden. It is the one essential constant. It has long been taught that the healing power of the Elixir stems directly from that ingredient. Indeed, our people sometimes refer to it as the Flower of Life, our most literal and beautiful reflection of nature's grand plan. Its creation is our most treasured story from the time of Mother's ascension as the center of all nature. The flower was a gift from her, and if the Garden has been destroyed, then the magic in the ingredients taken from it could also have been affected, rendering them inert. Useless."

Helia took a careful, calming breath to hold back the competing emotions now threatening to overwhelm her. She took a step toward the railing and grasped it firmly in both hands as she stared out across the top of the Great Tree. "But how is that possible?" she asked the Chief Scientist, seeing the other woman's face trying to regain some sense of composure.

"The flower is tied to the Conjunction, our most special of days, when the twin moons align Mother, and the pollinators are renewed and the cycle of life blossoms throughout Silvyra. All nature, from the First Forest to the gardens of Bloom, are connected in that moment, through Mother, through her mycelium networks, and on a very literal basis the very *spirit* of nature itself. Without the Cerulean Rose connected to the rest of Silvyra in a living form, it's essence must be simply . . . gone. And even if we could plant more roses, we are a full season away from the next Conjunction."

No, thought Helia, stunned. It can't simply be gone. First the Rose Garden had been destroyed. Its beauty and powerful healing and regenerative spirit burned to the ground. The dragon gone. Taken perhaps to goodness knew where.

Then she had witnessed Xav die. Her love, her partner, all their adventures together over the centuries . . . she had watched it all incinerate in an instant by that *nightmare*. Her grief from his loss was still as fresh and gaping as the wound on the Chief Scientist's arm. The absence of him burned within her deeply, making her feel at once lost and unwilling to want to find her way back to whatever constituted a "normal" feeling. At least the pain was a reminder of what they'd had.

She had managed to come on this journey to Silvyra despite all of that. Because she'd had the hope of the Elixir to hold tight to, a way to fix at least some of this.

But now it was gone. The healing potion famous throughout the world of Silvyra—and beyond—no longer worked.

The implications of such a thing were not something she could fully comprehend in that moment. Silvyra and its inhabitants were vulnerable. They had already lost Perennia, their protector, and now there was no way to heal themselves from whatever destruction was coming their way.

It would be easy to lose hope now, but Helia had never been one to give up so easily. There was always hope, always. So no matter the anxiety writhing within her, she would not accept defeat, even in circumstances that would cause others to despair.

"Perhaps we could try other vials," she suggested, offering a smile she hoped didn't betray her worry. "There may yet be life in the Rose Garden, among the fire. Perhaps some of the Cerulean Rose survived. If we try a few more, we might get lucky. It is a faint hope, of course, but even a faint hope is a hope."

As she shifted her hands from the railing, a little green shoot could be seen, sprouting straight out of the timber. Things like this happened from time to time. Helia's powers were directly connected to her emotions, and when they got the better of her, small acts of creation would sometimes form.

Even as she moved away, its little leaves continued to bulge and unfold.

Lyvanda must have noticed. "There is always hope," she said, returning the smile, similarly maintaining hope in the face of hopelessness. "Let us go and halt the last of the outbound airships. We will work through the Elixir until we find what we need."

Helia nodded and looked out for a last time to the dock, where an ocean-green and gold-striped airship had lifted and was beginning to pass as it slowly turned. She watched the long, elegant paddles underneath fan out and tilt to capture the wind. While at the rear of the cabin, the pennants of a distant land fluttered proudly.

Then, at the portholes of the underhanging cabin, a face appeared.

Someone waving to them. No, wait, they weren't waving.

They were banging on the window.

Shouting something.

Trying to warn—

The air shuddered as the cabin exploded.

Helia felt the heat of it on her cheeks, even from where she stood. The cabin simply burst apart, flames incinerating it in a flash, before enveloping the balloon above—which then ignited, turning the sky the color of blood.

There was a scream from somewhere. It could have been from Nu, or Helia herself, but it sounded distant, swallowed whole by the roar of the fireball above.

Then another roar shook them, and another airship—this one still sitting on the docks—vanished in a terrifying mass of flames. Then another exploded, having just taken off. Pieces of it fell immediately through the branches of the tree. Meanwhile, Helia caught a series of flashing lights in the distance as other airships were lost, followed shortly by a crescendo of booms as their explosions shook the air like a multitude of distant storms.

In all directions, the sky was full of trails of fire, and smoky wreckage was raining down around them. It was as if someone had lit firecrackers, having timed them to go off one after the other.

Except the firecrackers were all airships full of people, exploding and dying before their very eyes.

Lyvanda was the first to utter rational words, something about needing to get help, but before anyone could process what she'd said, there came another terrible noise.

Another roar of thunder that shook the Great Tree.

This time from below.

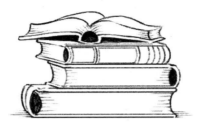

CHAPTER TWENTY
A STORY IN THE CHAMBER OF CHRONICLES

It took Arturo several seconds of panicking before he realized he wasn't free-falling into a bottomless pit. There was a slide beneath his back, which eventually curved upward and finished abruptly, shooting him off the end into a standing position—a perfect landing.

Which he immediately ruined by falling over.

Robin landed neatly beside him and carried on walking. "No time to rest, Arturo. We've got some research to undertake. Our destination is ahead."

Arturo sighed heavily, and he pushed himself to his feet, feeling every inch of his aching, middle-aged frame. As much as he loved how different this was to his normal day, he was getting a little tired of all the surprises.

"We went in a lift earlier, through a mirror, now down a slide. Is there no consistency here?"

"The Library was founded by one person, but created by many."

She gestured for him to follow her down some steps, to a tunnel that led through a huge fish tank. All kinds of bizarre-looking fish—and the occasional shark—swam around them, their shining eyes growing huge as they pressed up to the glass, before flitting away again. "What started as a single bookshelf in a cave evolved somewhat over the years, with each generation finding new and ingenious ways to expand the building into the mountain and help people navigate it. The entire place is an architectural melting pot of ideas and visions and, occasionally, the results from a little bit of joking around. The slide, though, is a convenient way to move from one floor to another. Quite honestly, I'm surprised more people don't utilize it. Why walk downstairs when you can feel the rush of the slide?"

They reached a pair of huge iron gates that seemed welded together, and Robin placed her hand on the symbol at the center: a small circle, within which a butterfly spread its wings beneath an eye and a crown. As she touched it, Centauri glowed a faint crimson, and the iron gates pulled apart.

She lifted her finger to her lips for Arturo to be quiet, then gestured for him to follow her. Even Centauri grew dim as they stepped through, and they found themselves in a faintly lit, wood-paneled room. A single round table stood at its center, with an avalanche of books cascading across it. Several people, in colorful clothes similar to Robin's, sat in arched-back chairs around the table, poring over the books or whispering to each other, clearly discussing important ideas. More small flying machines bobbed and weaved silently around their heads, communicating to each other, to the scholars below, and occasionally disappearing into the sliding wood panels around the walls, before reappearing with new tomes.

Arturo hadn't seen much of the Library, granted, but this room felt very different to the others he'd seen so far—a basic, almost secret place, squirreled away from the magnificence of the main rooms and plazas and gardens.

He knew immediately that this was a room hardly anyone ever saw.

A face he recognized looked up from the far side of the table.

"Welcome to the Chamber of Chronicles," Mwamba said, spreading his hands wide as he excused himself from the two scholars he'd been sitting with and walked around the table.

He clutched a scroll, which he tapped Arturo on the shoulder with

and bade him to sit down. Mwamba and Robin sat on either side of
Arturo, their two Orbs rising over the center of the table and circling
each other, overlaps of fractal patterns and intricate weaves of light indicating they were catching each other up.

Mwamba explained, "Few visitors even know about this room. We
keep it off the beaten path, away from anybody who might stumble
here accidentally, as it's where all the information on the collections
can be accessed—and that kind of knowledge is really only for those of
us who work here."

Arturo nodded absently, now able to hear the distant sound of something riding tracks nearby. Another tram?

A chime sounded, and he watched as a woman rose from the table
and moved to the wall behind her. A panel near the bottom slid open to
reveal a small crimson wagon holding three egg-shaped cases. As soon as
she'd plucked them off it, the transport vehicle ran back into the secret
tunnel it had appeared from, and the panel closed again.

The scholar rested the strange items on the table and glanced at
Mwamba. "They're here, Sage. The books you wanted."

Arturo stood up, leaning over the desk toward them, gently bumping the edge by accident as he did so, causing the three large eggs to
wobble from side to side.

"Those are books?"

They weren't like anything he'd seen before. Yet they were bound in
stretched material, with letters he didn't recognize across one side, which
seemed to indicate a title. He even caught a glimpse of a jade "spine"
arching across the back. It glittered as the book-egg rocked again. Arturo
had seen stone inlays like that in the Aztec collection at the *Museo Na-
cional de Antropología*.

Robin tugged on his shirt to get him to sit back down again. "Shhhh.
Just watch."

Mwamba reached out to grab the first one, and with his large hands
on either side, he pulled it apart like a coconut. Inside, lining the inner
shell of the egg, were crystals and other strange stones. To Arturo's surprise, Mwamba's Orb, Canopus, dropped from his conversation above

the table and nestled into the strange device. Mwamba closed it on him and sat back.

The book-egg rocked again and lifted a few feet off the table. Then, to Arturo's surprise, it lit up, spilling light out of every pore of the book's binding.

It revealed a hologram before them, a list of interconnected words joined by fuzzy little lines that flickered like static. The words didn't make much sense to Arturo, and he wondered what language they might be. But as soon as the thought had popped into his head, he realized they were changing, as though he had been wearing glasses that had fogged and were now clearing up. Soon words that he recognized began to form, the word *Log* hovering at the center of them.

"It's an interactive catalog of activity," Mwamba explained, reaching out to touch one of the subsections in the hologram. "A catalog of all the Great Library's holdings. As the collection is so vast and extensive, any mundane means of indexing would be unfeasible. We have hundreds of visitors to the Library every year, not to mention hundreds more scholars who live and work here, and each time they interact with a book, the catalog records the event. We call it the Codex."

"Just like the librarian who stamps out your book, it gives us a record of who has looked at what and when," Robin added.

Mwamba's hands danced quickly between the different images that appeared, as though he was flicking through the pages of a book in three dimensions. His brow was furrowed and his eyes watchful, even as he talked to them. He was looking for something.

For a few seconds, there was nothing but the buzz of activity, until Arturo finally voiced the concerns that refused to leave his brain.

"I'm sorry, but why am I here?" he asked, almost pleading. "You seem to have all this under control, and surely whatever happened to your book will be recorded here. You can't possibly need me for anything."

Mwamba looked at him through the hologram. "You're here because we have lost contact with our Author. You think like an author, and you were brought here just when we needed one most, which makes me wonder whether the Library already understands how this puzzle can be solved. Maybe it knew that you would play a part in the solving."

Arturo pulled at his collar, feeling a little overwhelmed and lost. He wished everyone would stop talking in riddles.

"Yes, you've said that before, but I still don't understand how I could solve anything here. Look at this place—the magic and the technology working together. I mean, you don't have computers, but whatever this hologram thing is, it's probably better than any computer that exists back home. In the event I'm *not* dreaming or hallucinating, you must surely have everything you need to find out what's wrong with the Book of Wisdom. How can I—someone who only dabbles with stories—possibly help?"

Robin rolled her eyes. "Are all writers this woefully self-depreciating?"

"This is me on a good day."

Nobody in the room laughed. Someone coughed. Mwamba continued to look at Arturo intently.

"This isn't just a Library, as you are well aware. The basis of this place and what lies beyond it in Paperworld—and the basis of life too—has roots in the world of storytelling. Stories exist not only to entertain, but to tell us about ourselves, to uncover the heart of who we are and why we do things. To show humanity what life is about. Our Author understood this more than most. She saw the patterns woven into our interactions and relationships with the world and each other, and she was able to use these connections to answer questions we had." He waved away Arturo's continued protests. "I can see that your experience on Earth has led you to change the way you live, taken you away from the right path. You wear a mask to survive the daily drudge of what you've become and hide the real you behind it. What we need you to do is take off that blindfold and do it quickly, because we need your expertise."

Arturo opened his mouth, then closed it again. He wasn't going to win this argument. He might as well just go along with it.

Mwamba gave him a thin smile. "Good, then let us begin, for we are already running out of time. What we are doing here is trying to understand when the Book of Wisdom's ability to communicate became corrupted. This log—or hologram, as you say—might shed some light on any anomalies that have been recorded since it last spoke to us, which was some time ago, but it's a place to begin the investigation, at least."

Arturo placed his hands calmly on the table in front of him and brushed away some imaginary dust from its surface. "May I be honest?"

"Of course."

There was a thread of a plot already forming in Arturo's mind and a series of questions he needed to answer to progress through it. Touching the table was enough to ground him, to maintain his ability to remain in the present while his brain skipped ahead along the storyline. He couldn't help it. The process had begun, as it did with every puzzle that formed the heart of the stories he used to write. It made him feel suddenly full of life.

"I think the question you're asking is the wrong one," Arturo stated, getting to his feet to pace about the room. "In all the time you've known the Book of Wisdom, has it ever acted in such a way as it is now?"

Mwamba shook his head. "No. The Book has always been able to talk to us when the time has come for it to do so. There has been no record of it ever being prevented from such."

"Then it doesn't really matter so much *when* this happened, does it? The more important question is why now?"

In the glow of the hologram, Robin's face tightened. "Suttaru."

Arturo raised a finger to confirm that that was exactly what he was thinking too. "Cause and effect. This is what propels stories. You can't simply string random plot points together. They have to make sense; there has to be a natural progression of things. In this case, you have a clear and obvious suspect—this Suttaru fellow. He's already attacked your Rose Garden. For the Book of Wisdom to suddenly not be able to talk after all the time it's been around, well, that's too random to be a coincidence. He's behind it."

"After our earlier conversation and my talk with Helia, I had wondered," Mwamba said, running his thick fingers over his brow, massaging it as though trying to ease the worry he was clearly feeling. "And yet how could he possibly have come in without us knowing? There are many special passageways from Earth to here. But there is only one portal into

Paperworld, and it is here, in the Great Library. When Suttaru first went through—long ago, in the beginning of the Great Library—it was an anomaly. The portal was wild and raw. The Book of Wisdom was created to control it, allowing us to navigate the realms that lay beyond. And ever since, only Sages and their Orbs have been allowed to travel back and forth."

Arturo continued to pace, staring down at the various scrolls and old books the scholars were studying. "Do you think Suttaru's powers would allow him to somehow overpower the Book? To force his way in?"

"The Book was what had stopped him in the first place. His powers are clearly no match for hers."

Arturo nodded. "Then logically he must have had help. An ally on the inside. Or at least someone who could get into the Library."

"Who?" Robin began to laugh, but quickly stopped as she realized what he was implying. "A Sage? You think a Sage did this? That's ridiculous! We sure as hell wouldn't dream of interfering with the Book. We were all chosen for a reason, to protect the Library and Paperworld and Earth, and that's what we've been doing all this time. It's our calling. The Book of Wisdom created our Orbs, and they in turn selected all of us. And the Book's *never* been wrong!"

A cough from Mwamba stopped her from continuing.

For a second or two, there was quiet in the room as the elder Sage stared at Arturo. Waiting for what, Arturo didn't know. He suddenly felt very uncomfortable, the confidence that had burned through him only moments ago having dissipated, leaving him a hollow bag of doubt. Had he overstepped the mark? Offended them? Would they banish him . . . or worse?

When the man finally spoke, it was with a grave solemnity, one that seemed to push Robin's incredulity back into itself and told Arturo he'd hit upon something important.

"That's not entirely true . . ." Mwamba began.

CHAPTER TWENTY-ONE
SABOTAGE

"The refinery's gone!" a guard cried as Helia, Lyvanda, and Nu pushed their way through the terrified crowds.

They had all just witnessed the destruction of the airships. Now they were greeted by cries of anguish pouring up the Tree and rippling through the inhabitants who didn't know what to do, seeing both fire above and fire below.

"By the moons, what's happening?"

"Are we under attack?"

"Where do we go?!"

Helia pushed aside any concern she had for her own safety as she ran through the haze of heat that had engulfed them all. Balloon and rigging debris were still falling, catching on branches around them while continuing to burn, while thick, bitter smoke poured up the Great Tree from below. She checked quickly on Nu, who looked pale and horrified, but was keeping pace. Meanwhile, Lyvanda firmly relayed instructions to two of her guards, asking them to spread the word and get the folk back into their cubbies. Two more followed the three women down the spiral staircase that ran around the outside of the trunk of the Great Tree.

Vega was pulsing supportively at Helia's neck, having hidden in her amulet for now.

She touched her fingers to him now and then for reassurance.

The journey down the Tree was fraught with soot-stained faces and wide-eyed children, crying families looking for escape. Helia was gladdened to see that Lyvanda provided leadership even on the run. As they hurried past, she would stretch out her graceful arms and direct them back up to their cubbies or across the bridges to the other—hopefully safer—trees around Mother. When they happened across more guards, she instructed them to escort as many people as possible away from the sweltering heat below, which was now blanketing everything, to get them away from the scenes of devastation.

Meanwhile, she led the way toward the danger without hesitation.

After running down many sets of stairs, sliding across a snapped bridge and taking a private leaf-lift inside the great trunk, they finally made it down to the ground. They exited in shadow, beneath the giant roots that were knotted all around them like the tentacles of a great leviathan. A seed-tiled pathway led them around one root, then underneath another, before it soon became littered with shards of wood and bark and copper machinery, all bent in unnatural ways. Shocked workers stood around, clutching each other and staring at the smoke that poured out of a ragged tear in the Tree ahead. Through it, glimpses of a huge complex of machines, walkways, and gigantic brass containers could be seen.

The refinery of the Elixir of Life.

Ablaze.

Helia held up her hand to her eyes, as if it might do some good to shield them from the fierce heat and bright flames. Memories were swirling around inside her. Some were of her escape from the volcano all those centuries ago. Now, though, she couldn't help but see the cinders of the Rose Garden in her mind's eye and Xavier's blood-streaked face.

No.

She wouldn't think of that now. She suppressed the memory as firmly as she could, too strong and experienced with the challenges of life to let it bend or break her.

She was hope. She would always be hope. Even in her darkest moments.

As they both caught glimpses of the bodies among the carnage, she heard Nu gasp beside her. She forced her to step back a little, and they both took shelter in the crook of a root.

Lyvanda did not join them. She stood fierce and unmovable in the center of the devastation, her gaze reluctant to move away from the fiery heart of the Great Tree's operations. She crouched to offer some comfort to one of the injured.

"There was a creature here, Chief Scientist!"

While the man's shouts raised some looks, most of those gathered were more concerned with trying to fight the fire, tapping into the roots and pumping out water through grass hoses, as though it would do any good.

It might stop it spreading, Helia considered, but the refinery itself was gone.

"A beast of four legs and fire!" the man continued. "I was talking to one of the Runners, Tywich, when I turned around for a moment. And then when I turned back, he'd gone! The beast had taken him, and I caught sight of the flaming nightmare running off. I don't know if the Runner is still alive, but the beast itself ran off into the Maze, just before the refinery blew."

Helia's jaw clenched as she listened, knowing where such a creature must have come from. *Suttaru.*

She caught a glimmer from Lyvanda's golden dress, which was gleaming against the reflections of flame and the continuing explosions inside the refinery. Lyvanda finally left the man after he'd been carried off by his friends and stepped back to join Helia and Nu.

"I'm so sorry," Helia began, but Lyvanda shook her head.

"Save your sorrys, Sage. We will deal with these atrocities as we now must. But it is clear that what brought you here today is already rearing its head in our precious Tree. First the Rose Garden, then the laboratory, and now this? The Elixir we have has been rendered useless, and now our ability to make more has been blocked."

Helia straightened as best she could, despite feeling the despair nipping at her insides like a hungry wolf. In all her time as a Sage, she had never faced such a moment of horror and loss. "Can the refinery be rebuilt?"

"No," Lyvanda said. "There could be a way to set up a temporary station. We have some of the finest engineers in all of Silvyra here. But . . ."

She paused, the words on her lips too bitter and horrid to give voice to.

Helia finished for her. "But even if you could, we have a bigger problem. There are no formulas left and nobody to make them."

Lyvanda's lips thinned. "Our students are dead, and the archive is burned to cinders. Everything and everyone we need is gone."

"Except Dzin," Nu said quietly.

"The student who ran away? The one they say murdered his colleagues?"

Nu shook her head. She had that feeling again, the one that directed the words out of her mouth, even though she wasn't quite sure how. It was pure instinct, so real she could almost taste it. She could even picture it, vivid and colorful: Flames licking at the corners of the image in her mind. A young man, terrified, trying to save his friend as he faced a hideous creature with flames for fur, the laboratory ablaze because of it.

"I believe he was innocent," she said, shivering as she returned to reality. Whatever had just happened again, she knew she could trust the truth of what she had seen. She kept her voice firm and confident, knowing what she was saying was important. "You need to trust that he did not do this. And besides, he has the last remaining formula. You say he escaped with it into the Maze? We should go after him."

Lyvanda inclined her head slowly at Nu's directness. "That is true. He has the last formula with him. Which means, yes, whether he is guilty or innocent like you say, you must follow him. You must recover that formula and the student himself, because only he can brew the potion. Dzin is now the only hope of you recovering your memory, Helia. It may yet allow you to find Perennia and bring her back to protect us, to breathe new life into the Rose Garden, and to ensure our Elixir of Life can heal once again. I will organize our Runners to set up a makeshift laboratory for your return."

She reached out and gave Helia's arm a gentle squeeze. Despite their age difference, Helia couldn't help feeling it was the kind of act a mother would give. There was a stirring of pride within her that the little girl she had known had grown so wonderfully.

"It was good to see you again," Lyvanda continued. "But now we must part ways. Follow the creature—go back along that path, then turn and follow the largest trail to the First Forest and then on to the edge of the Maze. You will see the gateway into it easily enough, but getting there will take you some time."

"Thank you, Lyvanda."

"Don't thank me yet. The journey ahead of you is fraught with danger. You must blindfold yourselves before entering the Maze or risk losing yourself in there. We cannot afford that, my dear."

Helia nodded and ushered Nu ahead of her. She then turned back to offer her thanks, but Lyvanda had already moved on, directing her people to search for survivors, even as the embers of the ruined refinery continued to rain down around them.

With a shiver, Helia left her to it.

"Anything from the Great Library?" she asked Vega as they hurried up the path.

The response was a desolate buzz against her neck.

Helia nodded and accepted it.

Dum spiro spero, she repeated in her head. Her mantra. The saying Xavier always loved and the one that had kept her going for so long.

While I breathe, I hope.

Once again, it was enough.

"Then we go on alone," she said, offering Nu a smile of encouragement.

Surprisingly, Nu offered her one back.

The First Forest and the Maze lay ahead.

CHAPTER TWENTY-TWO
RESCUES IN THE MAZE

Helia breathed a sigh of relief as they emerged from the First Forest. Beside her, Vega hovered, flashing shades of forest green and brown at the effort it had taken them to speed their way through the dense trees and vegetation. Nu stared at her in amazement, never having witnessed the full power of a Sage working with nature as she and Vega had just managed. That such an ancient and primordial place had sensed Helia's need and flowed around the two travelers was nothing short of a miracle, one that cut their travel time to less than half that of even the locals. They had run from the Great Tree through the shifting forest, and even now the sounds of shifting vegetation could be heard behind them.

But it was what lay ahead that held her attention now.

The Maze welcomed them in. Its walls of dark leaves and vines, twisted branches, and unnatural flowers closed in around Helia and Nu as they entered.

Helia couldn't see any of this, though, as she was now wearing one of the blindfolds the Library had ensured was pocketed in her outfit, as if it knew she might need it.

As always, the Library was right.

Thankfully, Helia didn't need to see with her eyes in this place. The feeling of nature was so powerful here that through her link with Vega—who was still bouncing in the necklace, safely against her chest—her natural senses were heightened. All she had to do was quiet her mind enough to reach out and *feel*.

It was a difficult sensation to explain to anyone who didn't yet have that relationship with their Orb, which was why she had simply let Nu believe Vega was guiding them. In reality, the magic of the Maze had made the Orbs' sensors grow fuzzy, ensuring they couldn't see too far in any direction.

In here, she was the one who could "see" everything. As they'd entered, she could sense the gaping mouth of the Maze swallowing them whole. She could picture the nocturnal birds flitting about above them, hopping between branches and settling into their nests to watch the visitors pass by. Helia could also see the creatures of the night lurking nearby, scuttling through the hedges and foliage, or creeping around corners, stalking their prey. Here and there, she also felt the residual presence of previous visitors to the Maze who had not been found to be worthy or pure of heart. Their bones were now hidden, their skulls forever open-mouthed in horror at their mistake in believing they could pass through here unscathed.

Helia felt everything through the ground and the roots and the trees and leaves. She was one with this magical place.

You have a connection with nature, her mother always used to say as she'd marveled over her daughter's bountiful garden. There was always produce to feed the family and often enough to pass along to their neighbors in the village too. *Nature listens to you, Helia. You are like the sun above us. When you shine, there is always a green shoot of hope.*

To Helia, nature had always represented hope. As a child, when she was surrounded by the elements, she always felt attuned to the world and excited by its possibilities. No matter the obstacles the natural world faced, in all its different and improbable forms, it always found a way to overcome them. And this was something Helia embraced in everything she did. She became the green shoot of hope, even when life seemed cruel and hard.

It was this connection that first attracted Vega to seek her out as a potential successor to the Sage of Hope. It was why he followed her on her travels. And it was why, when her world turned to brimstone and ash, and as the mighty mountain she had been born beneath blew itself apart, shaking the earth and the seas, her little Orb had swept her away, saving her from death and guiding her into the portal to the Great Library.

It was here she'd discovered that while her talents were limited on Earth, here in the realms beyond, she was able to do so much more. Her talent for connecting with and harnessing nature was enhanced beyond her wildest imagination, thanks to the power of the Library and the connection to the Book of Wisdom she now had through Vega.

And so it was that she was now able to sense her way through the dark and dangerous Maze, while beside her, Nu tripped again and again, her arm going taut against Helia's each time she tried to catch herself.

"Keep watching out for those roots," Helia said patiently, holding tightly to her. "They will come out of nowhere to try and test you. You have to lift your feet and tread carefully. Slow steps."

It was a little unfair on the poor woman. Helia had been able to see the root squirming across their path, and she'd been able to step over it. But she didn't think it would hurt to let Nu realize just how challenging this place could be, and to make sure she respected it in the future, should she ever come back and have to navigate it herself.

"I can't watch the roots if I'm blindfolded," Nu muttered as she gripped Helia's arm, sighing as she righted herself. "And you're going way too fast for me to tread slowly. Are you sure you're still wearing a blindfold? Is this just some kind of test you're putting me through?"

Helia smiled to herself. "It's the Maze's test, not mine."

Nu tripped again and cursed. "Shivers, Helia. I'm sorry. I'm slowing you down, aren't I? Maybe you should leave me and run ahead to find those brothers and the formula."

"Nonsense. You're doing wonderfully well so far. Especially given the circumstances we've thrown you into." She brought them both to a stop. "Now, just keep your head calm and breathe and stay quiet. I'm going to take a moment to recalibrate."

"Okay," Nu said warily, unlinking her arm.

Helia stepped aside and crouched to touch the soil, letting her fingers ease into it. It was damp following a recent rain. This wasn't the ideal way of communicating with the plant life around her. It would have been far more direct to scoot to the side of the path and grab hold of a branch or a vine. But Helia didn't trust the Maze not to try something. It only harmed those impure of heart, those it couldn't trust, but it did *test* those who ventured inside to see if they were worthy.

She had already witnessed in her mind's eye at least one moonrat teased by a hooded bane. The bucket-like flower had snapped down at the creature's head, before sweeping around and grabbing its tail between the petals and throwing it into the night. Helia felt her powers could help her dissuade the Maze from trying anything with her, but with Nu in tow she didn't really want to take the risk.

So, she sat on the path and felt through the ground, her senses reaching out until they found a root, then following that up within the vast network of information that was flowing around them unseen, the billions upon billions of messages from each shoot, leaf, branch, and flower. Her senses could even touch upon the creatures living in harmony with the Maze . . . and those currently being eaten by them.

It was then she finally felt the presence.

A distant echo, yet one that was unmistakably human.

Two people.

And a vibration—what appeared to be a terrified moaning as they both hid within a plant. Another creature prowled about outside, a creature on four legs, from which she could *feel* the heat emanating across the Maze.

The creature at the refinery.

"It's found them," she whispered, feeling her gut churn. If that wasn't enough, she now realized what kind of plant the two had chosen to hide in. "They jumped into a voonusian mauler? Terrible choice. You don't ever want to do that. Come on, Nu. We're about to lose them."

But the only sound she heard was the muffled answer Nu couldn't give her . . . as her friend was suddenly dragged away.

"Nu?" There was no reply.

Helia leaped to her feet, severing her natural connection with the Maze, but she could still see the image burned into her mind's eye—and what she could sense through her link with Vega. That would have to do.

A big-toothed fern had unfurled from behind them and had silently wrapped itself around the poor girl, before curling her up into its deadly embrace and pulling her back into the mass of jungle.

Helia kicked off her boots as fast as she could, then ran after Nu, using the very faint connection through her bare feet to guide her senses. The sticks and stones, leaf litter, and withered twigs were sharp and rough underfoot, causing her to wince more than once, yet she kept her focus on the image of the struggling Nu.

This shouldn't have been happening. Nu was as pure of heart as they came. The Maze shouldn't have touched her.

Then, as she ran, she felt the blindfold on the ground beneath her feet.

Oh no.

She picked it up and shoved it into one of her pockets.

"Vega, help me!" she urged.

She needn't have asked. The Orb was already leaving her amulet, growing back to his regular size and pulsing fiercely. Helia could feel the warmth of his connection flow into her, could feel her power grow in strength, coiling like a spring ready to be unleashed.

She saw better now—more clearly, thanks to him—and as soon as she reached the hedge wall, she shoved her hands inside. The foliage closed around her hands and arms, tearing and scratching at whatever part of her it could find. She ignored the pain, pouring her emotions into the Maze, toward the fern.

Let her go, she thought firmly. *She just made a mistake. Let the girl go. Now!*

Nu's muffled shout reached her ears, even as Helia felt something give way around the greenery. It wasn't much, just a gesture, yet enough to make her realize she had been heard.

It wasn't enough to stop the fern, however.

There was now a conflict developing within the Maze itself. Helia could feel the push and pull all around her, pulsing through her hands and into her chest. The oldest parts of the Guardian, those with deep roots, who remembered her being here in the past, were urging the brash new growths to rein it in, telling the fern that it had overstepped its mark in taking the girl, despite her taking off the blindfold.

But they were being ignored.

The toothed fern continued to roll up its unfortunate victim. Nu's muffled shouts of panic were growing fainter. Helia could feel the younger parts of the Maze begin to win their argument.

The panic began to rise. She wondered whether she'd overestimated her strength here. Her heart raced as her vision deteriorated and she slowly lost the ability to see Nu. She felt the sweat dampening her blindfold. She squeezed her eyes shut behind it.

This wasn't working. Time to change tact.

"Blast it," she yelled, lifting her own blindfold to see and then lunging in the direction of the moving foliage. The tip of a shoe was the last thing she saw before she dove headfirst in after it and grabbed Nu's legs with both hands. "No, you don't. She's with me!" It wasn't a wrestling match she was going to win. She knew that instantly as the fern yanked her forward. Every muscle in her body ached. Her skin was scratched and bleeding. Her lungs burned with the effort she had already expended that day. She was a pale, exhausted shell of a woman who had lost everything since waking, and yet still had more to lose.

"Let her go," she urged again to nobody in particular. The Maze. Herself. She didn't know.

Vega was pulsing a furious brightness behind her, enough to splinter the undergrowth with shards of light, enough for Helia to see—through her tangled hair and the greenery closing around her—that Nu was almost lost. The only marker was a small glow against the young woman's wrist as Antares weakly guided them from her bracelet.

One last push. She had to try.

Closing her eyes, Helia continued to hold on to Nu's leg with one hand as the other let go to grab on to the nearest branch. An old trunk. One that might help.

Please.

It was enough. Something constricted ahead, and she wondered if the poor girl might actually be dragged through and ejected from the Maze, to be left alone in the night at the mercy of whatever creatures might have wandered upon her. But with a cold burst of relief, like surfacing after being underwater for too long, Helia realized it wasn't the plant around Nu that had constricted. It was the bushes nearby. Reacting to Helia's urging, they had come to Nu's aid by pushing against the fern, their tentacles slithering out to choke its bulb, until the long, rolled leaf began to loosen, and Helia was able to pull her free.

Thank you, she thought.

Pushing the branches and leaves out of their faces, Helia and Nu pulled themselves back to the path, where Vega was swirling around like a cyclone of fury and panic. Helia didn't wait to calm him. She pulled her blindfold back down, rushed past, and grabbed her boots in one hand, once again relying solely on the connection through the earth with her bare feet.

"Put your blindfold back on and run," Helia said, taking it from her pocket and thrusting it into Nu's outstretched fingers. "And don't take it off again!"

"I'm so sorry. My eyes were stinging with sweat. I just took it off for a moment, I prom—"

"No talking, Nu. We haven't much time."

There was still an image in Helia's mind of where they needed to go. A left up ahead. Follow the twist of the path through the gate of thorns, then under the stone bridge. As long as there were no trolls underneath it, they might just be all right.

She pulled Nu, now blindfolded again, along into the damp darkness, hearing Vega whistling through the air behind her excitedly. She hoped Antares was still safe on Nu's wrist.

Luckily, they found no trolls, nor heard any rasping growls nor felt any sharp, clawed fingers swiping at them. Although Helia did wince once as her feet found a pile of what initially felt like twigs, yet when she put her full weight on them, they cracked like bones. She kicked them aside, and spurred on by the horror, pushed forward until she felt the relative brightness of the early morning shadows of the Maze on her face again.

There.

The image was slightly sharper the closer they got to the brothers, her connection to the life around her still enabling her to see the two figures huddled together in the not-at-all-safe belly of a voonusian mauler. Meanwhile, the creature of fire still prowled about outside them, having somehow escaped being eaten so far. Helia wondered if it was because it was a creature rather than a human. Could creatures be found to be unworthy or even evil? Perhaps the Maze needed a little nudge in the right direction.

"Stay," she whispered to Nu, unlinking her arm before veering to the side of the path. A branch swung out at her, which she grabbed. She poured her power through it, along the twists of interconnected roots and up into a fern that stood not too far from the creature.

I've got a meal for you, she called out. *Something distinctly unworthy to chew on.*

The fern instantly slithered out in the direction of the beast. As it wrapped itself around its legs, the surprised creature howled, flames sputtering from its jaws.

The plant was unimpressed. In a burst of sizzling sparks, it yanked the beast down to the floor, then pulled it into the dense foliage. The inhuman cry faded into the distance as the creature was pulled through and then quickly ejected from the Maze. Clearly, it was not subject to the same magical rules that might have cost an unworthy or evil human traveler their life in here.

Grabbing Nu with her free hand, she started running and kept on until they heard panicked voices up ahead.

"Can you push it open from your side, Dzin?"

"No! It's not moving. I'm so sorry, brother."

"Stop your whining and try harder. Have you kicked it yet?"

"Yes! I said it's not moving. I've tried everything. I'm so tired. Maybe we could just take a little nap here before we try again . . ."

"Don't go to sleep!" Helia shouted as she and Nu skidded to an awkward, blind stop, thudding against the thick membrane of the plant. She let go of Nu, dropped her boots, and reached for the flower.

There was a small kerfuffle inside as the two men kicked out in surprise.

"Hello?" a sleepy voice called out, followed by the sound of a yawn.

Helia placed both her hands on the thick petal lids that encased the two men inside. She knew she'd have no chance of forcing them open physically, for there were hooks at the edge of the lids that locked against the bell of the flower. They couldn't be opened unless you had a sharp knife and a few hours to slice away at it. But by then, the brothers would be jelly.

With every ounce of energy she had left, she reached out through the petal, pushing her power through the cells, trying to urge one last favor from nature—focusing on the beauty of this flower, communicating that she understood its need to eat, and requesting it release its captives anyway, for the good of them all.

To enable the Great Tree to enact justice for what had been done.

That did the trick.

Something moved in the earth. Suddenly, the plant bulged and there was a snapping sound as the hooks retracted. Blindly, Helia and Nu managed to pull open the petals and reach inside to grab the two men, who were now very nearly on the edge of passing out forever.

"Whuh-huh?" one of them whispered as the women pulled him out and dropped him on the path. They then lifted out the taller and heavier of the pair, who at least had the strength left in him to claw his way out over the membrane. He stumbled momentarily, sucking in a lungful of fresh air, then he picked up his fallen brother.

"Are you okay to continue?" Helia asked.

They both made sounds that sounded like agreement.

Helia felt Vega hovering next to her ear. She didn't have the breath to tell him to hide himself in case one of the brothers lost his blindfold. She simply tapped her amulet. He understood and immediately shrank and slipped into it with a warm, satisfying click.

With that, she grabbed her boots again and led the others, arm in arm, back down the path, toward where she could sense safety. Her feet were raw and bleeding now, but she was still able to connect with the Maze, and that was the only thing that mattered for the moment.

They just needed to get the hell out of this place. So, she followed the images in her mind, taking them down one path, then another, then another. One of the men muttered something she didn't quite catch. Something about "going back to the Tree" and "punishment." She didn't answer, content to let the men stew in their concern.

Finally, the way out appeared in front of them.

The north entrance arched high, its woven vines and brambles tugging at their arms and legs as they sprinted through.

They fell to the ground in the open plains.

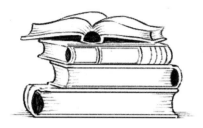

CHAPTER TWENTY-THREE
THE ROGUE SAGE

Arturo sank back in the chair, listening to the crackle of the fire beside him.

The reading room he and Robin had spent the last few hours researching in was about the most beautiful thing he had ever seen. Everywhere he looked around this enormous place he could see books. Tall, small, thin, thick, of all colors and decorations and designs. Stored up against the walls three stories high, and even somehow held across the ceiling too.

And this was just a single room within this fantastical Great Library.

How long had it taken to build up such a collection? He knew this place was old, but when all was said and done, here was the proof of it in all its musty, paper-scented glory.

He twirled the shot glass, which contained a thick golden liquid, letting its powerful scent waft up, causing his eyes to water in that delicious way all really strong alcoholic drinks were capable of. Then he downed it and leaned over to the coffee table to take another delicacy from the silver platter of savory treats prepared for them to sustain their research.

Popping it in his mouth, he realized he had no idea what the pink-and-red pastry contained. But Robin had said that everything in the Library was plant-based and sustainably grown, so he really didn't mind what it could be. All he knew was that he'd eaten six of them already and was wondering if he could convince Robin to order another platter.

For a few seconds, chewing on the soft vegetable filling contained within the crispy pastry shell, he found contentment in the normality of the experience—among the paranormal events of literally everything else he'd experienced that day.

His mind ticked over, contemplating the story Mwamba had told them. The tale of the Rogue Sage had been an interesting one, both for its content and for the way Robin had reacted to it.

Arturo was fast understanding that as much as Robin was a confident member of this group of Sages, she was still relatively fresh and idealistic. To her, the Great Library and those who lived and worked within her cast no shadows. And the Sages especially were beyond reproach. The Orbs had selected them based on the wonderful qualities they had shown on Earth, so how could they not be everything the Orbs thought them to be? Their small companions couldn't be wrong, because they operated through the Book of Wisdom, the almighty authority at the center of this world. They were therefore a trusted source of information. To Robin, there was absolutely no way they could make a mistake and choose a Sage who could go bad.

Brushing the pastry from his shirt, Arturo held his shot glass upside down over the nozzle on the small table and watched with amusement as another squirt of the drink poured *upward* into it until it was half full. He turned it around, still marveling at the ingenuity and, he now accepted, magic.

The warmth of the liquid burned his throat all the way down.

The thing with Robin was that she was positive and idealistic. He'd only known her a short while, but he understood that she saw the good in everyone. Arturo had grown a touch cynical himself, so he hadn't really been too surprised to learn that a person who was supposed to be good, one of the very Sages who were so esteemed in this world, wasn't entirely all they seemed.

"The Rogue Sage, Edwin Payne, arrived in our halls about a couple of hundred years ago now," Mwamba had said, beginning his story.

Arturo and Robin had leaned in closer, listening intently.

"He was a general in the British army, but also a great inventor specializing in the creation of electric light. He was selected by his Orb to become the Sage of Creativity, and indeed, he seemed to be the perfect fit for the role, being able to harness the power of fire and create warmth and light wherever he went. Yet it was clear his time fighting colonial wars across the world had left its mark on him. Aside from losing an eye, he had been tormented by what he saw. So, while he was always polite and well mannered, he became withdrawn. He suffered hideously from nightmares and became more blinkered and secretive about his work."

"What was he working on?" Robin asked.

"We weren't sure, if truth be told. But some rumored that he was looking for a book, a journal belonging to Suttaru when he was first at the Library, before he became corrupted by the darkness. This journal was said to contain secrets of magic unknown by anyone else, telling of a way to consume stories to fuel your strength."

Arturo frowned. "He was trying to fix himself? To rid himself of the nightmares?"

"Perhaps," Mwamba replied, an underlying tone of regret in his voice. "Either way, we didn't pay enough attention to him at the time. We were complacent, confident that his Orb had been so sure of his worth that we needn't worry. Yet we learned that even the Orbs can be wrong. He was discovered researching the darker materials in the Library, looking for a place known as Discordia, a place of dark stories. It was only then we stepped in to apprehend him and his Orb. Alas, in the ensuing chase, he was thought to have fallen to his death. He was never seen again."

Arturo had then asked the obvious question: "But did anyone actually see him die?"

"I don't believe so—and we couldn't check. His Orb had been found to be corrupted, and thus the Book of Wisdom had already cut it off from the network of communication that links our companions to the Great Library and each other."

"Perhaps he didn't die, then?"

Mwamba had stared at him for the longest time, before he finally nodded.

It was then he had sent them off to do more investigating.

Which is how they had ended up here.

With a loud sigh, Robin left the high bookshelves she had been perusing, the dull thuds of her boots coming down the copper rungs of the ladder, snapping Arturo back into the present.

He had been doodling, scribbling down notes in his pad. Thoughts, really, about what he had seen and done. Of course, they had continued to be brought to life around him, and as Robin approached he quickly made an edit.

The beautifully tall tree, stretching from beside his chair right up to the ceiling, fluttered as he altered it. The leaves turned a full and vibrant orange, and the branches arched over her as she gave a theatrical sigh and collapsed into the chair opposite him.

"You're getting good," she said.

"Thanks, but I'm just dabbling with the plants in here. Did you find anything of note in that section you wanted to check?"

Robin picked up a stray leaf from where it had fallen into her lap. "Oh, just a few more pictures like we've already seen. He was certainly the epitome of 'ye olde British soldier,' wasn't he?"

Arturo nodded, thinking of the images they'd seen. Sketches that had come to life on the page and a hologram of Edwin Payne's gaunt face turning this way and that with his eye patch over his missing eye. "Anything else?"

"Oh, there were also a few clues about what he was researching. Mostly to do with accidental discoveries of dark magic over the years— ways to change your physical appearance, like a kind of changeling, the ability to cloud men's minds and twist their will to your own. It sounded like he was particularly interested in nightmares, too, especially how to get rid of them. Plus, I found repeated occurrences in the Codex of him searching for poisons."

"What kind of poisons?"

"Not your regular kind. The records suggest he was hunting a poison that could harm even inanimate objects. Can you believe such a thing?" She turned the leaf over as she studied it. "But that's it. Lots of half hints and false trails and . . . well, gossip, if I'm quite honest. Nothing that ties Edwin Payne directly to Suttaru. Nothing about the journal he was supposed to be looking for nor whether he actually found it. No clues to suggest he deliberately disappeared, as you've suggested. Maybe he could have just fallen and died, as Mwamba said."

"Maybe and maybe not. That still seems too easy a plot twist. He's too good a suspect, considering what you've just told me. You said it yourself: no body was ever found."

"Fine. What do you suggest, then? Where would your mind take you if you hit a dead end like this, a writer's block? How do you get past that?"

Arturo gave her a smile, then gestured to his glass. She grinned, and they each got a refill, raised them in a toast, and chucked the shots down their throats.

"We're still left with the issue that only a Sage could access the Haven, where you say the Book of Wisdom is kept," he said, feeling his head go nicely fuzzy. "So, while the evidence might not be obvious yet, I still think our suspect is. It's Edwin Payne. Unless you know any other Sages who might be capable of throwing their lot in with Suttaru."

"Of course not!" she replied. "The Sages are my friends and colleagues. I trust them all with my life."

"Well then. All signs point to a dead man."

Arturo understood that Mwamba wasn't convinced by this theory yet. He had agreed to tell them the story but had advised that all the evidence pointed to the fact the Rogue Sage had perished. The elder Sage remained in the Chamber of Chronicles, returning to the records to continue his search into *when* the problem had occurred with the Book. He wanted to work backward to find the source. Very methodical, but too slow and rigid a process to accommodate the obvious answer that was staring them—or at least Arturo—in the face.

Edwin Payne was the obvious suspect. And his convenient "death" had been a red herring, a smoke bomb thrown down before the baying crowd to allow him to vanish from the eyes of the Library, thanks to whatever trickery he had learned along the way.

And if he had truly been looking for Suttaru's journal, perhaps he'd found it. But what if he decided to go a step further and find Suttaru himself? Clearly, this villainous *Ash Man* hadn't died long ago. Perhaps he'd been trapped somewhere, waiting for his chance at revenge. So, what if the Rogue Sage had come along and corrupted the Book of Wisdom in order to find him and bring him back?

Arturo knew as surely as he'd known anything that this must be what was happening, because that was exactly how he would have written it as a story.

If Mwamba wanted him to stay and play the author here, he was going to do just that, even if it felt somewhat ridiculous.

There was only one problem now, he considered, as he took one final shot and placed the glass on the table. He gave Robin and Centauri a tired but contented smile, feeling the hot liquid setting his insides aflame in all the best ways.

Having a suspicion about who was causing problems for the Book of Wisdom was one thing.

If he was going to do any good here, he had to confirm it by finding the man, proving he was alive, and stopping him before he could do any more harm.

CHAPTER TWENTY-FOUR
UNDERGROWTH

Helia pushed through the tangle of leaves and branches around the gateway to the Maze and pulled the others along with her. Together they collapsed on the ground and took off their blindfolds, blinking in the afternoon sunlight.

The two brothers were very different. One was shorter than the other, with brown tufts of hair that were now matted with pollen, and a long, strong nose splitting his wide face. His eyes flickered guiltily between Helia and Nu, clearly wondering which one of them was going to start hurling accusations at him first. Yet, wearily, he also seemed to have accepted whatever they would deal him.

His brother, the taller one, swept a hand through his surprisingly immaculate blond hair and scooted on his behind closer to his sibling.

"Dzin didn't do it. It's all a mistake, and maybe we shouldn't have run, but we had no choice. There was a fire beast at the laboratory, and Dzin only just got away with his life. I won't allow you to take him back."

"We're not here to take anybody back," Nu said. "Are we, Helia?"

Helia held up a tired hand, knowing the brother was about to continue his protests no matter what she said.

She addressed the shorter man instead. "Whatever happened, I believe you are innocent in all this, Dzin. Now, please tell me: Do you still have the formula?"

The shorter man blinked. "How did you get us out of there?"

"Excuse me?" Helia asked.

"I'm serious," Dzin said, looking toward the Maze and then back to Helia. "That is a place of magic, designed to protect the First Forest and the Great Tree. Only Runners should be able to navigate it as well as you just did. Yet you are no Runner."

"No, I'm not. But that's a story for another day. Now, please tell me: Do you have the formula?"

Dzin blinked in confusion, then turned to his brother. "Yantuz?"

Yantuz shrugged. "You might as well show them."

Dzin reached into his coat and retrieved a crushed but intact scroll. "You mean this?"

Helia could have laughed had she not been so exhausted. She settled for a grateful nod.

"That's it."

"You've come after us just for my formula?"

"Not just the formula but also you as well, Dzin. You just became one of the most important people in this realm—and all the others, for that matter."

Dzin shared a confused look with his brother.

"Are you suggesting we're *not* in trouble after all?" Yantuz asked.

"Oh, I wouldn't say that, boys," Helia said, getting to her feet. She gestured to them and Nu to do the same. "Listen, we won't go back to the Great Tree right now. I don't think any of us fancy another little escapade like that. We should regroup somewhere else."

Her gaze was drawn to the horizon, where she could see an unmistakable shimmer of a settlement nestled among the scrub of the rolling hills. Beyond it rose a vast cloud, within which shadows of mountains could be seen, but it was the towers of the town that drew her eye. Beanstalks, she knew. A clump of tall, thick emerald stems that lifted from the center of the place and twisted into the skies above it. A marker of somewhere she was familiar with.

Undergrowth.

She hadn't been there in a while, but that she knew the town gave her some comfort it could be a good next step. There was only one way to know for sure. She looked to Nu, who was staring at the town intently.

Then she turned back and dipped her head ever so slightly. An unspoken understanding passed between them—one Helia knew all too well. Nu could feel things, the truth of what came next. Helia had experienced it enough with Xav over the years, and it was eerily familiar to see it again so soon after losing him.

Yet it was a comfort too.

"Decision made, then," she said to the brothers. "Come on. We've got a walk ahead of us if we're to reach Undergrowth before nightfall."

The tavern was housed in an abandoned beehive—one the size of a warehouse, full of cracks and holes and the chill of the breeze as it blew through.

Dzin tried not to look too hard at the level of disrepair threatening to bring the place down around them: the beams above them cracked and rotting, the honeycomb roof itself blackened and crumbling, allowing a splattering of rain to fall in right beside their table.

It was certainly not of a quality similar to the establishments he frequented back at the Great Tree.

I wonder if I'll ever see them again.

He shuffled further up the bench toward Helia, who was nursing a hollowed-out chestnut mug full of a clear drink that smelled like potent wine.

"We better make this quick," she said, glancing over the rim of her mug at the gaunt, shadowy figures at the other tables in the room, each of whom sat nestling their own drinks and talking in hushed whispers. Her fingers played with the small sphere in the amulet at her neck. Dzin wondered if that was her way of calming herself, much like the way he rolled his walking staff back and forth between his thumb and forefinger when he was nervous.

Much like he was doing now.

Helia's gaze came to rest on Yantuz. "There were no nicer places to talk?"

Even in this darkened room, Dzin noted his brother was a picture. A handsome and glowing face, full of trust and love and loyalty. Of course the two strangers had taken a shine to him already.

"You said you wanted to be discreet," Yantuz said with a wry smile. "This looked like the best place to do that. Besides, the Queen's Nest is homely, and the drinks are drinkable. And we don't stand out, despite our unkempt appearances." He looked around at each of them. It was true. It looked like they'd been dragged through several hedges sideways, which wasn't far from the truth. "What better surroundings could you need for our discussion?"

"A roof without holes maybe?" Nu replied. A heavy raindrop hit the floor and splattered them all. "I fear we may leave this place in *more* of a state than when we arrived."

As the good-natured back-and-forth continued, Dzin warmed his hands over his own drink. The sweet smell of steaming chocolate wafted through his fingers, and he breathed it in, feeling the warmth slide down the back of his throat and soothe his nerves. He wasn't quite sure how he was still functioning after his misadventures so far. The anxiety was there, but it was quiet for the moment. There was something about these two women that he liked and trusted.

The steaming chocolate helped too.

He followed it up with another delicious sip and sighed contently at the sugary tingle, enjoying the little taste of comfort amid the chaos of everything else. Relishing the lack of anxiety that usually caused him so much grief.

"We need to talk about the formula," Nu said.

And now it's back, he thought with an inward sigh.

During the long walk through the scrubland next to the Maze, Nu and Helia had filled him and Yantuz in on what had happened at the Great Tree. They had listened in shock as they learned that the booming noises they'd heard while trapped in the flower had been the airships and refinery blowing up. Dzin felt himself go as pale as was possible when

Helia told them about the Rose Garden and the missing dragon—and then paler still when she told them the Elixir of Life was no longer working now that its connection to the magic of the Rose Garden was severed.

He had still been a little woozy from the pollen in the flower, but even so, he couldn't believe what he was hearing. He kept repeating, "But the Elixir always works . . . it *always* works," while Yantuz had been urging him to return immediately to help their community, despite understanding the scrutiny the two of them might face.

Dzin had felt guilty enough to consider it.

But Helia had once again persuaded them against a trip back through the Maze, convincing them that a drink in Undergrowth would allow his mind to clear. They could all catch an airship back after they'd spoken.

So onward they'd walked, reaching Undergrowth as evening fell. A town where the balance was definitely in favor of nature, leaving humans to squirrel their buildings away in between the giant beanstalks and hide their bustling streets beneath the canopies of leaves.

Dzin had more or less recovered his senses, which meant that as soon as Nu reminded them of what they needed to discuss, his nerves had been quick to return.

"What do you want to know?" he asked reluctantly, wanting to unburden himself of whatever information he had, but not entirely eager to think about what had happened. He was still reeling from the experience. The stink of charred flesh still clung to the back of his nose, and in his mind, he could still see that vicious beast's teeth as it tore the other students apart.

What had that thing been? And where had it come from?

Ever since he heard about the acts of sabotage at the Great Tree, he had been wondering about that in particular. He bristled at the thought that someone had sent that beast deliberately into the laboratory to end them all. But who?

His mind went straight to the advisor of the Chief Scientist. The man with the strange silver eye. But that made no sense. Why would one of the most powerful people at the Great Tree want to destroy the laboratory and everyone in it?

"Tell us again what happened. You mentioned you were at the laboratory when it caught fire?" Helia asked.

"I was there when it happened, yes. But it did not just catch fire. Things don't just 'catch fire.' It was set ablaze by a creature. One that then set upon my friends." He paused and shook his head. "The fire beast, or whatever you want to call it . . . that's what caused the blaze and killed them. It just appeared out of nowhere."

Nu's bracelet seemed to buzz against the table. Dzin and Yantuz both stared at it, but Nu quickly covered it up and smiled.

"Why did you run?" Helia asked.

Dzin picked up the staff that had been resting on his lap and held it up.

"I survived only because I had my staff in hand, and I was able to fend off the beast. But when the guards turned up, the creature just disappeared."

"And they thought you were responsible?"

"They did. But who can blame them? Who else could they point the finger at other than the one surviving student?"

"And you?" Helia asked Yantuz. "Why are you here?"

Yantuz took a swig of his drink and smiled sweetly. "I'm tagging along for the drinks and to make sure my older brother doesn't get into any more accidental trouble."

Helia took a thoughtful sip of her wine, then cradled the glass in her hands. She turned back to Dzin.

"Okay then. Tell me about your formula."

"What do you want to know? I've spent many rotations researching ingredients, gathering those I needed, and then crafting a specific formula to create my own version of the Elixir of Life. Same as any student in the history of the Botanical Education School. We create our Elixirs, and then they are produced en masse in the refinery. Until such time as they expire and a new batch of students is needed to create their versions."

"Right. And would it be easy to brew your particular Elixir again?"

Dzin's brow furrowed as he recalled the last few months of brewing and rebrewing his own unique formula. Late nights and early mornings, poring over his desk at the laboratory, scribbling adjustments to quantities and ways to mix things together.

Easy? None of it had been easy. And yet nobody else really understood the effort that went into it. They only saw the end result or the Elixir itself. They didn't see everything that led up to the finished creation.

"My Elixir?" he repeated, and Helia nodded. "Yes, I suppose. I managed to rescue my scroll, so that's an important part. Most of the ingredients are quite common, although, of course, each Elixir requires a very distinct use of each one. There were only two ingredients that proved difficult for me to get. But what does it matter? With the refinery at the Great Tree gone, we can't brew anything anyway, not on a large scale to replace what we've lost. And if the existing Elixirs have lost their magic, how can we know that a new batch would even work?"

Helia chewed her lip thoughtfully. "We don't, but I don't really see any other choice. We have to try to make another Elixir. *Your* Elixir. I need it to recover my memory of what happened in the Rose Garden. Those missing moments, I think, will tell me where Perennia went. I think it's the only way we can track her down and save her, which we must if we are to fight back against the evil that visited your world today." She leaned across the table, placing her drink down, and put a hand on his. To his surprise, he realized it had been shaking as he clutched his mug, causing little drops of spilled chocolate to fan out in a circle across the table. "I'm sorry to drop all this responsibility on you, Dzin. But I need your help. We are lucky you grabbed your scroll and ran. You now hold the only formula to the Elixir of Life in existence. We just need you to brew it. To help me remember. Can you do it?"

Dzin stared in confusion and horror, feeling the pressure almost like a physical weight pressing down on his shoulders, holding him in place, not allowing him to move or breathe freely. His hand was no longer shaking under Helia's gentle touch, but inside he still felt the waves of panic breaking on the shore of his sanity, threatening to overwhelm him.

It was a lot to take in. For a few moments he couldn't respond, as he fought to maintain control of himself. The storm swirled and raged, but thankfully didn't hit him this time.

Counting slowly in his head, he waited until there was a break in the tide.

He took a breath and was relieved to find he could finally move.

Helia let his hand go. "Dzin?"

He nodded. "I'm sorry. Yes. We can try. The only problem with re-creating the formula will be those two rare ingredients I mentioned. One was particularly unique to my family, and"—his eyes went wide, and he immediately shoved a hand into his coat pocket, before excitedly pulling out a handful of mushrooms—"and it turns out I accidentally brought that one with me! So that was lucky."

"We were due some luck. So, what's the other rare ingredient?"

His excitement dropped. "Well, that's just the thing. The core part of any formula for the Elixir is an ingredient from the Rose Garden. The Cerulean Rose. Which is hard to take a cutting from at the best of times because it blooms very rarely and never in the same place . . ."

Helia nodded patiently, although he could see the frustration in her eyes. "And this isn't the best of times, because the entire Garden has been burned away. Can the Cerulean Rose be found anywhere else?"

"I don't think so. I'm so sorry."

Helia and Nu shared a glance that indicated they were feeling the same heightened emotions of panic and anxiety that he was used to experiencing most days, blowing around inside him. He noticed Yantuz staring into the distance, drumming his fingers on the table thoughtfully.

Just as Dzin was about to tell him to stop, his brother did.

"I think I know someone who can help us," Yantuz said.

"You do?"

"Yes, remember that Runner at the School a couple of cycles ago? The one you told me about, who intimidated you, but who I secretly think you liked."

"Um, oh, well, I don't know if I said anything about—"

"Oh, come on. You remember the one. She was tall and loud. Ended up getting kicked out and getting work here in Undergrowth."

Dzin sat for a moment, trying to think.

"You know her," Nu said suddenly. She was looking at him with a strange, quizzical pull to her lips and a gaze that bore into him, as though she saw something nobody else did. Yantuz saw what she was doing and raised his eyebrows but said nothing. "You know the name, Dzin. Just think."

Suddenly, it popped into his head, and he sat straight up, bucking the bench and almost sending Yantuz flying.

His brother cursed under his breath, and Dzin pointed his finger in the air. "Rascal Troy! That's right, that's right—that's the one. Well remembered, brother. Oh yes, she was a hell of a Runner and always regaling us with stories of her adventures."

"Which you'd always come home to bore us with," Yantuz added as he mopped up his spilled drink.

"Fine, yes, maybe I did. Regardless, Rascal always made a great show of telling us the secret places she'd discovered ingredients, over all the time she'd been a Runner. It got to the point where she actually started helping the students with their research, dropping hints about where they needed to go to locate whatever they needed."

Dzin thought back to how he'd often hoped he might run into Rascal when he was deep in a panic about that final ingredient, before Tywich had ended up helping him. He wondered whether she would have known to take him to the roots of the Tree to find what he needed— that the key was the mushrooms, grown in this particular area that was close to his dear parents.

The mushrooms had seemingly worked, and though it had been a close call, he was happy with how it had turned out. He hadn't been able to test the formula like he might normally, because of the time constraints. But Tywich had assured him it would be fine.

It was something Dzin hadn't thought anything of at the time, simply too relieved to have made it and that he'd been able to graduate. His mind was already racing ahead to the logistics needed to collect and farm his ingredients—now that he knew what they all were—to allow the refinery to brew his Elixir for the masses.

Thinking back now, though, he felt anxiety growing deep in the pit of his stomach. Had the last batch even worked? Could he pull it off again?

I'm the only Runner left, he thought. *I have no choice.*

"She lives here?" Helia asked.

"Huh? Who?" Dzin snapped back to the conversation. "Oh, Rascal! Yes, I think so. She left the Great Tree, which is unusual for retired Runners, as they usually stick around in some capacity. Some become teachers. Others end up managing operations in the refinery or take jobs transporting the vials around Silvyra. Last we heard, this is where she'd come to work."

"And you think she might know where to find another location for the Cerulean Rose?"

"I think if anyone would know, she would."

"Great. Then let's go find her."

Helia pushed back from the table and gestured for the others to follow her.

CHAPTER TWENTY-FIVE
THE BOOK POISON

"I keep coming back to the poison."

Arturo, Robin, and Centauri wandered the third-floor balcony that overlooked the Main Concourse. Arturo paused to watch a flock of flying contraptions shoot past. The Volare, Robin had called them. They acted as messengers of a sort and were of so many different specifications — hefty and minuscule, mechanical and magical—they presented a bizarre yet wondrous sight. He was starting to get used to those.

"Ah, the *poison*," Robin responded, waving her hands before her theatrically, her voice booming out across the open space, causing more than a few heads to turn their way. "It was the Rogue, in the Library, with the arsenic! Elementary, my dear Arturo."

She burst out laughing. He narrowed his eyes and gestured for her to walk faster to keep pace as his brain ticked over.

"Are you always like this?" he asked.

"What do you mean?"

"You wanted me to be serious. I'm here being serious. Why not the poison?"

Robin blew out her cheeks as she glanced at the floor, frowned again, then twirled away. "Because there's no evidence to suggest that's what the Rogue Sage was looking for or even if he managed to re-create it. We've certainly seen no sign of it here. We've been over as much of the Library as two people can reasonably explore in one afternoon. Centauri has talked with the Volare. You and I have talked with the scholars. Nobody has seen anything out of the ordinary or unusual. If there is book poison at work here, enough to corrupt the Book of Wisdom, surely there would be a sign of it somewhere. Things would be going *wrong*."

"You said yourself this place is huge, a city even. We have barely scratched the surface."

"All true, Arturo. And yet without the Book being able to communicate, our Orbs can't tap into her vast repository of knowledge. She would be able to tell us if she could. But she can't, which is the whole problem."

Now it was his turn to be funny. "You're not thinking like an author."

She stuck out her tongue and kept walking. He grinned at Centauri, who flashed pleasantly, clearly having warmed to him.

Despite the looming threat that hung over their heads, Arturo was enjoying the change from his usual Earthbound routine. In his work here, he wasn't trying to shoehorn words into some campaign he didn't really care about; he was trying to undo the knots of a real-life story, working backward along the plot points to deduce just how it all fit together—and all against this wondrous backdrop of Orbs and Sages and magic and so many damned books; he might as well be in heaven.

Robin, for her part, was keeping him amused and in good spirits. She seemed to have an energy about her that infused everyone around her with a glow. He could almost see it coming off her in waves. People she touched, even barely—a tap to the shoulder or a handshake with a friend—all drifted away, seemingly happier for the meeting.

She had explained to him that all Sages had powers based on the talents they'd shown on Earth, that their Orbs had selected them on this basis to fulfill a greater destiny in the Library. Although Robin hadn't confirmed what she was the Sage of just yet, Arturo knew this quality was linked to it. A wave of happiness or kindness of some sort. He wondered what that meant.

"Let's go back to the beginning," he replied patiently. "There is a trail, Robin. One that leads from the Book of Wisdom to wherever the problem currently is, and right now that's our main concern. If we can find the source of the problem, we'll probably then pick up a trail that leads us to the man who created it in the first place."

"What do you mean?"

"Just that we need to follow the narrative. In this case, it's one that suggests we'll find a Sage at the end of it."

"The Rogue Sage, though, right?" Robin stopped short, causing Centauri to bump into her head. She frowned at her Orb, then turned back to Arturo. "Let's be clear that it can't be any of us current Sages, okay?"

His face flushed. "Oh, of course, I didn't mean to point the finger at you or accuse your colleagues!" He spread his hands wide as he tried to better illustrate his point. "If you were the culprit, it's unlikely you'd put yourself in this position, and if you'd had anything to do with sabotaging the Book, I'm pretty sure Centauri would have alerted another Orb. I would also wager you'd vouch for every one of the Sages you currently work with."

"I would."

Arturo smiled. "That's good! Which means the person we're looking for isn't *currently* a Sage. And as far as Mwamba knows, there is only one in the history of the Sages who could be suspected of doing anything out of the ordinary, a fact we've just proven in our research. This rogue was visiting places forbidden to him. We don't know why, but the likelihood is that it was for bad reasons. The fact he is said to be dead shouldn't throw us off the trail. It's too convenient."

"So, we assume he's alive. What about the lack of evidence for the poison?"

"Ah-ha!" he said. It was now his turn for the theatrics. He raised his finger like those television detectives when they finally get to the crux of the point. "Out of everything we've learned, the poison stands out as the most likely research he'd been undertaking on the sly, and it's the only substance that we've found that could theoretically affect the Book of Wisdom—which is still an inanimate object, for the most part, don't forget. The thing about poison is that it isn't always fast-acting. There are plenty of examples in history of slow-release poisons that have been used to great, horrible effect, while helping to hide the killer's tracks. A drop in a drink here, a dab onto someone's skin there . . . just enough to set things in motion, but not enough to make them keel over and die just yet."

He glanced to the side to see Robin's expression suddenly lighten. She'd finally understood what he was getting at. "The Book of Wisdom is still operating. It can't communicate, but everything else is still working for the moment."

"For the moment," he repeated with a nod, gesturing for her to continue.

"And what we're looking for isn't some wide-ranging damage but a single drop—a specialized event."

"It'll be a little bigger than a drop, I think. But certainly small enough to have gone unnoticed so far—until the poison spreads, that is, and we start to see more of its effects."

"You think there is more to come?"

"It is likely. Which means the quicker we can identify where the poison has been unleashed, the better. We might have a chance at identifying it and finding an antidote." He stopped and scratched his beard, looking down over the bustling Concourse below. For a moment, he watched a workshop of students, who were undertaking the reconstruction of what looked like holographic dinosaur bones. "Tell me, Robin: If you think of the Great Library as a body, what would you say the Book of Wisdom is as a part of the whole?"

"The Book of Wisdom guides us when we are lost. It provides the knowledge of the Author within it. So I'd say it's probably the brain of the whole operation." She stood beside him and looked down, thinking for a moment. "But the operations of the Great Library, the interconnectivity of our Orbs, it's all linked back to the Book. They run through it like blood through the heart. So I guess it's a bit of both?"

He nodded, glad she had agreed with the direction his mind had also led him.

"Well, I don't know about you, but I've seen enough crime shows to know that when you fictionally poison someone, you should try to do it subtly. So I would imagine you want to target a place on the body that's obscure. Somewhere that nobody will ever think to look. The last place anyone will suspect could be the source of the issue."

"I was never a big fan of such shows growing up, but I think I know what you're getting at. The place we're looking for isn't going to be anywhere close to the paths most traveled . . ."

"Right. So where are the parts of the Great Library that don't get a lot of visitors? Important parts, but out of the way? Somewhere like the Chamber of Chronicles, but older."

"Somewhere forgotten?"

"Exactly."

Robin's eyeline drifted off into the distance. Then her eyes lit up, and she turned back to him excitedly. "I think I know just the place!"

"Good work, Watson."

"It's old and quite well hidden. We'll have to take the tram."

He nodded. "Show me."

CHAPTER TWENTY-SIX
RASCAL THE RUNNER

It had taken the better part of the next day to track down Rascal.

Thankfully, she was known in these parts. Most Runners—even those who had left the job—passed through Undergrowth often enough. It was the closest town to the Great Tree, so it was common that they would frequent the taverns and market stalls here on their travels when they were searching for ingredients. Yet despite what they were told by barkeepers and traders, Rascal was in none of the places she was supposed to be—not at the job she was working down at the rigging yard, not even at the inn she frequented.

No, it turned out she was some way out of the city, in the even grungier outskirts, trying to earn enough for whatever kind of life former Runners like her lived after leaving the Great Tree. And so the group had finally found its way to a half-submerged warehouse in the center of swampland, where a party of violence was underway.

Helia and the others stood in the center of the warehouse, feeling the thudding base of the music shudder through the grimy pipes that twisted around the walls like the intestines of a mechanical being.

In the corner, two women were busy creating the tunes on a platform where they twisted and stretched to touch floating bells and pluck at strings of light that were webbed all around them. As the music was driven to its climax, one of them, with wickedly straight dark hair, threw her arms up and closed her eyes. Fire exploded out of her hands, before forming thousands of tiny radiant fireflies, which swarmed together to create a stunning image of a celestial supernova over the crowd.

The other woman, with sweeps of sandy locks drifting past her shoulders, mixed in another pounding rhythm beneath the noise to crank up the tempo. The heavenly vision rippled as the dazzling fireflies beat their tiny wings in time to the music, before they vanished in a sudden explosive flash, at which point stardust began to fall across the dance floors, to the great roar of the crowd.

And what a crowd it was. A mass of people swaying to the music, lifting their hands up to the sheer white petals, while dancing around the magical snakes of smoke that slid in and around them, pulsing and feeding off their energy, giving off a multicolored glow that intensified the atmosphere.

But it was what was in the center of the chaos that held Helia's focus. A dome of thorns amid the people. A makeshift arena. And inside, two fighters beating the hell out of each other.

Helia did her best to hold back the grimace that kept trying to force its way onto her face, a feat helped a little by the fact she wasn't the only one of them who found this distasteful. Dzin, too, was slack-jawed, unable to take his gaze off the tall, gray-haired warhorse of a woman and lithe, tattooed man who were punching, kicking, and elbowing each other as they circled the ring like wild animals.

"Is that Rascal?" Helia asked, gesturing to the woman.

Dzin nodded. "It is," he said.

Helia could only just hear him over the roar of the crowd, the jeers amplifying in volume as the man attempted to headbutt his opponent, only for the woman to throw her shoulder up, breaking his nose. Dzin winced as blood speckled her skin. "This isn't right though. The Great Tree is the center of our world, and Mother looks after everyone beyond the First Forest and the Maze too. To have this debacle happening so close to her boundaries . . . and involving a former Runner. Ours is a society that revolves around helping each other and ourselves. Around peace, not violence!"

Helia thought back to the Rose Garden and Xavier. The ash falling from the sky. The blank-eyed stare of the man who had killed Xav.

"And yet violence seems to follow like a shadow wherever humans move," she replied as the man in the ring suddenly pulled a secret knife out of his boot and slashed the woman's forearm, sending a spurt of blood arching across the green cage. The plants wrapping around each other, forming the arena, suddenly spasmed and writhed in pleasure, soaking up the blood—they had clearly been placed here to keep the place clean. The thought of how much blood they must have consumed over the years made Helia shiver. "Unfortunately, violence cannot be escaped, Dzin. Only fought and defeated. Even in this world of yours."

"You mean *ours*?" Yantuz had stopped nodding in time to the beat and was now staring at her with a frown.

Helia ignored him and turned her attention back to the fight. The chaos inside the cage had grown tenfold. The man's face was a bloody mess, but he kept up his attack with the knife, swishing it before him to try to cut his opponent even more. Rascal feinted and ducked as she tried to draw him into an attack. Once, twice more, she was cut across her arms and side, before she clearly got fed up.

To the gasps of the crowd, the clothes on the woman's back tore open to reveal two metal wings. Helia and the others stared in shock as they unfolded and glinted under the light, before they slapped the man on both sides of his head and he dropped unconscious to the floor, bleeding from his ears.

Helia knew there had been a few Runners in the past who had grafted wings onto their backs after visiting the realm of Adscendo. She'd never seen any of them before though. Peering closer, she could see that these were attached deeply, intertwined with the very essence of this powerful and intimidating woman. Likely connected directly to her nerves and mind, so she had full control of their movement and power.

It was a transformation that Helia knew must have hurt. Which meant Rascal was tougher than she'd already proven and was not to be messed with.

"Shall we go talk to Rascal now?" Nu asked, watching the man being dragged from the arena.

A gust of wind forced them all backward as the woman spun around inside the cage, wings still raised high, and grabbed the thorny, blood-sucking brambles in front of her, pushing her face between the barbs. It was as if she was about to tear the cage wide open and gobble them all up like a giant from a children's story.

Her bloodied lips parted in a grin. "And who exactly wants to talk to me?"

"I don't believe it," Rascal said again, aghast at what she'd just been told.

"I'm afraid it's all true," Dzin replied as patiently as he could. His anxiety was bubbling beneath the surface again, and it was all he could do to tamper it and keep talking. Being back in the presence of Rascal Troy was an experience. She was considered a legend among the Runners and feared in equal measure.

They were now in the fighters' rooms. Rascal had put on a pair of nonbloodied boots and was folding her impressive, deadly wings.

"The Rose Garden has been burned? Thousands of Elixirs have been blown up, and the remaining ones don't work anymore? All the formulas except yours have been destroyed? *And* you need me to help you find an ingredient to brew a brand-new Elixir in order for this woman here"—she pointed to Helia—"to remember what happened to Perennia, who is now missing?"

"When you put it like that, it sounds ridiculous. But that's about the size of the problem we're facing, yes."

"You spin a hell of a tale, my friend. I'll give you that. And you say we've met before?"

Dzin felt his cheeks burn. "Once or twice, back at the Botanical School."

"Hmmm," Rascal replied, looking none the wiser. "If you say so."

Helia cleared her throat and spoke up. "Unfortunately, the tale is the truth. The archives, the laboratory, the airships, and the refinery—it's all lost. I was there in the Garden when it fell, too, although I can't remember some of it. I took a knock, I think. If I could unlock my memories, it might help us find the dragon."

The former Runner leaned back against the rusted, graffiti-stained wall. Around them, other fighters of all sizes and builds were gathering to try their luck inside the cage as the grizzled ringmaster took their entry fees and matched them up with no real care for equality.

"Seems like a reasonably easy job for any Runner of the Tree." She harrumphed loudly.

Then she tugged on a long leaf-leather coat and stood up, towering over the four of them, who remained seated. Her shadow seemed to envelop them.

"Why'd you seek me out? There are other Runners to be found in Undergrowth, those who still run the ingredients for Mother and who get paid for it too. I haven't been one in some cycles now, not since the Chief Scientist and I had a . . . let's say *disagreement*."

Dzin sighed. "It's the Cerulean Rose we're seeking."

"Which is only found in the Rose Garden."

"Uh-huh."

"The Rose Garden that no longer exists."

"You can see our problem," Yantuz said. "Dzin suggested you might know where it could possibly be found elsewhere."

Rascal shook her head, her brow pinched and jaw set hard. "Well, I just don't know. The Cerulean Rose is rare at the best of times, only blooming once a cycle, for what amounts to the barest blink of an eye. Even if the Rose Garden *was* still around, it would be a tricky ask. I don't rightly know what you can do. It can't be found anywhere else. I'm sorry, but I can't help you. Now, leave me be. I'm going to collect my winnings."

She was about to move, but Nu immediately rose and stood in her way. Dzin held his breath, watching as Nu, the younger sapling, faced off against the mighty oak—a mismatch if ever he'd seen one. Yet the strange young woman held her ground and talked in a clear, low voice that only the gathered group could hear.

"Yes, you can help us."

She had that look in her eyes again. The one she had used on Dzin earlier, a look that seemed to suggest she saw more beneath the surface.

Not for the first time, Dzin wondered just who these women were.

To his surprise, Rascal raised a hand in surrender and stepped back from the confrontation. Her pale, scratched cheeks began to grow flush.

"It only grows in the Rose Garden, but I might know where we can find a seed," she began, then cleared her throat. The complete change in her demeanor was clear now. She seemed nervous, although why that might be, Dzin couldn't tell. She couldn't possibly have been afraid of Nu. "That said, I would advise against seeking it out, as the seed won't get you what you want straight away. You'd have to wait until it grew."

"You don't need to worry about that," Helia said, straightening. The hope in her voice was plain to hear. "Where is it?"

Rascal sighed, reluctant to say.

"Rascal?"

"All right, fine. It's in the kingdom of the Raptor Prince. But . . . he will not give it up for anything. He is a proud and difficult man to bargain with, a ruler who lives to enjoy himself, ensuring he has the very best of everything while the rest of his city fights for the scraps. He paid handsomely for the seedling many moons ago. I believe three chests of pearls were traded for the honor of its possession. It is now kept as the pride of his collection, in the highest chamber of the Clockwork Mountain. In the desert to the west."

"The Clockwork Mountain?" Helia repeated, looking to Nu. "I've heard stories of that place. So that's our destination, is it?"

What she was looking for in her young friend, Dzin didn't know. But it seemed as though Nu had been expecting Helia's unspoken question. She gave Rascal a penetrating gaze, a look that was so powerful there was actually weight to it, before she turned back and nodded.

A glimpse of pride flashed across Helia's face and something definitive passed between them. A moment of admiration and respect. Mentor to student, Dzin realized, having remembered just how it had been with him and Tywich.

"It won't matter if you go," Rascal said. "Even if you had more pearls than he paid, he will not part with the seed."

"Why pearls?" Nu asked.

"It's the currency here," Helia replied, standing to join her. She touched her amulet and rubbed it between her fingers as though for comfort, as she did often. "Pearls of all shapes and sizes, collected from the very bottom of Silvyra's oceans." She turned to Rascal. "As for the Prince and his seedling, we will simply have to travel to seek an audience with him at the Clockwork Mountain. Runner Rascal, thank you for your help."

"Wait!" Rascal replied, a little too loudly. Even in the din around them, it drew a few looks. She glared at each and every one of the inquisitive faces until they looked away; then she stepped back to the group, less imposing this time, more a willing participant. Dzin noticed she was staring at Helia's necklace with an air of puzzled recognition. She lowered her voice. "If the journey to the Rose Garden is hard, the one that lies in the desert would be even harder. It is not one that can be made on foot. You would have to acquire an airship."

"Which we can do here," Helia replied, eager to be off.

"But not just any airship." Rascal stopped her again. "You need one fast and maneuverable enough to get past the Rock Giants."

"Excuse me?"

Dzin and Yantuz looked at each other and simultaneously mouthed— *the what?*

"The Rock Giants . . . they hide in the desert sands, camouflaged, ready to protect the Clockwork Mountain from her enemies, which are many and varied."

Helia raised an eyebrow, to which Rascal replied with a shrug.

"And yes, those enemies have included me in the past. Still. If I must face that place again, I will. Not going to lie, it won't be easy, but I can get you into the mountain. We just need a certain type of airship, especially for a mission of your *specialized* requirements."

Helia looked the woman up and down, clearly unsure about her change of heart. In the end, though, she seemed to give into any doubts she was having. Having someone on their team with her particular skills would certainly be a benefit should they encounter any issues.

Even Dzin knew it was a risk worth taking.

"Do you have one in mind?" Helia asked.

"Oh, there is only one I ever have in mind for such things," Rascal replied with half a grin. "The *Golden Oriole*. The fastest and sleekest airship in these lands and beyond. A ship I used to frequent myself, in fact."

Helia nodded and gestured for the others to get ready to leave. "And where can we catch this airship of yours?"

Rascal's wings twitched as she pointed up to the top of the beanstalk towers. They all followed her gaze, to where two thin vines ran from the top of the towers off into the distance, gaining height before disappearing into a murky cloud. Tiny pods were swinging wildly beneath these lines caught in the winds at such a height. Some moving one way. Some another.

Dzin caught a glimpse of a shadowy peak at the end of the line.

"The bridge?" he asked, his blood running cold.

Rascal gave him a grin he didn't much care for.

CHAPTER TWENTY-SEVEN
THE BRIDGE

Nu was beginning to worry that Dzin wasn't doing so well.

He'd made a bit of a fuss as they'd taken a variety of lifts and stairs up the inside of the beanstalk tower and then the outside.

"But it's one of the most dangerous skyports in the whole of Silvyra," he had said, in between puffs of exertion as they reached the top of another spiral staircase. "The airships don't even stop there for fear of being buffeted against the cliffs if they linger too long! The wind at those heights wore down the rock itself, creating the bridge. The arch. Whatever you want to call it. How exactly are we supposed to catch this ship of yours?"

"I have a plan," was all Rascal would say.

The discussion carried on even as they reached the top of the towers and waited on the viewing platform that circled around the stalk. Nu took in the stunning view. Undergrowth sprawling beneath them. The Maze and the First Forest in the distance behind them, with the Great Tree looming large at their center, even seen from these many miles away.

Ahead—and above—constant, swirling clouds hiding the mountain range Dzin was worried about. And everywhere else fields and plains and hills, rivers and lakes.

Nu figured if she spent a week up here, she might still be finding new things to look at. Quite a sight for a girl who'd grown up inside. Yes, she loved her home. The Great Library was a magnificent, grand place, and she would never think ill of it. But this was a level of openness and freedom she had never expected. It was one thing to know what existed out there, to read about it in books and hear the Sages spin tales of their adventures in such worlds. Experiencing it for herself, however, triggered a wave of emotions. Her heart felt simultaneously awed and excited; there was a rush within her chest at both intimidation by the expanse and an eagerness to explore and breathe it in. The adrenaline made her feel more alive than she'd ever known.

Soon enough they were contained within one of the lumpy pod vehicles—like the hollowed-out shell of a giant Halloween pumpkin— that was dangling from the vines of this strange transport system. The pod had been made big enough to fit four people quite comfortably.

It was unfortunate they had five.

Especially considering one of their number was Rascal.

The formidable woman was hunched over, her knees almost up to her chest in an effort not to take up too much space. Her wing tips twitched above her shoulder, compressed as far as they would go. It was a sight that would have made Nu grin had she not predicted it could cause more of a wobble in the pod than the wind buffeting them as they traveled high above the land.

Rascal explained the transport as some kind of pulley process. Two counterbalanced vines stretched from the beanstalk towers to the mountain in the clouds, and beneath them were rows of the pods. Half of them were going up, half of them were coming down, with the gravity and weight of the downward vine helping to move the upward vine to its destination.

"It's just like a funicular," Helia had explained quietly. "There are plenty of them back home, including the town near where I'm from. It's an ingenious and energy-efficient system, using the weight and gravity on one side to pull up the other. We could do with seeing more of them around the world."

Nu nodded, still watching Dzin. He sat opposite her, and thanks to Rascal's bulk beside him, he had his face pressed against one of the windows. Unsurprisingly, he looked fairly anxious. Especially as they climbed higher and the wind increased. His fingers gripped his knees, knuckles whitening every time the pod swung wildly.

"Are you sure this is safe?" he asked again as the pod shook, which pushed them to an uncomfortable angle. "Is it tied on okay? Have any of these fallen?"

Rascal, wedged in between him and Yantuz, couldn't move much, so she gave him a sidelong frown.

"Sparks and seeds, Dzin," she said. "It's perfectly safe. People in Undergrowth take these all the time up and down to the bridge and the mountain farms of Galnaterra. How do you think they get the produce down from those terraces to the town and the goods back up to the airships? Not all these pods are filled with people, you know. Some are carrying far more weight, and they are doing just fine."

"I heard a story about one of these breaking free and falling." Dzin ignored Rascal's reassurance and peered out of the window to the ground below. "And from such a height, it didn't end well."

"We're not going to fall," Helia said. She held her hands on her thighs, one resting over the amulet containing Vega. "I promise you, Dzin. The cable up there is perfectly strong and well connected. I looked at it when we got in. We're going to be safe. Just enjoy the ride!"

The pod shook and tilted wildly again. As Dzin groaned and Rascal snapped at him, Nu leaned in and whispered to Helia, "Is it really okay up there?"

Helia whispered back. "I don't know, but I grew some extra vines around us, just to be sure."

The journey up took roughly an hour. About three-quarters of the way there, they left the skies behind and entered the clouds. There were glimpses below of the land rising with them as they climbed the mountain. There began terraces cut into the slopes, each one filled with crops and the occasional farm building. Further up, the terraces grew from farm to town, with gray rock-cut buildings huddling together as though in protection against the harsh elements up here. Above them, so large it traversed the void between two mountain peaks, a natural stone bridge came into view through the clouds.

"The Bridge of Galnaterra," Rascal said. "We're almost there."

Nu couldn't help but feel relief at that as the wind picked up even more, swinging the pod nearly perpendicular to the vine it was dangling from, causing even Rascal to begin looking worried. The remainder of the ride was completed in silent, collective panic, clutching their seats, while Nu decided Dzin had definitely been making a good point before.

The pod jolted to a halt at their destination and swung back and forth a couple of more times just to really make them feel ill. Rascal reached over and slid the door back to let them out. Yantuz, who had been silent the entire trip, led the way brightly.

"Well, that was fun!"

Rascal hurried him onward as she unfurled herself through the door. "It gets more fun from here," she said.

The view below—as seen through the toes of her boots while she stood as close as she dared to the edge of the bridge—took Nu's breath away.

It was a very, very long way down. Far more than she had envisaged.

Resisting the wind battering her clothes and attempting to coax her into falling, she kept her eyes open, unwilling to give in to the terror of being so high and vulnerable. Antares vibrated against her wrist, still bound to her bracelet, but able to offer a little encouragement and re-assurance.

Nu still couldn't quite understand the Orb. It felt like: *You can do this.* But it might very well have been: *Don't look down.*

She laughed despite herself, and the Orb vibrated again, acknowledging it was the latter. Just that little interaction sent shivers of excitement and pride through her. She had enjoyed a wonderful upbringing in the Great Library, but she'd never felt this special before. She was communicating with an Orb—an actual Sage's Orb! To do that in any capacity back home would have been an honor. Yet here she was, in Paperworld, on an adventure with one.

This didn't make her a Sage, of course. But it felt every bit as wonderful as she had imagined becoming a Sage might.

For a moment, she let her mind drift, dreaming about Antares choosing her for real.

What that might entail. What it would feel like to know she was truly a Sage.

Then the wind shook her again, and she knelt quickly, her fingers clutching the rock.

"How long do we have to wait?" she called to Rascal as the others hung on for dear life beside her. Dzin was almost lying flat on the rock, and right now she didn't really blame him.

"The *Golden Oriole* has a strict schedule to keep," Rascal shouted, trying to make herself heard against the roar of the air being funneled between the two mountain peaks they were straddling. "Before heading to the Clockwork Mountain, it passes through Galnaterra at this exact time. There are changes in the wind here that can be measured, and so the ship needs to be here at the right moment to take advantage of the relative calm."

"But it doesn't actually set down?"

"No. It's too dangerous, so it keeps moving. Picks up and drops off its cargo on the run. Very swift operation. Mightily impressive, if you ask me."

Nu looked to Helia, who was looking a little more concerned about where this was going. But Nu decided that if the older Sage didn't speak up, neither would she.

Dzin, however, was a little slower to piece it together. "We need to board the *Golden Oriole*, but it isn't landing anywhere for us to do that?"

"That's about right. It will pass directly below us without stopping."

"Then . . . I'm sorry, but by the pollen and the petals, how do you claim we can catch the damn thing? Unless we grow wings and glide down, we've no chance of boarding," Dzin said.

Rascal grinned and flexed her wings just enough to indicate what she was thinking.

"I think that's her plan, brother," Yantuz called across brightly.

Dzin's face immediately paled. He looked over the edge, then back to Rascal, then to the others, then back over the edge again. "I don't like this plan."

Rascal laughed and slapped him on the shoulder. "It'll be fine, Dzin. I don't think it'll be that far to jump. I've seen them clear the bridge without as much to spare as the height of the Maze's hedge walls. And let me be clear: The airship is magnificent, a true beauty of the skies, and she's one of the traditional types, too, with her cabin clung below a thoroughly netted balloon. There should be ample landing space, a cushioned fall, and plenty of rope to grip on to. From there, it's a little climb down to the cabin, and we're in."

"Easy for you to say—you have *wings*!" Dzin stumbled backward at the mercy of another hard gust of wind. He knelt and clutched the rock again. "If the rest of us miss the balloon, we'll fall and die. Am I the only one concerned about this act of wanton delirium?" He looked to the others, aghast. "It's a long way down, and I happen to like my bones unbroken."

Nu shook her head. Dzin was right—jumping aboard a moving airship, even if it did have a balloon, was too much of a risk. There had to be a better way.

A flash caught her attention. Vega was communicating with Helia again. Nu watched as the Sage looked around the nooks and crannies of the rock around them, then reached out and touched a thick, leafy plant somehow growing from a deep rut. She tugged at the stalk thoughtfully, feeling it stretch, then patted her bracelet.

"Helia?" Nu asked, wondering what she was thinking.

Helia turned to the others and held up a hand. "Please hold on to the rock, no matter what you're about to see. Do you understand?"

Their confused faces were enough to give her the go-ahead, just as Nu realized what her plan was.

Carefully clutching the stalk between her fingers, Helia closed her eyes and her bracelet glowed as she and Vega channeled their power. At first there was little to see—the growth was so small—but then they all watched as four new shoots emerged from the stalk and began to writhe outward.

Dzin fidgeted nervously, but he clearly worried more about the drop next to him than the long, thin leaves that were unfurling and curling around the group.

Then the growing stopped. Helia let go of the original plant and grabbed one of the leaves that looked a bit like a long, vine-like cord.

"We can use these to drop down there safely," she said. "They're not wings, but the cellular structure of this leaf is sufficiently strong—and, importantly, elasticated—that it will hold our weight as it stretches and shouldn't pull our hands off." She held on to the end of the vine-cord and began wrapping it around her arm, once, twice, then a third time, from just beneath her shoulder down to her wrist. She gave it a good tug. "See? It has some give in it. As long as the airship isn't much lower than the height of the Maze, we should be fine to leap down."

Rascal closed her open mouth. Dzin and Yantuz kept staring.

"What did you just do?" Dzin asked after a moment. He reached out to tentatively touch the closest vine-cord to him, then snapped his hand back as if it might bite him. "You got us out of the Maze alive, which nobody but the Runners should have been able to do. So, I assumed you had some special connection to nature that others do not have. Who *are* you?"

Yet it was Rascal who answered, doing so without yelling. The wind had suddenly grown less fierce.

"It's time. I see the ship!"

A speck appeared and quickly began to grow in form.

The *Golden Oriole* was clearly a magnificent craft, even when spied through the clouds. As it approached, Nu could see the great crimson silks of her balloon shine, with a thin film of moisture beneath the golden rigging, while below hung a sleek wood-and-brass cabin that ran the length of the balloon, resplendent with swirls and symbols along its edges. At the back of the craft, on either side of the trail of steam that drifted from the circular engine, long, flowing golden pennants fluttered. At the front, two small figures could be seen through the thick glass window.

Her rumble grew louder as she approached.

"Quick, wrap the cords around your arm like me," Helia urged the others. "Not too tight; give yourself room to unravel it. The airship is coming slowly, but there will only be a few moments when we can land on the balloon before it passes beneath the bridge."

They did as they were told; then all five of them perched on the edge, with Rascal at the center. She stretched out her wings behind their backs.

"Follow my lead," she said. "We go when the nose of the ship is directly below us. With the momentum, we should land right on her back."

They all readied themselves.

Nu didn't know why she chose that moment to ask the Runner what had been on her mind. It seemed a bit late. And yet if she was going to die here, she didn't want to go without knowing.

"Why are you helping us, Rascal?" she asked as quietly as she could so the others couldn't hear. She could see the golden binding of the airship closing in on the bridge. They were almost at the moment of leaping.

Rascal reached over and tapped Nu's bracelet. "I've met your kind before."

Antares vibrated again, stronger this time.

She knows.

Nu didn't have the capacity to try to hide her surprise or bluster her way through an explanation. It was all she could do to avoid falling off the edge by accident. Thankfully, Rascal didn't allow Nu an opportunity to deny it.

"It was another Sage. He wore a similar piece to your bracelet, with the ball in the center of it. That's an Orb, isn't it?"

"Her name's Antares."

The Orb buzzed again, and Nu felt she was being given a positive message.

Antares didn't seem to mind Rascal's assumption.

The Runner nodded and tapped the bracelet again. "I owed that man my life and promised I would always help his kind. So here we are." She smiled.

"Even though it may cost us our lives."

Nu turned back to face the drop, feeling her fingers begin to sweat as they clutched the vine. "And yet if we don't do this," she said in return, "it will almost certainly end with people dying. Better to risk it for the hope of succeeding than do nothing and give up on hope altogether, eh?"

"Well said." Rascal nodded down to the airship about to cross beneath them. It was much further down than Nu would have liked. She hoped the vine-cords were long enough.

"Ready, everyone?"

"No," Dzin said.

Rascal nudged him, and they all jumped.

Dzin fell.

Over and over, spinning and tumbling through the sky at the end of a vine-cord.

Regret and nausea battling in his head.

Fear and wind buffeting his entire being.

He had been holding his brother's arm for balance when they had jumped. But he'd almost immediately let go as he felt his staff begin to slip out of his waistband. It shouldn't have mattered. His other arm was wrapped in Helia's strange plant.

It had been instinct. The staff was his mother's. The only thing he still had from either of his parents, except his father's short stature and susceptibility to panic attacks.

So he had twisted to hold on to the staff. And now he was spinning.

The rush smacked him in the chest. He convulsed, feeling the wind trying to suffocate him.

The airship was coming up fast.

Briefly he could see the blur of the others beside him. They were still falling, but in a far more controlled way. His vision filled with rock and airship and cloud . . . and glimpses of the town of Galnaterra below. Way too far below.

He was about to die. He was spinning so wildly that the cord would snap, and he would drop past the airship, unable to catch it.

Bile rose in his chest, and he shut his eyes. His brain whirled, wondering if anyone would save him. Maybe Helia could control the plant from where she was. Maybe Nu had secret powers that she might reveal.

The rumble of airship engines was close, and he knew he was nearing the point of no return. The cord tightened around his arm. He was almost at the nadir of the plunge. If he didn't unwrap himself now and at least attempt to grab the *Golden Oriole*, he was done.

No choice.

He flung his arm in circles, unwrapping the cord. He opened his hand and let it slip away. Then he reached out with both arms, ready to grab the netting he'd seen.

Too late he realized he'd spun away from the path of the airship.

There was a commotion from above him—at least, he thought it was from above. He was spinning so hard now it was all the same. His mind was doing its best to shut down, wanting no part of being here when it happened.

But someone was definitely yelling.

One eye opened.

He saw a rush of blond hair before a figure smacked him in the chest. *Yantuz.*

"Hold on," his brother gasped, one arm wrapped around Dzin's midriff, the other holding his own vine-cord. It strained under their weight, but held long enough for Yantuz to swing them into the side of the balloon.

"Grab the ropes!" his brother yelled.

Dzin did, burning his hand as he slid down one, before he got a toehold below him and juddered to a halt. But Yantuz hadn't let go in time. He'd held on to make sure Dzin was safe and had lost his opening. The vine had been fully stretched, and now it was retracting again, just as the airship passed underneath the bridge.

The fear in Yantuz's eyes was plain, even as he was pulled swiftly away from his brother.

"Let go!" Dzin cried. But it was already too late. Yantuz bounced off the airship's midsection, spun off the back of the balloon, and was left dangling behind them for the briefest of moments, a desperate silhouette against the cloud, before he slipped from the cord and tumbled out of sight.

CHAPTER TWENTY-EIGHT
A MESSAGE

Edwin Payne surveyed the scene of devastation before him. The Great Tree, once a place of peace and tranquility, was now akin to a war zone.

He'd seen similar before, of course, having fought many times for King and country across the world back home. He was still unable to shake the horror of such things. Images of people suffering, the energy they exuded, it had a way of being burned into one's subconscious. He knew that was why he had nightmares of such voracity only a great magic could surely rid him of them. A secret laid bare in Suttaru's journal, which had led him to the man, the *legend* himself—and a promise that he could be rid of the nightmares, once his part in this was done.

Yet there was part of him that was almost used to the agony of such things now. The chaos of death and destruction, and the purest, primal emotions of those caught up in the midst of it all. There was nothing like it in the world. He wondered if he would miss his nightmares when they were gone, when Suttaru had done what he had promised, in return for Edwin Payne's help over the decades of hiding and planning.

The boughs of the Great Tree were scarred and littered with pieces of airship. Flaming banners, frayed and smoking, were tangled in branches, and the leaves all around the highest parts of this fabled place were wilting fast, curling and dying before snapping off and falling to the forest floor far below. Meanwhile, thick gray smoke was still choking them all as it curled up from the tattered remains of the refinery.

It was all going delightfully to plan.

More or less. Tywich had yet to finish the job.

Suttaru's insistence that they destroy the remaining Elixir, blow up the refinery, and kill the new batch of graduating students had gone almost flawlessly. Now the entire Tree was steeped in fear over what had happened. Of the unknown threat they faced.

There was just one minor problem.

The surface of his Orb, Myrtilus, swirled a question the color of a cold winter mist. Payne nodded reluctantly. The news he had to deliver to Suttaru was not of a good sort, and he expected to face the consequences. Even communicating through his Orb across the realm of Silvyra, a distance stretching from the Great Tree to the attack underway in Aedela, he felt a substantial fear wracking his body. His liege's powers were growing ever more substantial since his release from Discordia. Who knew how far they could reach?

Minutes later, Edwin Payne curled into a ball and clutched his head trying not to scream, hidden from view by those leaves not blackened or curling up from the fire that had rained upon the Great Tree.

You let him escape with the formula. Twice.

"I—I tried, my liege. No, please, I—"

The agony in his head grew, as though his Orb was aflame inside his eye socket and trying to grow back to his full size.

It didn't matter how distant they were. Suttaru was taking the news badly and was using the Orb to convey both his words and his ire.

"Sorry, m-my liege."

Your apologies are not accepted.

"Please, I beg you—"

You have failed me. The nightmares you so desperately wanted me to rid you of are nothing compared to the pain you have coming now.

His head seemed to be at the point of bursting. The grip of Suttaru's magic on the Orb was about to shatter his skull and splatter his brains all over the nearest branches.

Payne put all his efforts into forming words—the last words he might ever speak.

"I—I know where they went."

The pain lessened slightly.

Tell me.

"The student, Dzin, ran from the Tree with his brother before he could be killed. I sent my man Tywich after him in his beast form. But it did not work. The Maze ejected it. And the Sage of Hope helped the student escape. But I caught wind that the escapees fled to Undergrowth after that, my liege. They did not try to return here, as I thought they might."

That was all the information he had to bargain with. He held his breath, preparing for the worst, as a moment of terrifying silence followed.

But it did not come.

They are trying to re-create the formula, Suttaru's thoughtful response came.

"My liege?"

But whatever Suttaru was thinking, he did not elaborate. Finally, he released his hold on the Orb, and Myrtilus mercifully removed himself from Payne's face. The Orb's surface was blank for a moment, waiting impassively, the layers beneath showing no sign of further transmissions coming through, until finally the patterns started weaving and relaying instructions.

We hold to our plan. Return to the Library. Use the rest of the Dark Elixir on the Book of Wisdom. It should already be sufficiently weakened for you to finally retrieve my journal from where it has been hidden all these years. But there is no harm in making sure the insufferable Author inside the Book is damaged beyond repair. When you are done, open the portals to our legions and begin your attack. Flood the Library with death.

Payne bowed, despite knowing Suttaru couldn't see him. He simply had to hope Myrtilus conveyed his respect.

Then the transmission ended. A cloud of shadow crossed his Orb's surface.

The end is coming, Myrtilus noted.

For Payne, it could not come fast enough.

He instructed the Orb to take him back to the Library one last time.

CHAPTER TWENTY-NINE
THE FIRST BOOKSHELF

Arturo and Robin shivered in unison as they stood in the dimly lit, damp corridor, staring in horror at the tendrils of black roots that crisscrossed what had once been a door.

Robin hadn't been wrong about this place being far from the plaza. They had to take two trams just to get near, then had to run down several flights of rock-cut steps and through a labyrinthine structure, where the man-made walls were broken more regularly by those of natural rock.

Then they had to navigate an underground forest of sorts, letting Centauri guide the way as best as he could, shining brightly to allow them to follow him through the gloom and avoid the patches of floor that disappeared away to goodness knows where.

On the way, Robin told him that she'd never been down here before. She had only heard about it.

Arturo could feel the truth of her admission. He could sense her apprehension about being in this deep, dark part of the Library, so far from the Haven and the Book of Wisdom. It was one of the oldest parts of the entire magical city, maybe even the oldest part, which was saying something, considering how old she had suggested to him the Great Library of Tomorrow was purported to be.

He could also tell Centauri was being a little more hesitant than normal in the way he investigated the growths across the wall, trying not to hover too closely to them, perhaps in case one reached out and touched him.

"Anything?" Arturo asked, unable to shake the feeling these *things* were like some kind of tentacles, reaching out from an evil portal that should never have been opened.

The Orb's brief swirl of crimson suggested that, no, he didn't have the first clue about what the thin, rootlike strands were. Arturo looked to Robin, who grumbled impatiently and shooed Centauri away so she could reach out and touch one of the black strands herself. Before he could stop her, Robin's fingertips disappeared into its wet, sticky surface and she shivered.

"What are you doing?" he moaned, reaching out for her arm and pulling her away. Too late though. She was covered in the stuff. "Who knows what that is. It could be dangerous."

She brought her fingers into the Orb's light, and they both stared in confusion at the droplets of dark liquid that had come away on her fingers.

"The effects of poison." It all but confirmed his suspicions. He had followed the clues his writing mind had put in front of him and had reached this conclusion. The only one that made sense now. Yet there was another twist to reveal.

"Yes, but what is it?" Robin asked.

"What makes books? As in, the words inside them. How are the words printed?"

"Oh," she said, turning her fingers over in Centauri's low light, before rubbing the drops between her fingers and letting the darkness stain the tips. It looked like she'd dipped her hand in an old-fashioned inkwell.

Arturo nodded, although he felt significantly less happy about being right than he thought he would.

"Where are we, Robin? What *is* this place?"

She gestured to the door. "This is one of the oldest parts of the Great Library. The First Cave. They say this is where it all started, where the

Founder first arrived from the sea and entered this underground world. This is where he decided to start his collection, through the simple act of carving a bookshelf and placing the books he already owned on it."

Arturo remembered one of the paintings he had seen. The scene with the cave of books and the woman reading by lamplight.

"You mean this is where we saw Andora sitting down to read?"

"Yes. That is part of a story that's been told here for centuries. Although who's to say what's true and what's fiction anymore? You know how stories can grow over time and become embellished with each telling, depending on who the storyteller is. Sometimes the real details are forgotten, and the stories evolve beyond the memories behind them."

"Memories?" He reached out and touched the door, finding a place untainted by what he was now regarding in his head as book blood. "Perhaps that's why the Book of Wisdom can't communicate. Its memories have been compromised. It has forgotten how to talk to us."

"Because of the poison?"

Arturo gestured to the ink. "Words seem to be bleeding from the pages beyond this door. The stories they told are being lost."

"You think it will get worse?"

He thought it might, but didn't want to say.

"I guess we'll see," was all he said.

And with that, he pushed the door open and strode through.

Robin had mentioned on their journey down how she had known about this part of the Library for many years. Apparently, Sage Veer had told her about it during her first month here, while they'd spent hours and hours exploring and soaking up the magic. According to Robin, Veer had been trying to impress her a little. Or maybe even scare her. And Arturo understood that now, because this place wasn't like anywhere else he'd seen in the Library.

Of course, he figured it wasn't normally covered in book blood. But even without the ink spilling across it, the chamber was dimmer and damper and far spookier than elsewhere.

In Centauri's soft glow, their eyes drifted over the rough rock walls of the cave to the rocking chair in the corner and the unlit fireplace, which had coal dust swirling in little eddies around it, an unseen wind brush-ing past. In the distance, Arturo could have sworn he could hear the sea and the lapping of waves, but it also could have been his imagination.

It didn't matter either way.

Because his gaze had become fixated on the wide, carved bookshelf in the wall to the right of the doorway. Seven shelves high, stretching from floor to ceiling, and stacked with what had once been books of all heights and sizes.

Books that were now coated in a thick mass of ink, which squirmed and pulsated as it pushed out from their pages, over the carved nook, and across the walls, where it continued to spread throughout the entire cave.

"He came back to give it a sickness," Arturo whispered. "The Rogue Sage found the poison he was looking for, and he brought it back here. He corrupted the books, made them bleed their stories out all over the place, ruining them."

He felt nauseous as he stared at the mass, but he couldn't tear his eyes away, even as Robin spoke softly to him.

"But why here? And how did he get into the Library?"

"I'm not sure," said Robin, "but it's possible the same elements that allow the Book of Wisdom to regulate the portals and the Orbs to take us Sages to Paperworld could still be working for him somehow. Or, in a very practical way, he knows where the Library is on Earth. It's mag-ically shielded from the rest of the world, but if you know the exact coordinates . . ."

"So, how does the Book—and the Orbs, for that matter—regulate the portals?"

"It's complicated," said Robin. "And we don't have complete records from the time of the first portal's discovery. What we do know is that the early settlers, led by the Founder, discovered a large meteorite here on the island. It was made of an exotic metal that even now, with the combined technology of Earth and the full knowledge of the Library, defies our full analysis. It simply doesn't seem to be an element known to our world. What we do know is that Fairen, the scholar who found the first portal, used parts of the metal in making the Book of Wisdom and the Sage's Orbs. None of our other technology, even the more mag-ical things we have here, can manipulate the portals. The ore from the meteorite is somehow connected to Paperworld."

"Okay, so a magic rock falls to Earth, somehow it's linked to the portals, and it's used in making magical objects. That's not strange at all!" He looked at Robin, his eyes alight with the wonder of this strange place. "What about now?"

"Well, we still have a large amount of the original meteorite, and in the rare occasion when a new Orb is needed, it's used by the Book of Wisdom and very specialist scholars to bring a new one to life."

"So, do they grow old?" he asked.

"No, Arturo. Paperworld is a place of wonders and magic. A metaverse of nature and beauty like no other. But it's also a place of danger at times, and wild magic. Sages die, my dear man, and some-times their Orbs are lost with them."

Arturo looked at her and how she was suddenly so serious, the playful facade lifted, and his mind went to Sage Xavier. He wondered if Robin had lost friends and loved ones to violence. Then he had a thought.

"So, Payne's Orb didn't make it back and was replaced?"

"Yes, but we know that."

"I know, but if he's alive, his Orb is almost certainly alive, yes?"

"Well, yes." She wasn't sure where he was going with this.

"So, if his Orb has this magical metal, and we know he and Suttaru are moving around Paperworld, it stands to reason they have another way of regulating the portals, yes? And if the Book has blocked the dark Orb, perhaps it also can't see him sneaking in and out of the Library—or a portal we don't know about elsewhere on the island."

"Yes, it must be! I can't believe we didn't think of it. The Book of Wisdom is powerful beyond what we know, but if he has managed to sneak by her somehow, and weakened her with this poison, then it may be she just can't see him."

He shook his head, still trying to piece together that part and how it fit among the horror of what he was seeing. What was it about this particular place and these particular memories that Edwin Payne had needed to poison? Why desecrate these books? Arturo had moved right on from his writerly satisfaction of solving one issue only to come up against the next loose thread he needed to tie up.

"Why here?" he repeated to himself. "It's just an old cave."

"The First Cave."

"Okay, yes. The Library's First Cave. Containing its oldest, most important memories . . ." His voice trailed off as he looked from the seething mass of ink on the walls back to the tall bookshelf. Which is when he saw that the ink stains were spreading out from one particular book in the midst of this gruesome scene.

Both he and Robin tilted their heads to read the gold lettering down the spine.

The City of Forever.

"What's that—" she began, before the door to the room opened and a gaunt-looking man stood framed in the light from the corridor beyond, a vial of blue liquid clutched in one hand and a worn-looking book in the other. A look of surprise was etched across his face.

The same face they'd seen pictures of that very day, when they'd been doing their research. The thin, taut features and too-little skin pulled over his skull.

A rusty gray Orb rotated in the man's eye socket.

"Payne," Arturo gasped.

Arturo leaped forward, grabbing the Rogue Sage by the lapel of his tunic and slamming him back against the wall of the corridor. Despite Payne being tall and thin, however, he was strong. The element of surprise gone, he forced Arturo back, pushing the book he was carrying into Arturo's midsection.

Arturo caught it and tried to wrestle it off him. There was a ripping sound, and some pages came away in his hand, but he couldn't get the man to back off.

So he punched Payne back before shoving the pages into his pocket to keep them safe.

As the man fell backward, he still held on to the book, but he dropped the vial.

They both looked at each other, then at the fallen vessel.

And then, with a panicked curse, Payne ran.

For an old, supposedly dead man, the Rogue Sage ran faster than expected.

All Arturo could see was the back of him as they gave chase out of the First Cave and along the tunnel, away from the route they'd used to travel down, heading deeper into the lower levels of the Library.

As they began to gain on him, seeing his bobbing gray hair disappear around the corner, it was becoming more and more clear how familiar he was with the passageways of the Library. As Arturo ran, he wondered how often the man had been here. Or even worse, whether he had somehow been hiding under their noses the whole time.

They sped around a corner and were confronted with some kind of thick blue smoke. Not normal smoke either. There was a physicality to it, akin to that feeling of trying to run in a dream. Heavy and slow, with an underlying frustration about the fact you're going nowhere. It seemed that the book poison wasn't the only thing Payne had apparently stumbled upon on his travels.

It only spread out a few feet, but it was enough to buy the older man some time to reach the end of the corridor and exit by one of two doorways.

"We should split up," Arturo suggested.

Robin barked a humorless laugh, not prepared to consider it. "I'm a Sage, and you're my responsibility. What would your daughter say if I had to tell her you're never coming home? Sorry, no, we stick together."

She grabbed his arm and shoved the right-hand door open.

They were now in a wooden stairwell that spiraled upward, hugging the rocky void. Robin gestured for Centauri to speed ahead, which he did, right up the middle of the spiraling stairs.

An echoed gasp drifted from above, indicating they'd chosen the right door. They raced up the stairs as quickly as they could, still not quite thinking about what they'd do once they caught up with the Rogue Sage.

Then they heard the man's gasps transform into something else.

A growl.

They were no longer chasing a man, but a huge beast, a canine on all fours but bigger than any dog Arturo had ever seen. Its sooty fur rippled with flames. Its teeth like so many curved knives, jutting out from behind hateful, twisted lips.

A single red eye glared at them.

The fire seared the air of the stairwell, stinging Arturo's skin and making his eyes water. He tried to shield his face, but it seemed to do no good, and Edwin Payne knew it.

The beast was the Rogue Sage. Arturo knew that now. How the man had transformed, though, he could only guess.

There was a huge *bang* above, quickly followed by sparks of electricity that began to shower upon them. Robin ducked, only to see Centauri begin to fall lifelessly from the floor above.

Arturo reached out a hand and caught Centauri, then threw him to Robin. High above was the Rogue Sage's Orb, its surface swirling with victorious shadowy patterns. It flew after the demon dog, and the two disappeared through another door.

Arturo carried on after them. Robin paused only to check Centauri was okay, before following in his wake.

They were in the food cellars now. Rows of bottles of wine were down one side, with casks of other drinks along the other. The thick stone walls also held shelves of other food and drink. It was cold and damp, perfect for storage. He shivered as they ran out of the cellars and up the stone steps.

Arturo had a sense of where they were heading now.

They were back at the Concourse.

Pushing through the heavy oak door that had been swinging shut, he caught sight of the demon dog and its Orb as they flew into the main area of the Library. The quiet was shattered as those studying threw back their chairs to dive out of the way, shouting in fear as the beast growled at them all.

Robin must have seen a familiar face, because she slowed down for a moment.

"Get Mwamba!" she urged, grabbing the red-haired woman's arms to ensure the message was understood to be urgent. "Urulla, you have to hurry. Get Mwamba and tell him to go to the First Cave. A poison has been spilled there. The vial should still be on the floor where it was dropped. Mwamba needs to find the antidote to the poison. If anybody can, it's him. Go! Quickly!"

With that, she and Arturo sped off again.

Edwin Payne's haphazard flight of escape was scattering the crowds down the center of the Concourse. It allowed Arturo to see him at the far end, diving into one of the aisles.

Thank goodness, he thought, feeling every part of him aching. *He's cornered himself. We've got him.*

Yet when they rounded the corner of the aisle, he could only see the hind legs of the creature as it leaped through a hole in the air.

A portal.

To where, Arturo didn't know. He only cared about the fact that the bastard was escaping, and he wasn't about to let that happen. Arturo prepared to give chase, running up to the portal . . . only to stop short as he caught a glimpse of what lay on the other side.

A world of swirling black clouds, jagged mountains, and a plain that was heaving with hundreds of glowing people, all with the script of an unnatural language burned into their skin.

"Discordia?" Robin whispered from beside him.

Standing before them, Edwin Payne had taken his human form again. And as the pair watched, the Rogue Sage's Orb shrunk and slipped into his empty eye socket.

The man grinned.

CHAPTER THIRTY
THE *GOLDEN ORIOLE*

Dzin kept replaying the loss in his mind, finding comfort in the pain.

The fall from the bridge. The wind whipping at him, battering him, spinning him around like a plaything. The thump of Yantuz barreling into him, swinging him to safety.

Then his face as he lost his grip on the netting and was pulled back, only to fall to his death. Tumbling away into the cloud.

Dzin held his hands around his knees, curled up tight. The floor buffeted under him as the airship swayed and shuddered, but he kept his eyes shut. The loss was too much to comprehend, too much weight on his already addled mind. His brother, his only family, was gone. Dead. All because of him.

He felt a cold wave of anxiety flood through him. His breath quickened. His eyes fixed on nothing, while his mind was on everything all at once.

Here it comes, he thought, clutching his mother's staff tightly in his lap and squeezing his eyes shut.

Yantuz had been the constant calming influence in Dzin's life, not just since the fire but way before that. Dzin was the older brother, but Yantuz had been his rock in the storm even when they had been children.

A few years after their parents' deaths, Yantuz had been the one to keep Dzin going. As he was forced to step up and be responsible, any time he wondered whether he might be swept away by the anxiety he was starting to feel, Yantuz had offered his older brother calm and kindness.

These anxiety attacks only got worse as he got older and took on more. They peaked when he was accepted into the Botanical Education School as a student Runner, where he found himself excelling at what he did while bowing under the immense pressure he put on himself to succeed.

Panic storms, Dzin called these anxiety attacks, because they were so huge and overwhelming, battering him with a huge range of competing emotions and pressures. He was unable to avoid them. When one hit, it was all he could do to keep his feet firmly planted and try his best to ride it out, lest it carry him away.

Now he was here, alone, and the weight of everything was pressing firmly on his shoulders, trying to crush him.

His friends at the laboratory had been slaughtered. The Elixir of Life destroyed throughout Silvyra. The archives of past formulas demolished.

He was the only one left. The only student with the only formula. The fate of these strangers in his life depended on him. The fate of Perennia too. And Silvyra. And who knows what else.

The nausea broiled in his stomach, and he pulled his knees tighter against his chest anyway, the staff wedged in between. It made it harder to breathe, but he was already threatening to hyperventilate, and the pressure helped to stop it getting out of control.

The storm raged within him.

During such times, he had often relied on Yantuz to hold him fast as he was pulled in so many different directions at once. Yes, he also had his mother's staff, his comfort stick—he hated the name, but he had to admit it was accurate—and sometimes that was enough for the minor episodes. But when things got really bad—as they were now—his brother had been a crucial safe space.

Yantuz, who saw the whites of Dzin's eyes as they widened and heard the silence in what Dzin wasn't saying. Yantuz, who wouldn't do much more than simply be present and talk quietly to give him something to focus on, a lone voice cutting through the rage of the storm that wanted to devour him.

Yantuz, who was now gone.

It was all on Dzin now. Him, alone.

He clutched the staff even tighter, fingers digging into the bark, feeling its roughness burn against the wound on his palm where he'd caught the rigging earlier. The pain helped to give him something to focus on, but he knew this storm was going to last awhile.

He wondered what the others must be thinking of him right now. Pitying him? Or despising him for being so weak and foolish to let his brother sacrifice himself to save him?

Dzin didn't know, and right now he didn't care.

The hijacking of the *Golden Oriole* was going badly.

First Dzin had slipped away from the group and spun out of control. Then Yantuz had gone after him, only to be lost.

Helia knew she'd had no choice but to bring the brothers on this journey. Dzin was important to finding the dragon, and Yantuz was important to Dzin. So she had pushed down the guilt as she landed on the airship with a thump, right behind Rascal and Nu.

All she could do now was make sure the rest of them got inside the airship. The winds were rising, and the dark was closing in. They had to get to safety before the light went; otherwise, they'd be trapped out in the open.

"Temperatures drop out here at night, especially when we get over the desert, and the Rock Giants will come out before too long," Rascal yelled at Dzin, as he refused to move from his spot, clutching his staff in one hand and holding tightly to the rigging with the other. "Either the frost will kill us, or we'll be thrown to our deaths, neither of which will help you find our dragon. Neither of which will honor what your brother just did. We have to move and fast!"

Dzin finally moved, with Helia and Rascal guiding him between them, while Nu led the way down the rigging. The wind pounding them, they slid down the ropes that held the ship beneath the balloon and wrenched open one of the doors at the back of the craft—enough to slip inside and collapse onto the cold, metal floor of the cargo chamber.

Unfortunately, their situation didn't improve much on the inside.

Two people slammed open a door and strode in. One man, a small, gruff, bearded fellow with red cheeks and a tilted hat pulled over his eyes, the other in a finely tailored brown uniform, carrying a trident.

"And what do you interlopers think you're doing on *my* ship?" the small man, who was clearly the leader, growled, standing over them.

Helia opened her mouth to explain their situation, but the first mate moved quickly. She found herself point-to-eye with his pitchfork. Sparks of electricity popped across its sharp tips, and she flinched.

She shut her mouth again.

"Aye, that's what I thought," the captain continued. "Because there is no excuse good enough for boarding a vessel midflight. Especially when it concerns this . . ." His voice trailed off as he saw Rascal. His flushed cheeks grew even more furious. "You?!"

Helia felt worn in that moment, stretched too thin. There were so many questions she wanted answered, yet she could only sit there as Rascal met the man's glare.

"Captain Finesse, please hear us out."

His lips were already twisting into a scowl as he turned to his first mate. "Earnest, shut them in the brig and keep watch."

"Shouldn't we hand them to the authorities somewhere?"

"No time for that now. We have a schedule to keep. We'll just have to carry on and hand them over to the Prince when we dock at the mountain. We still have to chart our course through the Rock Giants if we're to make it at all."

Nu gave Helia a look of hope, to which Helia inclined her head ever so slightly. Things hadn't gone to plan, but at least they were still headed in the right direction.

Yet as she saw Dzin with his arms wrapped around his knees, tears in his eyes, quietly holding his wooden staff, she realized it had all come at a cost. She wondered whether they'd even be able to bargain with whoever met them at the other end. Because if they were locked up, they'd never be able to retrieve the ingredient they needed to complete the formula, which meant Perennia would be lost, and the realms beyond the Library would fall to Suttaru. Which meant Earth and humanity would be next.

Helia reached for her neck, hoping Vega might offer a little acknowledgment of comfort. He wasn't only something that enhanced her powers; he was also her closest friend and a source of hope whenever she felt lacking.

Yet as her fingers closed around the amulet, she realized something was very wrong indeed.

There was a hole where Vega should have been.

They'd been locked in the hold of the airship for close to an hour, with no way to escape. Nu hadn't the energy to talk to the others about what could be done. It was all too overwhelming. Whether through sheer exhaustion or sleep, something suddenly took over, like a cold sheet being draped over her body.

And then she was taken by another sudden vision. She was back in Aedela with Veer.

Despite the chaos of the town, it was easy to feel the vibration of the living, breathing flower towers around her. The towers were communicating with each other through their interconnected roots and the fungi nodes that joined them, warning the inhabitants throughout the town. It was impressive, and Nu couldn't help but make the connection to the Orbs and how they communicated with each other—and their Sages—through the Book of Wisdom.

Veer was again nearby, standing alongside the Petal Queen, who Nu understood to be the leader of this place. The couple were organizing what troops remained with them to hold back the forces pouring in from the south.

They would soon be overwhelmed; the grim looks on their faces showed they all understood that.

Regardless, they remained.

Veer let a rare sigh of frustration slip out. "I thought you were leading your people out of here, Your Majesty? That was the plan we agreed upon."

"You agreed. I merely let you think the agreement was mutual."

"Your people need you."

"My people need me to do what's right, and that means giving them the best chance possible of making it around the southern edge of the mountains, to the safety of the Great Tree, without being caught. I will stay with you and face whatever it is that's coming. To delay its advance as long as possible."

Veer dipped his head ever so slightly, holding her gaze.

"It would be an honor to fight alongside you."

The vision blurred.

Nu was suddenly thrown from one street into another. It was later in the day, and this street was full of mangled bodies—flower folk and monsters alike—lives snuffed out and only shells remaining. Grim markers of a fierce and terrible battle that was already underway.

She found herself running alongside a bloodied Veer as he moved quickly toward more danger. His hands moved as if of their own accord, the magic in them an instinct now. Lynx was still by his side, alight with flashing colors, and Nu felt raw power passing from Orb to Sage. Veer looked tired, his use of power taking its toll. Suddenly, the power flowed through him, and Veer straightened again. He nodded his thanks to the Orb as he reached out to the wind, pulling and twisting the strands of it as though teasing notes from an orchestra. It rose to a furor at his beckoning, playing to his direction, whipping up and carrying him along even faster.

The cries were coming from all around them, thick and fast. Some were from the troops who stayed to fight, now injured or dying. And underlying it all was a scratchy, inhuman noise that Nu wished she could block out.

Death itself. A collective voice of the corrupted beings sweeping across the wildflower plains and spilling into the town to destroy and maim and kill.

The enemy was nothing like Nu had ever seen before. Nothing like she could have imagined, even in her darkest nightmares. An army of people and twisted, wolflike creatures marked in horrific ways, with terrible words and stories carved into their skin, and a rage for destruction filling the gaping void where their hearts once were.

She tried to call out in warning as another beast moved along a side street. Veer hadn't seen it, and as it approached Nu yelled again, louder. She tried to close the distance to help him, but she had no power here. Her movement was slow, her feet unable to run. She was tethered to Veer, but unable to warn or help him.

She watched on in horror, furious and fearful that she could do nothing else. Yet Lynx had spotted the danger and Veer spun to meet it.

The attacker was a woman, though it was as if a switch of darkness has been flicked within her. A once plain face was now all snarling maw and fire-tattooed skin. She snapped at Veer's throat, and he spun away, feet kicking through the dirt as he twisted his hands. The wind bent to his will once more, wrapping the creature up and throwing her into two more fiends, sending them skittering away.

A tall, sticklike man leaped at him from a high window, only to crash back through the lower ground floor. Two more Unwritten hounds followed. Veer let go of the wind and ran, the beasts biting at his heels. One caught Veer's cloak and half ripped it from him until Lynx buzzed past its head, distracting it momentarily. Veer took the opportunity and pulled away the other half of the cloak, lest he be strangled by it, and kicked the evil monster away, then made his way to where the Petal Queen and her guards were defending the last of the escaping folk.

The town was lost. Nu could see it, and she knew Veer understood too. The cloud of ash was still moving slowly, deliberately, through the fire and taint, further into the settlement.

Veer was fighting fiercely, but Nu saw the Petal Queen had taken charge. A mirrored blade in hand, she cut through swathes of the enemy, before splitting up what remained of her guards. One half to cover the path of retreat. One to take the fight to the monsters, to cause distraction and puncture their waves of attacks.

It didn't work. Her troops, who until now had mostly been for show in this otherwise peaceful world, were not prepared. They were quickly *overwhelmed, and without their queen to direct them, they scattered, trying to find their own way out. Nu saw Veer try to gather them up using the wind, but there was only so much a stranger and his companion Orb could do here.*

In the midst of battle, they paid him no heed.

Nu could only hope they would make it without his help. She watched as he tried his best to give them cover, throwing the wind around the streets, guiding it, cajoling it to anger, making it crash against their attackers. But it was not enough. She saw a few of them fall beneath the hordes and heard their calls of terror before they were silenced.

Nu's eyes still burned with the heat surrounding them. The town was on fire. And even as she continued to run alongside Veer, as he pulled the wind around to clear his path, she could feel the flakes of ash begin to fall against them.

Not much time.

He was close now.

Who? Nu feared she might know. And although Veer was not one for panic, she saw it in his eyes. He knew they were surrounded.

And the worst was yet to come.

CHAPTER THIRTY-ONE
AN UNFORGIVING DESERT

Nu returned to the present with a shiver.

It took her a moment to place where she was. A harsh metal floor, shelves full of strange shapes hidden beneath old, leaf-woven sheets. Boxes were cluttered around. And it was freezing, her breath fogging in front of her face as she exhaled. She squeezed her eyes tight for a moment, feeling a slight pinch behind them. Then it disappeared again, and she sat up.

A small object vibrated in her hands. She looked down to see a silver Orb cradled against her skin, and in an instant, she remembered everything.

The journey, the fall, the loss. Being trapped in a cargo hold on board an airship.

Three friends around her, but it was a group that was now one short.

Dzin was murmuring in his sleep, huddled in the corner, leaning against a wooden crate, with his arms around his knees and his hair resting over his face. He was sweating, despite the cold, and a single word played itself again and again on his lips: *Yantuz.*

Rascal was glaring into space, the folded tips of her wings twitching. If she had heard Nu stir, she gave no sign. She was fixated on her anger at their predicament and the loss of Dzin's brother on her watch.

Helia, meanwhile, sat cross-legged, as Nu had. Her eyes were closed, giving the appearance of calm. Nu could tell she wasn't asleep, however. There was a telltale crease in her brow.

What had she just seen? Another vision? A dream? *I should say something. No, what would I say?* If it had just been a dream about one of the Sages, possibly born out of stress over their mission, woven into concerns about what she'd heard earlier, they might not trust her anymore. They might send her home, and she desperately wanted to stay the course. Fears of the threat facing them all. That was surely all this was, no matter how real it had seemed.

Just a dream.

But what if there was more to it? What if this meant something about why Nu was here? *What if I can see across Paperworld? What if I'm meant to see this and tell Helia?*

She instantly put the fantastical idea out of her head. No, that was silly. She was just Nu from the Library. Any thoughts about being something more were simply wishful thinking.

Antares vibrated weakly against her fingers, as if to tell her something. But just as she reached for him, the airship shook violently, and the door to their temporary prison burst open.

"All of you, up now," Earnest, the first mate, growled at them.

Again, he carried the deadly electrical trident, but this time it hung idly at his side. And as the airship bumped and shook again, Nu got the impression he had other far more pressing concerns than the intruders.

"What now?" Dzin asked with a sniff, wiping a sleeve across his eyes.

Rascal was already up on her feet, brushing herself off and looking concerned. "It's the Rock Giants, isn't it?"

"Yes, and something's wrong with the ship," Earnest growled. "Whatever the blazes you did out there earlier, you've damaged something. We're heavy on the starboard side, and it's taking the captain all his skill just to keep us in the air, let alone avoid the obstacles ahead. It's all or nothing now. If we're to get out of this, you need to atone for what you did and help us get through. Now hurry."

They rushed up the length of the lower layer of the ship, before clanking up a ladder to the next level. This must have been where the passengers normally sat, except most of the plush seats lining each side of the vessel were either empty or filled with wooden crates.

"Ah, good, you are here to make amends for wrecking my ship," Captain Finesse roared from the flight deck. "Best get busy before we all die!"

Nu couldn't move. She could only stare out of the wide cabin window at the desert ahead, bathed in the light of twin moons. And the towering giants, several tree lengths tall, with bulbous rocky faces and thick arms, rising from the sands to block out the sky.

"Brace!" the captain yelled as an enormous fat-fingered hand swiped slowly at them, crashing from the heavens above.

The group grabbed hold of whatever piece of cabin they could reach. Helia and Rascal wrapped their hands around a couple of seat belts. Nu's fingers found a brass handrail.

Dzin reacted too late.

The captain swung the airship to the left, but it was moving too slowly, and the Rock Giant's finger grazed the balloon above. The entire vessel shuddered. Something hit one of the glass windows, leaving a crack resembling a tiny lightning strike.

Dzin was lifted off his feet and thrown through the air.

Only Helia moved in time. She stretched out a hand instinctively, her fingers reaching for one of the crates strapped into the chairs. Instantly, the wood splintered as two wormlike branches broke the surface, shot out across the cabin, and wound themselves around Dzin before his head met one of the lamps that lined the wall.

As Nu bounced around, she saw the look of surprise on Helia's face—which was perhaps even more surprised than Dzin's, who was now held fast, upside down, in the center of the cabin, away from harm.

"I shouldn't have been able to do that," Helia said, half to herself. She looked to Nu, a puzzled frown creeping across her brow. "Not to that extent. Vega's gone. Without him, my abilities shouldn't have allowed me to react that quickly."

Nu looked outside to see another Rock Giant rising from the ground, oceans of sand spilling from its shoulders.

The creature's roar was like a gale, rushing against the metal container, which groaned in response.

"Hold together," the captain urged, lovingly slapping the copper-framed dashboard. He gestured to the group. "My ship is suffering tonight. It's time to break out the wind oars, or we're going to lose her and ourselves in the bargain. We're going to need all the help we can get to make it through this."

"Can't you just fly above them?" Dzin asked, still hanging in the middle of the craft by the branches, looking as white as a sheet.

"Not in this desert, my boy. There's worse above us, trust me."

Nu, Helia, and Rascal were directed into the cabin and took seats on either side of the captain. Earnest, who was sitting in front of Nu, directed them all to grab the poles, which had suddenly extended across their laps.

"Hold it steady with both hands," he urged. "When the captain directs us, pull back as hard as you can. It's extra leverage against the elements out there—won't help much, but it might just give us a few yards of steer when we need it."

"Starboard!" the captain yelled.

Nu and Earnest both strained as they grasped the oars and pulled back as hard as possible. Nu wasn't sure what this was doing outside the craft. She had images of boat oars bracing against the wind, but whatever it was seemed to work. Her shoulder slammed into the cushioned panel as the airship swung violently to one side, and dipped, just avoiding another grab by a Rock Giant.

Nu watched its fingers close into a fist, capturing only the air to the side of them, where the airship had just been. Another roar shook them, the creature venting its frustration.

"Port!" came another yell. This time, Rascal and Helia had to pull back on their side. The airship twisted and lifted again, narrowly avoiding the rocky arm they'd been heading toward.

The game seemed to go on for hours, the airship ducking and weaving and rising through billows of sand, lifting high enough to capture the moon's image in the cabin windshield, then dropping close enough to the desert floor to see the legs of the giants rising through the dunes, all while rocky hands, limbs, and snapping jaws attempted to snatch the craft from the night.

Nu's fingers burned, and she felt her hands slipping against the oar as they grew clammy. Her forehead was damp, too, from sweat dripping into her eyes, which stung. But even as she was thrown around the seat, she didn't take her hands off the handle. Not once.

She just gritted her teeth and kept going.

Finally, the last swipe of a Rock Giant's finger cut through a lighter sky as dawn broke. A roar issued behind them, but it was the last one.

Silence followed. And the air calmed again.

The captain sat back in his seat with a grunt, keeping his hands on the controls, but letting the weight of danger slip from his shoulders. He eyed the skies ahead as the golden light grew and the horizon solidified, broken only by a dark shape in the form of an arrowhead rising from the sand, dead center.

A jagged peak, it jutted out from the world to split the sky and cast the desert below it in shadow.

The Clockwork Mountain.

"The Giants don't venture too close to the mountain, so it should be smooth sailing now," he said, glancing at the reflection of the group in the window. "Of course, if it weren't for you pirates breaking my ship as you boarded, she wouldn't have struggled in the first place. But your help just now meant we weren't dashed to the dunes below, at least." Thick fingers rasped over his chin as he scratched his stubble, contemplating what to do. Finally, he growled under his breath. "Doesn't matter either way. I have good currency here with the Prince, and therefore I must hand you over to him when we arrive. They are fastidious with their rules, and we are contracted only to bring two crew on each journey. Which means it's either you or us, and I have a business to run. Rascal knows as much, which is why she should never have brought you here. But I am sorry for what lies ahead for you, because you don't *seem* dangerous." Nu watched the captain's gaze narrow as he witnessed the branches holding Dzin lower him back to the cabin floor, where he collapsed in a nearby seat. His wrists looked like they'd been rubbed raw from where he'd been held, but at least he was alive.

"The most unlikely pirates I ever did meet."

Nu looked to Rascal, silently urging her to negotiate, but whatever had passed between them was still a matter of pride for her. Rascal refused to meet her eyes and folded her arms, proud and stubborn, as she stared out of the window.

Clearly, she wasn't going to debase herself to talk the captain out of his decision.

It was left to Helia to slide from her bench, unsteadily making her way to the copilot's seat, grabbing handhold to handhold in case the airship bounced again. She collapsed next to the captain and said quietly, "We're no pirates. We just needed your ship to gain passage to the Clockwork Mountain. For my part, I'm sorry for any damage we caused, but we're grateful you got us through. Let me deal with the Prince. I may yet be able to convince him our journey here is a worthy one."

"Is that so? Well, I wish you luck, then, whatever your quest may be." He gestured to the steadily growing peak before them. "Because you will find it a hard task to convince that man of anything good—not without a fair few pearls or goods to trade. The Clockwork Mountain is run to a rhythm set by the Prince and to a time everyone needs to keep. There is little flexibility there, no deviation from the expectations set in the stone foundations of its cogs. Strangers are expected to behave, and pirates too."

Nu watched as Helia touched her amulet again, still anxious about Vega's absence. "Then we will have to find other ways to fulfill our mission. We'll be fine, I'm sure."

Helia looked to Nu to confirm that what she was saying had some truth to it. They had developed a shared but unspoken acknowledgment of her growing powers in their time together. But Nu had nothing to offer her right now. The way she had been able to see things over the last couple of days had been surprising and occurred when she least expected it.

Seeing how Dzin and Yantuz might be able to help on the journey, that had been more of a gut feeling. It had been her knowing. She'd had a good understanding of their energies ebbing and flowing around them. They weren't just harmless; they were potential allies. Friends and companions. That truth had been easy to decipher.

Sometimes this *knowing* had been useful. But more recently it had been terrifying, especially in her dreams. But all had the same limitations: It was what had happened in the past or was happening in the present. She had never seen anything occurring in the future or been able to command a dream at will.

So as much as Helia wanted to know the future, Nu couldn't oblige. She could only peer over the Sage's shoulder through the windshield and look to their destination, trying to ignore the occasional sun-bleached bones of huge, ancient beasts poking out of the dunes and feeling the thudding in her heart that had nothing to do with the journey they'd just been on, but rather a sense of what lay ahead.

Danger and death awaited them—she knew it.

"Nu?" Helia's eyes had narrowed. "Are you okay?"

Nu shivered, unable to answer her friend.

CHAPTER THIRTY-TWO
THE CLOCKWORK MOUNTAIN

The *Golden Oriole* swept into the shadow of the Clockwork Mountain, and the world darkened around them.

It matched Dzin's mood.

Unlike his newfound friends, he chose not to stand and ogle through the cabin windshield at the sight. He was too heartbroken, too busy replaying his brother's last moments, too distraught to properly care that they'd made it to their far-flung destination.

He'd heard stories of the mountain as a child, from his mother and more from others at the Tree. This city deep in the desert was split into three rounded sections—like gigantic cogs—that sat on top of one another, each containing its own section of the city and each grinding in opposition to the one above or below. Depending on what rumor or myth one believed, the bizarre, magnificent place was the remnants of a machine designed by an ancient people, long since forgotten.

Over time, people had sought refuge here from the harsh elements outside. Settlements soon grew in the gaps in the cogs, nestled between the mechanisms. And although it was difficult, travel between the sections was possible whenever these gaps above and below briefly aligned, before contact was lost again for another cycle.

As much as Dzin had always enjoyed traveling, having the same drive to see the world that had made him so excited to be chosen to become a Runner, he couldn't bring himself to care right now.

As the others marveled, he sat back on his bench alone, his arms resting on the oar handle. Staring into nothingness, he was barely able to see anything beyond the image of the shocked look on Yantuz's face as he missed the rigging and tumbled off the balloon to his death.

An image that was now burned forever into his mind.

I'm so sorry, Yantuz. I should never have brought you along with me.

And yet he knew if he had gone alone, he would be dead by now. Because Yantuz had saved him.

"I've never seen bravery quite like it," Helia said, sitting down next to him, content to keep looking ahead, letting her gaze drift beyond the others to the mountain. And for that, he was glad. "Your brother put himself at risk to grab you. And it was a risk that paid off."

Dzin closed his eyes, squeezing the tears away. "For me. Not him."

"True, but that was his intent. How many of us can say we did—or can ever expect to do—such a thing? He was clearly a good man. And a good brother. You should be proud of him."

"I am."

"Good." She gently ruffled the material at his shoulder. "I really am sorry. Will you be okay?"

Dzin didn't know how to answer that. He wasn't okay in the slightest, yet it didn't really feel like something he wanted to admit in front of everyone.

He sniffed and nodded.

"Thank you, Dzin. Because we need to make what he did count for something. I'm sorry to keep pushing you like this, but the fate of so many rests on our mission, and Yantuz has sacrificed himself to ensure all is not lost. The Prince isn't going to let us just walk away with his prized specimen. It's going to be a fight, and that's only after we struggle to get up through the different cogs of the city to reach the peak. I understand your grief, Dzin. More than you know, I understand what you're going through. But right now I need you to focus on what's ahead.

I'm going to need your courage, just like Yantuz showed us all. Do you think you can do it?"

"I don't know," Dzin replied honestly. "But I'll try to find it."

To his surprise, she smiled.

"I will take honesty over lying. Less surprises that way." She pointed beyond the others, to the revolving mountain slopes that were covered in constant streams of scree, through which tiny lights could be seen, indicating the presence of life within.

Dzin felt his stomach lurch as the airship began to drop. He could now see a gaping maw far below, one buzzing with the comings and goings of other strange and wonderful airships.

"We're preparing to land. Rascal says the dock is in the bottom layer, as strange as that sounds for such a place. But I guess they figured it makes the peak far more secure if the only way in was through the bottom. It'll certainly prove a journey for us, even if they don't put us in the nearest cell, which I believe they will."

"Prison?" Dzin asked, feeling his heart sink further.

Helia got up and beckoned him to do the same.

"Don't worry. I've got a plan."

This was a useful distraction from his distress, Dzin realized a few moments later, when the plan had been revealed. But if he had known it would be this uncomfortable and claustrophobic, he might not have agreed to it.

His elbows were grazed from being bumped against the inside of the crate, his legs bruised from the jabs the shipment of mechanical items were giving him. And through it all, his anxiety grew steadily, causing him to have to pinch his legs to keep from yelling out with the sheer terror of it all.

He could hear the docking crews of the Clockwork Mountain around him, grunting as they heaved the crate he was in, as well as the many others from the *Golden Oriole*.

The only upside was that, despite his predicament, he was the only one of his party still free.

If one could call this free.

Helia hadn't been wrong about the Prince's intentions. Captain Finesse had done his best to smooth the waters for them, but rules were rules, and he had docked three people more than his papers stated.

Three visible people, at least.

Dzin had crouched in his crate, his nerves fraying, listening as Helia pleaded her case to the officials, before Rascal then made a significant fuss as they were led away, in an attempt to prevent them from looking for anyone else who might have been hiding.

To his credit, the captain hadn't said anything when he'd noticed the group was one short. It was a small mercy that gave them a chance.

A small chance that involved Dzin not losing his mind, trapped inside this little crate, hardly able to breathe, and with no brother to comfort him as his vision began to blur again, his heart raced as though it might pop out of his chest, and the white heat of his anxiety threatened to turn him inside out.

It was up to him to escape and free them.

Me? I'm responsible for saving them.

He badly wanted to curl up into a ball in this box and just disappear. Maybe they would store him somewhere, and he could just hide for the rest of forever. At least that way he wouldn't have to deal with these feelings anymore. He could just let them swallow him whole and be done with it.

Rot and roots, Dzin, focus!

No. He had come too far to give up now.

He fought to breathe evenly, touching the rough interior of the crate to center himself.

Keeping his mind busy as he unpicked the knot of the situation.

Now. Where had his friends been taken? The three had been led away to meet the Raptor Prince. Then it had been said they would be taken to cellblock Beta—so he'd heard the officials say anyway. Meanwhile, the bumps and jolts told him his crate was being loaded onto a cart headed . . . he didn't know where. Given his luck, though, it wouldn't be close to anywhere he needed to be.

The rumble of the airship engines was fading. He was moving further into the mountain. He decided to get out quickly.

Forcing his sweaty palms against the underside of the wooden lid, he gave a tentative push, trying not to alert anybody who might be around. The lid moved, but only a little.

Rascal had done too good of a job nailing it down just enough to hold it in place.

He shoved again. The splinters from the rough wood cut his palm, but he pushed aside the pain.

Yantuz had never cared for consequences, only for doing what was right in each moment.

Despite the intense panic beginning to grip him, Dzin tried to draw strength from that.

So he pushed and pushed, pressing his back against the crate while shoving his hands into the lid as hard as he could.

It moved a little.

Then a little more.

Now there was a definitive gap, through which air rushed in, together with a cacophony of smells: oil and grease, engine fumes, even sweat—it all poured in.

His crate was one of many being transported through the inner workings of the docks, accompanied by a constant roar of clanking machinery and airship engines, and people shouting over each other. Underneath it all, he could hear the *tick, tick, tick* of the mountain cogs as they turned.

Time is running out, Dzin. Move!

With one last shove, the nails gave. The lid cranked fully open and clattered back down at an angle. He stuck his head out, hoping he hadn't been heard by the two unnaturally pale men who were sat not far in front, steering the rusty, shallow-bottomed cart further into the mountain.

Neither moved, both probably deafened by the din around them.

Behind him, the early morning desert light filtering through the dock was growing fainter, but he could still see the outline of the *Golden Oriole* sandwiched between a much bulkier transport ship and a small, sleek pleasure craft. Dock workers milled between them like ants, while beyond, even more airships flew in and buzzed off again into the outside world, in a seemingly never-ending procession of colors and growling engines.

The outside world. He suddenly hoped he would see it again.

Unfurling himself from his hiding place, trying not to jangle the bottles around his feet too much, he stumbled off the back of the cart and pulled himself into the shadows of a giant, clanking machine, which was pouring out a thin line of gray smoke that rose into a gloomy funnel above. Looking through the pipes that bent at odd angles from the machines and the chains that hung from the ceiling, he realized he couldn't see any sign of the others being led away. They were already gone, moving forward to face whatever fate had in store. Leaving him alone in this dank, dark place.

Growing up at the Great Tree, he'd been ensconced in the natural world, surrounded by life of all descriptions. Nature made sense to him. There was a balance to it, a sense of logic, even if sometimes it was a little brutal to the untrained eye. But it worked for millions of cycles and would continue to work for a million more. And although the world beyond had always been something of a thrilling concept, filled with many different locales, cities, and cultures—plenty of which he had experienced in his quest to be a Runner—he had never visited anywhere like this. So . . . unnatural.

The thought of being trapped in such a place, deep underground, with so much weight separating him from the open Silvyran skies, made his hands clammy and his heart pound.

Just think about it in natural terms, he thought, trying to calm himself. *That's all this is—just a man-made jungle. An overgrowth of mechanical branches and foliage. Those pipes are branches, the chains just vines, that arm—*

The almost translucently pale arm, so lacking in color it had clearly never seen much daylight, cut short his thinking.

Snaking around his neck, the muscles tightened. His eyes swam. And a face pressed next to his.

"So, what do we have here?" a warm, ale-infused voice breathed into his ear.

Everything went dark.

CHAPTER THIRTY-THREE
THE RAPTOR PRINCE

Helia kept Nu close beside her as they were led away from the docks and inside the mountain. Rascal followed behind, shadowing them like the grumpiest guardian angel one could imagine. On either side of them were four very gaunt-looking—and heavily armed—men. Guards, soldiers, Helia wasn't sure what to call them. She only knew they were rough and seemed willing to use the short daggers they each carried.

One guard jabbed the point of one into her side—not enough to pierce her clothes or reach her skin but enough to know that it could if they wanted.

"Left here," the man said.

Down another dimly lit corridor they went, before taking a lift a short way up to another level. They were led through a pair of sliding doors into a room that was large and surprisingly luxurious, considering it was open to the elements outside.

Ever-changing dunes of shifting pink blew around the floor, while across the walls blooms of great silver cactus flowers climbed and twisted.

A low wind whistled from the sun-kissed desert beyond.

Helia blinked and shielded her eyes. She shifted her weight to steady herself in the sand.

The doors closed, and the armed men formed a semicircle around the three of them.

From the middle of the room, the Raptor Prince turned lazily from where he was reclining on a sandblasted rock-cut chair, his face so pale it was almost glowing. He looked nothing like Helia had expected. He wore a white glittering gambler's hat with contrasting feathers, like an Earth fedora invented by a culture that had no practical use for such things, and swirled a stained-glass goblet of a strong-smelling green liquid in his hand, the index finger of which sported an elaborate ring, ending in a short but wicked-looking talon. He tilted his head slightly as he considered the visitors, before he curled a long-nailed finger through his elaborate waxed mustache, twisting it into a point to make his thin, birdlike face look even more severe.

"Ah, you're here," he said, his voice promising milk and honey, but his expression cold and suspicious.

He got to his feet, letting the fierce cut of his bright pink suit fall into shape, which hugged his figure as he glided over to them, the material of his outfit shimmering as though he had been conjured of glass made from the sand that surrounded them. He swept his fingers down his sleeves and straightened his cuffs. The Raptor Prince looked every bit the preening bird, flaunting his plumage for the crowd of eager-looking sycophants who ringed his throne room.

"He looks like a desert bird," Nu whispered.

"I *am* the desert, child," he replied, a sly grin splitting the shadow beneath his hat. A golden chain worn at his waist in lieu of a belt, the end swinging like a pendulum as he moved, keeping a beat. "I was born of heat, and it should be of no surprise to anyone who knows me that I like to dress the same way."

Shifting his gaze to Helia, he was clearly smart enough to understand that she was the person leading this expedition.

He was tall—nobody else they'd seen living in this mountain had been—and Helia wondered what that might say about his genetics. Was he even from these parts? As they'd been led through the corridors, they'd noticed the average height to be shorter than those people at the Great

Tree, and their skin was paler, more like the sand and rock of their home-land. Rascal's face had shown her dislike of the closed-in feeling of the place, and as the only person here with actual wings, she seemed oddly well placed to think about the fate of a bird kept in a stone castle. *Perhaps*, thought Helia, *the Raptor Prince was in a prison of his own making.*

What was undeniable was the Raptor Prince had a presence about him that seemed to suggest he thought he was towering over Helia and her group as well, both physically and with regard to their status.

His grin faded. "Of course, by the looks on your faces, you do not know me. So, pray tell, why have you appeared in my city, and why are you disturbing my morning reflection?"

Helia did her best to seem awed, bowing her head slightly. "With re-spect, Your Majesty, we came here seeking your help." She chose *majesty* with great deliberation, flattering the Prince as though he were a king.

"Help?" He laughed. "Oh, that's a good one. It was worth agreeing to meet you just for that alone." His demeanor changed in an instant, and he leaned into Helia's face, so close she could smell the drink on his breath, the talon on his finger tracing the contour of her chin. "And why, by the dunes, should I help you?"

Helia sensed Rascal tense behind her. She needed to diffuse this quickly.

"There is a man who seeks to bring destruction. Silvyra is on the precipice of a great deal of suffering, and we must stop him. To do so, we need an ingredient to make the Elixir of Life."

"You couldn't have picked an Elixir up elsewhere? They are all over the world, my dear." The waves of the desert continued to glow gold and red through the window behind him, shimmering as the wind blew the dunes in an ever-changing sea.

"Ah yes," Helia replied. "Unfortunately, there was trouble at the Great Tree. They have all been rendered useless, and the refinery has been destroyed."

"What?!" he yelled right into her face. "How can that be?"

"It's a long story, I'm afraid. But if you'd like to—"

He continued as though she weren't even there. "But it's been weeks since the last shipment. Our stores here are running on empty. Are you saying no more is coming? This is inexcusable! What kind of operation is that so-called Scientist woman running up there?"

Helia stood firm and held his gaze, not happy with him speaking to her—or about her friend—in such a way. It seemed to do the trick. His outburst faded as quickly as it had come, and he moved casually out of her space.

She continued. "That is correct. There is no more Elixir, and we must brew a vial as a matter of urgency. Which brings us to the ingredient we need. It is usually one we would source from elsewhere, yet we cannot. I believe you are in possession of a seedling of the Cerulean Rose, and I would humbly request access to it for just a few moments."

She wasn't willing to use her powers in sight of anyone if she could help it, but if she could just get ahold of that seedling, she could hopefully grow it and create another seed to take its place. They would have their ingredient, and nobody would be any the wiser.

It didn't seem like it was going to happen though.

"Nobody touches the Cerulean Rose," he said. "Or anything from my collection, in fact." His pale face flushed, showing real anger at the suggestion. "Do you know how long it's taken me to build my collection? How it wows my subjects and visitors alike? There is not a collection like it in the whole of Silvyra, outside of the Conservatory of Aedela. Indeed, I'd wager an ocean of pearls my collection rivals even theirs."

"Your Highness, please?" said Helia, persisting. She had to get him to see reason. "This involves everything and everyone. You will not be protected from what's to come, even here."

The Prince was already bored by the conversation, though, far too concerned about the lack of Elixir and muttering to himself—as he removed his hat and stared at his slicked black hair in the mirror—about whether he was going to start seeing gray hairs again.

"Your Majesty?" Helia said again, louder this time. For this she received a jab of a dagger in her side. She flinched.

But it didn't matter. They were done for the moment.

"Take them away." The Prince sighed, gesturing to the guards. "Let them enjoy the hospitality of the cells for even daring to come here and think they have a right to seek one of my prized seedlings." He'd turned from the mirror to face his audience, for that seemed to be how he treated his fawning subjects, his hands raised in anger. "Nobody touches my collection but me." He turned his back, approaching his throne.

Nu spoke up now. "Raptor Prince, you have to help us. The fate of everything rests on you now."

The man barely turned, before brushing some invisible dust from his jacket. "I don't care," he replied. "The petty concerns of the First Forest and garden regions of this realm are nothing to my people. We live in and for the desert's warm embrace. There is little that my power cannot protect us from here, in this place." He gestured to the impassive stone walls, and then he waved dismissively to the armed men, who immediately swept the three of them up and led them away, back down the twisting tunnels, into the grime and grot of the bowels of the Clockwork Mountain.

As they were hustled along toward their fate, Nu wondered if there had been anything else she could have said to sway the Prince's mind. Perhaps pander to his ego more or offer a bribe of some sort—although what she could offer, she had no idea. He was already in charge of his own city and by all accounts had a collection of rare and valuable items from all over Silvyra. What exactly could she have offered to change his mind?

Yet the feeling she hadn't lived up to some kind of expectation continued to nag at her. A niggle of anger at herself that she *should* have done more somehow. That if the flights of fancy she'd allowed herself—of being someone special, like the Sages—were true, then surely she could have changed his mind.

Which made it even more disappointing that she'd failed. Not only did it dispel her notions of grandeur but she hadn't been able to help Helia after all. She'd been a complete waste.

Now they would rot in the cold rock of this mountain, dumped unceremoniously inside a cell even smaller than the cargo hold on the *Golden Oriole*. And as the women and Dzin stared at each other, Nu realized there was nothing more she could do.

Then her thoughts drifted and traveled, her mind overtaken, and suddenly she was somewhere else. Again.

Nu was back alongside Veer in the midst of war.

And the battle was being lost.

Nu saw in the Sage's eyes that he already knew. The Petal Queen too. Yet both continued fighting as though it was not a lost cause.

The air was thick with smoke and drifting charred petals, while the blackening sickness the shadow had brought with it was already spreading outward. Nu sensed that the settlement of Aedela was gone. There couldn't be many guards left to keep fighting the evil hordes. Most of them were either dead or likely injured and staggering after the evacuees, hoping in vain to catch up with them before they were caught or bled out.

Nu could see the last vestiges of Veer's energy and spirit seep out of him as he tried to catch his breath. The frustration built in her again that she was nothing but a bystander here, and she couldn't help any of them. This power should have given her the chance to do good, and yet it did not.

The hordes continued attacking. Something was driving the legion of nightmares forward, forcing them into a never-ending killing frenzy.

"Leave now and keep running," Veer said to the Petal Queen. His breath came in shallow gasps.

How long has he been fighting now? *Nu wondered.*

"Catch up with your people; lead them to the Great Tree. Wherever possible, travel through the forests on the way. Mother has influence through them; she will protect you should you be chased."

"If you think I'm leaving you behind—"

"Just go, Your Majesty. I'll hold them off for as long as I can."

He didn't give her a chance to argue. A gust of wind sent her onward, while he stopped and turned to face the evil masses.

There were hundreds of terrible faces and jaws and teeth.

And hatred, so much hatred.

Nu sensed the conviction in Veer. He was still the Sage of Strength, and despite the odds—or perhaps because of them—he stuck out his chest, twisted the toe of his boot into the soil, and prepared to meet the enemy with what power he had left.

Except, suddenly, the horde was no longer moving.

Nu watched, confused. The enemy were holding off, waiting for something.

The mass of gray cloud that hung over them was beginning to grow thicker and more unforgiving. The cinders continued to fall around them. From where she stood, Nu could barely take it anymore. She wanted Veer to run, but he refused to move.

She knew why she was here now. She had been shown this for a reason. To bear witness to the truth that's approaching.

To see him.

When the figure appeared in the crowd, she could not help but convulse. Something rippled from deep within her, all the way through her body. Her mouth was dry, her eyes watering at the sheer evil of the energy he exuded. The tang of burning flesh assaulted her senses, and the glow of fire could be seen at the edges of the figure's dark cloak.

He was an abomination. A walking visage of misery and torment.

Evil personified.

It was his face, though, that struck fear into her heart. Because he didn't have one. It was a melted mass of flesh, a horribly blank canvas.

Nu knew who this was. And now she had seen him, her feet finally moved. She was able to take a step back and set herself to turn and run, to try to escape this horrible nightmare. But then, finally, she was noticed in this place.

The figure paused. His eyeless face turned toward her. And although there were no features to give away his thoughts, Nu understood what he was feeling.

He was angry. Angry and confused.

She sees us? *He said. The voice was loud and terrifying in her mind, and Nu didn't know what this meant or how he could have possibly seen her.*

There was then a sensation at the edge of her mind. A roughness, cruel and probing, casting a net against her thoughts. She tried to force it back, but they were already caught and dragged away to be studied. A hand stretched out, a finger pointing her way.

She could only stand there and cover her ears beneath the onslaught of his booming rage. Only the sense that he was incredulous, too, surprised by this turn of events, gave her a measure of comfort.

Veer seemed to sense his enemy hesitate. After filling up his chest with an abnormally large breath, he used the figure's confusion to weave a hundred thousand arrows of air, barely visible as they hung in the sky above them, barbs pointed downward.

He raised his hands, readying them to launch.

But then there was a flash of darkness before them, a rent in the air. Both Veer and Nu covered their eyes at the power of it, while feeling a swirling torrent of the cloud swoosh around them, battering and stinging their skin with cinders and ashes.

Then it subsided and vanished. And with it, the enemy too.

All of them.

Nu staggered, unable to believe it. Veer seemed to have had the same reaction, confounded by what had just happened and by the fact he was still standing here, alive.

The battle was over for now. All that was left was the near silence of the breeze blowing through the streets, carrying the smoke of the still-burning fires. A sense of dread continued to hang thick in the air, clinging to the debris around them in a city that was no more.

Veer turned to Lynx.

"We need to get back to the Library," he said. "And fast."

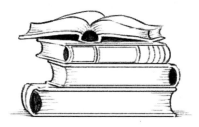

CHAPTER THIRTY-FOUR
THE SIEGE BEGINS

Arturo skittered back across the marble floor away from the portal, pulling Robin along with him.

He could see the legion of nightmares already moving toward the opening.

A more hideous sight he could not imagine. The people and their beastly devil dogs were not just carved with words but their bodies were in an increased state of decay, as though they'd been like this for years, perhaps centuries. Dressed in all kinds of material that may once have been gowns or dress suits or robes, but were now barely rags hanging from their withered skin.

They're going to pour through, he thought, panicking.

"Close the thing! Close it now!" Robin cried to Centauri.

But as much as the Orb spun and the symbols lit up and pulsed fiercely in its communication with the Book of Wisdom, nothing happened. It didn't deactivate the portal, as Arturo assumed it might normally be able to do.

Gray, stinking smoke was now seeping through, and they could hear the growls and gnashing teeth on the other side getting closer.

"It's not closing!" Robin yelled, looking around wildly as if that would help her spot the source of the problem. Centauri buzzed in a panic around her head. "Why isn't the portal closing, Arturo? The portals always close. Why isn't this one?"

"How the hell should I know?" he cried back. "I don't work here!"

They both turned and shouted down the aisle, "Mwamba!"

Robin pulled Arturo back further as another terrifying hellhound began to emerge from the portal. Its gigantic snout split in two, revealing jagged and rotting teeth.

Arturo gasped in horror, unable to look away, though Robin didn't hesitate. She grabbed a nearby desk lamp that had been resting on the shelf for late-night readers and slammed it at the beast as it tried to jump through. Something in its skull cracked, and it was pushed back to wherever it had crawled from.

But he'd seen the rest of them beyond the portal. The army of darkness. He knew there wouldn't be much time before the next one tried to get through, and he wasn't sure a thick scientific tome could take down all of them.

Spotting the sliding ladder further down the aisle, he reached out to grab it. He dragged it over the portal and wedged a book under its wheels.

"Temporary measure," he said, noting Robin's incredulous expression.

"Of course it's temporary. It's a ladder; they'll climb right through!"

At that moment, Mwamba and a group of scholars appeared, silhouetted by the light at the end of the aisle.

"Robin?" he called.

"Mwamba! Oh, thank God. Did you get the message?"

"Yes, Urulla told us about the First Cave. We found the vial you mentioned." His assistant who was holding the vessel of the murky poison as far from his body as he was able, as if it might explode at any moment. "We'll find an antidote. Even a temporary one. Enough to stop it affecting the Book. Although . . ."

His voice trailed off as a once-human arm reached out of the portal and grabbed the steps of the ladder. Robin repeatedly slammed the book down onto its bloodstained fingers until it withdrew, but then another took its place.

"What's going on?" Mwamba exclaimed.

"No time to explain," Robin said, smacking the thing back again. Centauri was also trying to help, repeatedly dropping like a medicine ball onto a head that had appeared, full of burning, glowing script across its skin. As that one fell back into the portal, another appeared, and Centauri and Robin both bashed that one together.

Arturo couldn't help but think of the fairground game Whac-a-Mole. Except these were certainly not your average moles.

"You have to stop the effects of that poison, Mwamba." Robin's breath was ragged. "We don't have much time. If we don't reawaken the Book and shut down these portals soon, then we're in serious trouble."

Mwamba nodded. He turned on his heels and ran, gesturing to his nervous assistant to follow him. Mwamba's Orb, Canopus, swirled a quick *good luck* to Centauri before he nudged the assistant into moving faster, and the group disappeared along the Concourse.

Moments later, another Sage appeared at the end of the aisle, who Arturo recognized immediately, thanks to his walrus mustache. The Sage of Strength also wore bruises over his cheeks and cuts across his neck.

"Veer!" Robin cried, then gave him a look of horror. "I was going to say, 'Thank goodness you're okay,' but I can't tell if that's the case."

"I'm alive at least, Robin. We managed to get a lot of Aedela out of there in time, but the town fell to Suttaru."

"How did you escape?"

Veer slammed a gust of wind through the portal, blowing back all manner of limbs that had been trying to get through.

"I don't rightly know, my friend. The army just up and left. Disappeared right as I was ready to go down, guns blazing."

"Disappeared where?"

Veer shrugged and gestured behind him, where flashes of light were sparking in the distance. They were accompanied by cries of horror and the sound of chairs scattering.

"No time to explain how little I know," he said, giving them an apologetic nod. "Good luck to you both here. There are other portals that need defending."

With that, he ran off to assist elsewhere.

Robin sighed.

"Great," she muttered to Centauri. "Let's hope Mwamba finds that antidote fast so we can fix the Book and close these bloody portals. Until then, I guess it's just you and me against the world, my little friend."

Arturo tried not to look hurt.

CHAPTER THIRTY-FIVE
REVELATIONS

Nu returned to the present with less of a jolt than last time, but the same momentary confusion and shiver of cold, and this time a feeling of dread had followed her back to her waking self. She was in a cell now, propped up against the wall, as though she had fallen asleep against it.

Had she fallen asleep though? No. The last thing she remembered was walking through the tunnels of the Clockwork Mountain with the others. She barely had a moment to see the cell they'd been thrown into before she'd disappeared into her own mind.

The others sat around her, watching her now.

"Welcome back, kid," Rascal said. "You were gone for a little while there. Are you okay?"

"I don't know," she said. *Am I going mad? Has Suttaru been manipulating me?*

Only Helia had stayed silent. She sat cross-legged again, weighing what she saw before her. Nu's face blushed.

"Helia, what's happening to me?"

Helia gave her a sad and kindly smile. "What did you see?"

Nu didn't think to question how she had known. The woman had spoken with such confidence, Nu felt compelled to simply answer.

"I—I saw Veer. We were in Aedela. There was a battle going on; there were hideous creatures attacking the town, and Veer and some ruler, the Petal Queen, were fighting them."

Helia's forehead furrowed even further. "And how was he? Veer, I mean."

"Scared," Nu replied. She knew it was the truth. Because for all the man's vigor and strength, and his determination to fight till the bitter end, he couldn't hide his disquiet.

Neither could Nu, especially when she remembered that awful, horrible faceless man.

"There was someone else there, Helia." Nu paused, feeling suddenly nauseous. "Someone controlling the army that Veer was fighting. I saw him. He didn't seem to have a face. I think it was—"

Helia tensed and held up a hand.

Nu suddenly felt embarrassed. All this time, these dreams she'd been having, maybe they had meant something after all. Why had she not told her sooner?

"It's not the first dream I've had either." She didn't know if Helia wanted to know more, but she had to get this out, no matter how much it made her feel silly. She just knew she had to be honest about all this. It was important. "I had a similar dream about Veer while I was on the airship. And at the Great Tree, just before the explosion. I've been seeing what Veer has faced in Aedela all this time. I even saw—*felt*, I suppose you could say—a little of Dzin's laboratory fire too. While I was awake." She groaned. "I'm . . . I'm so sorry, Helia. I should have said something earlier. I just didn't realize what was happening. I was afraid I was doing something wrong, spying on the Sages, or that Antares was breaking the rules, showing me things I wasn't supposed to see."

Rascal interrupted. "They're just dreams, Nu."

"You didn't know," Helia said, although it was unclear whether she was agreeing with the former Runner or ignoring her.

Nu tensed. "And there's something else. Something much worse."

"Nu, we don't have to continue. I said it's fine."

"No, Helia, it's not. When the figure appeared . . . he . . . he saw me. He looked straight at me, and I could tell he knew I was there."

Helia's eyes widened. "The Ash Man saw you?"

"The Ash Man?!" Rascal blurted out.

"Yes. And I know it was just a dream, but it felt . . . like he'd seen me for real. I felt his gaze on me somehow. He knew I was there. And then all of a sudden he was gone. He disappeared—him and his army. I think . . . I think he might be coming *here*."

A slow crawl of shock and recognition of what this must mean grew over Helia's face like a crack across a pane of glass.

But it was Rascal who spoke again, looking between the pair with a deepening frown.

"Just what is going on? Because it sounds to me like you both are taking these dreams a bit too seriously. And why in the twin moons of Silvyra are you dreaming about the Ash Man, Nu? That's the most obscure and ancient of all campfire tales. I didn't even realize the story of him stretched back to wherever you're from too."

Helia closed her eyes and crossed her legs again. Nu recognized it as a meditative position.

It was a sign Helia was trying to center herself, to focus.

"He's real, Rascal." Her words were calm and considered. "Or at least he was. A man, a scholar of great learning. He was from our world originally."

"And how the blazes did he end up here?"

"Stories have a curious habit of traveling beyond the pages of their books," Helia replied.

"That's particularly vague, even for a Sage."

"So you knew. I thought you might."

"Yes, as I told Nu earlier, I've met your kind before. Although the last Sage I had dealings with didn't get me into half as much trouble as you have."

Helia kept her eyes shut, ignoring the bait. "If he saw you, Nu, he will likely also know what we're doing. He'll know we're on the trail of Perennia, and he'll try to beat us to wherever she is. And that's not our only problem."

Nu felt her face pale. "What else?"

"Quite possibly he may have seen where you were too. And if he knows we're at the Clockwork Mountain, I can imagine we don't have long."

"You think he'll come for us?"

"In some way, yes. I have no doubt. We need to get out of here and find that seed."

Nu felt her skin tighten at the thought. What she'd seen in her dreams was too horrific to contemplate experiencing in real life. Surely this was just a mistake. They were just dreams, the anxious conjuring of impossible scenarios her brain had decided to torment her with.

"Are you sure?" she asked in a quiet voice, not wanting to sound like she was questioning a Sage, but unable to accept what she was saying. "Perhaps it *was* just a dream."

Helia's eyes opened, and she spoke quietly, her simple words carrying the short distance across the chilly air, and in that moment, these words changed everything. "You were having a dream, but you weren't asleep. It was vivid. You could see things you shouldn't be able to see and feel emotions you have no right to feel. When you woke, you were lost and unsure, right? You were colder than usual, and you had a temporary ache behind the eyes, which was gone as soon as you were aware of it. All true, yes?"

Nu's mouth fell open. "Yes! How did you know?"

"It's a common reaction to having visions. Xav used to have them on occasion, usually in times of stress. Now it seems you will too."

Visions?

That was it. That was the word that captured exactly what had just happened. What she'd experienced at the Great Tree too. Indeed, in a way, it was what she'd learned to deal with her entire life.

She'd always been secretly proud of her *knowing* of things. Small snippets of feelings and emotions flowing from others into her. Or moments when she could see something about a person, a time in their life, for example, that she shouldn't have been able to see. All in order to understand that person a little more.

She'd simply known things and enjoyed the power it gave her, the ability to give people more of what they needed, be it kindness or encouragement or support.

But these visions were something else. Stronger and more vivid each time. All since she'd rescued a little Orb in the Great Library.

Nu looked down at Antares. The Orb floated from her hands and grew a little in size, as if recognizing the importance of the moment.

There was only one thing on her mind now. A question she had been playing with throughout this journey, but one which she hadn't dared to take seriously.

Antares knew though.

It's true, she flashed.

It was true.

Nu was experiencing the same kinds of visions as Helia's partner, Xavier. The same as the former Sage of Truth. It had all happened after she had found the Orb.

No, that's not true.

After the Orb had found *her*.

The realization struck home, and she lifted her eyes to meet Helia's. Helia, the Sage of Hope, who was kind and understanding and didn't need the power of truth to know exactly what Nu needed right now.

"Yes," Helia said, reaching over to touch Nu's arm. "She chose you, Nu."

"But . . . why?"

"The bond between a Sage and her Orb is a strong one. They choose us for reasons only they know, but they never fail to find someone who has that special connection. Perhaps they can foresee the relationship, thanks to knowledge contained in the Book of Wisdom. Or perhaps it is divined through some ancient magic infused in them as they grow. Regardless, when they choose us to be their companions, it is with faith that we should accept. We have no need to question their choice, only honor it."

"So I'm—"

"A Sage," Helia finished for her. "Yes, Nu. You are."

Nu sat back against the wall of the cell. This was almost too enormous to contemplate. Her brain was racing, her heart pounding, trying to take it all in, this sense of accomplishment. Of pure happiness. It was a wonderful struggle to process and accept it as fact. *This is really happening,* she told herself. Sure, she'd thought about what it might be like to be told that. Of course she had! So many in the Great Library often did. As children, they learned about these champions of virtue among them. Protectors of Paperworld, the Great Library, and Earth. It was inevitable for any child who heard such things to occasionally slip into daydreams and fantasies about the "what-if." But Nu had never really taken those flights of fancy very far.

Now she was being told she was an *actual* Sage.

Strangely, there was a part of her that knew it made total sense. Her knowings in the Library had become entire visions of the past and present in Paperworld. Her talent becoming her power. Such was the way of the Sages, each with their particular skills, which were transformed into special powers while on their travels across the other realms. Powers that were aided and strengthened by the bonds with their Orbs.

Antares had chosen her. Bonded with her over their short time together. And grown in strength thanks to their new shared connection.

The Orb floated before her now. The pulses and flickers of gold that drifted around her metallic layers became stronger and more excited.

Sage.

Nu didn't know what to say. She was flustered and overwhelmed. Not least because this life-changing moment wasn't going to be very useful in altering their current situation.

"Thank you," she said, reaching out to touch Antares. The Orb buzzed against her finger, the vibrations following her finger as it ran over the metallic surface. "But I'm afraid as happy as I am to have been chosen by you for this momentous role, it probably has little bearing on getting us out of here. My dreams"—she paused and corrected herself—"I mean, my *visions,* can't unlock the cell door."

"Which is why we need our friend out there to hurry up with our plan B," Rascal said, her wings twitching impatiently. "Let's just hope Dzin can get us out of this."

Dzin awoke in a cell with three familiar faces staring at him.

Rascal grumbled as she leaned on a wall, thick, meaty arms crossed over her chest.

"Time for plan C, then."

Dzin sat up groggily. For a moment, there was a peaceful bliss to the ignorance of what was happening, until he remembered losing Yantuz and his own subsequent capture.

"His brother's just died, and he is still in shock," Nu said, coming to his defense. Her hand was on his back, rubbing in gentle circles. "What did you expect? It was worth a try, and it didn't work. You can't blame him."

He opened his eyes to find that he was propped up in the corner of a dingy container. Dirt and sand were scattered across the floor. The door opposite him had three bars in its tiny window near the top, but he couldn't see anything through it.

Everything was rusted and grime-ridden. It was as far from home as he could have imagined, and that knowledge just gave more power to his sudden wish to go back to the relative comfort of unconsciousness.

He had failed in his mission, and they were now trapped.

As he sat up, a groan escaped his parched lips. He felt the floor move and heard the walls reverberate as if something had shaken the mountain. Or at least he thought it did. It could have been his body finally giving up after everything he'd been through.

"I'm sorry," he whispered as Nu helped him to his feet.

"Don't be," she replied quietly, giving him a sympathetic smile. "I would have been captured far quicker, I'm sure. I was always terrible at hide-and-seek."

Dzin couldn't help but nod at that. He'd been the same as a child, trying to hide in their small cubby in the Tree. Yantuz always found him within minutes, no matter where he hid.

Yantuz. The thought of his brother made him almost double over. It felt like his heart had dropped through his stomach.

Helia reached out to steady him, even though she, too, looked anguished over something.

She kept touching her fingers to the amulet at her neck.

"Are you okay?" she asked.

He couldn't think straight, knowing Yantuz had died. And for what? Nothing.

Dzin wasn't half the hero his brother was.

But all he said was, "Sure."

"Look, you gave it your best shot." Rascal sighed and clapped him on the back rather too hard. "We failed, too, if it helps."

He looked around at his newfound friends, trying to ignore the disappointment in their eyes and the pity they regarded him with. He took a breath. "So, I take it the meeting with the Raptor Prince didn't work out as you'd hoped?"

"He didn't really give us time to convince him. I'm not sure he's the caring type." Nu shrugged. "Helia did her best, but he didn't want to listen."

The room shook again, and something akin to a siren sounded in the distance.

"Then . . . what do we do now?"

The reply he received was unexpected. It was a voice from beyond the door to the cell.

From beyond death, even.

"We go get that ingredient, of course!"

CHAPTER THIRTY-SIX
THE GRIEFBRINGER

"Yantuz?"

Dzin's voice was hoarse and cracked, but suddenly full of hope again. He stood, awestruck, as a smile far too bright to come from beyond the grave shone through the bars, and the bolt slid back on the cell door.

He rushed forward, barely allowing the disheveled Yantuz to step through before he crashed into him, sobbing a low moan of relief and happiness into his brother's tattered shirt as he hugged him fiercely.

"Oh . . . you're alive. You're *alive*!"

"It seems so," Yantuz joked, wrapping his arms around Dzin and squeezing back just as hard. "Although for a while there, I wasn't sure."

They held each other for a moment, Dzin's mind spinning with emotions. He was too confused and shocked to do anything but hold on as tightly as he possibly could, lest Yantuz slip away again somehow. Finally, his brother patted him and pulled him away, then reached into his pocket.

"Luckily, I found a friend out there."

He lifted a ball that was the size of a large marble, which then grew quickly until it was only a little smaller than his own head. It was strange and otherworldly looking, with a metallic sheen to its exterior and layers beneath, which now twisted and spun excitedly. Strange symbols appeared all over it, with an emerald light so intense it reminded Dzin of moss bathed in sunshine.

"Vega!" Helia cried.

The glowing ball leaped out of Yantuz's hand and started spinning around in the air above Helia's head. Dzin staggered back in surprise.

"Oh, Vega," Helia said, the relief tangible in her voice. "I knew you couldn't have gone far. I could still feel the strength of my powers, so I knew you had to be close. Or else it would have been like that time in the snow lands of the Lotus, when you got trapped."

The symbols on the ball became leaves that swirled around as if caught in gusts of wind. It looked as if the Orb was laughing.

Helia chuckled too. "Yes, yes, I know you're sorry. Let's not get into all that now. The question is: Where have you been, and why did you not come back to me straight away?"

"I wondered if he might belong to you," Yantuz said with a wry smile, scuffing his feet against the grimy floor as though a little nervous about voicing his thoughts. "There was something about you. I couldn't quite put my finger on it. Anyway, thank you. When I slipped off the airship, I was falling fast. I should have made a big dent in Silvyra."

Dzin watched his brother, still stunned he was standing there. The same old Yantuz. Not a vision or an illusion, but real and alive. He barely cared what magic or luck had brought him back. He was just overwhelmed with gratitude to have him here again. And yet his lips couldn't help but voice his curiosity.

"How?" he whispered. "What happened?"

"That little ball of light is what happened. Vega, is it?"

The ball buzzed as if responding, and Yantuz grinned.

"He literally caught me. Put himself between me and certain death, and did his best to hold me up. And he's pretty powerful too. He grew enough to let me lie on him and then carried me back to the airship. You were all on board, so all I could do was clamber on to the rear of the ship and hold on as tightly as I could. Although I think I might have kicked off a rudder, because something definitely fell off while I was trying to climb back on."

"You're the reason the bloody airship wouldn't turn." Rascal laughed somewhat hysterically. "You almost got us killed in there."

"I almost got killed *out* there! I had to wedge myself into the rigging as best I could—it was all I could do to hold on while you dodged those Rock Giants. And let me tell you, at that altitude, those nighttime desert temperatures are not pleasant. The ball here—"

"Orb," Helia said.

"Orb, sorry. Well, he not only caught me but kept me warm out there. Otherwise, I wouldn't have made it."

Helia gave her Orb a big grin, then gave Yantuz an even bigger hug. "Thank you for bringing him back."

"Oh, I definitely think it was the other way around. He was the one that led me back to you through this infernal, unnatural place. We've visited some pretty tight and not-at-all pleasant air vents in an effort to avoid drawing attention." He nodded solemnly at the Orb, who seemed to shiver dramatically at his words. "Anyway. If you don't mind, I'd quite like to leave, please. Something is in the air here, and it isn't pleasant."

Dzin couldn't help but keep staring at his brother. The joy that was filling him up, from his boots to his head, was almost too much to bear. He had so many feelings that he couldn't formulate thoughts or actions. He could only stand there, feeling stunned and relieved and so very happy.

But then there was an explosion in the distance. Outside the window, he could see a flash of strange light, and the corridor began to shake.

"Was that you?" Rascal asked, turning to Yantuz. "Some kind of distraction?"

By the look on his brother's face, he was just as surprised as everyone else. "No, I didn't think of anything beyond finding Dzin and the rest of you. Certainly nothing that involves explosions."

Rascal's face darkened with concern, even more so than Dzin thought possible. He could almost feel the shaking of the room as she thundered toward the door, trying to hurry them all along.

"Then let's not wait around to find out what's happening. We need to get on with what we came here for and then leave. This place has always given me the shivers."

The group didn't make it far beyond the cell, though, before Nu let out a gasp of horror, and they all spun to meet a flash of heat blowing up the corridor toward them.

A gigantic, multilimbed beast had burst through a doorway and was now crawling up the tunnel, dragging its ample behind with it.

At first glance, it looked like a giant spider, except this one had too many unnaturally crooked legs, too many teeth, and its crisp black skin popped and fizzed beneath the fire that covered its entire grotesque form.

If that wasn't bad enough, as the nightmare creature gave a howl of smoky rage, giving them a glimpse of the flames also flickering at the back of its throat, its back burst open and a mass of smaller fire creatures burst forth, beginning to skuttle up the corridor toward them.

They all ran for their lives, away from the horrific beast and its babies, as the nightmare beings chased them, setting everything they touched ablaze.

Suttaru, Helia thought. *He sent his nightmares quicker than I'd expected.*

She tried to focus, to feel the environment around her, seeking some form of life. A plant, a shoot of grass, anything she could channel her power through to throw up an obstacle to slow the creatures down.

But there was nothing but metal and rock.

The hopelessness of the situation threatened to overwhelm her. All she could think about was Xavier and how she'd not been able to help him escape, how she'd had to watch him die. And now it was happening all over again. She was going to lose her friends too.

Except Xav hadn't given up, had he? He'd saved her. Sacrificed himself and told her to go on without him. Because he knew that hope must and would endure. In his final moments, he hadn't given up on her.

She refused to give up on him.

"Dum spiro spero," she panted to herself, trying to clutch tightly to her calm.

Keep focused, Helia. You can do this.

"Quickly, here!" she heard Rascal shout as the Runner made it to a door and called back. There was a squeal as she wrenched the spinning mechanism to unlock it, then pulled it open and shoved Nu through. Helia caught a glimpse of nothing more than a ladder on the other side. There was no room to pile in. The only way onward was up.

"What do you want? An invitation?" Rascal urged, kicking Dzin through, before Yantuz and Helia followed.

There was then a strange noise, and Helia glanced back to see Rascal's left wing unfold briefly, snapping out to tear a hole through one of the many pipes that crisscrossed along the ceiling.

Water immediately sprayed out, down the corridor, toward the spiders, all of which reared up in fury, before Rascal slammed the door behind them.

"That won't hold the mother long," Helia gasped as she and Rascal began to climb after the others. The ladder shook, but she knew it wasn't because of any of the people on it. Clockwork Mountain was under attack. "We have to hurry and get that ingredient before Suttaru's legion can stop us. Suttaru is not famed for giving up so easily."

"The Ash Man?" Dzin blurted out, his response so similar to Rascal's she scowled involuntarily.

"It's a long story," Rascal replied. "And you won't get to hear the rest of it if we don't hustle faster, all right, boys?"

Neither had a chance to question further, as a burst of light appeared overhead, and a sea of noise poured down toward them. Nu had wrenched open the hatch that led out.

They climbed up from the drain to find themselves in the middle of a bustling underground street. To Helia, it could have been the markets of Napoli, like on one of those busy Sunday mornings when she'd been allowed to accompany her mother when she was a child. But the rock on the level above weighed heavy overhead, and the rusted lamps tied to each stall were no substitute for skies and sunshine.

She thought back to the Library, where life was similarly lived underground, yet where sun and starlight was collected on the surface and poured into the city below. Even on the darkest of days, it felt natural and open.

Everyone here was much paler. She wondered whether they ever made it out of the city or if there was simply nowhere to go beyond the safety of the mountain. The desert certainly made for a foreboding boundary.

Still, it seemed not to bother anyone. It was a world full of families and people chatting and shopping, surrounded by excitingly decorated stalls that sold all kinds of exotic plant foods and toys and tools and products. Salesmen boomed as they competed to drown out their neighbors, boasting of their latest offers. Children playing games ran in between people's legs. A hive of excitable activity, all beneath a metal ceiling far above—an unnatural atmosphere moving ever so slightly, in the way the moon and stars might seem to be moving across the night sky.

Yet these heavens were rust colored and entirely man-made. And while plenty of ghostly faces turned their way as they entered the scene in the most unlikely way—crawling out of the street and standing there stunned by what they saw—none of the inhabitants seemed to be bothered by the shaking floor beneath them. They were just going about their day, too caught up in the chaos to pay any mind to the sounds of danger closing in around them.

"Where are we?" Nu asked.

Rascal was looking around, seeking a way out. She pointed to a square spiral of broken stairs that ran up the corrugated side of a building and nudged the brothers toward it.

"The mountain is split into three layers. You saw the docks and the prison block where we came in? Well, that makes up the majority of the bottom section of this city, along with the engine room. This is where the important things happen to keep the city running, all operated by the people deemed least important to society. This place? This is the first settlement they built. They call it Lower Sprocket. It's the highest part of the bottom cog, where the workers and their families live. This is where we need to wait until the cogs align; then we can make it up to Higher Sprocket on the next level."

"And where's the seed we're seeking? Where does the Prince keep it?"

"Beyond that. In the upper cog. Known as the Dial."

They pushed their way through the crowd, taking the stairs as fast as they could. Helia couldn't help but keep glancing back to the street, toward the drain cover they'd just put back. But nothing moved there.

"Should we warn them?" Nu asked. "If the city is under attack, surely they need to know."

Helia nodded, too breathless to speak. Fatigue enveloped her entire body as she struggled up the last turn to where the stairs reached the roof.

But it was Rascal who replied. "Even if they believed us, where would they go, kid? This is a big place, and there is only one way in or out—through the lower section, where we left that terrifying monstrosity. The mountain is designed to keep everyone above here safe from threats in the desert, the Rock Giants among them. I don't think it was meant to protect against infiltration by those insidious *things*." Her face darkened as she regarded Helia. "Or the evil of legend who brought them here."

"I said I was sorry," Helia snapped, exhausted and scared.

She missed Xav more than ever. They'd never been in a situation like this before, but he would still have known how to deal with it. Or at the very least, how to get her through it. Nu was here, but she didn't want to dump all this on the poor girl. She was only in her twenties, and in the great scheme of things, she was just a child of the Library. She couldn't help like Xav would have done. It wouldn't be fair to ask her to either.

Helia wanted nothing more than to break down and cry.

But she couldn't.

She wouldn't, because she was the embodiment of hope, and her friends—and this world and those beyond—were relying on her.

Whatever was happening here had implications. There was a balance between Paperworld and Earth brought about by the Great Library, and Helia was one of the guardians designated to ensure it remained stable and safe. It had worked for centuries. Entire civilizations had grown because of it. All that was good in the world was born of Paperworld.

A universal union of love and connection between so many different realms, for the good of them all.

If she didn't get Perennia back, Suttaru would continue to destroy everything that stood before him. And who knew what that meant for the Library . . . and Earth.

But also, she refused to let him hurt anyone here. Not if she could help it—and she *could* help it. Or at least try.

She knew the lost memories in her mind were the key. Suttaru had done something to Perennia in those moments, and she was sure her brain had witnessed it. What was hidden in there? She needed to find out what it was. She *needed* the Elixir.

"Vega."

It was a request, not a command. They had been companions—friends—for so long that she would never demand anything of him. Yet the desperation in her voice must have been clear because he flew out of her amulet and grew to his regular size, despite the unfamiliar people around them, from whom he usually did his best to hide.

There were more important things to consider now, though, even as the others looked at her strangely, wondering what she was doing.

Vega flashed a question, and she nodded. "I'm going to need you at full strength, because I, quite honestly, am not, and there's not much here to work with. We need to seal off that drain, using whatever we can find. Can you give me what you've got, little one?"

She felt the warmth flow through her as the energy pulsed across their bond. She felt her connection to nature—the one she'd always had—grow, and as she sought a life-form she could utilize, she felt a little wave of sensation explode from her.

There. On that stall.

It was seemingly inconsequential. A branch of some exotic fruit, which had arrived on some airship, having traveled from its source several lands distant from here. A rapsnacker.

Its taste was bitter, and its only value was for the oil it produced, which was used for cooking.

Yet its roots were the toughest around.

Pouring herself into the task, Helia grasped the metal handrail and looked toward the drain cover. She encouraged the roots toward it. In her mind's eye, she could see them bulge and stretch at first, then expand and grow, first down the stall legs, then snaking through the debris that littered the metal floor.

There was a shout of surprise from one woman, the only one to notice, who dragged her son out of the way. But other than she, nobody else saw it. The tip of the root found the manhole cover and then quickly weaved itself around the handle, bolting it to the floor.

Not a moment too soon, as something underneath started to bang at it.

Helia collapsed as she let go. She wasn't confident it would hold long, not against Suttaru's creatures, but maybe enough to let them reach the next level and hopefully draw away any attacks on the people down here.

Nu put her arm around her shoulders, knowing what she'd done and why. Helia was heartened to see that the promising young Sage had also let her Orb out of her pocket to fly alongside them. Antares was still somewhat smaller than Vega—although she was continuing to grow as she recovered from her trauma—and the way she bounced around them energetically, finally given permission to be herself, showed that she was still growing into her new personality. But the fact she was there gave Helia the feeling that a little bit of Xav was there too.

Which gave her a dash of added hope.

"We probably don't have long," she said, pushing herself off the railing to face Rascal. "Any sign of the next level appearing?"

Rascal suddenly pointed. "Yes, there!"

There was a crack of light two buildings' distance away. It was only a small opening into Cog 2—showing a platform and a lift rising from that, alongside another ladder—but it was a sliver of hope, a brighter, better environment that slowly moved above them, bathing the markets in a warm glow. Helia wondered whether—for the people who lived here—it was like the sun coming out during a cloudy day. A chance to glimpse a brighter future above them that maybe they could aspire to reach.

But there was no time to think on such ideas. In the back of her mind, she could hear the banging of the monsters on the drain cover, and they were growing louder.

"We can't wait for it to reach us," Helia said, pulling Rascal along across the roof, toward the entrance that was slowly approaching above. "We can climb up on that building instead. Come on."

This time, she led the way, her limbs drained of energy and moving slowly, as if in jelly, though she felt the renewed vigor running through her blood, buoyed by the sight of Vega floating alongside her. She scuffed her feet through little red clouds of rust along a bridge to the next building, ducking under a clothesline and past a softly chugging generator, until she reached a roof. Just below it was another that was currently sitting only inches away, but which would soon align with the coming platform.

A family stood there already, giving the strangers a look of fear.

Then a gap in the ceiling appeared overhead, and the light shone down. Helia gestured to the family to go first, then made sure her group followed quickly after.

Up on the roof, they waited as the platform drew alongside them.

Only for the two guards there to raise their weapons.

"Passes only," one of them growled. "You know the rules: nobody gets on here without them."

Confused, Helia looked at Rascal, who shrugged. "The Prince likes to keep order, and nothing says order more than bureaucracy."

The family began to beg the guards, trying to force a couple of pearls into their hands, clearly having come up here without a pass and hoping to curry favor using whatever they had saved.

Helia leaned into Rascal. "Do *you* have a pass?"

She shook her head, her face grim. "Last time I was here, I came prepared. Not today, I'm afraid."

"Then what are we going to do?"

One of the guards had now grabbed the father by the throat and was trying to force him back. The other kept her weapon swinging wildly between the family members.

Rascal's face darkened. "This time we just have to wing it."

And with that, she turned and unfolded her wings, the metal tip of the right one smacking both guards in the face and sending them sprawling into their little hut at the back of the platform.

Rascal gestured to the family to get a move on, and they crossed, looks of fear and gratitude plastered to their faces. The rest of them followed until they were all climbing into the lift.

Yet before the doors slid shut, Helia saw an explosion below. The drain cover had finally burst open, and several fire spiders were crawling out and leaping into the crowd. Two people fell in flames almost instantly, before everyone else understood they were in danger and began to flee in all directions.

As the screaming started, Helia gritted her teeth, but the sound was cut off as the lift doors shut, letting the group ascend to the next cog in fearful silence.

CHAPTER THIRTY-SEVEN
ATTACK ON THE LIBRARY

As the screaming and yelling continued in the Concourse, Arturo held fast to his own hell portal with Robin.

He didn't know what was happening or what to do. All he could do was copy her as she kept on trying to beat the hordes back. So, he grabbed a similar-sized book, grunting under its weight, and raised it above his head.

Robin rolled her eyes at him. "I'm already doing that, and it's not going to work much longer. There's too many of them here."

"Then what do you suggest? It sounds like more are coming in elsewhere. Don't you have any protection in here? Guards or whatever?"

"I think we had them once, but they haven't been around in centuries, because we've never needed them! We just have to hold them off as long as possible. Perhaps Mwamba will deal with the poison and stop whatever is preventing us from closing the portals."

"But how can I help you? I'm not a Sage or a soldier. I'm not the kind of person who would be useful here. I'm just a writer!"

"A writer?" Robin's eyes brightened in a way that he suddenly found very concerning. "Yes, that's it!"

"So?"

"So, you can *write* a way out of this. Remember all those little tricks you pulled using your notepad? The tree. The dancing books. You made them all come to life."

He laughed somewhat hysterically. "Those were just me playing around while I was bored! Illusions at best. How could they help now? You want me to distract the monsters out there with another big moth?"

"Think bigger, for goodness' sake! And before you ask, no, I don't know how. But what I do know is that you need to hurry because I can't stay here all day doing this," she said through gritted teeth. "Don't look so shocked, Arturo. You clearly have a power in this place, one I don't understand."

Thwack. She swatted another grabbing arm.

"I need you to try, Arturo. Please?"

Oh God.

He nodded and reached into his pocket for his notebook.

And panicked when it wasn't there.

Shit. It must have fallen out of his pocket as he'd chased the Rogue Sage through the Library. He spun around, looking for something in the aisle that might help him, something other than books and death. But there was nothing.

"I need paper and a pen," he said.

"Can't you just, you know, say the words?"

"I'm a writer, not a bard. Look, wait here. Just stay alive."

She groaned as more arms reached for her. "Can't promise anything. Hurry, please."

He skidded out of the aisle into the Concourse. He could see battles raging all around him. Veer was trying to block off several portals, and a small group of scholars were physically attacking any inhuman beings or their hounds that came through another.

Arturo stumbled across the floor toward where the tables lay.

Thankfully, because everyone had rushed away when the attack began, all their research was still scattered on the tabletops. Including a pencil. And a notebook. He noticed it was already full of scribbles, something about a frozen flower.

He ripped that page out and left it on the table, hoping whomever it belonged to would have the chance to come back for it, and ran back to Robin. His brain was rushing like a train through a station, and he needed to find the brakes before it shot right past the idea he needed.

How the hell was he going to write his way out of this? The parlor tricks he'd conjured up earlier were one thing. But this was on a much bigger scale. Also, what exactly should he create? A weapon or a blockade?

Back in the aisle, Robin and Centauri were now facing multiple snouts and legs that were trying to pull themselves out of the portal. The copper ladder was coated in bloody smears, as was the Orb, and Robin's hair was plastered to her face.

"I'm here! Hold on!" he shouted, flicking through the pages of the notebook until he found a blank page to write on. Then he put it against the edge of the bookcase, lifted his pencil, and . . .

Nothing.

There was nothing in his brain. The blank page stared at him, taunting him to write. To get anything down. That was always the best way to start for him—just to start writing. It didn't matter if it was good or not. He knew he could always fix it later.

But he couldn't do that here, could he?

He had to get this one right the first time.

Shit, shit!

He'd never had to do anything as urgent as this before. He'd had deadlines, but this was something else. This was the purest form of writer's block he could think of, and as the sounds of Robin struggling sifted into his consciousness, and as he heard the snarls of the enemy, the groan of the ladder as it was jolted, the monsters nearly pushing it off the rails, he realized he wasn't up to the task. He should never have tried to wander from that path he'd carved himself.

This moment called for heroism, and he was not a hero.

"Arturo, what are you waiting for?" Robin gasped. "Write something!"

"It's not that easy!" he snapped back.

"You're a writer!"

"It's not that easy," he repeated. "I don't know what to write."

"Literally anything. Just write literally anything."

Screw it. He put pencil to paper.

Mwamba took a breath as he looked down from the balcony at the battle unfolding across the Concourse only one story below, hearing the cries of his community of friends and scholars as they fought back against the invaders. Thinking was difficult up here, yet that's what they needed right now, wasn't it? For him to think. So he blocked out as much of the fighting as he could and tried to concentrate.

Being the Sage of Knowledge didn't come with any obvious physical powers, like some of the other Sages. His talent had always been a love of puzzle-solving, of dissecting information in order to solve the problems in front of him. Which, with the help of Canopus and the Book of Wisdom, had become his superpower here in the Library.

The other Sages looked up to him for that, even though they were all equals in here.

He wondered what they'd make of his inability to think properly right now, despite the fact the Library and the fate of everything was depending on him.

He peered again into the bottom of the Rogue Sage's vial in his fingers, which still held a few drops of the nasty black ointment. He didn't bring it too close to his face and was very careful in handling it, lest he get any on him.

Canopus flashed a warning.

"I know we're running out of time," he said briskly, still staring at the ointment, tipping it this way and that, as far as he dared, to catch the light. There were elements to it he almost recognized. Almost . . . if only he could concentrate.

A flash of limbs drew his attention. Another of the Unwritten had burst through a portal below. The screech from the man's screaming mouth, surrounded by burning text, split the air as he looked up and saw Mwamba peering over the railing. The being leaped up to climb the shelves, scattering books in its wake.

"Canopus . . ."

The Orb hadn't waited for Mwamba's call. He'd already buzzed over the balcony and dropped like a stone onto the attacker's fingers. The figure fell onto a table below, sprawling on its back and groaning. Down, but not out. Its eyes sprung open, and it got up again.

Hurry, Canopus flashed repeatedly.

Mwamba didn't respond. He was close now. His eyes could almost see the patterns forming in the ointment in a way he'd seen before. The way the ointment congealed in one corner of the shattered vial. The way the glass sparkled when it caught the light.

He'd definitely seen these things before.

As he slipped into the zone he'd been striving for, suddenly the dots connected.

And it all became so incredibly clear. It was as if the answer had been staring at him this entire time.

The Elixir of Life. He remembered the last time he had seen it and recognized the movement now. That, too, moved in the same way and had been in a similar vial.

Except, no, this couldn't be the same Elixir. Because it wasn't anywhere close to being the pure and clear solution he remembered using. It was like this was its shadowy twin.

A Dark Elixir.

He had to check.

Running the length of the balcony, then leaping down the next spiral staircase back to the Concourse, Mwamba headed for the section of books he knew could help him.

Here he skidded to a halt and quickly let his eyes drift over the titles until he saw the one he was looking for: *The Trials of Yith the Extraordinary*. A tale of a legendary adventurer who was famous for the travels that had taken him across the realm of magic he had been born into. Mwamba knew it also contained secrets of a particular sect of sorcerers Yith had crossed paths with.

A group who claimed to be able to mirror the effects of any potion known to exist.

Whipping out the book from the shelf, he tucked it under his arm and carried on running, even as Canopus dropped down next to him and slammed into another corrupted ghoul.

The Orb swirled a question as he joined him on the run.

Why that book?

"Mirror potion," Mwamba explained breathlessly, trying not to slow down. He kept himself in shape, but at this pace, he had a feeling his old bones might not last much longer, let alone his lungs. "If the poison is what I think it is, its opposite is the Elixir of Life. A sinister but clever corruption of the very principles of the Seed of Life, the guiding philosophy of Silvyra's citizens. Only the Runners in Silvyra have the skills to create a true Elixir of Life, which might be able to undo the poison. But I think a mirror potion might get us close enough to counter its effects in some form. If we can just get to the Potionery, I think I can create a temporary antidote for the First Cave."

This will work?

Mwamba kept running. "Let's hope so."

Nu soon realized that Rascal hadn't been wrong about the layout of the Clockwork Mountain.

If Lower Sprocket was like the working-class dockyards she'd seen in all those Earth movies she used to watch at the Library's theater, Upper Sprocket was the wealthier part, where people with housekeepers lived and had the privilege of having the time to sit in a cozy chair, drinking tea.

As they ran along the well-lit corridor, with its white-painted rock walls and diamond lamps in the ceilings, Nu saw at least two people cleaning. She wondered whether the cleaners, a young man and an older woman, were both from the upper class of the lower levels or at the bottom tier of this class.

Thinking about it made her frustrated that such a place existed, especially in this fantastic otherworld. But she knew deep down it was just a microcosm of how life worked elsewhere, so she supposed it was to be expected. After all, this place was born of humanity's stories.

The family they'd helped move up to the higher cog had disappeared already. Nu was relieved they'd been able to save someone, at least. The mother had offered her some fleeting words of thanks before they'd left, as though they didn't want to hang around in the vicinity for longer than they had to. Nu didn't blame them. She could still see the image of those fire spiders killing indiscriminately as they scuttled through the market.

As she ran on, keeping an eye on Helia to make sure she kept up, she found herself caught between exhilaration and terror.

None of this seemed fair. She had finally made it beyond the Library to fulfill a destiny she'd always hoped she was meant for, yet the truth was that it had come with danger and death. She didn't know what was normal to be feeling in this moment, only that she wanted to make Helia proud.

In an ideal timeline, she would have had the chance to sit down with the Sage of Hope—and the other Sages—and learn about her place in the Library, how she could make a difference. Yet she had been thrown into the deep end of this adventure and had found the sharks were already churning up the water.

Glancing occasionally over her shoulder to ensure Antares was still there, Nu followed the group as they made their way through Upper Sprocket, climbing another ladder and creeping behind a natural waterfall, before hurrying through a cavernous chamber full of sparkling lights.

"The Crystal Cavern," Rascal explained, letting the echo carry her words to the others. Even she was beginning to tire, and they had all slowed their pace, both to catch their breath and to soak in the sight around them—a small enclave that had been carved out of a seam of crystals deep in the mountain. Strips of diamonds, emeralds, sapphires, and plenty of other beautifully transparent gems glinted and gleamed as they passed, their footsteps soft as they quietly skirted around a group of worshippers who were gathering outside what appeared to be a chapel, although what or who these people were worshipping, Nu could only guess.

Rascal didn't elaborate further. She merely gestured ahead to where some steps had been cut into the crystal wall and heaved herself up them, followed closely by the others.

Up they went, climbing through the various settlement levels of the middle cog, pushing their way past oblivious citizens, navigating the bright, internal streets. All the while, Nu hoped that Rascal wouldn't get them lost, because despite the brighter light here, there was still the sense of oppression clogging up the musty air. They were very clearly underground, and the constant sense of the cog's movement, combined with the lack of natural light and fresh air, was making her feel a bit lightheaded.

It looked as if Yantuz was feeling the same. He was especially pale, and his body language gave the impression he might vomit at any moment, which was probably reasonable, considering he'd spent the night clinging for dear life to the outside of an airship. But Dzin stepped up, linking arms with his brother, encouraging him along, and although he was clearly tired, Nu could see a determined light in his gray eyes and a flush of intent on his dark, bark-colored skin. The sense of renewed energy he was giving off highlighted this change in his demeanor. It showed a rekindling of hope, lost not long ago and found once more, now that he had his brother back.

People didn't often get a second chance. He was clearly determined to make the most of his.

"How far, Rascal?" Dzin called to their guide as they crested another set of rock-cut steps and dove into a tunnel lit only by gemstones in the floor.

His words echoed around them.

"We're almost at the center," she replied, pointing ahead to where the tunnel forked. She headed down the left side. "From there we can make our way up to the peak. To what they call the Dial."

"Will it be guarded?" Helia asked.

"No, I've brought us the back way to avoid that."

The tunnel came to an abrupt end. An iron-plated door barred their way, and the lock that hung from the clasp looked formidable. But it wasn't enough to stop Rascal, who stretched out a metal wing and slammed it down, severing the device and sending the lock clattering to the floor. She grunted as she then yanked the door open, leading them into another huge space.

They were in the center of the mountain now, and it was a huge cylindrical hole, one that ran the entire height of the three cogs. In the middle was a gigantic spine carved from bone that was rotating slowly as it took this section of the mountain around with it.

Nu watched as Rascal moved toward the edge of the chasm and the various spokes that connected this section of the city with the spine in the center. The rest of them followed warily, staring up at the turning mechanism at the heart of the mountain, then down into the chasm below.

"It's a long way down," Dzin noted.

"Then don't fall," Rascal said.

She led the way again, gesturing to the beam ahead that seemed a fusion of both rock and metal, then walked across it, slowly and carefully. It was only about a foot in width. One slip would prove fatal.

Nu didn't mind waiting for the others to cross first.

Unfortunately, this gave her time to look down into the void again, where she saw something disconcerting.

Tiny silhouettes lit by fire. Hundreds of them. All climbing up the walls.

CHAPTER THIRTY-EIGHT
SURVIVAL

Arturo wrote as if his life depended on it.

He tried to remember when he'd written like this before. Usually when under a tight deadline at work. Never in a way in which he needed to tell a story. Storytelling was usually something reserved for the quiet of night or whenever Rosa was busy playing, times that allowed him to write free and easy.

It had never been like this.

Not with the clawing hands and snapping mouths of beasts and people from Discordia, pushing to break through from the portal. Robin and Centauri were still keeping them at bay, but it was quickly becoming a losing battle, and so far, Arturo had failed to conjure up anything to properly help them.

The first thing he'd thought of were books with teeth. It was ridiculous, and he had no idea if it would work, but it was the only thing that popped into his brain. So, he wrote.

The books woke from their slumber, their pages glistening like teeth as they sprang from the shelves around Sage Robin to help her fight back against the hordes of monsters.

It was clunky and awful, but it worked. Suddenly, the bookshelves around Robin burst into life. The books shook themselves from their positions and leaped into the fray.

Robin shrieked as they snapped around her, attacking the creatures whose arms were suddenly red and bloody from the frenzy of deep paper cuts. She then shrieked again as one accidentally nipped her.

"Are you trying to kill me too?" she yelled.

"I'm trying my best here."

"You can do better!"

Fair enough.

Arturo was now really beginning to panic. He crossed out his words, and the books disappeared. One couldn't defeat devils with paper cuts anyway. What else could he do?

Something less violent maybe. A way to shield the portal?

So he tried to write a passage about the ladder coming to life and growing across the portal. He looked up and could see that immediately the copper poles on either side of the steps had sprouted new limbs. They weaved around each other as they grew, crisscrossing over the bookshelves around the portal and slowly blocking it off. The bloodied digits and torn fingernails still pushed through, though there were fewer now.

"Better," Robin gasped, stepping back to watch the magic at work. Centauri flashed his surprise and possibly his approval too. "I think that's working. Keep going!"

Arturo did as he was told. Yet for some reason, as he wrote, he felt the paper pushing back, resisting his words. He glanced toward the portal to see that the metal weave—that had once been the ladder—was beginning to shudder and groan as it was pushed backward. Something else was coming through. Something bigger.

Through the gap, he could make out a new figure that was now appearing between the bookshelves and the ladder, and it howled loudly. A black snout shoving its way in. Spittle flew from its lips, splattering against the spines of the ancient books.

Robin tried to push the ladder back, but it surged forward, the beast snapping its jaws around her arm, its teeth tearing through her skin. Robin hissed through gritted teeth, smacking the book down again and again on it, until finally it let her go. She threw herself back to the other side of the aisle, her blood dripping to the floor, before kicking a foot out and slamming her boot against the ladder to keep it in place.

"Make something bigger, Arturo. I know you can do this."

"What if I can't?"

She closed her eyes, and something incredible happened. There was a glow from around her, one that spread down the aisle and wrapped around him like a sudden burst of sunshine on a miserable day. His fears instantly melted away. He felt warm and cared for and safe, but more than that too. It was like an injection of excitement and confidence, a feeling that he could take on any challenge that came his way.

He knew it then. The question that she'd refused to answer upon their meeting.

Robin was the Sage of Love.

She must be. Because what else could have done this to him? A purity of compassion and kindness and certainty, soaking in through his skin and filling up his insides with all kinds of wonderful feelings.

One of which, perhaps the greatest of them all, was understanding.

In encasing him in a pure burst of love in that moment, he not only felt his self-belief strengthened but he felt her understanding—and that was everything to him.

She understood he was scared. She understood this was terrifying, and he was lost and desperate. She also understood he could do this.

"This is beautiful," he said breathlessly. Then he saw the glow had slowed the attack a little. "Can you not turn your power on them? Look, it's making them sluggish."

Robin shook her head. "I think there's too many of them beyond this gateway. I could try, but I can already feel the sheer weight of their evil draining what little power I'm using on you now. We need another way."

And that's when his eyes rose up the pillar he was currently leaning on and properly regarded the carving that hung above him.

He'd seen something like it in passing earlier, when Robin had taken him on the tour of the Great Library, and it had set him a little on edge.

It was a mysterious figure that seemed to have half climbed out of the wooden pillar. Just a torso, with wide-set shoulders, claws for fingers, and a face hidden by a hood.

Looking around, Arturo now saw that these figures were everywhere, carved from the pillars flanking the aisles of bookshelves. All of them peering over the Concourse.

Maybe this was what they'd been watching out for.

The carving of the Watcher moved, he wrote. *Quickly pulling itself out of the wood above them in a crunch of splintering . . .*

Above him, there was a noise as the thing moved. Just a twitch at first, but the hood definitely shook, and the shadow within gazed downward at him.

"Arturo!" Robin called again. The feeling of being wrapped in her powers was subsiding as she weakened, but it had held out long enough for Arturo to do what he needed.

"It's coming," he breathed, standing back as the giant torso pulled its legs out of the wood and dropped to the floor. Arturo crouched, the pad held against his knee, and wrote more, the words spilling out as quickly as he could write them. This time the ideas flowed more easily, the story teased out of his head as if by an invisible force. The statue moved again and followed his directions. And then he began to involve the other carvings around the Concourse.

Soon the air was full of the sounds of cracking and splintering wood as more Watchers pulled themselves from the pillars they'd been guarding and marched into the aisle to fight the hordes.

"Robin, get out!"

She didn't need to be told twice. The battle of the bookshelves had begun. The Sage and her Orb shuffled back as more of the gargoyle-like Watchers poured in and descended upon the enemy.

Against the portal, the makeshift ladder shield creaked. One of the rungs bent and snapped, followed by another, until finally the entire frame gave way with an ear-bursting scream of metal, tearing free of its rails. As the otherworldly legion began to tumble into the Library, the Watchers formed a barrier with their thick, brutish bodies and fell upon them so hard they couldn't squirm free. The flaming hound—the Rogue

Sage—led the way, yelping as he was punched in the snout, before being picked up by a pair of Watchers and hurled back through the portal. He was soon followed by the other corrupted souls as the wooden guardians followed their plot to the letter.

Arturo's pencil had long since fallen from his hand. He could only stare in relief, along with Robin and Centauri, as they watched the tide of the battle turn. There were still more creatures trying to get in, yet as soon as each climbed through, they were dispatched again.

"We're done!" cried a voice from behind them. Arturo didn't need to look up to know that it was Mwamba and Canopus, racing back through the crowded plaza as the other battles raged on around them. "We created a mirror potion to the poison. Not quite enough to undo it—the dark magic is too strong for that—but it's a temporary fix. And if my calculations are correct, it should have done enough to allow the Book to regain its senses enough that the Author can close the portals any second now."

He was right.

The blue glow of the portal grew hazy, and the split began to shrink. The evil hands continued to push through, grasping for purchase, trying to catapult their bodies through, but the Watcher that stood guard continued to act as a barrier between them and the Library.

The portal grew smaller, until it seemed that the Unwritten could no longer climb through. The hands reaching out made one final grasp for the Watcher, making it wobble and eventually sending it toppling toward the portal.

Arturo didn't have time to grab the notebook and write anything to save it. Their magical savior disappeared into the doorway just as it closed shut.

A near silence descended upon the room, broken only by Robin's gasps; the low, incredulous buzz of Centauri; and the crinkle of paper at Arturo's fingers. They could hear the cries of relief from elsewhere in the Concourse. The other portals must have shut too.

Thank the heavens.

Robin turned to him, reaching for his hand and giving it a squeeze.

The touch gave him a tingle—whatever magic she'd used on him remained faintly. "You did it," she said. "I knew you could."

Mwamba stared in shock at the Watchers that still crowded the aisle, before his face turned to look at the shattered pillars all around them.

"What have you done to the Library?"

Arturo raised the notebook. "I'll fix it in the edits, I promise."

CHAPTER THIRTY-NINE
ASCENT

"Faster! Faster!" Rascal cried. She, too, had seen the ember eyes below them.

Dzin felt a shove on his behind as she gave him hasty assistance in getting up to the next part of the turning column. He felt his face go red but had no time to offer any kind of resistance.

"Rot and blight, I'm going as fast as I can!"

"Not fast enough, Dzin. Go quicker!"

The central pillar that sat in the middle of this unnatural place wasn't built for climbing. The Spine, as he knew it was called, although he couldn't remember exactly how—probably from one of his books—was part bone part machinery, and there were enough handholds and platforms to make up for the lack of ladder. Yet it was built for one single purpose: to grind the sections of the blasted place together—for whatever needs the original builders had designed it for. And it certainly must be a design of a different age, because who else would have built this place? He couldn't imagine any of the humans in here were that happy about the oppressive atmosphere or the lack of sun. Maybe the desert outside had its dangers, but at least there was light and fresh air.

Dzin was a man of the Tree. He liked the wind, the rustle of the leaves, the feel of the bark beneath his boots, and the calls of the various animals ringing in his ears. He had always held a fascination with the story of the Clockwork Mountain, but now that he was here he honestly couldn't imagine spending his life trapped in this underground labyrinthine city.

Especially one that was now swarming with spiders trying to burn them alive.

"Dzin!" Yantuz called over his shoulder. "Are you still with me?"

"Always," he replied with as much conviction as he could muster, though he was feeling so tired he wondered whether it might be best to just drop away and let the darkness claim him.

"Good. Keep going. We're almost there."

"I'll try."

So, he carried on climbing, his staff tucked into his waistband, following his brother and Nu and Helia, while Rascal brought up the rear. An unlikely group snaking its way up the spine of the Clockwork Mountain, while below the enemy pursued, scrabbling from the dark well, eyes blinking and fangs clicking.

"Almost there," Rascal urged behind him. "I can see the platform at the top level. Look, Helia has reached it already."

"Good for her," he wheezed back, unable to look up to see exactly how close they were because his eyes were starting to see spots. *One hand at a time. Climb slowly and keep your eyes on where you are.* His mother's words came to him. She had always been there to encourage him when he'd had to practice climbing along the limbs of the Tree outside their cubby. Yantuz had always scooted ahead, climbing along like a squirrel, always leaving Dzin in his wake.

But he was always there. Just up ahead.

"Brother, up here."

Dzin suddenly realized he had made it. Yantuz reached down and grabbed at his shirt, lifting him the last foot to the platform. They rushed across the beam back to the main cog. The spine disappeared into a magnificently ornate copper and brass machine that held it in place. Glowing carvings around the circumference—words of some long-forgotten language—pulsed gently, their magic still intent on en-suring the slow and steady movement required to keep the cogs of the mountain revolving.

He wondered briefly at the similarity between the patterns of the machine and those of the two Orbs, which continued to swirl around the heads of the group. But the thought was gone as soon as it had arrived.

Rascal pushed past him and led them all into the tunnel, to what Dzin assumed must now be the highest tier.

"Won't there be another locked door?" Nu asked.

They turned a corner and reached exactly that.

Rascal nodded, yet she didn't stop. She ran full tilt and kicked at the lock. It took a few minutes of repeated battering, but it eventually opened when she sliced the tip of her wing through the cracked pin.

The door clattered to the floor, and she sighed with relief.

In the settlement, the group continued to run before finding them-selves on a balcony that overlooked a beautiful collection of houses and lanes and shops. Above them the roof of the mountain was covered in tiny glass windows, through which the desert sun filtered through.

Meanwhile, around them, a giant, sprawling street party was under-way, stretching in every direction. Fast-tempo music hummed through the walls of the buildings and electrified the air as groups of fancily dressed dancers in jeweled dresses and fine jackets jived to the beat. Dzin watched as two- and three-person chariots raced around the streets. He marveled at the elaborate plazas sleek with moving geometric designs painted across them, and spilling over with laughing, cavorting folk who were trying not to drop their drinks. A shimmering false sky had been created with magic, full of sparkling stars and orbiting moons. Foun-tains of light poured forth over everyone, making people's skin glow, and hologrammatic mirrors spun from invisible threads in the sky, showing twirling reflections of the glorious chaos.

Meanwhile, pairs of drunken lovers could be seen sneaking off to quiet corners to have fun away from it all.

It was mayhem on a joyous scale. Pure decadence.

Dzin had never seen anything like it. Yet he couldn't enjoy the spectacle for what it was. Nobody here was aware of the danger that was coming their way.

They were too busy having fun.

As Rascal pulled them onward, he saw that this wasn't even the main party.

The swirling dancers and drummers who thrummed out tantalizing beats were all surrounding a huge villa that sat atop a rocky mount in the center of the place, a villa bursting with golden lights, smoke dancers, illusions of heroes of legend who wandered the crowds, and thousands of revelers, dancing and drinking and kissing, generally enjoying themselves.

"The Raptor Prince's palace," Rascal explained loudly as they made their way up the stone steps that wound their way up to the villa, pushing their way through the partygoers as they went. "The collection is up here. That's where we'll find the Cerulean Rose. Hopefully, these noisy shenanigans will allow us to get in and out unnoticed."

They crested the hill and entered, crossing the dance floor and trying not to engage with those who would grab at their arms and paw at them, slurring their words as they begged the visitors to join in the festivities. Yantuz slapped away one particularly vigorous person who lunged in his direction, while Helia and Nu drew closer together to avoid any stray hands.

Rascal couldn't make herself heard over the music, so she simply gestured to a doorway on the other side.

More steps led upward, until they found themselves in a roof garden, where more people were lounging around, with several swimming in a steaming pool. Dzin blinked as he realized several of the guests were naked.

"It's around here somewhere," Rascal said, not even bothering to look at the cavorting people, as though this was all a very normal scene for her. She was too busy seeking the collection. "I'm sure this is where I heard he kept everything."

For a moment, Dzin's panic storm threatened to carry him completely away, as the beats of the music swirling around him crescendoed in his chest. But he knew he couldn't let it. They had a job to do. *He* had a job to do.

If there was a seedling, they had to find it. That's the only thing he needed to focus on.

Which is when he saw what he needed.

An elaborate room toward the back of the garden, like a glasshouse full of strange-colored gases—a place to keep seedlings perfectly healthy, in complete stasis. He'd seen one before, back at the Tree. An ancient facility he had been taught was used to store particular ingredients brought back by the Runners that needed special care and attention in the form of a carefully controlled climate and light adaptation.

"I think that's it!" he yelled through the crashing waves of the music.

The attack that followed came from nowhere.

The Raptor Prince—Dzin knew it must be him, for he looked the part in a tight-fitting black-and-white dress suit that carried the insignia of the Clockwork Mountain royal family—pounced. He must have been downstairs dancing when they had come through and followed them up.

"Thieves!" said the Prince, the word thrown like a gauntlet, his thin mouth a hard line as he approached.

Dzin raised his staff instinctively and, through chance more than skill, cracked him across the face, sending the Prince stumbling to one side. He was up in an instant, though, scrambling into a fighting position and now wary. Dzin panicked and backed away, realizing he wouldn't get lucky again, before Rascal stepped in before him.

"You don't want to do this," she said.

Whether or not the Prince heard her warning over the thundering beats of the party, Dzin had no idea. But he did hear the growl the Prince gave in return as he leaped for her.

Rascal held her ground, spinning to one side as he approached and raising a wing to batter him. But he was too fast and ducked under it, before sticking out a leg and sweeping her off her feet. The ground shook as she landed on her back.

She shot out her other wing, tripping him up. He stumbled without falling, then came straight back into the fight again, pushing Nu to the floor in his haste, drawing a long, curved dagger from his belt, a twin blade to his taloned ring, as he leaped again at Rascal, looking to finish her for good.

Helia didn't let him.

She reached out, briefly touched her fingers together in a triangle, then spread her arms and beckoned nature to join the fight. While the partygoers around them had been watching with amusement, now they began to scream as the garden around them came to life, stems growing in an instant, leaves curling, as a mass of foliage swept out and onto the Prince. They encased him and shoved him against the wall. His muffled yells quickly became choked sobs as he realized he wouldn't be getting out of here anytime soon.

"The seed, Dzin," Helia said as he stared at her in amazement.

Had she just done that? Who *was* she?

But as soon as Dzin tried to shake himself into moving, he saw that Nu had already beaten him to it. He didn't know how she'd known what to look for in the collection, only that she'd broken into the glasshouse, and out of the hundreds stored there, she had retrieved the small blue-and-brown-striped seed they needed.

She passed it to him. "Is that it?"

He nodded. "How did you know?"

"Long story."

He placed it in his pocket and then joined the others.

From where she still had the Raptor Prince trapped in the growth of his own garden, Helia turned to Rascal. "Climb to the roof of the mountain!"

"How?"

Helia didn't respond, but simply reached back with one hand and pushed her power out again. With Vega now glowing with fast-moving emerald symbols pulsating over his surface, his light growing in intensity, there was a shimmer in the air. Suddenly, several of the flowers grew ridiculously fast, right before their eyes, shooting up toward one of the glass windows. There they spread into the cracks around the window, before yanking the window out, spilling glass down over the swimming pool that was thankfully now empty of people.

"Up," Helia whispered weakly, barely loud enough for them to hear. But they'd already realized what her plan was. They saw how thick the plants had grown, stretching to the window above. This was their way out.

With Rascal again leading the way, up they went, climbing the stalks, slipping and sliding, sending bits of leaf and sap spraying down below. Dzin climbed until he finally emerged out into what should have been fresh air, free of the mountain.

Except, as they gathered on the peak, they saw moving flames on all sides of them.

The fire spiders had broken out and were swarming the entire mountain, led by their hungry giant of a mother.

Helia was already pale from her efforts to summon the flowers, but she grew whiter still.

"They're here," she uttered.

"Where can we go?" Nu asked, looking around hopelessly. "We're trapped!"

Helia grasped the young woman's shoulder and pulled her in to protect her. "Hold on to your hope, Nu. There is always hope. We are not done yet." She spoke firmly, though her voice was barely above a whisper.

"Damn right," Rascal said.

Then, through the air, there came a beautiful sound.

An airship engine.

A beautiful-looking craft swung up from the other side of the mountain, and a ladder smacked down in the middle of the group. Dzin looked to Rascal and saw the faint flashing beacon tucked under her wing. She gave him a grin.

He didn't wait around to ask more.

After climbing onto the ladder, they were quickly lifted away from danger, into the sunlight, as the *Golden Oriole* flew away from the Clockwork Mountain, while below them, the spiders swarmed the peak and became a writhing mass of flames.

CHAPTER FORTY
THE BREAKING OF THE SPINE

"Do you really think the Book will be able to talk again?"

Arturo raced along the winding route to the Haven, following Robin and Mwamba. Robin was still clutching her arm from where that bastard Edwin Payne—in his demon hound form—had sunk his teeth into her. The sleeve of her dress was in tatters, and the blood had matted the material around the wound. Arturo had a mind to stop them both and convince her to see a doctor or a nurse—or at least the equivalent of one here—before she got rabies or whatever it was a Rogue Sage might infect her with. But right now they both deemed it more important to talk to the Book.

If the antidote has worked, of course.

As if reading his mind, Mwamba said, "The Book will talk; I have faith. I saw the reaction when we sprayed the mirror potion onto the leaking ink. There was a powerful reaction, a light of such purity that it drew out the darkness, first across the door and then in the main cave, and we could see the ink pouring back into the books. We didn't have time to check them, but I can only assume the stories are back to normal, or on their way to being so."

"And the whole reversal ended with the portals being closed," Arturo added in gasping breaths, unhappy at being made to run again. "If I understand how things work here, the portals closing means the Book has control again and whatever was affecting it has been stopped. Temporarily, at least. So all the ways in or out are shut, and we are safe for now, yes?"

"Yes," Mwamba said, then glanced over his shoulder. "Are you suggesting there might be more attacks?"

"There may. The legions of Suttaru were waiting on the other side of that portal for us, Mwamba. Hundreds of them, man and beast alike. They didn't just appear when we chased the Rogue Sage. I think they'd been waiting for him to return, before attacking. It was premeditated. We might have pushed them back and kept them out, but that won't be the end of this story. Sooner or later, they will return."

Arturo slowed to a walk. He couldn't talk anymore, not while running. He didn't know how people did that in movies; it seemed impossible to both relay information and jog at the same time.

Robin continued for him. "We went to the Observatory earlier. We already knew the climate was being disrupted back on Earth, but it appears it's now on the verge of breaking completely. The volcanoes were waking simultaneously in an unprecedented global event. If they do . . ."

She threw Arturo a look that showed they were both thinking the same thing: if all the volcanoes erupted at the same time, it would surely be catastrophic.

For their families. For everyone.

He thought of Rosa and had a sudden need to drop all this foolish playing the hero and go home to be with her. To make sure she was okay and get her somewhere safe. Except *where* exactly was safe now? A mass eruption on a unified global scale would surely affect everyone, in every country. Ash would be thrown up into the atmosphere for years. Life as he knew it would cease to exist, and it would become a scramble for survival. Borders would become meaningless, and humanity would finally be unified against a common threat.

But it would be too late.

What could he really do if he went back?

"We can stop this, right?" he asked.

"Perhaps," Mwamba said, with less certainty than Arturo had hoped for. "We've found over the centuries that life on Earth is deeply connected to the realms beyond the Library. Paperworld holds all the stories ever written and thus is forever linked to humanity's spirit, creativity, and energy. What happens there can and does impact life on Earth. Which means that what you saw in the Observatory could well indicate what is happening with Suttaru and Helia and Nu in Paperworld."

"You think he's found them? Stopped them from finding your dragon?"

"We can only hope not," Mwamba replied. "But I would wager that our friend the Rogue Sage and his actions here are connected to it, as you suggested earlier."

"It was simply the logical narrative conclusion."

"And yet you were the one to figure it out. The writer. Who used powers I have never seen before to help ward off the attackers and protect the Library. It seems the Book knew what she was doing when she brought you here. I should never have doubted her."

Arturo shrugged, slightly embarrassed at the praise.

Robin, meanwhile, was looking increasingly troubled. He knew she must be thinking of Helia and how she hadn't wanted her to go off alone. He felt a twinge of guilt that she'd been forced to stay with him. And yet without her, they wouldn't have been able to stop Edwin Payne or fix the Book.

"So, they attacked us on two fronts," she stated, looking nauseous at the thought. "Or perhaps the attack here was a decoy, and the real battle will be over there. With Helia facing him again as a lone Sage and only the poor young woman Nu to accompany her."

"We don't yet know Nu's part in all this," was all Mwamba would say. He stayed quiet after that.

Thankfully, they reached the Haven not long after.

The three of them walked into the sacred room, and Arturo wasn't sure what he was expecting, but it was certainly more than he could currently see.

A large room, with bookshelves around the outer rock wall, an empty rectangle made of stone at one side, and a lectern with a book on it in the center. Nothing more, nothing less. It was quiet, empty, and still.

"It's exactly as we left it earlier," Mwamba said.

The man's voice was calm, but Arturo felt a surge of panic rise through him.

What if it didn't work? What if we're trapped, and all we can do is wait for whatever attacks us next?

Yet when Mwamba placed his hands together briefly, facing his palms up, and began his incantation over the gilded red book, everything changed.

The room burst into life.

Robin had told Arturo she had witnessed the Sages talking to the Book of Wisdom only a couple of times in the past, including after her own initiation.

According to Robin, the Book opened up to talk very rarely and only on special occasions.

The Breaking of the Spine, she called it.

And true to everything she had told him, it was a spectacular experience. Before he knew it, the air was suddenly thick, the way a storm feels just before it breaks. The cover of the Book flew open, and a rising wind flicked through the pages so fast the letters written on them became a blur. Something began to take form above it. As if something was materializing, almost as if it was being downloaded. It was a manifestation of an impassive, majestic face held within the words of another book, this one a copy of the one below it, but much bigger as it now hung in the air with its open pages filling the room.

Arturo felt his breath catch in his throat as he stared up, as did Robin and Mwamba. Tears stung the corners of his eyes. Not many people would ever feel an energy—a *power*—like this in their lives. It was as if they were standing on the edge of all the stories ever told and were able to brush their fingers against the current of emotions protected within their pages, feeling every ounce of the humanity they held.

He closed his eyes and drank it in as a strange wind rose from the pages and blew outward with such force that Arturo reached for Robin's hand to steady himself.

Then, with a timeless, lyrical voice, the Book spoke.

Helia placed her hands on the railings of the *Golden Oriole* and felt the warmth of the brass seep into her fingers as she tightened them. With the sun beating down around her, the airship rocked gently beneath, caught in another updraft as they drifted over a nameless sea.

The deck on which she stood was small. Just enough space for the crew to come outside for some air and perhaps a chat as they surveyed the world below them on their travels. She considered it must be a good life, drifting among the clouds. It was quiet up here. Peaceful.

She was tired. Bone-tired. Every part of her being ached, and she knew it wasn't just the centuries of being alive catching up with her. But there remained a shoot of hope inside her, and for that, she was grateful.

They'd somehow managed to escape the monster sent by Suttaru. They'd also fought the Raptor Prince and succeeded in taking the seedling—a seedling that Helia had now grown.

She had taken it in the palm of her hand and dazzled the gathering by weaving her power into the tiny thing. She reached out with her senses, finding hope to channel. Her power surged, linked by her Orb, which shone a deep, vibrant green, and her companions glowed like human-sized fireflies on a summer evening, full of hope, or trust in her. But there was something missing. The seed lay dormant, and she remembered the Chief Scientist's words and the importance of the Conjunction and Mother. She reached out farther, felt the old wood of the airship and the embers of Dzin's staff fueling its incredible engine. Mother. She felt the Great Tree, perhaps the greatest source of hope for all of humanity. The center of nature and balance across Paperworld. She saw her as never before, and for an instant, Mother connected with her. It was unlike any power she had felt before. Moonlight warm as sunshine, pollen on a summer day, the flapping of wings and buzzing of pollinators hard at work. It was an old power, made of elemental forces and not to be comprehended by a mere mortal.

Mother's life force burst through her, and she felt the seed in her hand down to its very molecules, the circles of life themselves, this seed of life itself. And she saw it for what it was. A seed of pure hope, pure life, and as she understood, it grew.

Her companions watched, entranced as it sprouted and grew right before their eyes, its triple stalks intertwining as they twirled upward. The bulbs appeared, stretched, and lengthened, unfurling one by one to reveal furious petals of cerulean blue, at the center of which spectacular pollen gemstones glittered and shone. And this blossoming had been accompanied by the most incredible scent, one that reminded her of the freshly baked cakes Xav used to make, with a salty undercurrent like the spray of the sea near where she had grown up. In her mind, she could almost see the waves lapping at the shore, beyond which shimmered the undeniable curve of the isle now known as Capri.

She opened her eyes. For a moment, she had been a part of something unimaginable, something far greater than herself, and she had been home.

"That's quite a trick," the captain had said, bringing her back to the present. He was studying her amulet, which still held Vega, before his gaze lifted to hers and an unspoken understanding passed between them. Somehow he knew. "I've certainly never seen that in this realm . . . or any other, for that matter. It's almost worth us risking our lives and this fine ship to rescue you."

"For which we are, again, very grateful," Nu had repeated for perhaps the fifth time. It made Helia smile. The girl certainly had the diplomatic skills to make a great Sage.

After the use of her powers, Helia had made her excuses and left the group to come out here, onto the balcony. The fresh air was like a cool balm on her skin, yet it could not soothe the anxiety she still carried about their mission. They had survived the Clockwork Mountain, but there was still a long way to go. And until she had her memories back, she wouldn't know how far.

The *Golden Oriole* skimmed the air currents over the Unknown Sea, going around in circles until they had a destination.

Are you okay?

Vega bobbed in the air ahead of her, skimming the currents alongside the airship, relishing the freedom of flight. Helia smiled and nodded. Her Orb swirled his love back to her.

In truth, she was beginning to worry she might not make it as far as they needed to go. She was exhausted and spent, physically and emotionally. She would have liked nothing more than to crawl into bed in her room back at the Great Library and sleep for a month or two.

Of course, she *would* continue as best she could, giving the journey her all. She always did.

Her friends were counting on her, and they *were* her friends now, never mind how they had been flung together on this quest. They might have little in common other than a desire to help, but they had put their lives on the line for the greater good. There was something to be said for that.

She wondered if her Silvyran friends would stay with them, now that their part in the story was almost at an end.

That they had come to save them from the fire spiders and the Raptor Prince in the first place was a twist of fate Helia had not seen coming. Nor was the revelation that there was a small refinery on board, which meant that at this very moment Dzin was brewing his Elixir. Still, they were due some luck by now. In this case, it came in the form of Rascal.

Captain Finesse and Earnest had been escaping when they'd picked up an old beacon used by one of their previous crew members. Helia wondered if the pair had deliberated over whether to ignore it and save themselves. Thinking about it now, she remembered both had laughed a little *too* hard when she'd joked about that.

Regardless, they hadn't. The captain had circled back and swept down through the smoke to pick them all up, including the strong, winged woman who had gotten them this far.

It hadn't been too much of a surprise to discover how Rascal and Captain Finesse had known each other. Helia saw the reaction Rascal elicited from the man when they'd performed their doomed takeover of the airship. And how quiet Rascal had gone, even during the flight through the desert to the Clockwork Mountain.

"She was my second, once upon a time," the captain said when Dzin asked why they'd responded to her distress call. He hadn't elaborated any further, leaving the exact nature of their relationship open to interpretation. *Second what? In command?* Helia sensed there was more to their bond than either of them was letting on, yet in the end it wasn't her place to comment. All that mattered was the fact they'd been saved, thanks to a beacon that Rascal still had in her wings.

A beacon from when she'd been a part of the *Golden Oriole*'s crew long ago. Back when she'd officially been a Runner for the Great Tree and—Helia had been surprised to find out—an illegal brewer of the Elixir of Life.

Which meant they had no need to return to the Great Tree for Dzin to brew the Elixir—they had their own unofficial refinery hidden in the lower deck of the ship.

Now Helia was on the brink of retrieving her lost memories. She had come to Silvyra to do that, and she was mightily relieved that she was so close. Yet she was also nervous.

Anticipating what she might come to remember.

Coming face-to-face with the truth could sometimes be hard. Xav had taught her that over their many decades together. The truth was a wonderful thing, but it could also be a harsh and terrible wind as it blew away the doubt.

What had her mind suppressed and hidden from her? What would she see?

Undoubtedly, it would involve the Rose Garden, and she wasn't sure she could bear to relive that again, even in her head. She would get to see Xav once more, but those moments would be his last.

And what of the dragon's fate? What clues to her whereabouts would Helia be able to grasp? And if they did find a location, what then? She wondered whether she could persuade Captain Finesse to take them the rest of the way.

It was all so very much to deal with. Made more difficult by the fact there was still no word from the Great Library.

"Anything?" she asked Vega again.

If an Orb could have rolled his eyes, Vega would have done so in that moment. He flashed once more in the negative, and she blew out her cheeks and let herself fall back into her thoughts. She was asking too often, but the waiting was frustrating, and she couldn't think of anything else to do.

The clanking of boots behind her signaled she had company. Rascal appeared beside her.

"Always loved it out here. The captain used to let me jump off and glide around in between jobs. Heck of a thing to leap from safety and let the wind carry you away, let me tell you."

"I bet."

Rascal rapped her knuckles against the railing. "They're all cleaned up and waiting for you. Captain's there too. He said they have everything you need."

Helia followed Rascal back into the cabin.

"So, how did this used to work?" she asked as they made their way slowly down the steps to the lower deck. Not the *lowest* deck, of course. She now knew that was reserved for the minirefinery. "You used to run ingredients for the Chief Scientist—I understand that part—but what could you possibly get from setting up your own hidden refinery up here? Wouldn't you still need the formulas to brew the Elixir?"

"Freedom is what we got," Rascal said, the tips of her wings lifting in a shrug. Then she tapped her head. "And when the magic of my formula expired—all formulas expire after a few seasons—sometimes we took on newer Runners and used their formulas. Of course, that was all a long time ago. When the Chief Scientist caught wind of what we were doing, she made it far more difficult for us to procure help. After that, the lab wasn't really used anymore, and then Finesse and I had a falling out."

"But the refinery at the Great Tree has been doing this for generations. They've perfected the art. Surely it's not worth the hassle for you to do it yourself."

"Being able to brew the Elixir ourselves allowed us to operate faster than others. Anyway, why take a peddler's gift of song and ask for an extra verse? Just be glad we have it. Now the Cerulean Rose has been regrown, and the small amount of Elixir left at the Great Tree will be working again. But we don't need to waste time going back. You can brew it up right here and then head to wherever you need to go as quickly as possible. You'll have a better chance at finding the dragon that way."

"And it's all hidden in the belly of this ship? The refinery, I mean?"

"That it is," the captain said. The pair had walked into the seating area of the main cabin, and he had clearly heard the last portion of their conversation. "It took some doing, believe me. Not many ships could fit in the machinery, let alone still be able to lift into the air. But we managed to cram it all in. Along with—I am happy to say—a sample of every ingredient we have ever collected. Which means this young man here"—he clapped Dzin on the back proudly—"just got to brew up his own formula to help you save the world. The fate of everything rests on what you've just done, my lad. As long as it works, of course." He laughed. Nobody else did. "How'd you feel?"

Hidden underneath the grime of their morning's escapades, Dzin's face colored.

"Sick, if I'm quite honest. It was a bit choppy at times, certainly not as easy as brewing somewhere where the floor doesn't keep constantly moving." He straightened and smiled, turning to Helia. "But they have quite the store down there. Everything I needed was available to me. And I already had the mushrooms and the Cerulean Rose, obviously."

"You were very fast," Yantuz commented, seeming a little unsure. "I remember you telling me the last batch you brewed took a few rotations to get right . . ."

"Oh, well, stress is a great motivator." Dzin laughed nervously. "Besides, I've done this recently. When your process is fresh in your mind, you can still feel most of it at the ends of your fingertips." He raised a stained scroll that was looking a little worse for wear. "And of course, I had my formula and all the notes I'd made to get it right. Chopping the Zymeed Beans into five-by-seven quarts. A drop of Moonlight Water, but not before you've mixed it with the Gargantuan Root; stirring it seven times in the direction of the sun's arc through the sky. Squishing the Baygums and the Follypops into a paste that's exactly the color of the two moons. And, of course, then there were the mushrooms, finely peeled and sliced sideways, before being crushed by the flat of a kissed blade. After which you layer a Cerulean Rose petal across the top of the mixture and let it dissolve of its own accord to finish off." He looked up at them all proudly. "And although the laboratory was crude, in a manner—with pipes whistling at the walls, a lot of stored airship parts, and very little space on the cutting table—I made the best of it. You could say I've got it down to a fine art now."

The captain's cragged face split into a grin. "I'm certainly impressed by the speed Dzin operated with. But we've taken over now. We have a machine down there that mimics the refinery at the Great Tree, and it speeds up the final stage—the settling of the magic."

"It's a shame, because that was always my favorite part," Dzin said in a small voice that verged on complaint. He added under his breath, "I like when it bubbles."

"And yet, from what I understand, we do not have the time to wait. Earnest is supervising that part of the process. You can rest up, Dzin."

"How long will it take?" Nu asked.

Rascal stepped in. "It could be ready within a blink of a batshark's eye."

"And how long is *that*?"

"Trust me, you don't want to find out," the captain replied good-naturedly. "But I have it on good authority it's fast."

Helia let out a breath of relief. Hope. It felt good.

They had certainly been lucky. But there was always more to luck than chance. In their case, they'd needed to embark on this adventure that had almost gotten them killed . . . so if this was luck, Helia was going to take it.

And she didn't have long to wait before there was more good news.

Nu suddenly leaped from her seat, her hand raised and pointing to the other side of the cabin. Through the porthole window, Vega was furiously flashing against the glass.

Helia frowned, unable to quite make out the message he was trying to convey. Then Antares came zipping in like a puppy. She was still a little ways off from her regular size, but they all had to duck anyway to avoid getting hurt as she spun three times around Nu's head and flashed like early morning sunshine.

Nu beamed, and the fresh green shoot of hope within Helia grew some more. It was clear that Nu finally understood the secret language the Orbs used to communicate with their Sages.

You would be proud, Xav, she thought, staring at his replacement.

Then she grew even more delighted as Nu relayed the news.

"It's the Great Library," the young Sage said excitedly. "Antares can sense the Book of Wisdom again!"

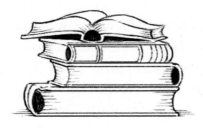

CHAPTER FORTY-ONE
THE COMPLACENCY OF TIME

"You saved me."

The face of the Author rose from the pages of the Book of Wisdom and spoke in a singsong voice that seemed to echo through time. It was like tapping into history and hearing what it had to say. Her words, quiet yet firm, resonated in Arturo's ears, bringing to mind all the goodwill and knowledge he thought might have ever existed.

"Like a mind in a dream, I've been trapped. This place, our Great Library, kept moving around me. Yet even though I felt the threat coming, its insidious fingers reaching into our sanctuary, I could not talk with you. I'm so sorry, my friends." She paused, as though trying to find the words to continue. "I . . . tried to break free, but the hold on me was too strong. I do not recall anything of this sort in all the history of my pages. Its power was strong. I could not even speak with my Orbs. I should have been more prepared. I'm sorry. The complacency of time has worn my defenses thin, it seems."

Arturo stood behind Robin and Mwamba, partly not wanting to get in the way and partly in awe of the spiritual face that hovered above them, her eyes sparkling from within the swirling galaxies and stardust that had been projected above the pages of the open Book.

Mwamba stepped forward, touching his fingers to his eyes and then to his chest. "I read not with my eyes, but with my heart," he said aloud, bowing his head in deference. Robin followed suit so Arturo immediately did the same. Centauri and Canopus flashed their own acknowledgments of reverence.

The stardust face smiled, and Mwamba added, "It is good to see you again, Author."

"It is good to see you again, too, my friends. I could hear your chatter all this time, like birds in a forest. It kept me alive in a way, knowing you were still out there. Thank you."

Centauri's surface swirled a blush red as the Author regarded the Orbs. She then turned to the Sages and nodded, before her eyes flickered down to Arturo.

He couldn't help it; he stepped back, clumsily bumping into the table behind him. The lamp on top wobbled, rocking back and forth, ticking like a clock, providing a suspenseful metronome as the Author regarded him for what seemed like centuries.

Finally, the lamp stilled, and the Author spoke again. "And to you, Arturo, I give my everlasting gratitude. For I know the part you have played here, even if the details are still lost in the fog of my memory. The Great Library must always have an Author to protect her, and in my absence, I am glad it was you who took my place."

He could only mumble something in return, unable to form actual words. Robin grinned over her shoulder at his discomfort, and it was only when the Author's gaze drifted away from him and back to Mwamba that he was finally able to move.

The sparkle grew darker, more serious.

"There are only two of you here," the Author noted.

Mwamba nodded. "Sage Veer is down at the First Cave. My antidote was enough to help you speak again, but the cave itself is still in need of saving. Veer is trying to see what damage may still be lurking. Helia and her . . . new companion are still in Silvyra."

"New companion?" The Author's eyes blinked, then her head bowed. Her voice became heavy, weighed with grief. "Oh, Xavier. Yes, of course, I remember now. He was a good man and a wonderful Sage."

"That he was," Mwamba said. "And Helia felt his loss more than most. Which meant we decided to send Nu with her. Antares had chosen the young woman; we simply had to trust it was for a reason. And while we do not know how their search for the dragon goes, events on Earth suggest it is not going well."

"And the other Sages—they have not returned?"

"We have been unable to reach them in the realms beyond, Author. I could not risk leaving the Library unguarded to get word to them, and Robin had to stay to help Arturo in discovering what had happened to you."

"I will send word to their Orbs now that I am able. And what of Earth?"

Now it was Robin's turn to speak. "They are suffering strange and terrible events, dear Author. Not only due to disruption of the balance of the ecosystems but there is now volcanic activity building on a widespread scale, the likes of which we haven't seen before. There have been no eruptions yet, but it is surely only a matter of time. We think it's to do with the threat brought by Suttaru."

The author's eyes blinked with solemn familiarity. "Now, that's a name I remember. Suttaru has truly returned, then?"

"Helia saw him. She said Xavier died by his hands. That he destroyed the Rose Garden and maybe even took the dragon. I believe her story."

"Then let us waste no time in turning the page and moving to the next chapter. What are your thoughts, Sages?"

Mwamba and Robin looked at each other, before Mwamba replied, "We need to talk to Helia and see how their quest is continuing. We do not know how the dragon was bested—maybe she, too, was poisoned—but if Helia can get her back and we stand united, we might have a chance of opposing Suttaru and his legions. Right now, we need you to communicate with Vega and Antares. Get word to Helia that we have you back and to see how we can help."

The Author's face inclined slightly, the stardust shimmering around her angelic features, then her eyes closed as she reached out across the divide between the realms.

Poison. Sabotage. A Sage gone rogue, returning from the dead to try to bring the Great Library down from the inside.

It was a lot for Helia to take in. She had been at the Library for centuries now and had seen and heard a great many things that would confound many mortal souls.

Yet this was surely the lowest point in the Great Library's history, second only to the last time Suttaru and the entity behind him had tried to destroy it.

She remembered the business of Edwin Payne. Couldn't quite picture his face, which had been lost in the mists of time along with so many others. But she remembered how it had felt to know that a Sage among them had been corrupted in such a way, enough for the Book to have cut off his Orb.

That he hadn't died was a surprise. She'd put that matter to rest in her mind long ago, and to have it come back to the fore now was unnerving. *What's he been doing this whole time?*

Antares continued flashing and buzzing her way through the story being told by the Author. Helia watched Nu carefully as the newest Sage translated the story for them all, now communicating with her Orb as well as any Sage before her. She felt pride at that fact, knowing that the Author must also understand how far Nu has come to be able to relay the information being transferred to Antares. But she also felt sadness as she saw Nu's features grow taut, her eyes narrowing with concern, as she became the conduit for such devastating information.

That the Author had reached out to talk to the Sages directly was unusual and filled Helia with even more concern about their precarious situation. The Book of Wisdom would often communicate with the Orbs when they were on their adventures around various realms, to keep track of their activities, pass messages back and forth, and conduct research for them if needed. But it was rare for the Author herself to reach out from the pages of the Book and communicate.

Things were about as serious as they could be.

As Nu finished translating, Helia went to take over. She could see the younger Sage flagging, exhausted from having such an intense experience, so she touched her gently on the shoulder and gestured for her to sit down. Which she did, pressing up against the porthole windows and reaching for Antares to settle in her lap.

Vega knew what she was doing, because of course he did. The two of them had a bond that went beyond talking or gestures. So he struck up a direct line of communication back to the Library, to the Author, taking over for Antares and then relaying their adventures in Silvyra so far.

Nobody else in the room could understand him as the patterns covered his surface, save Nu—and the young woman had closed her eyes now, too tired to watch.

Yet Helia saw her Orb speak of their conversations at the Great Tree, their trouble in the Maze, the boarding of the *Golden Oriole*, and the retrieval of the Cerulean Rose at the Clockwork Mountain, despite Suttaru's efforts to kill them there.

That the Great Library had been attacked at the same time made Helia feel sick with the knowledge that danger seemed to be coming from every direction.

She looked around the cabin now and at the group of people who had become her friends. Nu—the newest Sage of Truth, it seemed— whom she'd swept up from her life in the Library and thrown into trouble—trouble the young woman hadn't once shied away from. Then there were the brothers, Dzin and Yantuz, who had fallen in alongside the Sages and proved their worth. Meanwhile, Rascal, too, had shown that even those who had fallen out of favor with those at the Great Tree would help when called upon. And Captain Finesse and Earnest *had* saved them from the Clockwork Mountain when all hope had seemed lost.

And there it was again, as it always had been in her life.

The knowledge that there was always hope to be found, even in life's darkest moments.

Dum spiro spero. While I breathe, I hope.

All she had to do was keep breathing. Or, as the Author sometimes said, *"Keep turning the page, Helia. There is more of your story yet to tell."*

Moments later, the next page was turned.

Captain Finesse appeared from below. He wore an awed smile as he held up a glass vial filled with a beautiful blue liquid.

"Your Elixir is ready," he said, rousing Dzin, who—just like Nu—had been dozing in one of the chairs. Perhaps similarly exhausted from the pressure of having to brew his Elixir in the strange confines of the ship's hidden refinery.

He woke quickly, though, and stood, taking the vial in his hands in such a loving way it was as if he was being presented with his own child.

Helia was eager to get this done, but she let him have that moment, until finally she knew they could delay no longer.

"Dzin?"

She held out her hand.

Everyone's attention was drawn to her as Dzin handed over the vial solemnly.

She held the Elixir, feeling the smooth glass slightly warm in her hand and a pulsing of energy within.

"Are you sure this is going to work?" Yantuz asked his brother quietly, touching his shoulder in support.

Dzin nodded. "The Elixir heals all ailments, including those of the mind, so it should unblock Helia's memories. My worry now is that it won't help us in knowing how to save Perennia or tell us where to go next. What then?"

"We can only hope it will," Helia replied with a smile. "There is always hope."

Uncorking the Elixir, she held it up to the soft afternoon light that was drifting in through the porthole windows, then tipped the neck of the vial against her wrist.

What happened next was unexpected.

Nu awoke with a shout, scrambling up from where she'd fallen asleep, her eyes wide as she reached for Helia.

"No!" she cried.

Too late. The Elixir was already working its way into Helia's skin.

Except it wasn't the Elixir she had been expecting.

The agony was unbearable. It felt like an itch under her skin. A burn. One of fire and ice combined. It seeped through her, and she instinctively tried to scratch it out, but it was too late. She could already feel the concoction moving through her veins. Her mind raced. No memories surfaced as she'd hoped, only the words *something's wrong* on repeat—the same words the others were shouting around her. But Helia couldn't do anything about it now. She could only struggle, clutching her arm as her veins began to darken. Then she dropped to her knees.

"Helia!"

Vega was buzzing anxiously around her head, but it was Nu who was talking to her, kneeling beside her. Helia started to retch.

"What did you make?" Nu shouted at Dzin, who tried to stammer and plead his innocence. "What did you do to her?"

"It's . . . it's just my Elixir!? It's what I made before, back at the Tree. I followed the formula on my scroll. I followed the process as I remembered. I don't understand. She should be fine. It's the Elixir of Life. It shouldn't do this!"

Helia's vision had gone blurry, but she could see Nu looking at her with that faraway look in her eyes that suggested she was seeing something more.

"It's not the Elixir of Life," she said firmly. "This isn't what you think it is. It's something evil, Dzin. I can see its energy writhing and burning in her. It's a . . . a bad Elixir."

That was the last Helia heard. As though she had been dunked underwater, her hearing became as spotty as her vision. There were only colors and noise now.

Her hands flexed involuntarily, and she let go of the vial.

As soon as the vessel of Dark Elixir landed in her hands, Nu had another vision.

Not like the one that had woken her up as Helia had been about to take the potion. That one had been more of a warning in her gut. Indistinct but real enough for her to know what had been about to happen.

No, this vision was something else entirely. A twisting and writhing sensation, as in her mind's eye she was transported not only to another land but beyond Silvyra itself. To an entirely new realm.

She gasped.

"I see it. I see *her*!"

It was a sight unlike any other she had experienced before. Perennia was beautiful. As beautiful as anything that towering and terrifying could be. A strong, powerful creature with scales of purest gold, sharp and shimmering, rippling like waves across the deadliest ocean. Her wings stretched large enough to block out the sun. And upon her head sat a crown of tear-shaped petals inlaid with sapphires and rubies.

But it was in her violet eyes, so wide and bright, that Nu saw what she needed.

When they blinked and turned Nu's way, there was a reflection of something.

A city.

"She's alive!" she whispered. "Oh my, I think she's alive! She's in a city, although I can't see it that well. It seems to be hidden within mist. And there's a lake surrounding her too." Nu gulped as she not only saw but *felt* the landscape around Perennia. "It's so beautiful there, but . . . I don't know. It's also sad too. There is hardly anybody there. I think it's abandoned. Oh, but, Helia, the dragon . . . Perennia is there!"

As the vision began to swim away, Nu's eyes blinked furiously as she stared between the vial and then at Helia lying before her, only just conscious. She understood that this made no sense. The dragon they were seeking couldn't just be standing in the center of this city. She was free and not chained up. It was as if she was waiting for them.

Had they gotten it wrong? Had Suttaru not taken her? But if that was the case, then where was she? Why had she left? And yet she felt a deeper darkness in her vision, a touch of ash in her mind's eye. Had Suttaru connected with her again? She bit her tongue. There was no helping it now.

Helia reached out to touch Nu's arm. "Tell the Book," she said. And her suspicions faded into the background, her focus back to the here and now. As Antares revolved excitedly like a somersaulting bee, Nu realized the Orbs were already doing just that.

"I'm afraid I cannot help you," the Author said, a note of frustration in her voice.

Mwamba's face crinkled into an expression of confusion, which was mirrored by Robin's.

Arturo looked between the three of them, noting that this couldn't possibly be normal, and became increasingly worried that they had finally hit a dead end.

As the message had come through from Helia's Orb, he had found himself hoping this adventure was nearly over. They had gotten the formula and taken the Elixir, and someone had seen the dragon.

It all sounded so promising.

But at the mention of the city shrouded in mist, a beautiful, empty city in the middle of a lake, hidden from the world, the Author had shaken her head. She couldn't remember. Her memory was still tainted by the poison, and despite her efforts, she couldn't latch on to the name they needed to guide the others to Perennia.

"You really don't know where it is?" Robin asked again.

"I think I must," the Author replied. "There are echoes of knowledge of such a place in the Library. I can feel them, almost taste them. The problem is, I can't tell you anything. If I knew its name, maybe. But my memory is itself shrouded in fog."

That's when it hit Arturo.

The Author's poisoned memories were in the First Cave, the oldest

part of the Library, the place where the Rogue Sage had sought to in-
flict damage with his insidious plan.

And in that cave, there had been a book. One that had been at the
center of the threads of ink that spilled from its companion stories on
the bookshelf, as though it had been the target of the attack.

They'd had no time to investigate it further, because of the Rogue
Sage's interruption. Then there had been the attack, and Arturo had
forgotten about it entirely since.

But now he thought back to that moment, picturing the book in
his mind's eye, tilting his head ever so slightly as he tried to remember
the name.

"The City of Forever," he said.

The others stopped talking. Robin turned to him with a deep frown,
until slowly she realized what he was talking about. Then she began to
nod furiously.

"Yes, yes! That was the book. *The City of Forever*! That's the book in
the First Cave, where we saw the poison. Do you think that could be it?"

A light erupted from the Author's visage, the stardust seeming to
explode over them as her eyes brightened in recognition. She mouthed
the words to herself, then blinked as if having sent her mind off to search
her records for the information she needed.

"I have now accessed that memory," she said. "The City of Forever is
indeed a city within a lake, hidden by the mist. But it is not in Silvyra.
It is in another realm entirely. And . . . I'm afraid the exact coordinates
have been lost. The book itself has been damaged in the attack, and the
ink that contained the exact location has bled from the page."

The elation was short-lived. Robin let out a howl of frustration, and
even Mwamba sighed heavily, slapping his hand on the table.

"At least we know which realm they need to go to now," Arturo offered, trying to find the positive in the situation. "All we need to do now
is identify where it can be found within that realm, which shouldn't be
too hard . . ."

Robin didn't share his enthusiasm. "It's in another realm to Silvyra,
though, Arturo. Even if we knew the coordinates of where it was in that

realm, none of us can reach it. We've had to shut all the portals in or out in case Edwin Payne and his band of monsters try to get back in." She turned to the Author. "So we can't get out, and Helia and the others can't reach that realm without coming back here. What can we do?"

But the Author had clearly already been speaking to Helia's Orb on this very matter.

"They have said not to worry about that," she said, in a knowing tone that suggested she knew something the rest of them didn't. Arturo could have sworn he saw the corner of her lips flicker up ever so slightly. "Apparently, they have the ways and means to circumnavigate that problem. All they need are the coordinates for when they get there."

"I think I can help with that," said Arturo, to everyone's surprise.

CHAPTER FORTY-TWO
VISIONS OF OTHER REALMS

"There really *are* other realms?" Dzin repeated for what was probably the third time in as many minutes. Everyone in the cabin of the *Golden Oriole* stared at him. "I thought they were just tales and gossip. They're actually real?"

He noted Yantuz buckling himself into the seat next to him, seemingly taking it all in stride as usual, drifting along like pollen on the breeze.

Dzin wondered if he should give that a go. It would certainly make life easier than suffering all this anxiety and stress.

"We need to focus on the problem at hand," Helia said, giving him a pained look. She didn't seem that well. "The City of Forever is where the dragon has been taken. I don't know why, and it doesn't rightly matter at present. The challenge before us is getting there."

"But is it? Because you've just admitted you and Nu are from somewhere beyond Silvyra. So how did you two get here?"

"Magical portal."

Dzin gave a small squeak of a laugh, before calming himself again. This was all ridiculous, but if everyone else was taking this seriously, then so should he. "And why can't we travel to the city via this portal, then?"

"Because it's closed. The Great Library of Tomorrow is the conduit through which we usually pass to and from different realms. But they suffered their own attack and had to shut down their portal to protect themselves. They can't reach the realm in which the city is located. And we're trapped here in Silvyra."

Rascal had been hunched over in her chair, just behind the copilot's seat, listening intently to the conversation. Dzin had assumed she was just as shocked as he was and might offer her usual brand of scathing commentary, but what she said next proved that was not the case.

"Not necessarily."

"What do you mean?" Helia asked.

Rascal shared a look with Captain Finesse, who pursed his lips briefly, before giving a reluctant nod.

She continued, "There is a way to get to that realm from here. A way to travel out of Silvyra. Only a few Runners know of this, those who were chosen to export the Elixir beyond the boundaries of these fine lands."

"Export to other realms?" Dzin's gaze narrowed in Rascal's direction, unable to believe what he was hearing. "Now *that's* surely just a myth! A tale all told to us students to entertain us as we went about our work."

Rascal smiled and winked at him.

Oh. Goodness. It's real.

"A few airships from the Great Tree were constructed with the ability to traverse the divides," she explained. "It was on a need-to-know basis, only for those Runners and crews who needed to make the journey. Or at least it used to be. It's a dangerous venture, and the Chief Scientist wasn't too thrilled with losing craft, so she put a stop to it. She forbade any further training of pilots for the journey. Captain Finesse here happens to be one of the few left still flying who is capable of such feats."

"You've traveled between realms?!" Yantuz asked. Dzin took small satisfaction in seeing his brother finally catch up.

The captain nodded. "When we've needed to, yes."

"In *this*?" Dzin said, gesturing to the craft around them.

The captain's brow furrowed.

Dzin immediately blushed and held up his hands tiredly. "I'm sorry.

I just meant . . . there doesn't appear to be anything different about this ship. How is it possible you can do what you're saying?"

"All realms are connected through Silvyra, through the roots of the Great Tree, who is the true Mother of all. Right, Helia?"

Helia nodded, and he continued. "If you have a certain type of key, you can properly attune the ship to that natural connection and bypass the physical boundaries from realm to realm. Those stories you mentioned are all true. Rascal was one of those Runners, in fact, and we, her ship."

"On which I used to travel a little too much sometimes. Even after the ban on interrealm journeys," Rascal added. "Which was kind of the reason I was kicked out of the Guild."

"*And* off this ship," the captain added.

Rascal clicked her tongue and shook her head. "Sure, yes. If that's how you want to remember it, Finesse, then *fine*." She turned back to Helia. "Regardless, we can get you to the realm you speak of, Sage. And then, to reach the City of Forever, all we'll need are the coordinates once we arrive at the other end."

Cradled in Helia's lap, Vega flashed something, which Dzin knew only she and Nu could understand. She patted him gently.

"Vega says not to worry about that. He'll get them."

Dzin was somewhat overwhelmed. Bile was rising in his throat, and his heart was thudding against the inside of his rib cage. This was all a lot to take in. From escaping his home after witnessing the unthinkable, to almost being eaten in the Maze, to falling onto an airship, and then being chased up the inside of a mountain by demons, he had really landed himself in it.

And his brother too. He had gotten Yantuz involved in his mess— had nearly gotten him *killed*—and the worst part was the fool didn't even seem to mind.

Helia seemed to sense his thoughts. She reached over and put a hand on his leg, which he realized now was jiggling. Her touch calmed him a little, and as she smiled weakly at him, his leg stilled.

"We could drop you off before we go. You and Yantuz and Rascal.

This is your home, and you have already helped so much. It would not be fair to take you with us, would it, Nu?"

For her part, Nu didn't respond straight away. She was staring at him in a peculiar way, as though trying to figure out a puzzle.

"No," she replied eventually. "But you could be of more help, if you were to join us."

"I'm staying," Rascal said. Her folded wings twitched, and she crossed her arms. "I haven't had the chance to travel with a Sage before and certainly not on an adventure of such magnitude. You will need my help, for sure. No offense meant, but you Sages are slight, and if we come up against any more monsters, you'll be in need of some good old-fashioned brute strength."

"And Perennia is still missing," Yantuz added, looking pointedly at Dzin. "Setting aside the fact we would be considered outlaws if we returned home, without her, we may not even have a home to which we could return. Silvyra needs its protector, and the Rose Garden needs its dragon back. And—"

Dzin held up a weary hand to stop the onslaught he knew was coming. "Black spots and blight, Yantuz, you don't need to belabor the point. I understand. You want to stay on board and help."

"And what do *you* want, Dzin?"

Dzin considered that for a moment. He was scared. He didn't want to be, but he was. What did he want? All the answers he would normally consider were now impossible. The other students were dead. The refinery was gone. Perennia was missing, and the Rose Garden was destroyed. Everyday life in the heart of Silvyra had been irrevocably changed, so there would be no "normal" for him anymore. Nor anybody else. Not without the dragon to help stop whatever destruction was heading their way next.

He needed to stay and help if he could. Despite his fear of what might lay ahead, there was a responsibility here that he could not shirk.

"You don't have to come," Helia said quietly, stifling a cough. "You have already done so much."

"Please don't say that. I made the worst Elixir in the history of the

Conjunction! I want . . . I *need* to make this right." He paused and stared at her. She looked weak, beads of sweat beneath the chestnut curls of her hair, which were now plastered to her forehead. Her hands shook; they, too, were pale and clammy looking, except for the veins beneath her skin, which to Dzin's horror seemed to be darkening. His face twisted in a grimace before he could wrestle it under control. "My goodness, Helia. Are you okay?"

With great effort, she pulled her sleeves down to hide whatever was happening. There was still life in her gaze, but it was waning fast.

"I'm fine, Dzin."

"Are you sure?"

She didn't respond. He switched his gaze to Nu, whose flash of concern at her older colleague suggested she was worried too.

Dzin sighed.

"So how does this work?" he asked. "Perennia has been taken to the City of Forever, which is in another realm. Let's say I can get my head around that. How do we get there? Do we just fly until we reach the edge of this world and fall into the next? Are we going to set down somewhere and ride saddled fish across the sea to reach it?"

"Well, that's the problem," Captain Finesse said. "We need the coordinates, which the little Orb says he'll get. But we also need a key."

Helia and Nu's expressions darkened. They turned to face him.

"Oh," Helia said.

"What kind of key?" Nu added.

"There is no set design or shape like a regular key. The importance is in the material itself. This particular key needs to come from the Great Tree. It is the only way to tap into that natural link to the other realms, to grant us access between them."

Dzin clutched his staff tightly in his fingers. Nobody was looking at him, but he felt the heat of responsibility anyway.

It needs to come from the Great Tree.

His father had carved the staff from a branch that had fallen on the walkway just around the trunk from their cubby. He had given it to Dzin's mother, and it had been her very favorite possession. She'd used it as a walking stick from then on. Its *tap, tap, tap* had been seared into his memory. The sound of family and reassurance.

"So do you have a key?" Helia asked. Her voice was weak, the tone hinting at a desperation that hadn't been there before. "It's all very well having an airship that can travel between realms, but if you don't have the key to make it happen, we're still stuck here."

Rascal looked hopefully at Earnest and then Captain Finesse, but the set of the older man's jaw told them it was not good news.

"It used to be that the Chief Scientist would provide us with such keys whenever the journey required it," he said. "But that hasn't happened for many moons. In truth, even before she outlawed the journeys, she didn't want us making the crossings. They are risky, and she said we shouldn't meddle with universal boundaries. She was concerned that we'd bring them down around us." He barked a laugh. "Of course, that's *not* going to happen here. The boundaries are safe to cross, but the divide isn't without its challenges. It's a rough experience to skip realm to realm."

"One that we won't get to appreciate if we have no key," Rascal said with a sigh, looking apologetically at Helia and Nu. "I'm sorry, we'll have to go all the way back to the Great Tree to get a key before we can go on."

Dzin felt Yantuz's gaze on him. His brother was silent, yet he might as well have been yelling in Dzin's ear, such was the intensity of the unspoken words.

"I know," he whispered.

To his surprise, Yantuz didn't say what he thought he might.

"You can't give it up. It's your constant. It's what helps center you during your panic storms."

"I know."

"It's our last connection to Mother. You've had it all your life, Dzin. You can't—"

Now it was Dzin's turn to reassure, touching his brother's shoulder.

"I know, Yantuz. And it's okay."

He cleared his throat. Everyone's eyes turned his way.

"I have your key," he said.

He felt sick at the thought of giving it up. It was the last thing his mother had given to him as a boy before she'd passed. It was his only real tie to her. And as much as Yantuz had always mocked him for it— "You're not bringing your *comfort* stick again, are you?"—Dzin didn't care. It was his. It held his memories. It was something he could hold on to when life became too much to deal with. The wood beneath his fingers had kept him from falling into the abyss of his mind more times than he would care to admit.

What choice did he have though? His friends and his world needed him to make this decision. Lives were at stake.

He held the staff up for all to see. He'd been carrying it this entire time, but only now did Helia, Nu, and Rascal seem to see it properly. Rascal's eyes almost fell out of her head as she gestured for him to pass it across.

After a final squeeze, he gave it up.

"How did I miss this?" she exclaimed, then beamed at him as she passed the staff to Earnest. "Dzin, you've saved us."

Dzin nodded curtly. "Will I get it back?"

"I'm afraid not, my friend." Captain Finesse seemed to be wasting no time, already flipping switches on the dashboard to prepare for the crossing.

Dzin wondered if he'd noted the staff already and had politely waited for it to be offered, rather than pressure him into a decision by pointing it out to the others. If so, Dzin was grateful for that.

The captain continued, "The energy of the wood is absorbed into the ship. It's a big walking staff you've got there—perhaps enough for two trips, with a little left over. One there, one back. I'm sorry to say you won't be going home with much of it, if that's what you're asking."

"Thank you. That's all I needed to know."

Dzin clasped his hands together in his lap, already anxious about the absence of the staff in his fingers. The others were looking at him with a strange mix of pride and sadness.

Especially Yantuz.

Helia, meanwhile, looking even more sickly than she had a minute ago, gave him a smile that spoke of her gratitude. The knowledge that he had just helped them all was enough to prevent the usual panic from taking hold.

In fact, he felt rather emboldened by his decision.

At least until Earnest brought the staff down over his knee and snapped it cleanly in two. Dzin's stomach churned a little, but he held firm as Earnest gave him a quick shrug of apology, then hit a button on the dashboard. From the center of the floor a panel opened, and a platform rose between the seats. It held a metallic disc, which—as soon as the wooden artifact was placed in the center, where it was held firm in the air by some invisible force—began to fizz with sparks of blue fire.

Dzin swallowed his feelings and watched as Earnest tweaked a dial, making the thrumming noise that accompanied the strange contraption's increase in volume. The sparks flew, causing Earnest to squint, but he kept up the increase in power.

The staff began to disintegrate in a furious glow.

Goodbye, Mother, Dzin thought.

All they needed now were the coordinates.

Arturo watched as Mwamba beckoned the passing Volare and let the flying machine land on his hand. As its clockwork innards continued whirring, the Sage tapped a few instructions into a panel on the messenger's back and then hoisted it into the air again. It beat its four wings and disappeared immediately through one of the vents in the wall, heading for the First Cave.

"How long will it take?" Arturo asked.

"Not long," Robin said.

Mwamba saw the unspoken question in Arturo's eyes and smiled. "The route to the First Cave is a little arduous for us, but there is a whole network of vents to ease the path of our little messenger friends." Canopus flashed brightly, and he added, "And yes, sometimes the Orbs use them, too, when needed."

Only a few minutes later, they heard the echoes of the machine returning, and Arturo watched as it flew out again, hovering over Mwamba. It opened its bay doors and dropped the book into his hand, before flying off again to continue its work.

The words *The City of Forever* could only just be read on the spine as Mwamba turned it this way and that, studying the ink-stained book in the low light. He nodded solemnly to himself as he flicked through, then held it up to show them the last few pages.

The ink had bled badly here, too, and there was nothing but smudges of knowledge left behind. Unintelligible. Unusable.

Mwamba put the book down on the nearest table and gestured to Arturo.

"This is your moment to shine, my friend."

Arturo pulled the pencil he'd kept from earlier out of his pocket and stepped forward.

Leaning over the table, he held it up . . . then paused. "I am okay to write in this, yes?"

Robin and Mwamba shared a grin. "Yes, Arturo. I think this was meant to be all along," the elder Sage replied.

"You can do this, Arturo," Robin added warmly. "I believe in you."

"But what if I don't know what to actually write? I mean, it was only a theory I had. I have some power here, and things I put to the page come to life. But do you think it will really be as easy as I said? That I can just write some coordinates, and that will make it universally official? The city will be found at that location?"

Robin walked over and placed her hand on his shoulder. He felt a wave of compassion and kindness spread through him. And love. It flooded his insides with warmth and strength, giving him that feeling of confidence he remembered from before.

She didn't need to say anything. Their eyes met, briefly, and something passed between them, before she nodded for him to continue.

Bolstered by whatever magic she'd just used—or was it just her touch?—he leaned over the book again, placed his pencil over the page, and wrote.

It was the shortest story he'd ever written. A few words of the discovery of a city in the mist, using coordinates that he felt might be appropriate for a place in another world. There were no numbers, rather a series of fantastical markers.

Beneath the green stars at the edge of night,
past the mountains with golden peaks so bright,
fly through the clouds of blue to seek, the trails of the nomad fleet.
And when you see the whirlpool seas,
listen for the whisper breeze,
and follow it to the island mist,
where the City of Forever sits.

Arturo bit his lip, staring down at the words as he put the period at the end.

He took a deep breath. He wasn't sure what to expect—whether there would be some kind of magical twinkling chime or a flash of light or something else extraordinary.

Yet he knew that this time his writing would cause no physical effects that he would be able to see. He looked to Robin, who gave him a reassuring grin. Then he looked to Mwamba, who nodded solemnly.

Then all three looked up to the Author.

The smile that broke across her face told them all they needed to know.

"It worked," she said. And began to transmit the coordinates.

Some previously blank dials on the dashboard of the *Golden Oriole* suddenly lit up with a power they evidently hadn't seen for a while. Flashing on intermittently, they grew in power until bursting out in a furious amber glow.

"Here we go!" the captain shouted, flicking a row of switches underneath them all.

"The coordinates are in. We're all set."

Nu checked her seat buckle again.

"So how rough exactly is this journey going to be?" she asked Helia, squeezing the woman's hand.

"Pretty rough, I believe."

"No Glimmer?"

The older Sage choked back a laugh, though it was weak and sickly sounding. "Sorry."

The cabin vibrated around them as the captain reached up to grab a lever on the ceiling above his head.

"Brace!" he shouted.

Nu grasped the arm of the chair with her free hand, digging her clammy fingers in as though it might help, while clutching Helia even more tightly with her other.

A bright green glow shone in through the porthole windows.

And the airship collapsed upon itself and disappeared.

CHAPTER FORTY-THREE
THE CITY OF FOREVER

Nu struggled to open her eyes, and when she did so, she wished immediately to shut them again.

The world was shimmering and shuddering around her, the cabin convulsing, as though it were an image on a shoddy television screen. Helia's hand found hers and squeezed it reassuringly, yet her fingers felt wrong. Strange. As though they were not just kneading her skin but actually *inside* it.

There was no pain though. Only an uncomfortable and bizarre sensation, which seemed to tie in with everything she could see.

The nausea was horrendous. She tried to focus on the windshield beyond the Captain and Rascal, hoping for some hyperdrive-style image to focus on. Only there was nothing concrete there. It was like being caught beneath the ocean, watching sunlight fracturing through the churning waves. Except it wasn't just light now; there were feelings and emotions of all kinds of patterns and intensities that she somehow could actually *see*.

Was this one of her visions? She couldn't be sure. All she knew was that it was horrible.

It remained incredibly disconcerting, until everything began to shake, and a terrifying roar nearly burst her eardrums. For a few seconds, it all became worse, before easing off.

"Almost there," Helia tried to say. The words were almost visible as they tripped out of her mouth and drifted before Nu.

Another huge jolt almost shook her from her seat. She grasped Antares, who was resting in her lap, harder than ever, only barely aware of the way she was furiously flashing in terror—or perhaps just in discomfort at being squeezed. Yet Nu kept holding on tightly as everything turned upside down and then inside out. The shaking imagery around her continued for a moment longer, until suddenly it was gone.

Then it was just the shimmering and shuddering.

And then not even that.

Bright light poured through the windows, but a real light now, nothing supernatural.

Nu blinked and glanced to the side, where she saw blue skies and blue seas with little green islands dotted about. A sigh escaped her lips, fogging the glass as she moved—almost fell—closer to the window and stared.

Had it not been for the ringed sun above them, she would have assumed they might have traveled to one of the beautiful places on Earth she had often stared so wistfully at from the Observatory.

But they were not on Earth.

"We're here," Captain Finesse said with a little relief, before pushing forward on the controls and jolting the *Golden Oriole* ahead at a faster clip. "Now let's find this city of yours."

The journey took the rest of that day and then one more, traveling through the night, following the rather fantastical element to the coordinates they'd been sent. Every so often Earnest and Rascal would point out green stars and mountains with golden peaks. They all witnessed the blue clouds above, which they then passed through.

Then, early the next morning, they saw trails of ships far beneath them, which they followed until a series of strange noises drifted into the cabin from outside.

"The whisper breeze?" Nu asked Dzin.

"I guess so," he replied, shrugging and looking a little perturbed by the sound.

Finally, toward the end of the next day, they arrived.

"An island shrouded in mist," Rascal shouted excitedly. "There it is, friends. I think that's our city!"

Beside her, Helia woke suddenly, dizzily unfastened her belt, and got to her feet. Nu did the same, letting Antares fly from her lap. The two Sages moved toward the front of the airship.

"That's it," Nu confirmed as she leaned over Rascal's shoulder to get a glimpse outside the window.

It was the place from her vision. Just a glimpse of a jagged coastline, against which waves crashed, with only the shadows of towers visible within the gray cloud that blanketed everything, but this was it—she recognized it well.

It didn't take long to land. They dropped from the twilight skies and pushed into the thick cloud. For a second or two, Nu wondered whether they were making a huge mistake, but then the gray cleared, and she could see hills and a lush green forest below.

"There," Rascal said, pointing to a clearing on the edge of a body of water. The thin sliver of a bridge could be seen stretching out into it, before disappearing into the mist again, while a strip of white froth marked the hill beyond. "Set her down there, next to that waterfall. That'll do nicely."

The captain brought them down swiftly and silently, and there was barely a bump as they finally landed. He turned back and gave Nu a nod.

"Welcome to your City of Forever, kid."

He and Earnest stayed on board as the rest trooped down the gangplank in silence—Helia and Nu first, Rascal following, and Dzin and Yantuz at the rear.

Whether their silence was down to awe or trepidation, Nu didn't quite know. *Maybe both*, she thought as she noticed the waterfall gushing behind them was actually flowing *up*.

Helia caught her staring in amazement. "These realms can be strange sometimes, Nu. There is a lot of magic here you will discover—magic that defies our natural laws. I can't wait for you to witness and experience it all. But for now, we need to move. Come on, can you help me up?" She coughed and staggered a little as she tried to stay on her feet. "I can see shapes beyond the bridge. I guess we need to cross the lake to get to the city."

"Are you okay?" Nu asked.

Helia was grabbing on to her arm tightly and looked even worse than before. The fear grew in Nu's chest for her friend's health. And, if she was being truthful, for herself. They had come so far, and Helia had led the way the entire time. Nu was scared of doing this without her. "Helia, we can wait awhile if you need to rest."

"No, we should go. I'm fine."

It was clear she wasn't. Helia's veins were blackening by the minute, and once again she lost her balance, almost falling. Nu only just held her up, enough for Rascal to sweep in and lift Helia's other arm.

"She's still feeling the effects of the Elixir," Nu mouthed to Rascal as Dzin and Yantuz hurried over.

Dzin looked mortified. "Have I killed her? I have, haven't I? I'm so sorry. I could have sworn I'd made it properly. What could I possibly have done wrong? None of the ingredients were dangerous—I've used them all before. Especially the Cerulean Rose, which is used in all Elixirs." He paused, dug his hand into his coat, and pulled out what looked like a little mushroom. "Oh, and one of these."

Rascal inhaled sharply as she snatched it from him. "Oh, you didn't use *this*, did you? Dzin, that's horrendously poisonous. Even a small amount can maim. What in the blazes were your teachers thinking letting you use such a thing?"

Dzin's face grew pale, and he shrunk into his clothes, looking terrified. "It was an ingredient that meant a lot to me," he said quietly. "It can't be bad. It was my teacher who guided me to it—in a manner."

"What the hell does that mean?"

"I was . . . I was nervous. And panicking. I was caught in this overwhelming fear that I had bitten off more than I could chew and that I was going to fail at making the Elixir . . ."

"But you say your teacher led you to the ingredient?"

"Yes, I needed help at the time, so my teacher, Tywich, offered me a little guidance."

"Tywich, eh? I remember him. Odd man, but nothing that out of the ordinary," Rascal said, a frown creasing her already well-lined brow. "But that can't be true. We both know that doesn't work; only the student can find their ingredient."

"That's what I did. Tywich just helped me find the right place to start looking. At least, I thought it was the right place . . ." His voice trailed off, the energy ebbing out of him. Nu could see he was mortified at what had happened. He sighed heavily, his shoulders slumping. "In my panic, I didn't give the ingredient a second thought. It seemed to have all happened as it should, and so I had no reason to question it."

"I'm surprised Tywich didn't question it though."

"Oh, he was just happy I'd found the mushrooms. And when I had created the Elixir, the advisor himself was there. He and Tywich were talking, and he asked for the honor of testing it, so what was I going to say?"

"You didn't test it yourself?" Rascal blew out her cheeks. "Goodness, Dzin."

"I know, I know. But surely if there was a problem with the Elixir, the advisor would have gotten sick too? Why wasn't he?"

Nu watched the interaction, a theory forming in her mind. She remembered the advisor to the Chief Scientist. The way he had looked at her strangely, with his sheer silver eye. She didn't trust him in the slightest.

Rascal seemed to share her opinion. "I think you were led astray. The advisor always seemed to have his own agenda, and I doubt it ran along the same lines as the rest of us. Whatever you created, it wasn't the Elixir then, and it sure isn't now. That ingredient has ensured you've created something else entirely."

Rascal was about to say more, but Helia groaned as though she might be sick.

Nu rubbed her friend's back, fixing the pair of Runners with a firm look. "It doesn't matter who is responsible for what's happened. What matters is Helia."

Dzin nodded so hard his hair fell around his face. "Please let me fix this. Maybe I can redo my formula, find another ingredient out there. Maybe we can get Helia the true Elixir of Life, before too much damage is done." He gestured to the airship. "Let me try. I can brew another rather quickly, with the refinery's help. I could heal her."

Helia took a breath and stood, despite Nu's protestations.

"That would be good. Thank you, Dzin," she said. "And while you do that, with Captain Finesse and Earnest as your guardians, I think the rest of us should proceed onward to find our dragon."

With that, she made her way through the gathering, toward the city.

The air was soft and warm in the clearing at the edge of the lake.

A light breeze carried across the body of water, rustling the leaves in the beautiful, gnarled, moss-covered trees, before climbing up into the hills that disappeared into the gray cloud.

To Nu, the lake seemed far too still. It was like the surface of a mirror, broken only by strange, copper monuments, which looked like telescopes—*reflectorias*, Antares informed her—and which rose at regular intervals around the lake. They all seemed to be angled to a single point in the city.

If that wasn't enough, there was something even odder about this place.

More than once, Nu would turn at someone's voice, only to find that nobody had spoken. She soon realized the words were being carried on the wind. And not just single words but snippets of phrases, familiar refrains she couldn't quite place but which she knew she'd heard before. Then there was music, a lilting tune that immediately made her think of home. Had she been sung that as a child? She was suddenly sure of it, despite knowing it must have been a good fifteen years since she'd last even thought of that song.

"Did you hear that?" she asked Helia.

But her friend didn't respond. Neither did Rascal nor Yantuz. As they stepped onto the stone bridge, they were all staring into the mist across the lake. Nu realized they, too, were listening . . . but she could tell they all heard something different.

Helia's face had grown hard, as though she was trying not to cry. Nu could see her lips mouthing one word over and over again as she walked.

Xavier.

Helia was still shaky on her feet, reaching for the railing and digging her fingers into the exquisite white rock that looked like a spiraling cloud, teased and stretched into a ghostly wisp, which led off into the distance.

Yantuz, too, was walking slowly, and he kept glancing over the bridge, as though someone was calling to him. "Mother?" she thought she heard him whisper. Momentarily, his face would glow with recognition, before he shook his head in puzzlement.

Even the unflappable Rascal had been shaken by whatever it was she was hearing. Her head was cocked to one side, her lips twisted into a crooked stare. At her back, her wings twitched as though eager to lift her into the air as they were once able.

Meanwhile, the Orbs, which were bobbing between Nu and Helia, stopped their excited pulsing and were colorless. Antares had grown even bigger on the flight, her strength seeming to be returning—she was almost the size of Vega now—yet Helia's Orb still took the lead over his companion, spinning slowly as though taking in their surroundings and not quite sure what to make of it all.

"We should keep going," Helia whispered to Nu, leaning in so the others couldn't hear. She grabbed Nu's arm tightly, a little more tightly than maybe she meant, perhaps to steady herself. "I don't know what's going on, but hopefully the voices will stop if we get to the other side of this bridge."

"You think it's the lake creating the voices?"

"I don't know. It could be. Whatever it is that's causing them, they are voices I've not heard in a while, and some that couldn't possibly be real." She looked up to Vega. "Are you still in touch with the Library? Can you tell us a little more about where we are?"

The Orb pulsed in confirmation and was still for a moment, the only sound a gentle humming from its circuitry or magic—or whatever it was made of; Nu still wasn't sure.

Finally, he began to talk, and Helia relayed the information to the others as they continued warily across the bridge, venturing further across the wide expanse of water and into the mist.

"The world this city is in doesn't have a name. It did once, many lifetimes ago, yet it is no longer remembered by the inhabitants. The only city they remember is ahead of us. The center of their civilization."

"The City of Forever," Nu said, peering ahead as shapes rose in the distance, their outlines sharp behind the fuzzy gray. Next to her ear, Antares buzzed in confirmation, clearly listening in to the transmission too.

"Mwamba says the writer we met—Arturo—he found a book in the Library that is inscribed with the name of this city. The book was damaged, but they've been able to read some of what's inside. It contains research of our Sages past, telling us about this great and wondrous settlement. It's a perfect balance of technology and nature, one crafted from the very best of its people. A place of love and reflection. A city built of . . ."

Helia's voice trailed off.

"Oh no," she said finally.

Vega's emerald symbols kept pulsing around his surface as he continued to relay the message, until he realized his Sage had slowed. He asked what was wrong. She didn't answer.

Nu was barely paying attention now, though, because she was staring at the shadows, which, as the bridge reached its destination, were growing more and more defined before them. She could see towering, curved buildings built of the same beautiful white material as the bridge. They rose from the mist like shrouded furniture in an abandoned house, broken only by veins of green and brown, nature gathering them in its embrace.

She glanced over her shoulder to make sure the others were seeing this too. Rascal was similarly focused on the sight that was beginning to materialize, but Yantuz had held back with Helia. He was looking nervously between her and the city ahead.

"What is it?" he asked her.

Helia didn't answer. Her already pale, clammy face was now completely drained of all its color, her eyes like shallow rock pools left behind after a withdrawing tide, the life within diminishing second by second.

"Memories," was all she said.

Except it wasn't a statement. It was a question. To Vega.

Her Orb clearly didn't know what he'd done wrong. All he could do was repeat what he'd just told her, which seemed to destroy her even more.

Nu didn't understand what was wrong. She moved back to take Helia's arm, as did Yantuz on the other side, and they gently guided her across the rest of the bridge.

Until the four of them stood on the edge of the City of Forever.

At which point Helia lifted her head back and screamed. A long, agonized cry of hurt and anger and despair. The noise pierced the air.

Yantuz jumped back into Rascal, and her wings unfolded in readiness for attack. Antares spun protectively around Nu, who could only gape at her friend in horror. Helia pushed them all away and fell to her knees on the overgrown footpath they found themselves on, allowing only Vega to stay by her side.

But there was nothing Vega could do to stop the howl of frustration and emptiness pouring out of his Sage.

In shock, Nu looked around to see what the source of the problem could be. The city buildings loomed around them, graceful and beautiful . . . but also lifeless. There were no lights in the windows. No sounds of people or vehicles or machinery. There were more of those copper *reflectoria* monuments, but they were still. Here and there she could see white arched bridges that stretched through the architecture, each winding around or even encompassing the limbs of ancient trees in its design. Yet there was no movement upon them, nothing but the gentle waft of the rust-colored leaves of the flowers and bushes that Nu could now see were bursting up through cracks as they grew through the stones.

What was this place?

"Helia?" she asked, crouching beside her now, the fear suddenly churning in her gut.

Where exactly had she led them?

Nu found out soon enough.

Something appeared in the mist ahead. An image rising against a rocky wall of glistening water, which might have been a fountain of some kind in the past, yet was now projecting a handsome, dark-haired man.

A hologram or more magic? Nu wasn't sure.

She could feel Antares moan softly beside her, and she wondered why. Then it became clear. The burst of tears that came from Helia told them she recognized the man, and she knew what that meant. "Xav?"

The man turned at his name and seemingly saw Helia. Xavier smiled at his lover.

Nodded as though he, too, understood her pain. Then he shimmered and disappeared.

Nu suddenly understood everything.

"Memories," Helia moaned.

Her already weakened shoulders slumped, her body like a rag doll the final time it was left on the floor, never to be played with again. Nu rushed to her side and knelt, terrified by how pale she was now.

"Helia? Helia!"

All the energy and life had gone out of her. The Dark Elixir had taken its toll, but now her spirit had been eaten away too. The patch of grass around where she sat seemed to darken before their eyes.

Nu placed her hand under Helia's neck and lifted it. Helia's eyes blinked weakly as she regarded Nu.

"This is a city of *memories*," she said, her voice hollow, bereft. "It contains nothing more than the whispers of things that have been lost. Memories of what is past."

"But the dragon is here," Yantuz said, confused. "Nu saw it!"

Helia tried to pull herself up into a sitting position. Nu eased her up, until Helia gently pushed her away and brought her knees up to her chest.

"It wasn't the true Elixir, remember? It was something else, something darker, intended to torment whoever touched it. Perhaps when Nu was holding the vial she touched a drop of it on the glass and saw what she thought was the truth, but it was a twisted version designed to cause anguish. Perennia won't be here. Only the memory of her will be. That's what Nu saw in her vision. That's what this city contains. Only memories of what once was."

Rascal scowled. "Then where's the real dragon?"

Helia looked up, broken and beaten. The realization that this had all been for nothing etched across her empty face.

"I think Perennia is dead."

CHAPTER FORTY-FOUR
A MATTER OF TIME

"Rot and blighted branches," Dzin muttered to himself as he crawled through the dirt on his hands and knees in the woods beyond the airship, blowing his hair out of his face and brushing away the leaves and pine needles before him as he tried to find something useful.

"This can't be happening. This just *cannot* be happening!"

He paused only to wipe his sleeve across his brow, before circling a particularly knotted tree. But there was nothing of interest to be found there either.

The sound of the waterfall could still be heard a little ways away, but as he kept searching, he warned himself about moving deeper into the trees in case he got lost. That wouldn't do at all. But then again, neither would leaving poor Helia to die out there after having poisoned her. He'd rather lose himself than face the others if that happened.

Dzin had always quietly prided himself on being a top student, one of the best in whatever class he was in. Not through talent alone, that was never enough. Being the best was always a combination of natural skill and hard work, combined with a pinch of curiosity. He wasn't an infallible individual by any means, but he'd never made a mistake with his work—despite years of nightmares worrying about it happening.

And now it had happened, and it was so much worse than he'd feared.

"No, got to do it. Got to find another ingredient and quickly," he said to himself, trying to keep his momentum going. Trying to ignore the pressure he was heaping on himself once again. The panic was there, and he didn't even have his mother's staff to hold now. His constant was gone, and he was alone. "I need to follow my nose, that's all. It's easy, I've done this plenty of times, haven't I? Well, that's not true, is it, seeing as I needed guidance to find the mushrooms . . ." He knew he was rambling to himself, but he couldn't seem to stop it. "That awful advisor tricked Tywich into that though. He knew what they were, and he took advantage of us. Oh, come on, Dzin. Focus, *focus*! What can you smell out there? What can replace the mushrooms?"

The ingredients in an Elixir could be anything natural: fruits, nuts, leaves, berries, roots . . . if it had grown, one could use it. Everyone's Elixir was different, and people came up with their own formulas in vastly different ways. Some researched for many moons and ventured into the world to seek out their ingredients. Others simply explored and followed their noses. Sometimes one didn't necessarily know what it was they needed until they happened across it and caught its scent. It was like falling in love, some said.

Yet while that part of the process was complicated and chaotic, there was always one condition to every ingredient of the Elixir of Life—aside from the Cerulean Rose, that is. The ingredients needed to be particularly personal to the maker. Ingredients that their nose led them to, such as a flower with a scent that reminded them of their first love; a berry that grew outside their parents' house; a crooked leaf, shaped like their favorite number. Whatever it was, it was unique to the maker and their experiences.

Which was the problem here, because Dzin could find nothing of note that reminded him of anything in his life or that spoke to him in a way that felt special. There was nothing personal in this world at all. Just leaf litter, sharp little pine needles, and moss—and a whole lot of animal droppings.

He clambered to his feet, at a loss for what to do. He rubbed his wrists, still raw and hurting from where they'd been bound by Helia's magic during their airship ride around the Rock Giants. There was the sound of distant thunder, but he knew it wasn't real. He felt it inside him. In his head. In his chest. The threat of the white heat he knew so well. A panic that was moving from the horizon toward him. His hands were sweaty, shaking. He blinked tears from his eyes and realized he couldn't focus. The clouds of anxiety swirled around him, clashing against his defenses.

Only now he didn't have Yantuz or his walking staff to help him.

Focus on the things you can control, Dzin.

He held fast to that thought, even as he wondered if this was the attack that would finally carry him away. He labored over his breath, trying to keep it slow and even. He closed his eyes.

There were things here he could control. He could do this. He had always been a skilled student who worked hard; it was just that his panic often got the better of him. He refused to let that happen here. There could be no worrying about "what-ifs" or letting people down now. It was no longer about him.

Helia's life was on the line.

He blinked his eyes open, looking around him.

"Personal to me," he repeated to himself, as if by just announcing the word before the trees sweeping around him they'd suddenly reveal a secret they'd been hiding. "All the ingredients have to be personal to me. Yet what could possibly be personal to me here? I was not led here by chance or scent. My gut feeling didn't bring me to this realm. I never even *knew* other realms existed! By the boughs of the Great Tree, what am I even seeking here?"

Which was when he realized.

The boughs of the Great Tree.

He ran back to the airship.

"Earnest!" he yelled, running up the gangplank and into the cabin. "Earnest, where's my staff?"

The copilot was sitting with his feet up on the dashboard. "Huh? What staff?"

"*My* staff! The one you broke in half without any hesitation. The one that helped us traverse the divide between realms. *That* staff."

"Oh," Earnest replied. He lazily reached down underneath his seat and pulled out the other half. "This one?"

Dzin snatched it off him.

Yes, this was it. He could feel it. All this time, his own personal ingredient had been sitting under his nose, and he'd never been able to sniff it out—until now.

"Do you have a knife?" he asked. When Earnest frowned, he added, "I'm just assuming you have a knife. You had a trident before, remember? So you seem like the type of scoundrel who might also have a knife tucked away in his boot or something."

Earnest looked hurt. But then he reached into his boot and slid out a small pocket blade.

"Scoundrel?" he said, trying the word on for size. "I like it."

He handed the blade over, and Dzin set to work, trying not to feel guilty as he took a couple of thin scrapings from the bark. He hoped it would leave enough to get them home, but right now he didn't care even if it didn't. The immediate problem was Helia. He couldn't let her die. He had to save her, or he would never forgive himself. And besides, without her, they were likely lost anyway.

As the curls fell into his hand, he felt a glimmer of hope—something he knew Helia needed now more than ever—then, throwing both the staff and the knife down on the seat, he ran to the airship's refinery to brew his true Elixir of Life.

There's still time to save Helia, he thought. *There has to be, or this has all been for nothing.*

Nu and the others trudged through the City of Forever, half carrying Helia. They were wandering aimlessly, unwilling to return to the airship, even though they had clearly failed in their mission.

Helia remained quiet. The strains of darkness were now inching up her neck and over her jawline. Her eyes were bloodshot.

She was on the verge of being lost.

They all were, Nu considered, if the dragon was dead. There was no bringing her back to save Paperworld. They would find nothing here but memories of her, twisted into the vision Nu had seen. One designed to give her false hope.

It's the hope that will kill you, she thought. She continued leading them on anyway, a pointless exercise, but what else was there? She filled the silence with history, relaying what Antares was telling her.

"This city was once full of life. A true balance of technology and nature, a glorious blend of love and cherished memories. Only the inhabitants wanted more. They loved their lives so much they tried to prolong them, yet the experiment they conducted went wrong and cursed them instead. They received their unnaturally long lives, but it came at a cost: their own memories would continue to fade as they must, and so each of them would forget who they had been, who they were, rendering their lives completely meaningless."

"Where are they now?" Rascal asked, her words thick with dejection.

Antares swirled the next part of the message the Great Library had sent. Nu nodded. "They say they abandoned the city, unable to stand what they had done to themselves and unable to stand being reminded of their own mistakes. Now they roam the world as nomads, binding themselves to a simpler life lived day by day. Only once in a generation do they return here as part of a pilgrimage, to reconnect with their stories—with their memories—to try to remember who they are."

Nu now understood more about the voices they had heard while walking over the lake. The voices were even stronger in the city, and the echoes of them had been carried on the winds that swirled and howled through the empty buildings. Snippets of words and phrases and songs and stories past. For Nu, it was also scents of roasted vegetables and nuts and gravy, combined with the sound of laughter, reminding her of close family celebrations as a child. The rumble of the tram that often lulled her to sleep when she traveled around the Library. The whispers of learning she often listened to in the Concourse, followed by the day-dreams of all the exciting images the knowledge conjured up in her mind.

All touchstones from her life in sound and scent, all while images continued to rise from the mist—sometimes flowing across buildings, some-times appearing in reflections, sometimes just ghosts passing them by on the footpath. And all the ghosts were special people to someone in the group.

Rascal's old friends, including one woman even taller than her, had blown the Runner a kiss, which caused her to grin madly. Yantuz's parents, for whom he stopped and gawked for a moment, before tears streamed from his eyes, and he had to hurry off to wipe them away. Even Nu's old parrot appeared, a white cockatoo she'd been given as a child by a trav-eler from Earth, a pet who she'd taught to speak and who had been her best friend growing up—until he'd died, giving her the first taste of grief.

As sad as it was, she found it all oddly comforting. Haunting, but beautiful. A strange, not entirely unpleasant, experience, like taking a walk through a cemetery in the midst of autumn's decay.

Helia was suffering, however. Xavier continued to stalk her and re-appeared many more times than any of the other apparitions, almost as though he was guiding them. Nu could tell seeing him again was both giving Helia strength, allowing her to relive one of her happiest mem-ories, while wrecking her at the same time. For she knew it wasn't real.

Twice Helia had wanted to stop and curl up in front of his image, and twice Nu and Yantuz had needed to pull her away, lest she stay there for good.

"He had the nicest hands," she said wistfully, glancing over her shoul-der at him as he waved after them. "He would reach over and gently scratch the back of my neck with his fingers whenever we sat together. Sometimes we didn't even talk. We were just present with each other." She coughed into her sleeve and almost lost her balance again. But as Yantuz went to pick her up, she pushed him away. "When you've found someone who will do that for you—just be there with you—that's when you know."

Rascal glanced at Nu and shook her head. Nu refused to acknowledge what she was suggesting.

Helia was going to make it. She had to. And despite the troubling appearances by Xavier, there was something within Nu that was telling her it meant something. As awful as it was to endure—even Antares grew still and mournful each time his image appeared—Nu continued to lead the group after him. Following him throughout the city, even though it was threatening to drive Helia to madness. Eventually, the older Sage draped her hair across her eyes as she shuffled onward. Vega floated silently beside her, gently bumping her shoulder every now and then to let her know he was there.

"I've failed," Helia said, her voice barely a whisper on the breeze now.

The rest of them said nothing. She spoke no lie. Their quest was at an end. The dragon here was only a recollection, a trick of the Dark Elixir in Nu's vision.

Perennia *was* here. But only in memory.

And yet . . . Nu resisted joining in with the sympathetic nodding of the others as the hope seeped out of the Sage in their midst.

Because a new thought was growing inside her, like the seedling that had sprouted beneath Helia's hands at the Great Tree. A knowing of the truth beneath the truth. That perhaps the vision she'd had on the airship, when she'd caught the vial of Elixir, was not a twisted and evil version of the truth designed to torment them. No. Perhaps it was something else.

It might simply be the truth. Yes, Perennia existed here as a memory. But perhaps Nu might somehow be able to bring her back.

What if the City of Forever could actually revive the dragon?

It was then that Nu caught a glimpse of another vision. A waking one this time. She felt the cold shroud fall over her, another reality overlapping this one.

This new reality was bright and bold and full of hope.

In the vision, Helia was smiling at Nu. And the dragon stood behind her, head raised to the heavens as her magnificent crown of petals sparkled and gleamed.

How could this be?

Nu didn't know. But as she let go of the vision, she realized their story might not be over. They had to press on. The answer was ahead. She could feel it.

She held Helia's hand and kept on walking, following the ghost of her predecessor, until Xavier eventually led them to where they needed to be.

They found what they sought in a plaza. It was a wide circular space, about the size of the amphitheater back at the Great Library, although much less magnificent. The ground was littered with broken cobbles, and there was little else save for the thick-trunked tree with curling limbs at the center of it.

Yet as she looked around, Nu saw they were surrounded by a ring of stunning roses carved from stone that lined the edge. Roses that Helia now peered toward.

"I know this place," she said.

They walked the short distance to the tree. It was an unusual shape, and the more Nu looked at it, the more she thought it resembled some kind of large creature.

Then it began to change.

It was indistinct at first. Small movements. Leaves unfurling slowly, rustling and glistening like scales in the low breeze. Then the limbs of the trunk grew before their eyes, forming legs and wings and stretching into a long neck. Suddenly, the entire thing bloomed, and a face of petals looked down, from which two purple roses eyed them with something akin to regret.

Helia began to cry. She alone walked toward the dragon, reaching out to touch the long foliage nose, which blew out a little snort of sadness. Her hand brushed against the scaly leaves, and the roses blinked closed for a moment as the two of them put their heads together.

"He killed you, didn't he?" Helia said, tears running down her cheeks. "I'm sorry we didn't get there in time. I'm sorry I couldn't stop him. I'm so sorry."

Even as Nu tried to hold back her own tears, her vision came back again.

Perennia, alive. The city around them beautiful and bright, with grand, noble statues standing amid the beams pouring from equally impressive telescopes—the colossal shinning *reflectorias*—into one glorious beam of light that lifted into the sky. At their center was a magnificent white tower, resplendent and gleaming in the reflected light. Helia was surrounded by a glow of such warmth it almost hurt.

It was gone just as quickly, and Nu shook her head, trying to make sense of what she had seen. Yet she knew it was the truth. She knew it as well as she'd known anything in her life. Things clearly weren't as bad as they seemed. They still had a chance to fix things! A crack of thunder answered her thoughts.

Helia jumped back, and the dragon shrank back to become just a tree again. Vega buzzed around her anxiously. Next to her, Yantuz shuffled into the relative safety of Rascal's open wing. And Antares flashed a single swirl of terrified orange, nudging Nu to look back.

Which she did, to see another very different glow pouring through the mist some distance behind them, as though a wall of fire had risen behind it and was trying to break through.

There was another crack of thunder that rippled around them.

Then something landed on her nose. She wiped it off and held up her finger to give it a closer look. Ash, she realized, as more of the tiny white smudges drifted down silently.

Her eyes widened.

Then Suttaru attacked.

As the Author finally stopped talking, Arturo looked over at Robin in shock.

"The dragon's dead—did I hear that right?" he asked. "How can that be? What are we going to do?"

Robin waved her hand to shush him, as around them the lights on the walls and those that decorated the chandelier above flickered and dimmed. Then he could hear the sound of distant thumping.

"Oh no, what now?" he moaned.

It was the Author who answered. "He's found them."

CHAPTER FORTY-FIVE
DUM SPIRO SPERO

The group ran as the fire burst through the mist, parting it long enough for them to see his cloaked and shifting figure stride toward them, flanked on either side by creatures born of the worst nightmare stories the worlds had ever known. Helia assumed magic had been involved in hiding the city in the first place, created to prevent it from being found by the wrong people.

Suttaru didn't care for such things.

Rascal was half carrying, half dragging Helia along after Nu and Yantuz. Her wings covered their backs, protecting against the balls of fire that spat after them.

Through the streets they ran into pristine, abandoned buildings and out the other side, ducking through glorious, broken bridges, across cracked plazas, and around trickling fountains. They finally found a moment to rest in a cramped cellar.

Helia could barely catch her breath, which was now ragged and shallow, causing her head to feel light. She wondered if she had long left and hoped she did, if only to ensure the others got away. She had been alive for so many years, a great deal of them spent with Xavier. But he was gone now, and there was a part of her that was close to welcoming the chance to join him in eternal sleep. All this endless chasing and fighting was overwhelming. Her body was close to giving up.

"Quickly, move," Rascal urged, hearing the howls of Suttaru's monsters outside.

Again they ran. Stumbling over broken slabs of street, tripping over weeds threading through the stones. Pushing on, always pushing on. Darting through ruined buildings and glimpsing forgotten remnants of the lives of past inhabitants. Across secret courtyards and over bridges that spanned pools where any sign of life had long since departed.

On and on they ran, but it soon became clear there was nowhere to go. The fire and ash followed them relentlessly, its deranged master following them with a slow, deliberate pace that was more terrifying than being rushed by a horde of his Unwritten.

The City of Forever had been built on an island in the middle of a lake. It was surrounded on all sides by the haunted body of water, filled with moments of the past that guarded the settlement. Almost as though it had been designed to test visitors, to see if they were truly ready for the memories the city had to offer them.

As they cowered in their next hiding place, the sheltered cove of what might have been a reception room to someone's home, Helia peeked through the vines that coated the broken windows and looked out at the lake.

It was clear now that the only way out of the city and back to the airship was the bridge they had walked in on.

The same bridge on which she could now see a cloud of ash moving slowly toward them.

They were trapped.

Suttaru was coming.

Back into the ruins they ran as they were stalked by the enemy, until Helia was quite sure they were simply going in circles. Pointless, useless circles, just trying to find an opening, a way to get out. They ran from hiding spot to hiding spot, fighting off the odd feint or seemingly half-hearted attack from one of the shifting horrors that stumbled across them—mainly thanks to the strength of Rascal, who repelled them in ways that made

Helia feel sick to her stomach. Running until her breath was so painful she wanted nothing more than to lie down and let the enemy take her. Just let them tear her apart or burn her to cinders, like Xav.

But the thought of the others kept her going. And Vega, her beautiful Orb, who was still keeping up and occasionally nudging her for reassurance.

Whose, she wasn't sure.

All too quickly, they found themselves skirting the large circular plaza where they'd found the memory of Perennia. Truly they'd been driven in circles and were now forced to hide beyond the ring of rose statues, in what must have once been a greenery or indoor allotment. There were troughs of soil here, long overgrown with weeds and wildflowers.

Helia could feel the energy of the plants around her, but she could do nothing with them. She was spent. Even with Vega nudging her, trying to keep her going, she couldn't do a damn thing. She could feel the evil Elixir she'd taken working inside her, muting her powers, stifling her ability to hope. The running had made it even worse, pumping the vile poison faster through the blood in her body, until she felt on the brink of succumbing to the darkness for good.

Yantuz was watching. She could tell by the puzzlement on his face that he was wondering whether she'd been lying about being an all-powerful Sage from another world. She probably didn't look anything of the sort, being as weak and sickly as she was, with blackened veins coursing through her skin.

Only Nu looked the part now. Despite her youth and being thrown into this role unprepared and untested, with death chasing them, her spirit still shone through.

Helia offered what she figured must be a half-dead nod and patted Nu's hand.

"I'm proud of you," she whispered. "It was never my intention to drag you into such an awful mess. It's not right. I'm so sorry. Orbs select their Sages, but there is always a gradual transition from your old life to your new one. Despite my age and all the years of experience, I think I've failed you."

"You haven't," Nu insisted, her eyes kind, yet still darting around on alert, trying to gauge whether they might need to move on. "*Dum spiro spero*, remember?"

Helia couldn't help but break out into a smile, now on the verge of tears.

"How did you know?"

"I've heard you say it often enough. I asked Antares to translate it for me."

They both said it at the same time.

"*While I breathe, I hope.*"

Nu smiled and gave Helia's hand a squeeze. "None of this is your fault. I know you've done what you could. I will do what I can now. And while we're still breathing, we have a chance."

Helia's laugh was low and raspy. "I'm not sure I'm going to be breathing much longer, Nu. The Elixir has almost finished its work. I will be with Xavier again soon, at least."

She retched, her body convulsing in agonizing spasms, like white-hot fire burning through her entire being.

Before them, there was a shout. A familiar voice, agonizingly awkward and scared.

Helia opened her eyes again.

"Helia? Yantuz? Where are you?" Dzin was running across the plaza, stumbling over the cobbles, something clutched tightly in one hand, while the other shielded his face from the flames that he ran past. He reached the tree at the center, then spun around, looking for any sign of them.

Letting go an exhale of relief, Yantuz stepped out of the shadows and waved him over.

"Dzin!"

Then they all saw it. A creature entered the plaza behind him, bounding after their friend. It was transforming as it ran. It was four legs on fire, above which appeared a human torso, arms, and a head. Then suddenly the four legs became two, and it was a man, smoking and smoldering.

The man reached Dzin and grabbed him.

"Give it here," Tywich, the fiery creature cried, his eyes wide and half-crazed with fear. "That's the true Elixir, isn't it? Give it to me now!"

Dzin was too stunned to do anything but stare at his old teacher. His worst nightmare, the creature that had literally torn his friends to pieces, was his *teacher*!

"Wha—what are you doing here?" He was stunned.

The chaos continued around the pair as Dzin looked his old teacher up and down. He saw the tattered rags of the man's clothes and grimaced as he saw what lay underneath.

Scratches on the man's skin, still raw, burning an angry red.

Words that had been blazed into him.

They were appearing one by one as Dzin watched in horrified confusion, seeing the marks appear further and further up the man's body.

One appeared at his neck, and Tywich moaned and scratched at it.

"Please, I didn't want to do any of this. I didn't even know what it was I was doing when I turned into that . . . *thing*. I was promised they'd make me Chief Scientist. That's all I ever wanted. I didn't know what the cost would be. The fire in the lab . . . my students."

Dzin took a step back. It was all becoming horribly clear now. He remembered seeing Tywich run in after the guards, part of his clothing on fire. "They were your students, and my friends. What were you thinking! Are you insane!"

The man's face suddenly contorted as more words covered his neck, and he screamed with rage.

"I killed them all, as I was meant to! Except you, you anxious pile of Naggler dung. You who were never fit to be a student, who panicked at the first sign of pressure. Who was *so* easy to manipulate into doing my bidding. Your parents would be ashamed of just how easily I tricked you into making the Dark Elixir!" Froth covered the man's lips, and flecks of it found Dzin as he laughed, his eyes growing wild with rage. "The same Dark Elixir we used to weaken the dragon, so she stood no chance of protecting her precious Garden. The same Dark Elixir the advisor has been using elsewhere, in the Library your friends come from. Once your part had been played, the advisor turned me into that beast to kill you all." He glared and stalked forward, approaching Dzin. "And yet you escaped. First in the lab and then in the Maze. I barely made it out of there alive, only to be branded a failure and corrupted into *this*!"

As the alien words carved themselves up the man's face, he cried out again and made a desperate lunge for the vial of Elixir.

Dzin stumbled back.

"Give it to me. Only that can stop me from becoming one of them." Tywich was pleading now, gesturing to the hordes they could hear not far from the plaza. "Please, Dzin. Give it to me, now!" His eyes lit up again. "Give it!"

But Dzin had heard enough. He looked at the man, then down at the vial clutched in his hand. This had all been because he'd let himself be tricked, his anxiety manipulated, his work unknowingly bent to the will of evil.

The panic blew and raged inside him, but it was now met with far more force of will: The knowledge that he had come so far and was still here. That he had suffered along the way and still made it through, alive.

Not only that—he'd made the true Elixir of Life, as he had always wanted to do.

He was a true Runner. Without help or guidance, he'd finished the task he'd set for himself long ago.

And his parents *would* be proud of him.

As Tywich lunged again, Dzin held his ground and brought his free hand up, curling his fingers into a fist.

It connected hard with the teacher's jaw, and Tywich collapsed, falling into an unconscious heap beside the tree. Eyes wide, surprised at his own strength, Dzin only hesitated for a moment before doing what his destiny demanded. He ran. Ran to the other side of the large plaza, where his brother and his comrades were hiding in the shadows.

"F-fixed, the Elixir," Dzin gasped as he reached the others. Yantuz was staring at him in amazement, but Dzin's eyes were focused on Helia. "I fixed it for you," he said, his voice full of triumph.

Helia watched as he shoved the bottle toward Nu, who quickly uncorked the top.

Then she pulled it back again.

"Does it really work, Dzin? For real this time?"

The man held out his wrists to show her. Helia's magical bindings had saved him in the airship, but she knew they had rubbed him raw. Now they could see his skin was perfectly healed. "Tried it on myself first, of course."

Helia nodded and gestured for Nu to pass her the vial, and she slowly dabbed the ointment onto her arm. This time, the Elixir worked.

The agony in her instantly subsided, as if it were a fire suddenly smothered by a blanket. The cool ointment against her skin revitalized Helia from the outside in, like a wave of energy sweeping through her entire being. She felt herself again. The writhing darkness had been burned away by the light. The despair faded into the background.

And even though the healing brought with it that elusive memory at long last—a memory full of sadness and loss—it did not break her.

Those lost few minutes in the Rose Garden flooded back into her mind now. A few of her last moments with Xavier. Using her power to fight off the ambush with what little life the Garden still held, before turning and seeing a clearly weakened Perennia—drugged with something a lot like Dzin's Elixir—flailing weakly among her favorite roses.

Suttaru stepped forward and incinerated her.

She burned into nothing, as Helia now knew Xav would also do, only a few minutes later.

Yet with the Elixir coursing through Helia's soul, she found no distress at the memory, as she had anticipated. She only understood. What was done was done. If they were to survive this, she could not dwell on the past. She would have to accept it.

And only with acceptance would hope be found.

Hope.

She felt it again.

A sigh of relief passed through her lips now as they curled upward into a smile, and she sat up straight and strong and true to regard the man who'd saved her.

"You did it, Dzin."

"I did," he said a little unsurely.

"You saved me. Thank you."

Despite his exhaustion from clearly having run all the way from the airship, and somehow sneaking past the enemy, he was still awkward enough to blush and fall back, as though he feared she might try to kiss or hug him or something. Which she almost found amusing, had it not been for the seriousness of their predicament.

Then Yantuz and Rascal cornered him and started asking questions about Tywich, wanting to know what had happened out there.

That left Helia and Nu alone.

"If you're back again," the younger Sage said quietly, "that means we have a chance, right?"

"We always have a chance. But honestly, I don't know what kind we find ourselves with here. Suttaru has more power than I've ever seen before. We can only do what we can do. If only we could have saved Perennia and united with her, we might have been able to fight. Yet she is just a memory now. A dream of what was. We can't bring her back."

"Bring her back . . ."

Nu repeated the words, a thought evidently forming in her head as she turned and looked around her. Then she shivered, as though she'd been shaken by unseen hands, before she suddenly stared past Helia, through her, at something nobody else could see.

Another vision. Helia could now recognize it—the look of awe in Nu's eyes as she stared at some unseen thing, before all too quickly blinking herself back to the present.

"We *can* bring back Perennia," she said, her eyes wide.

"What? I don't understand."

"We can bring her back!"

Helia knew the young Sage could be trusted. She knew she was already a bastion of truth in the world. But what she was saying didn't make any sense. The dragon was dead; Perennia was gone; there was no bringing her back. Helia had seen evolutions of technology and incredibly rare magic used across Paperworld in the centuries she'd been a Sage, and nobody—not one—had found a way to cheat death.

Although Nu's face was dusty and slick with sweat and exhaustion, the smile of her conviction shone through.

"I've been seeing it, Helia. I didn't understand what it was, but I've seen us do it. We bring her back to life." She gestured to where the tree shaped with the dragon's memory swayed in the breeze, then to the telescope-like monument near it. "There is a power in this city, hidden in the memories contained here. I've caught glimpses already, but I know I can see them clearly if I try hard enough. There are rays of light pouring from each of those *reflectorias*, crisscrossing in the sky and forming a glorious, powerful beam above us. And that combined light is the truth of life. It's a reflection of love and memory from all around this great and desolate city. They are hidden beams, but they are truthful, perhaps more truthful than anything I've ever known, and I can see them, Helia. Everything here, all the memories, are real. They exist in the light. It's how we've been able to see and hear and smell all those moments from our past. I think if we can channel your memory of Perennia into the main beam, it could work. The truth contained within could bring her back."

Helia frowned, hardly daring to believe what the young woman was saying, but believing anyway.

"But Perennia is dead," she repeated, less confidently than she had before.

But Nu only grinned and clutched Helia's shoulders, giving her a little shake. "Don't you understand? Nothing here is dead. As long as there are memories of something, it can never truly die. We are all just collections of memories, after all. As soon as we've lived a second, it's in the past, and we're in the next second. We build our lives like that—one second after another, one memory after another. Some more important than others, of course, but that's how it works." She pulled Helia up and gestured to the tree again. "*You* know the dragon, Helia. Your memory of her brought that tree to life before. She came back to life for *you*. Can you do it again? Bring Perennia back and grow her form enough so it touches the beams? Perhaps if I bring the truth of the city's beams to life at the same time as your memory of Perennia touches the energy . . . we can get her back."

Helia frowned, looking to the tree, then to Vega. He buzzed excitedly. *We can do it. She's seen the truth of what we can do. Trust her.*

A little further away, Dzin shrieked as one of the plants suddenly blossomed into life right next to where he'd been standing with Yantuz and Rascal. They all stood back as the one next to it began to bloom, too, then turned to Helia.

"Feeling better, then?" Rascal asked.

Helia smiled, feeling the rush of power within her once more. The Elixir had worked its magic. Now it was her turn.

They moved together into the plaza, across the cobbles, toward the tree.

Nu could see Helia was as weary as time itself, but there was an ember of warmth emanating from the woman now, thanks to the Elixir.

Perhaps stoked by the hope of their plan.

There was no time to contemplate what had to be done. Nu simply decided to feel her way through this new experience. No longer letting herself react to her knowing feelings and the visions, but proactively stretching out to use and wield her power.

Nu touched her forehead before stretching her hands out, seeking a grasp of the powers that she now knew she had. Unthinking, she moved her fingers in rhythmic motions, as if playing an invisible piano. *There.* She could feel the strands of the power, the same knowing feeling in her gut. She sought a way to tease it out of her being, pulling it into reality, until she was able to throw it out and connect it with the world around them.

The air shimmered, ripples of it pushing out and out and out. The truth overwhelmed the plaza and then the city beyond it, until it finally revealed what had been above them this whole time.

The sky above the City of Forever was suddenly full of crisscrossing beams of light from the hundreds of *reflectorias* around the city. Lights that seemed to feed off each other and grow as they poured into a powerful central beam, becoming a raging river of sunlight with the warmth of a thousand treasured memories.

It crossed directly overhead, curved up into the tower at the center of the city, and blazed into the heavens.

This was truth. Revealed by the ferocity of Nu's power, which continued to explode out and out and out across the ruins.

It was simply beautiful.

"You're truly a Sage now," Helia shouted. "Xavier would be proud."

Nu grinned to herself as she fought to control her powers. Then she nodded to Helia. "Quickly—your turn!"

CHAPTER FORTY-SIX
THE LAST BATTLE

Suttaru's forces must have seen the lights, too, for there came a great clash of howls sounding out across the city, but Helia ignored them.

Now that she could see the beams, she knew they had a chance.

"I'll need time," she told Rascal. "Even with Vega's help it's going to be difficult. In order to have Perennia reach the beam, I'm going to need to grow her to her full size, much larger than how we just saw her. It will take me a few minutes."

Rascal nodded without question. She didn't seem to be the type to be used to taking orders, but that all seemed to change whenever it gave her the chance to put herself in harm's way. "I'll take Dzin and Yantuz. We'll distract those demons while you get the job done. Won't we, boys?"

Yantuz nodded grimly, while Dzin looked like he was finally able to face his fears without being sick.

As they all reached the tree again, Rascal peeled off with the brothers. Just before they parted, Helia could hear her directing them to pick up anything they could find to use as a weapon. Yantuz chose a broken piece of lintel that had fallen from an arch overrun by ivy. Dzin snapped off a short, blue-painted wooden plank from a bench. Rascal, meanwhile, didn't need anything other than her wings, which she stretched out as she cracked her knuckles. They eventually gathered to form a U-shape at the edge of the small clearing.

Nu stood back from the tree, Antares hovering in readiness near her. "You can do this, Helia."

Helia gave her a thin smile. "You'll make a fine Sage, Nu."

The color that rose in the young woman's cheeks was almost reward enough for all they'd been through.

"It's the truth," Helia added, no hint of irony in her voice.

Helia turned back to the tree and leaned her head toward Vega, who was silently hovering—he hadn't left her side this whole time.

"Are you ready to do this, little one?" she asked.

Vega's intricate patterns fractured in slow motion across his surface, suggesting he'd been the one waiting for her.

His humor had always brought a smile to her face, and right now it was just what she needed to fuel the warmth that was slowly filling her up. The ember sparked a new fire. She let it grow, feeling the power flow through her connection with Vega. His emerald glow increased in intensity, and before closing her eyes, she took a moment to admire the beauty of his many weaves and designs of light that were born, lived, and died in the blink of an eye.

She returned her thoughts to the tree, reached out, and touched a stem.

The ripple across its leaves shimmered in her mind. She felt her strength grow, the magic of machine, human, and nature becoming one. Her being poured into the branch at her fingertips and into the trunk, down to the roots.

There was a creak as it began to take shape.

A yell from behind her.

She put it in the back of her mind as she worked and didn't let it faze her. Dzin had spotted one of the monsters—or rather, it had spotted him. There was the sound of scuffling and a smack of stone on flesh before it went quiet again.

But only for a moment. The noise had drawn the enemy's attention. Helia could hear the snarling and shuffling of Suttaru's chosen pets as they moved in on the group.

As she knew she would, Rascal quickly went to work. The sound of her wings cutting and slicing rang out in the clearing, while the grunts of Yantuz and Dzin suggested they were also laying into the enemy as best they could. They weren't many, but they were terrifying. Meanwhile, Nu held firm to the beam above them, controlling it, holding it in place so that it remained real and true.

Unfortunately, more footsteps were spilling around the buildings at the edge of the small plaza now. They would soon be overwhelmed.

Focus, she felt Vega tell her as her concentration began to waver. *Focus your eyes.*

"I've got them closed," she responded dryly.

That was the beauty of the connection as they worked together like this. She didn't have to see him to understand what he was saying or respond in kind. They were deeply bonded. In that moment, as death closed in around them, it made her feel less alone. She had a friend with her who understood who she was and everything she had been, and for that, she was grateful.

The tree grew in her mind, just as it did in the world. It began to take shape. Once again, its limbs became legs. The wings began to form, just small at first, nothing more than thin, translucent shoots and leaves, like a baby bat. But they quickly stretched and solidified, the bark crusting out over the branches, the chlorophyll in the leaves turning them a thick, powerful green.

"Keep going, Helia!" she could hear Nu yell as a chorus of angry growling erupted around them. Dzin was yelling in terror, Rascal in fury. In the midst of it all, Helia could hear the *smack* and *thwack* of wings doing damage she was glad she couldn't see. "You're almost there!"

She was.

The tree version of Perennia had taken shape. She was almost as big as they'd seen her before, but this time she was fuller and even more realistic. The previous version was a mere sketch, while this was a photograph.

Powerful, Vega said. *Your memory.*

And it was. She could feel it all spill out of her. A myriad of emotions of the times she had spent with the dragon in the past. Of the love

and hope and respect they shared . . . so many layers of connection between them. Of all the places in the realms beyond the Library, the Rose
Garden had been her favorite. It was where she had met Perennia and—

Helia?

It was where she had met Xavier for the first time too.

Helia, what's wrong?

She didn't realize it fully, but she had paused in her work, the dragon's form stopping at its current size. A new thought had overtaken her
senses, one she couldn't deny, letting it fill her whole being.

Xavier . . . She hadn't even considered the full possibilities of Nu's
plan.

Could she bring him back too?

She felt the tree wilt as her focus on Perennia fell away. Ignoring
Vega's pleas to keep going, she opened her eyes, breaking the connection.

Where she had earlier felt her hope fading, here it was, back again.

Xavier didn't have to stay dead. If she could save the dragon, then
surely she could save him too.

As if sensing where her loyalties truly lay, the city brought him back
to her again. While her friends fought behind her, Helia turned to see a
vision appear in the mist at the far edge of the plaza, between the roses
of stone. A figure materializing through the gray, beneath the falling
ash all around them.

Just for a moment, it was him. Even from this distance, she could
see Xavier with his scruffy hair and his blue eyes and a smile that never
seemed to falter, even at the end.

Then the vision rippled, as if something was moving beneath the
surface.

Helia froze in horror.

Suttaru stepped through.

Skinny beneath a cloak that glowed black and red, as though it was
made from embers, he regarded her. Not with sight. It was as if his features had been melted off long ago, leaving only a white, faceless visage.
But there was an energy to him. A sickly spirit that told her he was sizing
her up. And even though she was now terrified to the very core of her

being, knowing that she had let her distraction get the better of her, she could do nothing as he strode silently across the cracked plaza, leaving a scorched trail of crisp and burning grass in his wake.

I'm sorry, she spoke in her mind, hoping Vega could hear it before the very end. Because of her selfishness, they had all been caught and would now die—as Xavier had, as so many others would at this monster's hands.

Not your fault, he swirled in reply, trying to reassure her, even though she could feel his fear too.

Suttaru raised his hand toward her, as he had done to Xav only a few days ago . . . or was it a lifetime? She didn't know anymore.

Despite her revulsion at the monsters before her, she accepted her fate. She had nothing with which to fight this kind of evil, nothing of equal strength. None of them did. And in that second, she knew she was going to die, and she wondered again why that might be. Why evil always seemed to have more strength to devastate, while good never seemed to have a similar power to stop it.

Then Nu stepped into harm's way.

"No!" she called firmly, striding across the circular plaza toward Suttaru.

The young wisp of a Sage, her long black hair flung over her shoulders, her Orb hovering near her head, regarding the monster without fear. She seemed taller somehow. Her back straight, her chin defiant. Without hesitation, Nu stared him down, before touching her fingers to her forehead as she had done before when she'd accessed her powers to release the beams. She reached out her fingers, as if playing the universal keys only she could feel. The air around her hands shimmered as if affected by the silent music.

And then power poured out of her.

Light.

So much light.

The world changed around them in a flash. A burst of illumination rippled first between Nu and Antares, then out across the evil in their midst. It was as though Nu had dabbed a drop of silver into the water and watched it spread across the reflection before them, stretching out-ward, until it filled half the sky.

And when Helia looked back, she couldn't see Suttaru anymore.

She saw a green-eyed gentleman in an old-fashioned tunic, with a sweep of dirty-brown hair falling over his face, a face that held an expression of utter shock. And in the world around him, she saw the City of Forever as it had once been, long ago. Full of life and cheer, pedestrians wandering the markets around them, creatures flying be-tween the blooms of flowers that sprang up, and water everywhere—in fountains, glistening as it rose and fell across the majestic build-ings, gushing through the greenery in which the entire city nestled. And in the midst of everything, above their heads, the beams from the *reflectorias* shone brightly, a shining cobweb of beauty around the city.

Nu's power had laid everything bare.

Including the monster.

"H-how?" the man stammered as he stared down at his unmarked hands. He was no longer Suttaru, no longer the infamous Ash Man, but was whomever he had once been many centuries ago. Fingers reached up to touch a face that was now full of color, flush in the cheeks with shock. His eyes stared between them as he ran his fingers over his brow and nose, feeling his lips and teeth. He drank in a breath, savoring every moment of it. It was so long it seemed to draw in many centuries' worth of air, before finally he spluttered, "I—I don't understand."

But Helia did. Because Nu had shown the truth of it all, both now and then.

Truth. Nu's power. Xav's power. One of the foundations of humanity, the glue that held society together, and when it was lacking, threatened to break it apart. *That* was what good had on its side.

The young woman didn't turn around, too busy holding the power over the enemy.

When she spoke, her voice was firm, yet desperate, on the edge of giving out.

"Now, Helia. *Finish it now!*"

Helia realized she didn't have long left. Nu had saved them for only a moment. She had bought them a little extra time, and she had to use it.

Helia looked back one last time, toward where Xav had been. He was still there, standing in the glorious sunshine of the vision as life moved around him. He looked happier than he had ever been.

Helia smiled. Then closed her eyes.

The dragon tree shook as she poured everything she had left into her, growing that fine tail, her long, thick neck, her snout and teeth, and her blinding violet eyes.

Yes, Vega cried. *Yes!*

One last push. She screamed silently as she gave the last of her spirit, as if she was reaching into the tree itself and pulling it up with her hands, stretching it up and up and up into the sky and spreading out those magnificent wings.

The tip of one hit the central beam into which all the others were pouring.

The feeling that followed was one she couldn't properly understand and would never be able to. It was as if she'd touched an electric cable full of pure joy and sadness and nostalgia and melancholy—yet so much happiness. A current of human feelings all swept up in a beam of energy that now poured its way into the life she'd created and nurtured and grown in the face of death.

And now the tree came to life. The leaves became scales. The bark became skin, stretching and flexing. Her purple eyes blinked, and her roots became talons. She beat her wings, and almost immediately she tore herself free of the ground.

"Helia," Nu called.

But her voice was lost beneath the furious roar of Perennia as the wondrous creature unleashed her own emotions into the world she had been returned to—a cry of anger and pain and joy and hope.

Helia let herself smile at the sound, understanding and empathizing, while simultaneously feeling the weight of responsibility lift from her shoulders.

They had done it. Somehow, despite everything that had been put in their path, she had managed to lead the others through to this moment. The realms beyond the Library, even the Library itself and Earth too, might have been lost if she had not. Yet there was now a chance for their survival. To be able to fight back and protect them against Suttaru, who wanted so badly to destroy everything.

There was hope again.

"Helia," Nu called again, weaker this time.

But Helia had caught a glimpse of Xav once more as the vision of truth splintered and fell away ahead of her. He seemed proud. Not only of her but of Nu too. She could see him looking over at where she stood. The young woman had saved them all. She had already made a fine Sage of Truth.

A worthy successor.

As Perennia roared again, Vega's emerald light patterns grew fainter, and he began to fall. Helia plucked him from the air and pulled him into her arms, cradling him. The poor thing had exhausted himself too. Yet she knew he would be okay. As would Antares, who was in Nu's arms.

Everything was going to be okay now.

Helia looked over to her friend.

Nu turned to her and smiled.

It was a glorious smile. Weak but full of hope. And, for some reason, now it was glowing too. A glow so bright and powerful that light and warmth continued to spill across Helia's vision, until the girl was just a silhouette and—

Nu watched in horror as the flames lit Helia up.

Fire burned through her in an instant, turning her and Vega into nothing but a shadow of ash. A shadow that lasted only an instant longer before the fire was gone and the ash collapsed into itself, drifting toward the scorched earth.

No!

The fear and anger in Nu's mind were suddenly matched by a

ferocious noise as the dragon screamed. It was a scream straight from the earth itself, pouring through snarling teeth and her wide, furious eyes.

Nu glanced toward Suttaru. Saw his hand was still raised and now moving in her direction. Saw the sparks of flame still licking against his skin, before blossoming into another ball of fire that enveloped his entire arm as he drew it back, preparing to kill again.

To end her.

She didn't care now. It was her fault; she should have held on longer. Maintained the vision for just a few seconds more. But she just couldn't; she hadn't the energy.

And Helia was gone because of it.

The ash suddenly stopped falling around Nu as a shadow passed overhead. There was a downward draft so powerful it knocked her off her feet and threw her to the ground. She scrambled back across the broken plaza of the city, the fingers of one hand scrabbling against the broken stone, the other clutching Antares. The dragon's neck curved toward Suttaru as she flew down.

Her jaws opened. Green flames erupted and spewed forth, meeting the man's fire with her own.

The entire city shook as the two forces struggled and fought.

Perennia's wings beat gusts that pushed back the corrupted beings crawling and scampering toward her. She impaled one that had leaped onto her back, spearing it with her long, sharp tail. She flung it directly at Suttaru; however, he burned the creature into nothing before it could reach him.

His powers then swirled the ash tighter around the pair, trying to smother the dragon and her friends, who, even now bleeding and battered, were still fighting back against the hordes of Unwritten. As the group began to choke, Perennia's green fire lit up the cloud and forced it back across the plaza toward the enemy, until Suttaru dissipated it with his flames.

The dance of death continued like this for minutes. Or was it hours?

Nu didn't know. It could have gone on forever or no time at all. She was slipping in and out of focus, too weak and shocked to hold on to what was happening. Every time she blinked, she saw the image of her friend and her Orb. The look on Helia's face just before it had happened. The hope in her eyes.

Nu suddenly felt two hands grabbing under her arms, lifting her to her feet. Rascal pulled her tight to her chest, sheltering her under the huge, bloodied wing that hung over them. In her daze, Nu saw Yantuz helping a hobbling Dzin on her other side, blood streaming down from a cut on his leg. The survivors held each other as Suttaru's horrors came toward them. They were unlike anything Nu had seen before today. These weren't simply the poor creatures Suttaru had unwritten with his dark stories—ordinary people and creatures turned into unnatural combatants—these were something different. They oozed in bizarre synchronicity with one another, creeping, crawling, and surging in a mass of whirling teeth and tentacles, of smoke and fire. They rippled and phased as Nu stared, as Rascal, Yantuz, and Dzin—battered and bleeding—gazed at these horrors with something more than simple panic. They were overwhelmed, surrounded. The monsters were either going to tear them limb from limb, or Suttaru was going to incinerate everything around him. They would surely lose now. It was just a matter of time. As the enemy advanced, she felt her insecurities come at her in rapid succession. Her desire to spend time outside the Library showed her as unworthy, a disappointment to herself and her family. Her foolish thoughts that Triss might feel for her as she did for the bright and energetic woman. Her foolish belief that she could be a Sage, a paragon of virtue, when her own mind and inability to master her talents had brought the enemy to their door. She crouched, her hands at her head, trying to push the thoughts away, even as they solidified in front of her, as real as the ground beneath her feet.

Yet as Nu felt herself give up, something gave way. Antares was at her side, swelling to normal size, with an energy that defied description and left the colors of the rainbow to shame. She felt him connect, felt the sorrow of his loss and the joy of finding her, of becoming one with something larger than the human mind could possibly comprehend alone. And then she saw it. The truth of what faced them.

"They're our fears," she said to herself, staring at the once faceless monstrosities. She saw in them not just her fears but those of her comrades.

Rascal's fear of being an outsider, her onetime feeling of hopelessness and that the sky might one day reject her and her beautiful wings. Yantuz and Dzin's dead parents came back to haunt them, joined by Dzin's classmates and tendrils of things from the Maze itself, all reaching for them with sharp edges. They were flailing under the assault, and Nu knew exactly how to help them.

"Rascal!" yelled Nu, pointing past the older woman, a burst of pure light leaving her right hand, exposing the creatures for what they were—the stuff of nightmares and lies. Dzin and Yantuz looked over in awe as Nu directed her strength of will and perception to their opponents. She raised her other hand, feeling the power flow through her, bolstered by the Orb, her hands wheeling in intricate patterns her mind couldn't yet quite comprehend, unraveling the lies wrapped around these creatures as though she was untangling a ball of knots. Yantuz let out a yell of sheer emotional release and ran at the now-faceless monsters, his makeshift weapon in hand.

"Lies!" he called out, "Get. Out. Of. My. Head!" His opponent became clear to all, it's writhing mass of flesh, made from twisted ink-like tendrils, recoiled as he stabbed at it with the lintel. As it surged back toward him, he yelled again and beat the creature again and again with the arch support.

Rascal, an amazed look on her face as the young man ran past her, let out her own battle cry and surged forward, the metal of her wings stained with ash and fire and even her own blood. She slashed at the creature to Dzin's left, her wings a blur of sharp metal, cutting off pieces of the monster as if it were made of nothing. Nu stared as the fallen parts smoked and sizzled on the ground, dissipating into nothingness.

Dzin looked back at Nu, grinned tightly, and picked up the roar of battle from his brother and Racal. He hurled himself at the monster his fears had conjured. His wooden seat plank, barely blue now, more like the color of burnt wood, smacked into the demon in front of him. It wavered in his vision, shifting between the faces of his dead friends and his parents, until all he, too, saw was the mass of pure evil. He brought down the plank with all the force he could muster, again and again.

Nu sent wave after wave of pure truth to the enemy, her hands a blur, the monsters now mere shades of dark stories; their own inner fears and doubts made flesh by the evil of Suttaru, now exposed for the lies they were.

"For Mother!" rang out Yantuz's battle cry, a chant that came with every swing of his makeshift weapon as he pummeled what was left of his opponent, weakened as it was by his own truth.

Rascal fought without words, but with screams of raw emotion as she slashed at her own demons with her battered wings, her fists, and her feet.

Nu could see Dzin, fragile and insecure no longer, in a state of pure focus, his Runner's body finally at peace with his keen mind, with no hesitation. An apprentice no longer. He made short work of his opponent, about which no one was more surprised than himself.

Nu looked on to the larger battle. The power of Perennia was stronger than any of them had dared believe. The life that Helia had imbued her with was fiercer than even she might have ever thought possible.

Slowly, Perennia began to overwhelm the evil in their midst.

Nu didn't know whether her vision had weakened Suttaru, made him remember who he truly was—just a scared, lonely man—but now he was being overpowered. All she could see were the dragon's green flames, her strength, becoming a torrent that burst the dam of Suttaru's darkness.

His powers eventually spluttered and caved, the fire he wielded no longer thick with death, but flickering and weak. He was left open to attack, and Perennia wasted no time in smothering him with her own fire.

There was an explosion. It threw Suttaru back with such force that he flew through the nearest building.

The entire structure crumbled and collapsed on top of him.

The Unwritten howled as one and were silenced. For a split second, the group saw them as they truly were. It wasn't another of Nu's visions this time. Perhaps the shroud of their curse was falling away, as Suttaru's hold on them dissipated. Normal people and otherworldly animals

were revealed briefly. Masses of people, gaunt like Suttaru, sickly looking and frightened.

Dzin's teacher, Tywich, stared at himself in surprise.

And then they were released from their torment, their clothes shed-
ding, their skin cracking and falling away in strips from their bodies.
Their muscle tissue shriveling beneath, before their bones themselves
crumbled to dust. Soon these poor beings were nothing more than withered mounds of spent life, ashes that were quickly scattered to the wind.

After that it was quiet. And all that was left was the group, their
mourning, and the knowledge that they had won.

CHAPTER FORTY-SEVEN
GOODBYES

They were safe again, Nu told Dzin and the others in a quiet voice.

She was pale and shocked, barely a shell of the vibrant young woman he'd first met. But there was a strength in her eyes now and a confidence in the way she relayed this information that spoke of the Sage she had become.

Dzin knew the truth of her words, yet any relief he felt was quickly swamped by the agony in his body, as the cuts and bites from the twisted, malevolent creatures began to overwhelm him.

All he wanted to do now was get back to the airship. There was nothing left to fight. With Suttaru gone, the Unwritten died as well. He'd seen them crumble away before his very eyes, as though they were simply nightmares burning away in the morning light.

Now returned from the dead, Perennia stayed in the plaza as they left to return to the airship. Nobody said anything to her. Somehow they knew she'd join them in her own time.

The last he'd seen, her magnificent head was bowed over the same spot Helia and Vega had last been standing.

Dzin had only caught a glimpse of what the dragon had done, so consumed was he in the immediate battle he found himself in. Yet it was enough to realize she could protect them from anything. He silently urged himself to let go of the feeling of terror he'd been clutching on to—the way that Nu was now clutching her Orb—and he allowed Yantuz to steer him away. His brother said nothing at all, still stunned.

Across the bridge they went, away from the battle-scarred city, with Rascal supporting the poor, distraught Nu, until they crossed the clearing to find Captain Finesse and Earnest waiting for them at the controls of the *Golden Oriole*. The captain's grim features faded into a smile the instant he saw them staggering out of the mist . . . before disappearing when he realized they were one short—two, even.

Nothing was said. Nothing needed to be. They knew he must have seen the bursts of fire across the distant city, and the rain of ash that had fallen even here.

As he helped them back to the ship, he relayed how he had guessed what had happened and had been debating with himself whether to fly in and help them when he'd heard the dragon roar.

"They did it, then?" he asked, his voice cracking a little. "Helia and that little Orb of hers?"

Nu looked up to him, her lips trying to form the words but too weak to utter them. She simply nodded.

With that, they waited.

They had come here for Perennia, and they would leave with her, too, when she was ready, when she had paid her respects to the person who had saved her. Yantuz grabbed the remainder of the vial of Elixir and dabbed it over his brother's wounds first, then offered it to Nu and Rascal, who both refused. He gave it back to Dzin, who corked the vial and slid it into his pocket.

It was then the dragon appeared, a titanic flying shadow in the mist that burst through into the clearing. She landed right next to the airship with a thud that shook the ground and sent ripples across the lake. Antares flew over to her nuzzle her, which she accepted by leaning forward, before Nu very bravely approached and patted the creature's neck.

"Thank you," she said.

Perennia closed her eyes and bowed her head before the sound of a chime broke the moment. The dragon rose sharply as a light began to shine.

Everyone spun to face the rising waterfall behind the airship.

$$ \longrightarrow \bullet \stackrel{\backslash\!\!\!\;/}{\underset{/\!\!\!\;\backslash}{\diamond}} \bullet \longrightarrow $$

A vertical split of light had appeared in the center of the water and was quickly widening.

Nu's shoulders slumped. *What now?*

But as she saw a woman and two men hurrying through, she almost collapsed in relief.

Robin, Mwamba, and Veer.

The looks on their faces as they saw the group, the airship, and the dragon were too much. It almost broke Nu to see the flash of shock and joy pass between them—she wanted it to stay that way. She didn't want to see how their expressions would fall when they, too, realized there was someone absent from their group.

As Nu was swept up in a tearful embrace from Robin, she caught a glimpse of another figure coming through from the portal behind them. The author Arturo. Seeing his scruffy beard and his unkempt hair, she realized they must have been through a fight of their own back there. Yet right now his face was a mix of awe, curiosity, and terror as he stared at the world around them and then up at the co-lossal dragon. He almost looked as if he wanted to leap back through the portal and hide.

It was enough to almost make her laugh, even as Robin squeezed her tightly. Veer harrumphed beneath his mustache, and Mwamba put a fatherly hand on her shoulder.

"Helia did it," was all she could say to them.

Mwamba nodded. He didn't ask for any more than that.

The goodbyes to the others were harder than she thought they might be. These people had been thrown into her life, and they had somehow formed a friendship she didn't think she'd ever have with anyone else.

Perhaps a friendship forged in a shared experience, no matter how short, held a greater power than any other. She wondered whether she would see them again.

She decided she would.

One by one, she embraced them, while the other Sages waited for her at a distance, giving them some space. When she got to Dzin, she gave him an extra squeeze.

Out of them all, she'd known he'd been the most frightened. And yet he'd faced the demons anyway, choosing to take a stand where she knew many wouldn't. She would always remember that.

"You did it," she said.

The smile he gave her indicated he wasn't exactly sure what he'd done, perhaps even concerned that he might be in trouble for whatever it was, which made her beam at him all the more.

"Thank you all," she said, stepping back to take in their faces. Then for the first time, she noticed the size of the dragon compared to the airship. She let out a little moan as she did the mental calculations and came up short, but luckily Rascal had seen the question forming on her lips and cut her off.

"We'll get her home—don't you worry. We came all this way; we're not exactly going to leave her here." She gestured to Captain Finesse, who didn't seem to share her enthusiasm. "We've carried our fair share of interesting cargo between realms before. I'll have to tell you about it sometime."

Nu smiled back. "I'd like that."

Yantuz put his arm around his brother and grinned. "Next time you come back to the Great Tree, you can stay with us, Nu. It's a bit cozy in our little cubby, but Dzin here will be glad to sleep top to toe with me so you can have his bed."

Dzin nudged him in the ribs. "You snore too much. I'll sleep on the floor, thanks."

With that, Nu backed away, still holding on to Antares, who flashed her own goodbyes.

As Nu turned and made her way toward the portal, Robin took her arm while Mwamba and Veer stayed close to her other side in case she needed help.

Between them, they stepped up to the waterfall.

Nu glanced back only once, at her friends and at the City of Forever.

It was then she saw a familiar figure in the mist over the lake. And as the wind whipped against the water, it carried on its breath a final, fleeting message, whispered in her ears.

Dum spiro spero.

The words rang in her mind as she felt the presence of another figure, who could only be Xavier, joining the first, before they faded into memory together. They clasped hands together in memory.

A smile came to Nu's lips as she let her fellow Sages guide her back across the divide between realms as Robin whispered in her ear.

"Welcome back, Sage."

Nu couldn't help but shiver at the jolt of excitement that rushed through her in that moment. She stepped back into the Great Library to begin her new life.

The portal shut behind them.

CHAPTER FORTY-EIGHT
A LEGACY OF HOPE

Arturo stood in the Concourse, watching life return to normal as scholars and students discussed their own versions of what might have happened, while the Volare Machina buzzed around them.

It had been two days since Nu had returned. Robin had convinced Arturo to stay just a little longer by taking him back to the Observatory to show him how Rosa was getting on back home. Nobody had missed him yet, and he had one more night before he was due to have her stay at his place.

He wondered whether Robin had an ulterior motive. She said she just wanted to show him the Library properly, not in passing like they had the last few days as they'd rushed around trying to save it from monsters and poison—which, he'd learned, was the same Dark Elixir that Dzin had inadvertently made for Helia.

Robin said a proper tour was the least he was owed for helping them.

He'd smiled and accepted her offer, but he knew it wasn't the whole story.

The battle was over, yet the Sages were going to carry the scars for a while. Robin put on her usual brave face, making sly jokes and teasing him relentlessly, but he knew she was shaken by the whole affair. Then there was the young Nu, who now carried herself with more confidence and steel than he remembered.

She hadn't even been a Sage when she'd been thrown into this.

That was about to change.

"Ready?" Robin asked, tapping him on the shoulder and leaving her fingers there just a moment longer than necessary. He gave her a smile and nodded, then winked at Centauri, who was bobbing just behind her.

"I'm ready. Is Nu?"

"She's terrified but holding up well. It's probably the least terrifying thing she's faced in the last few days. She'll be fine."

Knowing it was what Helia would have wanted, Robin had immediately taken it upon herself to take the young woman under her wing, even as they both mourned. That kind of coming together was something Arturo had seen his entire time here. He saw it now, too, as they began to walk through the Library, noting how the damage from the battle was being patched up by a collective of workers and students and scholars, all pitching in together. No airs or graces here. Just people uniting for a common cause. That was what the Library was about, after all.

He was going to miss that when he returned home later that day.

"Quiet now," Robin whispered as they pushed their way through a set of impressive red-and-gold double doors with colorful winged symbols, which seemed alive somehow, emblazoned upon each one.

This was the Gallery of Sages. As they entered, he saw the place was already filled with an excited mix of people from all walks of life, all talking in hushed whispers or gazing in awe at the ten marble statues that stood larger than life in front of them. The figures all had Orbs cupped in their hands or pressed against their chest, and their faces were ones Arturo immediately recognized.

Helia, Mwamba, Veer, Robin . . . the statues of them were all here, along with all the other Sages he had only met briefly and whose names he hadn't had a chance to remember properly.

"It's you!" he said rather too loudly, pointing at the very lifelike and quite beautiful visage of Robin towering above them. "Wow."

"Shhhhh!" she hissed back, blushing. "You're going to have to be much quieter than that for the rest of this, Arturo. Don't make me regret allowing you to come. This is a sacred event! Now stay here. Don't make a nuisance of yourself. And enjoy it."

She gave him her best grin and hurried down the parted crowds, with Centauri in tow, to join her colleagues.

All the Sages stood at the front. Well, eight of them did, dressed in their very distinctive Library surcoats—gown-like fabric garments embroidered with intricate spiral patterns in silvery thread. And in this low light, the embroidery reflected the eager patterns and swirling symbols shining out from each of the Orbs, as if they were all speaking at the same time, and the Sages' surcoats were flashing in reply.

Only one stood apart.

Nu appeared on a raised black platform before them, a dais that sparkled with inlaid stars and galaxies. It was quite an effect, positioning Nu as some kind of grand energy or spirit, hovering amid the wider universe.

The ceremony was beautiful. It started with a celebration of Helia's and Xavier's lives, recounted by Robin, who Arturo could tell was doing her best not to cry as she told the tale of how Xavier and Helia had met. Mwamba then took over, speaking of his long-standing friendship with the pair. He was followed by the other Sages in turn, telling their own stories of the friends now lost—with Sage Maïa relaying a particularly amusing anecdote about Helia's escapades in Planaxis, which had most of the crowd laughing despite their tears.

And as the stories flowed and the memories were shared, the light in the Gallery grew stronger, as though the sun might have been passing overhead, beaming down with all its warmth and strength. Beneath it, Arturo could see both Helia and Xavier's statues start to glow with a spirit of magic, as though being gifted one last moment of life.

It was a glorious sight to behold. It was the powerful feeling of what swept through the room—and, he felt, the wider Library—that Arturo knew he'd remember for a long time. A uniting of friends. A celebration of life. A feeling that Helia and Vega hadn't really gone. That nobody ever did. Because their energy always remained, in a different form, but just as strong and loving and powerful, guiding those who followed after.

All too soon, however, the stories came to an end. The lights began to fade, and with it the statues' life. Helia's face seemed to smile one more time, if that was possible, and then her features faded away.

Waiting for the new Sage of Hope.

Standing on the platform, surrounded by her new colleagues, Nu spent a few moments picking out the familiar faces in the crowd. Her parents were there, waving without trying to seem like they were waving. She spotted her friends here and there, their faces beaming. Will was easy to see, being nearly a foot taller than those around him. While beside him, Triss signed, "Good luck!" to which Nu grinned in response.

Despite her pride at the ceremony, though, she couldn't help but feel the weight of sadness too.

I wish Helia was here, she thought as she'd glanced up to where her friend's statue stood, looking at her familiar features, all dark curly hair and kindly face, before they faded away, leaving a little hole in Nu's insides.

She looked to what had been the carving of Vega, now free of markings, just an Orb awaiting a name. She'd asked Robin earlier what would happen, given the Book of Wisdom needed a new Orb to choose Helia's replacement. Robin had only smiled sadly and said, "That's a tale for another day."

Nu said her silent goodbyes and turned back to the ceremony, standing straight and true, knowing it was what Helia would have insisted upon.

This was made easier by the realization she was now a part of the legendary order of Sages of the Great Library of Tomorrow. A protector of the realms beyond and Earth itself.

Who would have thought such a thing was possible?!

Up on the dais, she looked down at Mwamba, who whispered a little note of good luck, while Antares drifted to the other side of the platform and hovered, facing her at head height.

"The choosing of a new Sage is an important moment in our time here," Robin intoned, her voice echoing through the Gallery. The crowd held its breath, Nu among them. "It is the moment the Book of Wisdom, through her Orbs, selects a person of the highest caliber of spirit, someone who embodies one of the core values of the very best of humanity. A Sage who will join with their companions on the path to enlightenment, through growth, maturity, and study, all while living life to the fullest, standing united in the protection of Earth, the Great Library, and all the realms that lie beyond."

The Sages all now stood as one, their Orbs bobbing along next to them.

"Are you ready?" Robin asked.

Nu gave a quick nod and held out her hand, palm open, fingers outstretched.

Antares's many layers now swirled with a variety of intricate designs and symbols. When she'd first come across her, she'd been weak and flickering, almost burnt out, but now she was alive and beaming with the intensity of a glorious golden sunrise. The Orb was clearly excited, and the sight almost made Nu giggle. She had to dig deep to stop herself. It wouldn't do to burst out laughing at such a moment.

Then the light faded again, and the Orb flew forward. She hovered for a second and then placed herself down on Nu's palm.

Nu let her fingers close around her companion. Then she lifted her other hand and gently placed it on top, cupping the Orb, before she brought Antares to her chest.

It was a moment of uniting in its purest form. Of two friends finding each other and knowing they would be together forever.

"Nu has been welcomed!" Robin shouted, and the crowd erupted in cheers. Within the sound, she could make out cries of "Nu!" and "Welcome, Sage!"

A thunderous roar could be felt spreading through the rest of the Library as the celebration began in earnest. The fires around the hall suddenly burned higher and brighter and bigger, and everyone could feel the warmth and glow of the flames upon their faces. From out of nowhere, golden butterflies materialized in the air above the crowds, spreading across the Library, their wings catching the light from the fire and reflecting thousands of little light flashes around the hall. The collective fluttering of their wings created a hum that soon joined other sounds drifting around them now, filling the air with music—a beautiful symphony of celebration that seemed to pour from the walls and pillars of the Great Library itself, perhaps from the very rock beneath their feet. The smooth rhythms flooded each soul with a vibration perfectly pitched to drive them all to feel a united joy and excitement for what was a new chapter in their lives.

To top it off, there was the unmistakable smell of freshly made foods wafting through the halls toward them—spicy, salty, and sweet scents all combined in exotic and delicious ways to set many a mouth watering.

Yet as the glorious chaos washed through the underground city like a wave of exhilaration—as well as relief, after recent events—Nu made sure to take a moment to herself.

To glance up to another statue whose face had been blank: Xavier's.

She watched it change into one she knew very well.

Her own.

Dzin stood with Yantuz and Rascal in the Rose Garden, along with Captain Finesse and Earnest, trying not to fidget.

It wasn't the wounds he'd sustained in battle that were the problem. The Elixir had seen to those. Well, to his and Yantuz's anyway. Rascal had steadfastly refused to take any, seemingly proud of the scars she had won.

No, it was the nerves.

He was standing at the edge of the Garden—now almost fully regrown and full of colorful, buzzing life—at the front of a gathering of Silvyrans. The Petal Queen from Aedela was here, standing head and shoulders taller than even Rascal. She looked fearsome in her ceremonial armor, with long sleeves of golden thorns and a helmet crowned by emerald petals—an echo of the dragon's own headpiece. While on the other side of Dzin, the Chief Scientist was wearing a quite exquisite dress of handsewn petals and a train of crushed pollen, with a forest of flowers embroidered into the fabric, which shifted as if blown by a secret wind.

The Chief Scientist kept glancing his way and giving him a smile of pride, which he was too awkward to return in case it turned out to look more like a grimace. He merely nodded each time, feeling his cheeks redden and burn, and would then go back to staring at the ceremony that was unfolding before them. At least, until she moved closer and tapped him on the shoulder.

"We never thanked you properly," she said quietly. "So, from the deepest roots of my heart, thank you, Dzin. You have honored the tradition of the Runners in ways nobody could have imagined, and although we mourn those lost, I look forward to working with you to help us rebuild."

"Working with *me*?"

He almost fell over with shock, which she noted with amusement. Daylight sparkled off the silver tiara she wore as she inclined her head ever so slightly.

"The realm needs our Elixir. *Your* Elixir, Dzin. Our stocks are low after the sabotage, and yours will be the one that leads the healing of our great land. As Perennia has healed this Garden, you will heal Silvyra. Are you up to the challenge?"

"It would be an honor."

The faintest hint of smoke still hung in the air. But that was all that was left of the devastation he'd seen here, just before they'd landed. Before the dragon had once again placed a claw into the tainted soil and made it whole again.

The journey back from the battle had been uneventful. Once they had returned to Silvyra, Perennia had been released to fly the rest of the way. And it was good she had, because as they flew together over Mother, toward Bloom, they could see the swathes of devastation wrought across the forests and flowery flatlands, worryingly close to the Great Tree.

Perennia had swept down and breathed new life into the land. The *Golden Oriole* had carried on to the Rose Garden, before the crew watched the dragon land and fill the Garden with healing and hope again.

Fierce and dangerous to her enemies she may be, but at her heart, Perennia was a protector. A symbol throughout the land—and beyond, Dzin now understood—a defender of nature and all things good. A part of her was imbued with the healing properties of the Rose Garden. Or perhaps it was the other way around.

Either way, their symbiotic relationship bloomed the flora and fauna back into life right before their very eyes. Not quite bringing the Garden back to the same gloriously overgrown and wildly beautiful state it had been the last time Dzin had been there. But enough to show that life had won. For everyone to see that the Garden was alive again, as was the dragon within it.

And as Dzin looked around him, seeing the gathered people from the different lands across this world, he understood that they would need to stand united with Perennia now to protect her just as much as she protected them.

For they would need to survive what would come next. In his gut, he could feel that there might be something coming their way again soon.

Another adventure?

He wondered if that was anticipation he could feel building inside him. And yet while once that dreaded word might have caused him to shiver and make a face, or retreat into his shell for protection, it no longer did. Hadn't they just had the greatest adventure and survived it? Perhaps they weren't so bad after all.

Dzin looked up to his brother, noting his handsome face filled with pride, and then glanced over to Yantuz's equally handsome beau, Junic.

He grinned to himself.

If there was another adventure to be had, so be it. He would be ready.

In the Great Library, the festival of celebration continued long into the evening.

There was no real focal point; the joy could be felt all through the Great Library. It was truly a time of coming together, of uniting. Nu could feel the power behind it electrifying her skin, raising the hairs on the back of her neck as she wandered through the halls of the Great Library. It was unlike anything she had ever known.

She watched as the Orbs created their own show for the masses, throwing symbols of light that danced across the walls and ceilings. Antares was glowing so intensely with delight that she had almost become a tiny sun among her counterparts.

The ethereal music continued to pull the Library and her inhabitants into its warm embrace. It stirred everyone into a mass of elation and happiness, as they experienced waves of pure joy pulsing through them. Couples kissed and friends hugged, and Volare of all shapes and sizes swooped in formation through the air, adding their own jubilation to the celebration. Revelers even took over the Auditorium, where one of the more ingenious scholars had created a holographic globe on the center stage, through which a silvery beach party could be seen in full flow. Nu had taken a moment to watch as more visitors had stepped through the multidimensional rippling outer skin before appearing in the middle of the party and joining their friends.

Meanwhile, in the Concourse, other groups gathered not only to chat and make merry but also to continue the cleanup from the siege. This they did in good spirits, however, making a party of their collective victory. They all took turns returning the precious books to the shelves, some on the ground floor, others swinging from ladders, drinks swishing in their hands, full of gladness, knowing they'd saved the Library. Then they streamed en masse through the hall, enjoying the warmth and glow on their faces. The flames of the fires, hung from the chandeliers on the ceilings and within the lamps against the walls, all burned higher and brighter here, fueled by powerful magic. Groups took pleasure in the singers and acrobats entertaining everyone with their delicious melodies and stunning feats of physicality. Magicians wandered the aisles, too, casting the most dazzling illusions, sending flocks of birds of light flying through the bookshelves, and conjuring rivers that flowed through impossible seams in the floor, filled with all manner of sea creatures.

And just as the party began to peak, they were accosted by the most sensational scents wafting from the direction of the kitchens as an army of servers burst forth and began the celebratory feast in earnest. People helped themselves to the tastiest and most colorful meals, sizzling side dishes, and aromatic desserts, all the while nodding and dancing to the music that echoed through the Great Library of Tomorrow as the entire city came together in spirit.

As far as the people here were concerned, they had all the time in the world to make things right again. This was simply a new beginning.

Nu drifted through the celebrations, taking in the glances and looks of admiration, smiling at and thanking all those who wished her well— which was everyone, because she was now known throughout these hallowed halls. Antares hovered close to her head, glowing and now fully back to herself. Every now and then, she would nudge her shoulder excitedly as if to say *This is all for you!*

Nu grinned and shook her head. She could still hardly believe it.

Her. A Sage.

Her parents had been so proud, wrapping her up in their arms after the initiation, before rushing off to prepare their own family celebrations, which she'd join later. Her friends Triss and Will leaped on her like excitable puppies, before they both realized her new position as a Sage and respectfully loosened their hugs—although Triss held on a moment longer than was necessary, and Nu couldn't help the warmth of excitement building inside her.

She was definitely asking me on a date, she decided.

Then Grindlepuffin turned up, having snuck away from the kitchens to give her a proud grin and a secret handful of her favorite dark chocolate beans. All of which she relished with good cheer and a joyful heart.

Well, as much she could muster anyway.

Because as she continued her journey through the festivities, smiling and nodding and shaking hands and bumping fists, she drew closer to the Haven, where the other Sages were waiting. Her insides fluttered a little nervously. And she prepared for the difficult conversation ahead.

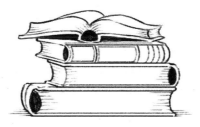

CHAPTER FORTY-NINE
TO MAKE A DIFFERENCE

In the Haven, Nu stood a little apart from the other Sages, listening to the conversation unfold.

Robin had said they would need a debrief. The ceremony of induction had been one glorious and slightly nerve-racking part of today. But the other was more serious and solemn, as the gathered Sages—including those called back from their travels in Paperworld—tried to understand what had happened. Above, the Author looked on from her restored place over the Book of Wisdom.

"Are we sure it was a Dark Elixir?" Amin, the Sage of Loyalty, said. "I'm still struggling with the idea they created a Dark Elixir and not just a bad batch."

"There are no certainties in life," the Author interjected.

"Ain't that the truth," said Veer. "The Ash Man, who most of us considered merely legend, had returned after all."

"We should believe what the young Sage says," said Paix, the Sage of Joy, who looked not much older than Nu herself. She was from Brazil and had closely cropped hair and a glint in her eye that spoke of a love of danger. "Nu experienced this all herself, and we should trust what she makes of such things."

The Sage glanced over at her. Nu nodded her thanks, trying not to feel too self-conscious and not wanting to add anything more.

She'd said enough already. About their adventures. Suttaru. And the Dark Elixir that Dzin created due to his corrupted teacher. It was now clear that the Rogue Sage, Suttaru's right-hand man, had also been interfering with lands beyond the Great Library. It turned out he'd been at the Great Tree all this time, hiding in plain sight as the advisor—which explained the glitch in the map room at the start of this wild journey—biding his time. But to what end, Nu wasn't sure.

Neither did she have the energy to think about it right now. It was up to the more experienced minds here to figure out what was going on and what it all meant. She was still a little in shock by it all, enough to not really take much in. The excitement from her initiation was still filling her up inside, as well as the anticipation at being a part of this wonderful group. The other Sages had all gone out of their way to make her feel proud of what she'd accomplished, and they all mourned together for the loss of Helia, Vega, and Xavier. They had encouraged her and supported her, and Nu was sure they were all going to become great friends.

The discussion finished with Veer informing the Sages that Aedela would need their help to rebuild following the attack, and then the Sages began to clear out.

Nu hung back, smiling and nodding as they left, until it was just her and the Author.

She stepped up to the Book and touched her hand to her eyes, then to her chest.

"I read not with my eyes, but with my heart," she recited, as she had been taught.

"You wish to ask me a question," the face said.

Nu walked over, unsure of how to broach the question in her heart. One that had been running through her mind ever since that moment in the battle when she'd laid Suttaru bare and seen him properly—as he had been.

It had started as a niggle. A strange moment of knowledge that she didn't know what to do with. But it had been growing ever since. And now she had her chance to at least get it out into the open.

"I saw him," she said, then cleared her throat. "At the City of Forever. I used my power to uncloak Suttaru. To see him as he once was, before he grew evil. Or at least, before he let the evil inside him claim who he was."

The face nodded, but said nothing, prompting Nu to continue.

"He didn't seem bad—maybe confused, maybe a bit jealous. Those are the feelings I got, anyway. I'm not sure. He just seemed normal, really. A normal person."

"We were all normal once," the Author said in acknowledgment. Then, more softly, "What is wrong, Nu?"

Nu took a breath. "I know what happened, Author. I felt how he was tricked into helping the evil that took him. The entity that wanted to consume the realms. I felt how his love for you—you back then, when you were the Scholar—was used to twist and deceive him. He was lost and vulnerable. And yet I think his initial intention had been to save you, no matter the cost to himself. An act of purity and goodness. An act of sacrifice."

The Author went quiet at that, as though she hadn't been expecting to hear such a thing.

Nu continued. "You loved him too. Didn't you?"

"I did."

"And yet, if you loved him, why didn't you help him? That first time, I don't think he was truly gone. He could have been turned back, turned away from evil. Why did you give up on him?"

The Author's sigh was full of human emotion. A metaphysical gust of regret that briefly made her face flicker in and out of focus.

"I would have saved him if I could," she said. "But you weren't here. He came with rage, and I couldn't save everyone. The consequences of losing the Library and the realms beyond were too great. I acted as best I could, to merge myself with the Book to defeat the enemy. To create the barrier to prevent that entity from consuming any more of our stories. And yes, this act cost me the person I loved."

"Trapping him in Discordia, with the evil that had turned him?"

"For the greater good, Nu, yes."

Nu blinked and looked away, understanding the sacrifice the Author had made, but unsure of how to feel. She could still see the truth of the man who had tried to kill them all. The man who had once been tricked by pure evil and had paid for it dearly. Tormented and tortured, until he had become a terrifying story brought to life, one they had just defeated.

It was a hard thing to reconcile. But as much as she was struggling, she knew the Author must have too. Nu had seen Helia struggle similarly in her last moments, lured by visions of Xavier, knowing she could save him and yet ultimately giving him up to save them all.

"I understand," Nu said. "I don't know how to feel about it, but I understand."

The Author had been just as human and flawed as anyone. Capable of making mistakes and required to make difficult decisions, just like the rest of them, sacrificing her happiness for a more important cause.

"Perhaps there is nothing to feel other than what is there, Nu. Perhaps all we can ever do is embrace that as our own truth and make the best of it, come what may."

"Thank you," Nu said with a sad smile.

She bowed, and the Author inclined her head, then began to swirl her way back inside the shuddering Book beneath her, until the covers fell shut, and all was silent again.

Leaving Nu with her thoughts and the difficult feeling that came with knowing too much.

"You don't really want to leave us, do you?" Robin asked, after appearing as if from nowhere and poking Arturo in the ribs. He rolled his eyes and ducked away as Centauri buzzed far too close to his head, apparently both excited and upset about his departure. "Please be careful," he joked. "Everything still hurts. And yes, I'm looking forward to going back home, where the only thing I'm responsible for is paying the bills and deciding what to make Rosa for dinner."

As Robin led him across the Concourse to where he could now see Mwamba and Nu waiting, she made a face. "It's just . . . I could use the help with my research, and it'd be fun to have you around. Well, *I* don't think that, obviously. I couldn't give a crap. But Centauri is really going to miss you."

They both grinned, knowing that wasn't the truth. The thought had occurred to him too. He was desperate to see his daughter again, but he couldn't help wondering whether one day he might find his way back here somehow. If Robin split her time between the Library and home, then why couldn't he?

"I will miss Centauri too," he replied dryly. "I suppose I've had a lot of fun here, if you can consider potential death and the destruction of multiple realms fun. Hey, maybe I'll write about this place."

Robin's face dropped. "Mwamba didn't tell you, did he?"

"Tell me what?"

They drew up beside the elder Sage and Nu, who were standing at the end of an aisle of shelves. Arturo was a little relieved to find there were no people or devil dogs with flaming words carved into their skin trying to pour out of this one. Just books, and at the end of it, an open portal that was waiting for him. He could see it led into the same bookshop he had come in from.

"I'm afraid you won't remember any of this," Robin said, glancing pointedly at Mwamba. "Not properly, anyway. Only Sages get to hold on to the details of our time here. We're like characters in the Library's story, while visitors . . . well, once they leave, so do their memories. For the most part, anyway. You will likely forget us."

"Oh."

He tried to bury his disappointment as the others looked at him.

"I'm sorry," Mwamba said, inclining his head apologetically. "It's true. You'll carry your experience with you, forever, but very rarely does anybody remember any of their time here. It keeps our secret safe."

Arturo straightened, putting on a brave face. "Do you really think I want to remember having to put up with her for the last few days?" He gave Robin a nudge with his shoulder.

Nobody laughed, just smiled politely. They could all tell the two were going to miss each other greatly.

Satisfied that there was nothing more to say, Arturo gave Robin a quick hug, then reached up and gave Centauri a pat goodbye, before walking down the aisle toward the portal.

His daughter was waiting. That was good enough reason to be excited to leave this wonderful, magical, dangerous adventure, as much as a part of him yearned to stay.

He stopped and glanced back, just before the interdimensional doorway.

"I just step through, then?" he asked "No magical words or spells I need to utter? No potions I need to brew or douse myself in? No mythical creatures I need to either fight or have guide me on my way? Seems almost . . . boring."

Robin groaned. "Just get out of here before I kick you through."

Their eyes met, and he nodded his thanks to her. For being his friend and companion and savior. Then he did as he was told, leaving the Great Library behind as he stepped back into his old life, knowing that even if he forgot, nothing would ever be the same again.

The door chime to the bookstore rang out.

Arturo blinked awake to the pure light blue skies and the early morning sunshine. As he let the door close behind him, he stopped, unsure of what was happening, feeling that perhaps he'd been daydreaming, then glanced over his shoulder in puzzlement.

Had he just come out of the bookstore? Exactly how long had he been in there? Because the last thing he remembered it had been the afternoon. And why had he gone in anyway? He checked himself to make sure, but no, he certainly hadn't bought any books.

Had he been browsing for something in particular, or had he simply stumbled in there after going to the bar?

No, he decided, scratching his beard, which for some reason felt a little thicker, as though it had enjoyed a few extra days of growth. He didn't feel like he'd been drinking at all. His mouth was fresh. His mind was too—more so than it had felt in a long time. What's more, as he stared at the bar next door, beginning to see signs of life as one of the staff came out and started setting up tables, he realized he didn't even feel like a drink. Which was strange, considering the frustrating day at work he'd had earlier.

Except it was morning now, so how much "earlier" had it been?

It doesn't matter, he thought to himself. And it was true, because it really didn't. While the memory of work was still vivid in his mind, the feelings he remembered leaving the office with were gone.

Arturo felt free. As though something had changed inside him. There was a strong urge pushing him to do something. To start making a difference. Not just in his own life, although there was definitely a lot he could do differently, but in the wider world too. He wanted to contribute and collaborate with others toward a shared goal. Or to create something beautiful and have it change people's lives.

He certainly wasn't going to go back to his office again. He wasn't going to suffer that feeling of being trapped and helpless in the cycle of going to work just to pay the bills. If that job had ever been the right path for him, it was no longer the right one now. He suddenly realized if he wanted to change his situation, he had to do something about it.

An image popped into his mind, of him writing his way out of that life, and it made him smile. That's exactly what he was going to do today. He'd start this new existence by writing his resignation letter.

And maybe, after that, he might start writing stories again. Just maybe. Because as he wandered down the footpath into the start of a brand-new day, he could suddenly picture his future. In it there were stories for his daughter. Something fun and hopeful, where the heroes overcame the bad men, where taint and corruption and lies and hate were always fought and defeated, and good was always stronger than evil. Something his daughter, Rosa, would enjoy.

Wouldn't that be something?

He felt elated at the thought and turned the corner with a skip in his step.

"See, I told you he'd be fine," Robin said with a faraway look in her eyes.

Nu and Robin peered through the door of the bookshop, watching as Arturo wandered blissfully down the road and disappeared from view.

"I didn't doubt you for a second," Nu replied, bending the truth a little. She absently touched the amulet at her wrist. Antares buzzed a little response back, and she patted the hidden Orb to keep her quiet. "So, he truly won't remember anything?"

"I don't think so. That's not how it's ever worked."

"That's a shame. I'll miss him."

Robin said nothing.

"So," Nu continued as they stepped back into the bookshop and headed down to the aisle where the portal waited to take them back. "What now?"

The other Sages and the people of the Great Library of Tomorrow had officially welcomed her into the role now. What came after that?

She realized she'd never gotten to ask this question to Helia. The actuality of being a Sage was something she hadn't even had the chance to try to comprehend. They'd been thrown into the adventure so quickly that she had never stopped to wonder what the reality was, the mundane day-to-day of the job.

She and Robin stepped into the Library again, landing on the marble floor without breaking stride.

"Well, you have two choices," Robin answered, her eyes flashing mischievously. "We can stay in the Library—rest or do some studying—or maybe I can bore you senseless with everything I know . . ."

"Or?"

"Or how do you fancy exploring your new life a little more?"

"What else is there to see?" Nu asked.

Her friend grinned as she took Nu's hand and led her toward the Haven, to the portal that led to the realms beyond.

"Everything," Robin said.

EPILOGUE

Arturo hurried from his bedroom, down the hall, and into his daughter's room.

Rosa was sitting up in bed, sweat having plastered her dark curls to her forehead.

"Dad?" she asked.

"I'm here, *mija*. What's wrong? Did you have another bad dream?"

"A nightmare," her voice responded. "Volcanoes again."

He sat on the edge of her mattress and pulled her head into his. He didn't blame her. The volcanic activity all around the globe seemed to have abated for the moment—that's what the geologists on the news had been saying—but the event had still spooked everyone, including him, and it appeared Rosa had perhaps taken it a little to heart.

That made three nights in a row she'd been having the same nightmares. All since he'd returned home that strange day, feeling brighter and fresher and ready to change the world.

Rosa tugged his arm. "Can you stay with me until I fall asleep again?"

"Yes, *mija*, of course."

Then he reached over to grab the soft toy fox she'd been cuddling and placed it back in her arms, stopping only to give it a strange look. He realized he had no idea where it had come from.

Dzin stood high in the boughs of the Great Tree, enjoying a breath of fresh night air. Yantuz was sound asleep inside the cubby, his little snores punctuating the air that was full of the chirrups of insects and the occasional woosh of a flying squirrel on a nighttime jaunt.

It was the first time he had been alone in three suns. Since the events at the laboratory had propelled him into that crazy adventure across the world—and into another—being chased by evil, all in the search for Perennia, a being he had helped to save, which in turn had given him his life back at the Great Tree.

Not the life he'd had before, of course. There was no getting that back, and he still had moments of guilt over the friends he'd lost. He saw their faces in his dreams sometimes. Last night Monae had smiled at him proudly from across the lab, and he woke that morning feeling full of joy and sadness. He missed them greatly.

No, the life he had now was altogether different. In fact, it was everything he had ever wanted and aspired toward. He had achieved his goal of becoming a Runner and was now an instrumental part of the operation to make the Great Tree flourish again. Best of all, the pressure that he normally would have felt at being given so much responsibility was something that he was handling better than ever.

After all the trials he'd faced, he'd somehow survived. More than that, he'd discovered something along the way he thought he'd never find.

Belief in himself.

That wasn't to say the anxiety wouldn't rear its head again. He knew it would never quite disappear, no matter how well he learned to handle it. But Dzin figured that after everything he had been through, it would take something pretty terrible for the panic storms to shake him as they once had.

Now he was back home, well respected, able to deal with the pressure of being a crucial part of helping to rebuild the Botanical Education School. He and Rascal would be joining the faculty, in fact, which he thought could be a lot of fun.

Dzin knew he should have been content. He should be relishing having survived the journey and having his entire being changed for the better.

Yet there was a yearning within—a feeling that was new to him, something he could not deny.

It was a strange feeling. Of course, there had been times during the quest he'd longed to just return home, to be able to stand here as he was doing now and simply breathe in the scents of the berries and nuts and blossoms and leaves he knew so well.

Yet now he was here, in the quiet of his home, all he could feel was an itch to go travel again.

After taking a deep inhale, he wandered a little way from the cubby, trying to understand what exactly it was he was feeling. He let his hands run over the branch shoots and fingers of leaves that spread out along his path. He nodded at the buzzing insects that tilted their tiny heads at him as he passed by.

Then he reached the end of the bough.

He looked down and frowned, seeing a most strange sight. An image that caused a familiar whisper of anxiety, while over the horizon storm clouds gathered once more.

Down below, upon the forest floor, he could see the roots of the Great Tree.

They were turning black.

GLOSSARY

Adi (now Suttaru): One of the original scholars who worked with Fairen, who later becomes corrupted by Discordia and transforms into Suttaru, also known as "the Ash Man."

Aedela: The capital of Bloom in the western region of Silvyra, it is home to a vibrant community of families who grow the most spectacular flowers and plants in all of Silvyra. The town gets its name from a special flower that is traditionally cultivated and maintained by Bloom's ruler.

Amare: She is a large, miraculous, magical bird from Paperworld. Amare has multicolored feathers, golden aspects, and fierce intelligence. She is capable of carrying a full-sized human on her back and can travel magically to anywhere in Paperworld and beyond by opening a rift in time and space and flying. She has a special relationship with the Sages of the Great Library of Tomorrow, who can call upon her in times of great need. She can, however, only carry one passenger at a time.

Amin, the Sage of Loyalty: A former architect born in Jordan, he came to the Library in the 1990s. His aptitude for sustainable living has translated into an affinity for his surroundings, allowing him to become part of the physical landscape he inhabits.

Arturo: A middle-aged man from Mexico City, Arturo has worked in marketing as a copywriter for most of his adult life. He is divorced, with a daughter named Rosa, and feels increasingly unfulfilled in his job until he happens upon a magical gateway to the Great Library. Once there, he discovers that he possesses the magical ability to write things into reality.

Auditorium: Located off the Main Concourse, this is where Sages and scholars give lectures and answer questions from the audience. The Auditorium is a cavernous space with high-arching ceilings and curving, dark wooden walls. It is arranged like an inverted cone, with semicircular rows of seats descending one after another, with a raised podium at its center. Atop the podium itself is a pillar of brass and steel, with a ring of crystalline lenses mounted around a concave mechanism at its top.

Author (see also "Fairen" and "the Scholar"): This is an honorific given to Fairen, often known simply as "the Scholar," who first discovered the portal to Paperworld and built the Book of Wisdom. During a time of great danger, she became one with the Book of Wisdom, becoming its voice and operating consciousness. While the Book of Wisdom is considered one entity, it speaks with the Author's voice.

Beanstalks: These very tall, towering stalks can be found in and around the town of Undergrowth, located in the realm of Silvyra. They are taller than most trees and used by the local population for a variety of purposes, from shipping goods and transporting people via airship to also functioning as residences.

Bloom: Located in the western region of Silvyra, the land of Flowers, which includes Aedela (its capital), Lake Arroya, and many smaller towns and communities. It borders great forests and mountains to the east, where the Rose Garden is located, the stewardship of which people of Bloom are dedicated to.

Book of Wisdom: The Book itself appears as a humble, moderately sized tome with a gilded red cover. Hidden beneath its bindings, interwoven, the secrets of its construction are only known to the Scholar (also known as "Fairen" and "the Author"). The Book rests on a grand pedestal that dominates the center of the chamber, a podium fashioned from wood taken from the island trees.

Botanical Education School: This is the main school of learning for the community that lives on and around the Great Tree. Prospective Runners attend the school, as do other researchers and general students.

Bridge of Galnaterra: A large natural stone bridge spanning between two mountain peaks like a great arch; the bridge serves the airship transportation needs of the town called Undergrowth.

Captain Finesse: The current captain of the *Golden Oriole*, assisted by his first mate, Earnest, and a longtime friend and companion to Rascal.

Cerulean Rose: This magical flower, named for its striking shade of blue, is a cornerstone of the life and culture of Silvyra. It was created many generations ago by Mother, the Great Tree, and given to the people of Bloom for safekeeping in what is now known as the Rose Garden. The petals of the Cerulean Rose are the one essential ingredient—the rest being personal selections—in a Runner's recipe for the Elixir of Life and flowers during the peak of every conjunction.

Chief Scientist: The Chief Scientist is the appointed ruler of the community living within the borders of the Maze in the First Forest and at the Great Tree. Typically a woman, the Chief Scientist is often a former Runner with great scientific curiosity as well as a deep affinity and knowledge of horticulture.

City of Forever: The City of Forever is a sophisticated and magical city located in an unnamed and sparsely populated realm. Although uninhabited, it serves as a repository of memory from across Paperworld. The scholars and Sages of the Great Library are currently working to uncover its secrets.

Clockwork Mountain: A very large, artificially manufactured structure consisting of three giant tiered cogs that serve as living space for a city ruled by an individual known as the Raptor Prince. The origins of the

Mountain are mysterious, but it is believed to date back to before the Age of Spirits, when raw elemental forces controlled the realm.

Codex: This is both the catalog and operating system of the Great Library of Tomorrow.

Conjunction: This event occurs once every five seasons in Silvyra during the harvest season, when the realm's two moons and sun line up together and cause the natural life of the realm to prosper and renew. Various cultures in Silvyra celebrate this event with a great celebration and consider it to be the most important event of all the seasons. The timing of the Conjunction is somewhat random, with the people of Silvyra sensing and observing its coming by both their reaction to its effect on nature but also by observation of the moons and sun.

Copper Sea Monster: A denizen of the dark world inhabited by Suttaru, an agent of the dark world of Discordia.

Discordia: The Realm of Dark Stories, it is believed that Paperworld constructed this place to house and keep separate the very darkest of stories. It was first discovered accidentally by scholars from the Great Library while studying the portal to Paperworld.

Dzin: One of two orphaned brothers, he suffers from anxiety yet has overcome these obstacles to become an apprentice Runner in his realm of Silvyra.

Edwin Payne, the Dark Sage: A former British army general from the time of the American War of Independence, after losing an eye during battle, he turned his interests to the development of electricity, eventually becoming the Sage of Creativity. On learning the history of Suttaru, he eventually abandoned the Library with his Orb, Myrtilus, to join Suttaru in his quest for power.

Elixir of Life: The most precious resource of Silvyra, the Elixir is a paste created by Runners from unique recipes. Its creation is a gift given generations ago by Mother, the Great Tree, and is a potent remedy for ailments, both spiritual and physical.

Fairen (the Scholar; the Author): An early scholar—often referred to as "the Scholar" in histories of the period—and contemporary of the Founder, Fairen was responsible for creating the Book of Wisdom. When the realm of Discordia threatened the safety of the Library, she joined her consciousness to the Book and became known as "the Author."

First Cave: One of the oldest parts of the Great Library, the First Cave is located where the Founder arrived from the sea and houses some of the earliest and most personal of his collection.

First Forest: This large and diverse forest surrounds Mother, the Great Tree, and is home to a multitude of plants, animals, and people.

Flower of Life: This is a symbol of Mother and the people of Silvyra. It is thought to have been first drawn by the original Chief Scientist after being inspired by the Great Tree herself. It consists of eight interlocking circles that, when drawn correctly, represent the petals of a flower. This image also serves as a guide to prospective Runners for their eight ingredients, which are needed to create the Elixir of Life.

Formula (also Recipe): The Formula (or Recipe) is the formal name given to the ingredients a Runner chooses and combines to create their own unique batch of the Elixir of Life. The Runners go through the Maze and into the realm to collect eight ingredients that have special meaning to them, one being the petals of the Cerulean Rose, and typically the final combination is written down on a ceremonial scroll.

Founder: The originator of The Great Library of Tomorrow. Little is known of his early life, not even his given name, but he was an avid collector and appreciator of books and knowledge. When drawn to a mysterious secluded island during his travels, the Founder decided to build a place to celebrate humanity's values, stories, and knowledge. The Founder was lost to the portal before the construction of the Book of Wisdom.

Foyer: This is the oldest part of the Great Library, built upon the carved stone rotunda that the Founder discovered at the base of the mountain when he first arrived on the island. There is a grand circular chamber with a high ceiling and a large classical-styled mosaic mural that celebrates the many forms of storytelling that the Founder brought together in his collection.

Gateways (Silvyra): These are the entrances to the Maze that surrounds the First Forest and Mother. They are placed roughly north, south, east, and west of the Great Tree.

Gallery of Sages: The Gallery of Sages is a grand space where ten marble statues of the Sages stand larger than life.

Galnaterra (small town; farms): A small town and farms on the mountains near Undergrowth, to the north of the First Forest.

***Golden Oriole*:** A magnificent airship made of wood and brass, it is one of the rare vessels from Silvyra that docks at Mother, the Great Tree, and can travel to other realms to deliver the Elixir of Life.

Hall of Finding: A vast and cavernous space filled with high shelves of bound atlases and travelogues in a seemingly endless array of cartographical information about Earth and the realms beyond. It also houses the Orrery.

Haven: Perhaps the most important room in the Great Library, the Haven is the very center of the Library, where the Book of Wisdom and the original portal to the other realms resides. It is a place of sanctity and magic, a place that students whisper about as they pass its doors, slowing to wonder about what astonishments lay beyond.

Helia, the Sage of Hope: Originally from Italy, where she escaped one of Mount Vesuvius's eruptions, Helia has been the Sage of Hope for several centuries and is the second-longest-serving Sage, after Mwamba. Supported by her Orb, Vega, Helia has incredible powers to influence and control plants and nature. She and Sage Xavier are a romantic couple up until his death in the Rose Garden.

Maïa, the Sage of Integrity: Before becoming a Sage, she was a circus acrobat in late nineteenth-century France. As a Sage, she possesses incredible physical skills due to being "one" with her body and is capable of feats unmatched by normal humans. Her Orb, Trix, is her constant companion.

Main Concourse: Beginning with classical architecture, evoking the cathedrals of the Middle Ages, then slowly changing to reflect the different ages of the Library's construction, this is the main thoroughfare of the Great Library. With towering shelves on both sides above marble floors illuminated by sunlight from outside the mountain, shining in through shafts bored through the stone itself and redirected throughout the area by a series of mirrors. There are balconied galleries leading to the arched roof far above, and all through the Concourse is the sound of bustling activity, from those who live and work here to visiting scholars and the machinery of the Library itself. The Concourse provides access to the other important areas of the Library, with the Haven at its center.

Maze: A creation of Mother, the Great Tree, the Maze encircles both herself and the First Forest and acts as a security barrier. Only the pure of heart can safely navigate the Maze while wearing a blindfold (or similar). If one is not worthy, the Maze will devour the traveler.

Moon Swallows: A bird commonly found in Silvyra and particularly in the mountain regions near the Rose Garden.

Mother (The Great Tree): She is the Mother Tree, the representation of the circle of life not just on Silvyra but in all the realms of Paperworld. Indeed, each realm has a descendant of Mother unique to its environment that acts as its realm's Tree of Life.

Mwamba, the Sage of Knowledge: The oldest-serving Sage in this era, Mwamba has the ability to absorb, understand, and retain information from any book at incredible speed and the experience to put his knowledge to practical use in the service of the Great Library. Consequently, he and his Orb, Canopus, rarely leave the Great Library, where they can be of the most use.

Nest: A special place, away from the Main Concourse, for the rarest of magical creatures, Amare, to visit the Library in times of great need.

Nu: A young woman with a talent for "knowing" the truth of things, she was born in the Great Library of Tomorrow to her Australian mother and Burmese father, who found the Great Library in their twenties and became permanent citizens. She finds the orphaned Orb, Antares, and forms a bond with her.

Orbs: Originally designed by Fairen, the Scholar, there are ten sentient Orbs at any one time, and each is bonded to a Sage, whom they have selected on behalf of the Book of Wisdom. The Orbs have exotic materials in their makeup, and they can communicate fluently with their Sages, each Orb using a specific color and unique patterns displayed on their surface, combined with a strong psychic link and in a more limited way with other Sages and non-Sages. The Sages' Orbs can alter their size to hide and boost the Sages' power and are the mechanism by which Sages can travel through the portal safely.

Observatory: The Observatory is a special room where one can see events on Earth through an ingenious mix of technology and magic. The device is slightly bigger than your average crystal ball, and is like watching a film, but one that makes the user feel as though they are really in the place being viewed.

Orrery: Located in the Hall of Finding, this great machine dominates the room—a complex assemblage of brass and steel and crystal filled the vast space around it, a multitude of concentric rings that spin and twist on individual axes and orientations. Its purpose is to help the Sages find new realms in Paperworld and to track the Sages' Orbs while in Paperworld.

Paix, the Sage of Joy: Born in Brazil, she appears to be in her late twenties but has in fact been a Sage since the early 1900s. She is a talented pianist, and her powers are literally electrifying.

Paperworld: A "metaverse" of realms, Paperworld is the parchment patchwork of all stories ever told, where the River of Letters flows freely along endless channels, branching off into both physical and metaphysical streams, forming into words, sentences, and ultimately stories, which can each turn into a unique world of their own.

Perennia: Silvyra's dragon protector, Perennia's origins are shrouded in mystery and much folklore. She lives in and guards the Rose Garden and can be seen soaring above the mountains west of Mother, keeping watch over the skies.

Petal Queen: Bloom is a matriarchal society, and its leader is known as the Petal Queen. This is an elected position held for life, and the office holder is sworn to govern and protect Bloom's citizens and watch over the Aedela, Bloom's national flower.

Pink-tipped humming bees: Large colorful pollinators found around Silvyra and especially in the Rose Garden and Bloom.

Portals: First discovered in the Great Library by Fairen (also known as "the Scholar" and "the Author"), it is a magical doorway to the realms of Paperworld. It is unique to the island where the Great Library is located and can be regulated and controlled by the Book of Wisdom. There are also portals from Earth to the Library, usually traveled by visitors to the Library, who emerge in the Foyer. They are also regulated by the Book of Wisdom.

Queen's Nest: A tavern in the town of Undergrowth.

Raptor Prince: This is a title held by the current ruler of Clockwork Mountain, the three-storied mechanical city in the desert to the east of the First Forest. He is vain, cunning, and obsessed with his private horticultural collection.

Rascal: A former Runner for the Botanical Education School at the Great Tree on Silvyra, and former crew on the *Golden Oriole*, she is full of life and seeks adventure in all aspects of her life, including having metal wings fitted to her back that allow her to glide through the skies of her world.

Reading Room: This is a place for the Sages to research and converse. It is a beautiful, enormous space housing large numbers of books—tall, small, thin, thick, of all colors and decorations and designs—stored up against the walls three stories high and even somehow held across the ceiling too.

Recipe (See "Formula"): The more general and casual term the Runners use for their Elixir of Life formula.

Refinery, The: Located at the lower levels of Mother, the Great Tree, the Refinery is a huge complex of wood, bark, and copper machinery, with giant brass containers where the Elixir of Life is manufactured in large quantities.

Reflectorias: Found in the City of Forever, these large copper monuments, which look like telescopes, are known as *reflectorias*. They are positioned at regular intervals around the city's lake and angled to a single point within the city. Once activated, they beam light toward a magnificent white tower at the city's center—a reflection of love and memory from all around the great and deserted city.

River of Letters: This is the source of all magical stories and life that make Paperworld. It flows freely along endless channels, branching off into both physical and metaphysical streams, forming into words, sentences, and ultimately stories, which can each turn into a world of their own. It is constant change and creation.

Robin, the Sage of Love: A former special needs teacher, she is Indian British and has a mischievous, infectious smile. She is a relatively new Sage, but still considerably older than one might think. Her powers allow her to touch the emotions of all people, often appearing as waves of golden light. Her Orb, Centauri, shares her upbeat manner.

Rock Giants: Living in the desert sands around the Clockwork Mountain, the giants are taller than most trees, camouflaged, and come out mostly as the temperature cools at night. They are seen as protectors of the mountain, but their origins and motivations are unknown.

Rose Garden: Once known simply as the Hidden Vale, the Rose Garden is located in a secluded space between the mountains to the west of Mother, the First Forest, and the Maze. It is the home of the Cerulean Rose and to Perennia, the dragon protector.

Runners: This is the name of the very best of Silvyra's horticulturists, who have studied and committed to searching out a unique formula for the Elixir of Life. Typically, only a small number of Runners are chosen for every cycle of seasons, and they must be brilliant, brave, and pure of heart. They spend several seasons researching, traveling, and navigating

Silvyra on a personal quest to find eight meaningful ingredients for their unique formula for the Elixir. This includes passing through the Maze and traveling to the Rose Garden, where they must obtain a petal of the Cerulean Rose.

Sages: The Great Library of Tomorrow has ten Sages, a position created by the Book of Wisdom to watch over humanity's core values and its stories across all worlds. The Sages are a fundamental part of the Library's leadership after the Scholar joins with the Book of Wisdom. An Orb selects each Sage under guidance from the Book of Wisdom, and once selected, they bond for life. The Sages' natural affinity for their core value—hope, truth, strength, knowledge, and so on—manifests in magical powers related to nature and their specific value. This becomes an innate power for the Sage, which the Orb can also enhance by channeling energy from the Library. Sages can live a very long life—sometimes many hundreds of years—but are not immune to physical harm or accidental death.

Seed of Life: Connected to the Flower of Life, the Seed of Life is a central philosophy for the people of Silvyra and reflects the need to find balance and unity with nature and respect the cycle of life.

Scholar, The (See "Fairen" and "the Author"): A formal name given to Fairen, who discovered the portal in the Great Library and built the Book of Wisdom, for the period before she became one with the Book.

Scholars: A general term for a resident or visiting researcher at the Great Library of Tomorrow. For citizens of the Library, this honorific places them as part of the research, librarian, and archivist careers within the Library.

Scuttlebug: A small, beetle-like creature found on Silvyra.

Silvyra: This is the realm of plants and flowers, home to Mother, the Great Tree, the Elixir of Life, and the dragon Perennia. It is a large and varied world with continents, islands, oceans, rivers, lakes, and even deserts. Across all these terrains, there is an abundance of flora and fauna, as well as thriving communities, from large settlements to smaller communities. Silvyra has twin moons and a bright yellow sun, which combine once every five seasons to create new life and prosperity.

Suttaru: Formerly known as Adi, once a close friend and colleague of the Scholar Fairen, he is the corrupted remains of that man, shrouded in a cloak of burning ash and servant to Discordia, the Realm of Dark Stories. In the Great Library of Tomorrow, he is known as the Ash Man, a title given to him mostly in jest to scare naughty children.

Tufted Jackrabbits: A native mammal of Silvyra, common across the realm.

Veer, the Sage of Strength: Veer was born in the first half of the twentieth century and has been a Sage for over seventy years. Before becoming a Sage, he worked on the development of early wind power for NASA. His powers, amplified by his Orb, Lynx, echo his former profession, and he can command the air and wind itself.

Volare Machina: These are the messengers and workers of the Great Library, a variety of mechanical and magical flying machines of all shapes, designs, and roles. Some have wings, others rotors, but all use a sprinkle of ancient magic in their workings.

Undergrowth: An airship port town north of the Maze, at the foot of a small mountain range and surrounded by large beanstalks. Above the town is a natural stone bridge, which is used for airship docking, loading, and unloading.

Unwritten: These are the victims of Suttaru and Discordia. They are helpless people and creatures whose personal stories have been rewritten, turning them into obedient servants of their new masters. The Unwritten can be identified by the burning script that appears all over their bodies while being controlled. It is written in a language unknown to the rest of Paperworld or the Great Library.

Wardrobe: Located in a newly constructed section of the Library, in a small room off the Main Concourse, is a room only visited by the Sages. It is a hexagonal dressing room, large enough for two people, with five tall, gleaming mirrors. When one enters, the images of the people in the mirrors change—not their faces but the clothes they are wearing. This is the room where the Sages change their Library clothing for the local fashion of their Paperworld destinations.

Xavier, the Sage of Truth: A true embodiment of the Sages, he is self-less in his duty and deeply in love with Helia. His powers of truth and foresight, however, were not enough to stop him from being struck by Suttaru during the assault on the Rose Garden. He dies heroically and is survived by his Orb, Antares.

AFTERWORD

BY STEVE AOKI

The great thing about the Tomorrowland festival experiences is I can never tell where they're going to go next. They're going to blow my mind. Always. They're going to blow *everybody's* mind because they're the leaders in this space.

With this new fantasy book by Rosalia Aguilar Solace, Tomorrowland has once again exceeded all my expectations. When I got this book, I devoured it. The characters, the world-building, and the story had me immersed from page one. In true Tomorrowland fashion, the book embodies the culture and ethos of the festival that inspired it, breaking out into sensational new worlds and experiences that will have the reader thrilled and on the edge of their seat. A whole new universe of worlds for us to explore, from the magical and evocative forests of Silvyra to the stunning City of Forever. And not forgetting the Book of Wisdom and her Great Library of Tomorrow.

As a creator myself, I can see the love and passion that has been poured into the book, the inspiration and dedication to making this not just a great story but an event for everyone who wants to feel alive, empowered, and a part of something larger than ourselves.

The book's action pulls you inexorably forward, its beat rising and falling in a story that builds to a crescendo that will have you, like me, at the end, shouting out for more.

This is a book for everyone: an epic fantasy with a story and characters that embrace the very heart of Tomorrowland in a magical tale of life, love, and unity.

AFTERWORD

BY LOUIE SCHWARTZBERG

It's always exciting to discover projects that coincide with the themes of nature, especially the forces of love and destruction I have myself discovered in filming nature's wonders. When asked to share those insights with the Tomorrowland team during the inspiration sessions for this book, I was amazed and delighted to be working with people on themes so close to my heart.

What captivates me so much about this book, aside from its mythological heroes and epic quests and wonderful worlds they visit, is that in the pages of this story we find the true magic of our universe: Nature. Raw and untamed. Cultivated. Often strained by the pressures we humans put on it, yet defiant, unending and working together to nourish, support, and defend one another.

Nature is the story of our world, and in this book, our one world becomes many, interconnected like a forest, and like nature, experiences everything from sudden destruction to timeless serenity. This is the magic of nature—its perseverance, its infinite capacity to forgive, provide, and to simply persist in the face of impossible odds. To paraphrase Shakespeare's *Hamlet*, by holding up a mirror to nature, in this book, we can see a reflection of what is real and magical in our own world. The truth of nature.

It is a stark reminder of the challenges we all face in the real world, but tempered with heroes who are searching for the truth of what it means to be human and part of nature at the same time. In crafting this tale, Tomorrowland has created a testament to our enduring quest for a deeper understanding of our place in this world and how to embrace the hero within us all. I'm so thrilled to have been a part of it.

ACKNOWLEDGMENTS

This first part of my trilogy, in which I share a glimpse into the magic of Paperworld—a magic I first experienced for myself as a child in the Great Library of Tomorrow—would not have been possible without the help and inspiration of many people.

First, thanks to the creative team at Tomorrowland: Their inspirational ideas and magical world-building made it all possible. And to the writing and editing team: Dan Hanks, Emily Yau, Karen Ball, Chris Roberson, and Michael Rowley. A huge thank-you for your wisdom, creativity, and all-around support.

Agents Paul Lucas, Nathaniel Alcaraz-Stapleton, and the whole team at Janklow & Nesbit: Your belief in the project and ongoing support have been invaluable. Thank you for being a crucial part of this journey and helping bring about translations in German, French, Dutch, Polish, and Czech, with more languages to come!

My editor, Daniel Ehrenhaft, has been a delight to work with, as has the whole Blackstone Publishing team: Lysa Williams, Josie Woodbridge, David Baker, and Rebecca Brewer. You're all fantastic, and I couldn't be happier to be working with you.

I also must thank Armin van Buuren, Louie Schwartzberg, Leen Gorissen, and Jill Peeters, who took time out of their busy lives to host inspiration sessions and share their unique thoughts on many of the themes in the book. Your insights were amazing.

Thanks to the legendary Steve Aoki, and again to Louie Schwartzberg, for your very kind afterwords.

And to you, the reader, for picking up this book: There will be many more journeys ahead. Thank you all for coming along for the ride. Magic and adventure await!

ABOUT TOMORROWLAND

Established in 2005 by Manu and Michiel Beers, Tomorrowland is one of the most beautiful music festivals in the world, famous for its fantasy themes, magical worlds, and unique feeling of global unity, with visitors from every country in the world. Located in the wonderful town of Boom, Belgium, the summer festival sells out in minutes and welcomes more than four hundred thousand visitors across two amazing weekends every year.

Tomorrowland's motto is "Live Today, Love Tomorrow, Unite Forever." "Live Today" stands for living life to the fullest; "Love Tomorrow" means having respect for oneself, including one's mental and physical health, others, and nature; while "Unite Forever" celebrates unity, diversity, equality, and freedom for all.

Yet Tomorrowland is so much more than just the summer festival. With new events landing each season in fabulous locations around the world, from Tomorrowland Winter at the magnificent Alpe d'Huez to the beautiful Itu with Tomorrowland Brazil, it is truly a global phenomenon.

Tomorrowland also connects with the People of Tomorrow all year long via One World Radio and its own record label, Tomorrowland Music, while projects like the Tomorrowland Academy DJ and producer school help mentor the next generation of musical talent. Meanwhile, the Tomorrowland Foundation builds music and art schools around the world, giving vulnerable children the opportunity to express themselves creatively, with schools currently running in India, Nepal, and Brazil.

With Tomorrowland Fiction now adding another layer and sharing unique stories full of magic to a global audience, Tomorrowland continues to spread its messages of love and unity around the world.